PRAISE FOR JILL SHALVIS

"Bestseller Shalvis (*Love for Beginners*) launches the Sunrise Cove series with a charming, emotional romance featuring a cast readers will quickly come to see as old friends."

—*Publishers Weekly* on *The Family You Make*

"Fall in love with Jill Shalvis! She's my go-to read for humor and heart."

—Susan Mallery, *New York Times* bestselling author

"The novel whizzes by. Shalvis's fans will be pleased with the message that everyone deserves a second chance."

—*Publishers Weekly* on *Love for Beginners*

"*Love for Beginners* is quintessential Shalvis, with humor and heat (whew, Emma and Simon give us heat), and a cast of characters you'll hate to leave behind when you turn the last page. But even so, we promise you'll finish this book feeling warm from the inside—and maybe the outside too. This is the summer's perfect beach read."

—Christina Lauren, *New York Times* bestselling author

"Jill Shalvis has a unique talent for making you want to spend time with her characters right off the bat."

—Kristen Ashley, *New York Times* bestselling author

"Shalvis capably weaves the complex, intertwining relationships into an appealing story of second chances. This is sure to satisfy."

—*Publishers Weekly* on *The Forever Girl*

The
Friendship Pact

ALSO BY JILL SHALVIS

SUNRISE COVE NOVELS
The Family You Make • *The Friendship Pact*

WILDSTONE NOVELS
Love for Beginners • *Mistletoe in Paradise* (novella)
The Forever Girl • *The Summer Deal*
Almost Just Friends • *The Lemon Sisters*
Rainy Day Friends • *The Good Luck Sister* (novella)
Lost and Found Sisters

HEARTBREAKER BAY NOVELS
Wrapped Up in You • *Playing for Keeps*
Hot Winter Nights • *About That Kiss*
Chasing Christmas Eve • *Accidentally on Purpose*
The Trouble with Mistletoe • *Sweet Little Lies*

LUCKY HARBOR NOVELS
One in a Million • *He's So Fine*
It's in His Kiss • *Once in a Lifetime*
Always on My Mind • *It Had to Be You*
Forever and a Day • *At Last*
Lucky in Love • *Head Over Heels*
The Sweetest Thing • *Simply Irresistible*

ANIMAL MAGNETISM NOVELS
Still the One • *All I Want*
Then Came You • *Rumor Has It*
Rescue My Heart • *Animal Attraction*
Animal Magnetism

The Friendship Pact

A NOVEL

JILL SHALVIS

AVON

An Imprint of HarperCollins*Publishers*

P.S.™ is a trademark of HarperCollins Publishers.

THE FRIENDSHIP PACT. Copyright © 2022 by Jill Shalvis. Excerpt from THE BACKUP PLAN © 2023 by Jill Shalvis. All rights reserved. Printed in the United States of America. No part of this book may be used or reproduced in any manner whatsoever without written permission except in the case of brief quotations embodied in critical articles and reviews. For information, address HarperCollins Publishers, 195 Broadway, New York, NY 10007.

HarperCollins books may be purchased for educational, business, or sales promotional use. For information, please email the Special Markets Department at SPsales@harpercollins.com.

FIRST EDITION

Designed by Diahann Sturge

Mountain peaks illustration © DenisKrivoy/Shutterstock, Inc.

Library of Congress Cataloging-in-Publication Data has been applied for.

ISBN 978-0-06-309546-5
ISBN 978-0-06-309554-0 (hardcover library edition)

22 23 24 25 26 LSC 10 9 8 7 6 5 4 3 2 1

The
Friendship Pact

CHAPTER 1

For the better part of her childhood, all Tae Holmes had wanted was to be an adult, only as it turned out, adulting was overrated. Take tonight, for example. She'd planned every-thing down to the very last little detail, and things had *still* gone FUBAR.

So she did what the Holmes women did when facing disaster—something she had a lot of experience with—she pretended all was perfectly well. Chin up, she strode across the ritzy hotel lobby like she owned the joint, shoving the inner echo of the emo teenager she'd once been deep. Because this wasn't about her. It was about making sure her fledgling event company be-came a success, starting with tonight's fundraiser for her biggest client.

Moving through the post-dinner-and-auction crowd in the lobby, she forced the confident smile of someone not at all wor-ried that the heels she wore were so high she risked her neck with every step, or that her updo kept quivering, threatening to escape the pins that held it together.

The epitome of a girl playing dress-up.

Her gaze caught on the sight of a guy standing by the twenty-five-foot-high rock fountain in the center of the lobby and her fake smile congealed. It was the guy she'd had an awkward first—and last—date with a week ago, Michael Someone-Or-Another. She was pretty sure the decision to never see each other again was mutual, so why was he here at her work event?

When he craned his neck her way, she hurriedly crouched behind one of the dozens of potted blue spruce pine trees and tried to bargain with karma. *I'm an okay person, right? I try to recycle. I give fifteen bucks a month to an elephant orphanage in Africa. I—*

"Tae?"

She closed her eyes tight, like that could make her vanish. She'd gone out with him because she'd made that stupid promise to her mom, that they'd both put themselves out there for some badly needed fun in their lives. Fun had been a rare commodity, what with work and the whole pesky keeping-a-roof-over-her-head thing.

"It *is* you."

Drawing a deep breath, she opened her eyes to find Michael closer, in a slim-cut blue suit, his long hair neatly contained in a man bun, his goatee perfectly manscaped.

"Wow," he said, looking her over with surprised appreciation. "You didn't look like this on our date."

True story. She looked like this never. Not to mention, he'd taken her on a hike to Five Lakes, a straight uphill climb, where he'd then decided to "test her outdoorsiness" by suggesting they go skinny-dipping. When she'd balked, he'd stripped anyway and jumped into the water. She'd promptly hiked back by herself.

"Seriously," he murmured, still taking her in. "*Wow.*"

One more "wow" and she was going to start her own drinking game. "Listen, I'm not sure how you managed to find me here, but I'm working, so—"

"*There* you are." This was uttered by a beautiful woman in a killer red dress with a camera strapped around her neck and a flute of champagne in one hand. Her smile was warm and welcoming. "Hello, darling."

Tae sighed. "Hi, Mom."

April Holmes shifted the camera aside so she could squeeze Tae in close for a hug. "Dress number three," she whispered. "It's perfect for you."

Okay, so Tae had rented three different dresses for the evening, no big deal. But her mom had promptly said the first two looked like they were meant for the sixty-five-years-and-older set. So here she was, in the third dress. Sexier than she'd wanted for a job, but that was what happened when you and your mom— only fifteen years your senior—had a codependent relationship. You did dumb stuff to keep the peace.

"Hold up," Michael said and looked back and forth between the two women as if he'd won the lottery. "You're . . . mother and daughter? I mean, sisters, sure, but no way mom and daughter."

April laughed in delight.

Tae, who'd heard the sisters comment a hundred million, billion, *trillion* times, just rolled her eyes. Yeah, yeah, whatever, they looked *very* much alike with the same five-foot-seven build and dark, shoulder-length brown hair. They each had brown eyes as well—though April's were dark brown and always smiling, and Tae's were light brown and usually *not* smiling.

"Tae, you look beautiful tonight," April murmured. "Doesn't she, Michael?"

Aaaaaaand there it was—her mom was matchmaking, part of her New and Improved Mom plan. "Mom, Michael and I have already figured out we're not a match."

Michael nodded in agreement. "Because you're uptight and don't know how to let loose. It messes with my aura."

Tae looked at her mom. "I mess with his aura."

"Wow," Michael said at her clear sarcasm.

Tae took the flute of champagne from her mom's hand and drank.

"But for the record, she's right," he told her mom. "We didn't vibe. But you and me, April . . ." His smile warmed and was actually quite charming. "We vibe."

Tae laughed, but it backed up in her throat at Michael's serious expression. "Wait. So now you want to date my mom?"

"Until two minutes ago, I had no idea she was your mom." He winked at April. "Nice to meet you, Mrs. Robinson. You're stunning, by the way."

"Aw." April smiled at him. "You're sweet." She turned to Tae. "Honey, I'm sorry. I had no idea he was the same Michael you went out with when I arranged to meet him here for a nightcap after the event."

Tae nearly choked on her champagne. "Wait. You're on a *date* with him?"

April smiled at Michael. "Would you mind giving us a minute?"

When he moved off, her mom sighed. "I'm truly sorry. I had no idea. And your eye twitch is back."

Tae pressed a finger to her eye. "This is what happens when you go rogue and set us both up for the same dating site."

"I've got just the thing." Her mom went through her purse and pulled out a piece of butterscotch candy. "Here. Your favorite."

Tae had to laugh. "Mom, that only worked when I was a little kid."

April took the candy back and popped it into her own mouth. "I'm just so sorry. I went out with Michael two days ago and you never came up in conversation, not once. We planned to go out for dessert tonight, and then a walk along the lake."

"Warning, he likes to skinny-dip."

"Oh boy." Her mom sighed. "Let's make a motion to strike him from the dating pool. The truth is, he's kind of smug, but I went out with him because I made you pinkie swear you'd get back into the dating pool, and I couldn't let you go swimming alone."

Tae had to laugh. "Always a giver, Mom."

"Remember that." She drew a deep breath. "Off I go to let him down." She fanned herself. "Look at me, I'm sweating behind my knees. I'm usually the one being dumped."

"Mom," Tae said softly, pained for her because it was true.

April's dating life had been erratic over the years, to say the least. But that was what happened when you raised yourself with no authority figure—you made a whole bunch of mistakes along the way. The men April had chosen weren't bad guys, just lazy and unambitious, often siphoning off April as a result.

As for Tae, who'd witnessed every one of her mom's mistakes, her own life often being affected as well, her views on love had been formed by what she'd seen. She'd early on given up having expectations regarding love.

Even as she still deep down hoped it existed.

"It's okay," her mom said. "It's taken a while, but I think I'm finally figuring out what I'm worth."

Tae hugged her tight. "Good. Because you're worth a lot. And if he gives you trouble, you're not alone. I'll kick his butt."

Her mom's gaze went from bemused to regretful. "Tae, you don't always have to be the tough one. I'm the mom, and I know what tonight means to you. Adrenaline HQ is your first big client."

"A client *you* got for me."

"No." April shook her head. "I'm just the receptionist. All I did was introduce you to my boss. You got the contract to run AHQ's fundraiser events all on your own."

Maybe, but she still had to prove herself to the company, which took athletes with disabilities and wounded warriors out on the mountain for winter adventures. Tonight's dinner and auction would fund next winter's ski program. She'd also proposed adding local at-risk youths to the program, and Jake Copeland, owner of Adrenaline HQ, had readily agreed. If they did well tonight, some of the money would be allocated as scholarships for those at-risk youths. But there weren't as many people here as she'd hoped.

"You're obsessing again," her mom said with a gentle shoulder nudge to stop Tae from mentally counting their guests.

"It's a way of life." They had maybe one hundred people here. Half of what she'd hoped for.

"We really need to revisit yoga and deep-breathing techniques for you."

That wasn't going to help. The only thing that could help Tae was success tonight. Success would mean security, safety, and stability—her life goals—so that neither she nor her mom would ever again have to work two or three jobs at a time.

Her mom put her hands on Tae's shoulders and turned her to take in the whole area. A bolt of lightning hit, making the lights flicker for a heart-stopping few seconds. But for a native Tahoe girl, taking Mother Nature in stride was par for the course.

"Take a good look," her mom said. "What do you see?"

Okay, so the venue was truly fantastic. "We're short a lot of people."

"The surprise storm is to blame for that, not you." Her mom gave her a little shake. "What else do you see?"

Tae looked around. "Well, Michael's either having a seizure or he's winking at you."

"Ignore him. People are having a *great* time, Tae, and I've got the pictures to prove it. Look." She brought up the screen on her camera, scrolling through some fantastic photos.

Her mom had been a lot of things in her forty-three years of life: a teenage mom, a housecleaner, a waitress, a nanny, and now a receptionist, but she'd always been a photographer at heart, taking baby and kid pics for friends and neighbors as side jobs. And yet her real passion was landscape photography.

Tae could only imagine where her mom might've been if she hadn't had a baby while still a baby herself. "These are amazing, Mom."

"I've got a great backdrop."

It was true. The hotel sat on a hill overlooking the dizzyingly gorgeous Lake Tahoe, which thanks to another lightning blast was lit up in all its heart-stopping glory for a few seconds. The massive, sprawling lobby was where they'd held the auction, the place made up of floor-to-ceiling windows, lit with miles and miles of twinkle lights and people in cocktail dresses and suits, who indeed were mingling and chatting and laughing. It was all so pretty it could've been a movie set. But had they made enough money on the auction items? Jake was currently adding everything up, so Tae could only hope.

"Smile," her mom said. "Remember, you can fake *anything* with a smile."

Tae bared her teeth in a semblance of a smile that made her mom laugh. "That'll do. Now, if you'll excuse me, I've got a date to dump."

Tae caught her mom's hand. "Only if you want to. I mean how often do you . . . *vibe* . . . with someone?"

Her mom snorted. "I don't want to vibe with anyone who can't see what a beautiful, wonderful, unique woman my daughter is, whether you liked him or not."

Tae's heart warmed, but she also had to laugh. "I know you're stretching when you use the word *unique*."

"It's true!" She pulled in Tae tight for another quick hug, then strode off, blind to the heads that turned and watched her move.

Tae took a deep breath and let it out, turning in a slow circle. Her mom was a lot of things, most of them wonderful, but she was also an eternal optimist.

Tae was the realist in their family of two, always had been.

Overhead, the lights dimmed except for the fairy lights. The music slowed, and the crowd on the dance floor slowed with it. A man and a young girl probably his daughter stepped onto the floor. The girl was maybe eight and had her feet on top of her dad's. They were beaming at each other, and Tae's heart tugged hard. She'd seen dads laughing and having a great time with their kids before, of course. But there was something about never having experienced it herself that made her feel like she'd missed out.

"Sweet, isn't it?"

She glanced over to find an elderly gentleman smiling at the duo. "I know men aren't supposed to admit it," he said, "but it chokes me up every time I see a father and daughter like that."

Same, but probably for a very different reason than he thought.

"I remember dancing with my daughter when she was that age," the man said wistfully. "One of my favorite memories." He sighed. "Did you ever dance with your dad?"

Surprised at the intimate question, she glanced over at him. "My dad died when I was a baby."

Now he looked surprised. "Well, that can't be."

"Excuse me?"

"You're Tae, right?" He pointed to her name tag, which had only her first name on it, encouraging a more casual setting for people to interact. "I'm Carl Schwartz. My grandson Denny has spinal bifida and attends all of AHQ's ski days. I go with him whenever I'm in town."

Tae gave a small nod, not understanding what that had to do with her dad. "Nice to meet you," she said politely.

"I knew your dad. Well, vaguely anyway. He hung out with my son Scott when they were teenagers. A few years back, Scott mentioned running into him."

Tae stilled. This simply couldn't be true. "He died overseas."

The man frowned. "We're talking about AJ Strickland, yes?"

Having never heard that name before, Tae felt a trickle of relief. "No. That's not my dad's name."

"Oh." He looked so surprised. "I must've confused things. We all knew that AJ had a daughter named Tae, so when I saw your name I just assumed . . ." He shook his head. "Well, we all know what happens when you assume anything. My sincere apologies."

With her heart thudding oddly in her chest, Tae took a step back. "No problem." She glanced around for her mom, finding her across the room clearly trying to let Michael down sweetly and gently. That was her mom. Sweet. Gentle. Trusting . . . the most open person in the world, which meant she believed just about anything that anyone told her.

Not Tae. Never Tae, and she turned back to Mr. Schwartz to

ask one of the hundred questions in her head, but . . . he was no longer standing there. "What the—" She looked around, but there was no sign of him anywhere. It was as if he'd never existed in the first place. Needing air, she headed toward the wall of glass doors to the exit. Halfway there, her phone rang. She would've sent it straight to voicemail, but it was her client Jake. They also had another connection that he didn't know anything about, and if she had anything to say about it, he never would.

"Hey," he said. "Everything okay?"

"Yes." She turned to sweep the room again and saw him in his wheelchair near the fountain, as physically imposing and handsome as ever. At his side sat his dog Grub, a ridiculously adorable rescue mutt who resembled Sulley from *Monsters, Inc.* Well, except he was red instead of turquoise with purple spots.

"That asshat you went out with last week is here," Jake said. "Don't tell me you decided to give Nature Boy another chance."

She'd known she'd be sorry she'd told Jake and his girlfriend, Carolyn, about her really bad date at lunch the other day. "Actually, he's my mom's date for the night."

Even from their distance of at least a hundred feet, she caught the flash of Jake's smile. "Awkward."

She rolled her eyes. "Gee, thanks, hadn't noticed."

He snorted, and she was happy to be the source of amusement for him, but . . . "I'm really sorry about tonight, Jake."

"What are you talking about? You did a great job. Grub loved the . . . well, grub."

"Only half the RSVPs showed up. The night's a disaster."

"No," he said. "If *I'd* run it, it'd have been a disaster. Tonight wasn't that. The storm kept some people home, sure, but everyone who showed up opened their wallets. But that's not what tonight's about anyway."

"No?"

"No," he said. "It's about talking with families, hearing their stories, and making connections. Being emotionally available."

Tae sighed.

"What?"

"I'm trying to figure out why you hired me. I'm not exactly the emotionally available type."

Jake Copeland had been Special Forces, then run a huge boating tourism company in San Francisco before settling here in Tahoe to start up Adrenaline HQ. He was as tough and badass as they came and didn't laugh often. But he was laughing now, in obvious agreement that she wasn't the most emotionally available person. "Look," he said. "I was older than you in high school and we didn't know each other then. But you're April's daughter, so I know that deep, deep, *deep* down inside you must have the same compassion and warm heart that she does. You're going to be a huge asset to Adrenaline HQ. Now go home."

"But the cleanup—"

"Will be handled by my staff. Not your problem. Good night, Tae."

Not willing to look a gift horse in the mouth, she ordered an Uber as she headed outside. For the first time all night, something went her way. A car would arrive in two minutes.

It took her that long to get down the stairs, through the slick parking lot to the street, without breaking her ankles in the most ridiculous shoes she'd ever worn. She couldn't wait to strip out of this dress, pull on comfy pj's, pour a glass of wine, and make herself a big, fat, gooey grilled cheese sandwich. She texted her mom a quick be safe, don't forget your carriage turns back into a pumpkin at midnight before looking up at where she was going. And damn.

Michael stood not three feet away.

He shook his head in disgust. "You *made* her cancel on me."

Oh goodie, they were going to talk. "I don't *make* her do anything."

"You know, I could tell from our half-date that you were cold and heartless," he said. "But I didn't think you were the type to also be jealous and vindictive. I honestly tried to like you, Tae. It's nothing personal that I didn't."

She opened her mouth, then decided nope, not worth it. Catching sight of a car pulling up, she mentally matched it to the color of the Uber she'd just ordered, and grateful—on top of freezing—she hopped in almost before it came to a full stop. Pulling on her seat belt, she laid her head back and closed her eyes. "Rough night, so I'm going to need you to be liberal with the gas."

The car didn't budge.

"Uh, it's the pedal on the right."

"This isn't an Uber," the guy in the front seat said.

Of course it isn't. Well, never let it be said that once committed, she didn't go all out, even for a horrible evening.

CHAPTER 2

Riggs Copeland sat in his rental car outside the glamorous hotel, knowing he was way out of his comfort zone, and since his comfort zone was a war zone, that was saying a lot. But at least he was at the event as his brother, Jake, had requested-slash-ordered him to be. He just wasn't *in* the event. He was also late, two hours late, and hoping he'd "accidentally" missed the whole thing. Yeah, he was an equal partner in Adrenaline HQ, but he was also a silent partner, and the one who didn't like to schmooze with people.

Or do much with people at all.

But some random hot chick had just stormed across the icy sidewalk and into his backseat, thinking he was her Uber.

The June Tahoe night air was thick with the off-season icy mist, touching everything in its path, including the woman who'd made herself at home in his backseat, looking like an angel in a glimmering silver almost-there dress and matching shoes that seemed to be defying gravity.

She'd commanded him to be "liberal with the gas," but since

he was two seconds out of the military and no longer under someone else's command, he did not in fact hit "the pedal on the right." Instead, he turned around to say *what the hell*, but the words stuck in his throat at the shock.

"You know what? Never mind," the blast from his past said, never even looking up from her phone. "I'll text my mom to catch a ride with her." She reached for the door handle.

Riggs hit the auto lock.

When he met her gaze in the rearview mirror, her piercing whiskey-colored eyes were as cold as ice, and she had a tool in her hand that he recognized as one you'd see on an infomercial that promised to break a car window in case of emergencies.

Tae Holmes was still badass, and for some reason that made him smile. "Been a long time, Rebel."

She didn't blink at his old nickname for her, didn't even move. Hell, maybe she didn't remember him, but he sure remembered her, even without the goth look she'd preferred back in the day. "I'm happy to give you a ride," he said. "Unless you're going to fib about where you live again."

At the reminder of that long-ago night, she froze, those eyes of hers blinking once slowly, like an owl. "*You.*"

"Shouldn't that be *my* line?"

She rolled her eyes so hard he was surprised they didn't fall right out of her head. "I almost didn't recognize you," he admitted. "I had no idea you were back in Sunrise Cove." Or that looking at her would remind him of both the best and worst time of his life.

"Don't let the dress fool you. Beneath it, I'm still that annoyingly emo girl."

"You were never annoying. And it's not the gown." Nope, he'd have recognized her anywhere, wearing anything, and damn, she'd grown up to be all-woman, complete with that tough-girl armor and the chip on her shoulder still in place. Back in high school, she'd been so different from anyone else, a little rough around the edges, a whole lot unreachable, and so damn smart . . . all of which had drawn him to her.

They'd been in a science class together, partnered up for labs. He'd been a jock; she'd been on the outskirts, quiet, withdrawn. Their circles didn't cross, mostly because, near as he could tell, she didn't have a circle. But in class with him, she'd been smart and sharply sarcastic. She'd made him laugh. She'd also made him work hard for every conversation, and he'd liked that. They'd been the most unlikely of friends, and though she had no way of knowing it, she'd been his only real friend. Until he'd blown it by sleeping with her one night.

They'd never spoken again.

Not that it'd mattered. He'd left Tahoe a few months after graduation. And if he'd thought of her in the years since, it had been with a wistful smile and no hard feelings.

Which apparently were not reciprocated. That was, if she even really remembered him.

"Unlock the door," she said. "I think I'd rather freeze than take a walk down memory lane."

His laugh sounded rough to his own ears. It wasn't like he wanted to take a walk down that particular memory lane either.

"It's the button that's labeled *lock*," she murmured.

He smiled. "Aw, *there* it is. Your sweet side."

"Unlock the door, Riggs, or I'll break your window."

She would too. He hit unlock. "So you *do* remember my name."

Ignoring that, she made to leave, and he sighed. "Tae, you're cold and wet. It's your call, of course, but I don't mind taking you home." And as a bonus, it'd save him from having to go inside the hotel for Jake's thing. "I'd hate for you to ruin that dress."

"It's a rental." She looked out the window into the night. "I guess a ride would be okay. If you stop for ice cream first."

"Rough night?"

"You have no idea."

He surprised himself by feeling a flash of sympathy, because *same*. He pulled away from the curb and drove to the end of the block and into a parking lot.

Tae frowned. "The ice cream shop's on the Lake Walk."

She was wet from the icy rain, her skin shimmering with it, and the way she was also shivering told him ice cream was the last thing she needed. But he had just enough experience with her, albeit more than a decade-old experience, to know that telling her what to do or what she needed was a surefire way to start a fight. He'd already blasted the heat, but now he rechecked to make sure the vents were aimed her way. "You asked for ice cream." He pointed to the convenience store. "Figured you were in a hurry for it."

"Oh. Right." She nodded. "Thanks, I'll be right back."

"Wait, let me give you my jacket—"

"I'm good." And with that, she opened the car door and got out.

There was a slit in her dress, a lethally dangerous one that revealed her leg to midthigh as she slid out of his car. But he didn't almost swallow his tongue. Nope, he saved that for when he caught the back of the dress.

Or the lack thereof . . .

She strode across the lot, ignoring the guy leaning against the wall of the store with the same ease she'd ignored Riggs.

Actually, she hadn't ignored Riggs as much as she'd refused to engage. No skin off his nose. He wasn't one for engaging much these days. His cell phone rang. He answered as his gaze followed Tae into the store. She might have traded in her Doc Marten knockoffs for a pair of four-inch heels, but she was as edgy now as she'd been back in high school.

"Where the hell are you?" Jake asked in his ear.

Good to know his older brother's voice could still make his eye twitch. He put a finger to it. "Hello to you too, Jake."

"You're two hours late."

"Yeah, I'm not sure I'm going to be able to make it tonight."

"Are you telling me you're choosing to be alone on your first night back in Sunrise Cove in two years?"

"Actually," Riggs said, "*my* choice was to go straight to D.C., but you made me come home first."

Jake scoffed. "Like anyone could *make* you do anything you don't want to."

The ensuing silence was filled with the resentments, misunderstandings, and the built-up anger that had festered between them since Jake had been nearly blown up.

Riggs hated it. They were all each other had, but sometimes it felt the chasm between them was so vast it couldn't be bridged. "Look, I'm here, okay? Just as you commanded."

"If I commanded it, it was because you were too scared to come on your own."

Riggs laughed. "I'm not scared of shit."

"Right," Jake said on a snort. "The big badass soldier doesn't ever show his fears, whatever. Look, it's been a long time and I'm glad you're here, okay? So let me get my eyes on you."

That wasn't what was holding Riggs up. Nope, what held him up was *him* getting eyes on *Jake*. In a fucking wheelchair . . . "I'm here for the summer," he said. "You're going to see so much of me you're going to wish I hadn't come at all."

"Uh-huh . . ."

"Tell me the truth," Riggs said. "Carolyn made you ask me to stay with you, right?"

Carolyn was Adrenaline HQ's activities director. Jake had snatched her away from an adventure company out of south shore. She was also Jake's girlfriend, and how the woman put up with his bossy, know-it-all, demanding brother, Riggs had no idea.

"No one made me ask you to come," Jake said. "The house is still half yours. As is Adrenaline HQ."

The house had been left to them by their dad, who was thankfully buried six feet under, his abusive black soul rotting. Adrenaline HQ was altogether different. Two years ago, Jake had sold his successful touring boat business in San Francisco to move home to Sunrise Cove, a little town on the California side of

Lake Tahoe. He'd needed an investor, and since Riggs had never spent much of anything he'd made, it'd been a no-brainer. He'd gone in with 50 percent of the necessary start-up costs, thinking it'd be a solid investment.

Guilt being the motivator.

Even more so, since in the past two years Jake had gotten a concussion skiing down a double black diamond with some fellow wounded warriors and also broken a leg getting knocked out of his chair during a wheelchair basketball tournament.

"Just come to the hotel," Jake said quietly. "I want to welcome you home."

Riggs hadn't thought of Tahoe as home since he'd been a kid. These days, nowhere was home. Being in the military and relocating had become his life. If things had gone to plan, he wouldn't even be here. He was supposed to have gone straight to a hush-hush security job with the State Department, but at the last minute, the start date had been pushed back from June to September.

"Did you go by the house?" Jake asked. "Did you see what we've done to the place?"

"Yeah." Jake and Carolyn had renovated their childhood home. Turned the POS into something surprisingly warm and charming. In fact, the female touch that Carolyn had clearly added reminded Riggs of what it'd been like before his mom had died when he'd been ten. Leaving no shield between her sons and their asshole, alcoholic father. "The renovations look great, but you should've insulated."

Jake was quiet for a single beat. "I *knew* I heard something when we were in the shower getting ready earlier."

Riggs had to laugh. "Getting ready, huh? Is that what the kids are calling it these days?"

"Why did you leave?" Jake asked. "And where have you been? That was hours ago."

"Drove around." He'd been restless, carrying a sense of not belonging, along with an odd feeling of loneliness he hadn't wanted to admit to, not even to himself.

"Look, the event's over," Jake said. "We can have a drink. Catch up."

Riggs looked into the front window of the convenience store and found Tae striding down the window aisle with purpose, arms full of crap food. It made him smile. "I'm not alone."

"That was quick."

"It's not like that."

"Oh, come on," Jake said with a rough laugh. "With you, it's always like that." He sighed. "At least tell me you'll come home tonight."

"I will." Tae stopped in front of a freezer. Riggs was the warrior, but even in that heart-attack-inducing dress, there was a strength and purpose and gritty resolve to her that spoke of a different kind of warrior altogether.

A self-made one, born of circumstance. Something he understood more than she'd known.

In his ear, Jake was droning on and on about an idea that had been brought to him, something about adding a summer program to Adrenaline HQ's already thriving winter program so there'd be year-round work for the employees.

More work was the exact opposite of what Riggs wanted for his brother, but as he opened his mouth to say so, the guy leaning against the outside wall of the convenience store pushed away from it and headed inside, his body language and nervous gait making Riggs straighten from his annoyed slouch.

Aw, shit. Was that a— Yep. There was a bulge in the back of the guy's jacket that Riggs figured had a good chance of being a gun. "Gotta go," he said, and disconnected, already on the move.

CHAPTER 3

Comfort food. That was the only thing on Tae's mind as she loaded up her arms in the convenience store. Comfort food and . . . Riggs Copeland. Big, strong, protective, annoyingly sexy Riggs Copeland.

She didn't think much could surprise her, but Jake's brother being back in town most definitely had done just that. He'd grown up too, and right into those long, lanky limbs, looking better than any man who'd seen her naked should. She'd forgotten the physical impact he exuded. Male, solid, and way too charismatic. Soon as she paid for her loot, she was going to sneak out the back door and hitch a ride home if she had to. She tried really hard to not repeat mistakes, but she wasn't sure she could resist this particular one.

But, hey, look, two-for-one donut packs. *Score.* As she took her bonus pack and moved to the ice cream freezer, she felt the weight of the cashier's gaze barreling down from the length of the aisle. "Ms. Riley," Tae said politely as she walked past.

"I *knew* it was you."

Tae ignored the woman's sharp, assessing, and judgmental tone and kept moving. Truth was, she deserved it. She'd been a rotten teenager. Desperate too. She could think of a handful of times she'd lifted food from this very store, then gone home and quickly put the food into grocery store bags so her mom would think she'd purchased it.

Her mom had worked multiple jobs at all times, pretty much either working or asleep at any given hour of the day, and even then there hadn't been enough money. Tae picking up baby-sitting jobs had helped, but not nearly enough, so they'd often couch surfed with friends or lived with whomever her mom had been seeing at the time.

She eyed her ice cream options. Thankfully, there were many. Double fudge chocolate. Mint. Cherry and nuts. But what was *nuts* had been Mr. Schwartz being so sure that her dad was alive. She'd been a newborn when he'd gone into the marines, but her mom had kept him alive with stories. They'd wanted to marry, but April hadn't been of age, and it'd been prohibited without parental consent. So they'd vowed to get married when Andy came back.

Only he'd died less than a year later.

Clearly Mr. Schwartz had been wrong. If not, either her dad had lied to her mom. Or . . . her mom had lied to Tae. Except her mom wouldn't. She didn't have the ability to lie, she literally got hives whenever she tried.

Ms. Riley was still watching her like a hawk, spine ramrod straight, bringing her to her full five feet in height—at least three inches of which was hair. For as long as Tae could remember, the woman's black-as-night hair had been piled up on top of her head resembling a beehive. It was shot through with gray streaks now, no doubt thanks in part to Tae herself. "You can't fool me with that expensive designer dress, you know."

"It's a rental!"

Ms. Riley didn't smile. "I've got my eyes on you. Tonight, you're going to pay for every single thing you take out of here, if I have to search you myself."

Tae pulled her debit card from her bra and waved it across the store at her, trying to ignore the heat of shame she could feel creeping up her face because, let's face it, Ms. Riley had the right to doubt her. "No searching necessary."

"Hmph."

Tae went back to the very important decision of choosing the right ice cream for her impending breakdown, doing her best to shrug off the piercing gaze she could still feel stabbing her right between the shoulder blades. And rightfully so. But Tae had long ago dropped money into the tips jar to cover the things she'd once taken. Still, it was hard to maintain the high ground with water dripping from her hair, down her arms and chest, her teeth rattling, and her body covered in goose bumps—not that this would stop her from her ice cream goal.

And now she had a real problem—there was no cookies-and-cream ice cream in the freezer. Which meant it was official. The evening had gone to hell in a hand basket. Tomorrow she would get out of bed with an adjusted attitude. She'd go back to her come-what-may facade. But for that to happen, she *needed* ice cream to go with her cookies, chips, and candy bar. Double fudge or Neapolitan? She loved Neapolitan, but sometimes a girl just needed her chocolate—

"Take one of each, let's go."

Riggs, of course. Of all the places in all the land, why had they collided tonight, with her confidence at an all-time low? She could feel him behind her, the heat of his big body both a bad and good memory. Okay, *great* memory. But she waved him off like a pesky fly without looking at him. "Some things can't be rushed."

Two long arms reached around her and took everything out of her hands, dumping them all in the bin of candy bars at her hip.

She tried to push him away, but he caught her arm and held tight. She stared up at him. His brown hair was military short. His eyes studied her calmly. He looked exactly like the teenager he'd once been, and yet also like he'd lived two lifetimes since she'd seen him last.

"You can yell at me in the car for being a pushy asshole," he said. "We're out. Now." Still holding on to her, he turned toward the door and then stilled, before turning them back to the ice cream. "Okay, don't look, but the kid behind you—"

She craned her neck.

"Jesus, Tae, I said *don't* look. The guy behind us might have a gun."

"You mean the kid? He can't be a day over fourteen."

"A gun doesn't give a shit about the age of the person holding it. Here's what's going to happen," he said, his voice low and steely. "You're going to take my hand and we're going to walk out of here, easy-peasy." He started to tug her along, but she dug in her heels, pulling free.

"And leave Ms. Riley alone to fend for herself?" she hissed.

He took her hand again. "No, we'll take her too. But if she refuses, there's a loaded shotgun under the counter, and trust me, she knows how to use it."

True story. "She won't budge from this store. She's glued her ass to that seat. But I think you're wrong about the kid."

Riggs stared at her like no one had ever dared question him before. "And if he's planning on using that gun to rob the place?"

"Don't be so quick to judge."

"I'm not the judgy one here."

She wasn't even going to try to attempt to decipher that comment. Or the look in those eyes of his, which were a startling, almost hypnotic green. She took another look around. There were no other customers in the store. Riggs was looking at Tae, or at least pretending to while actually eyeballing the mirror over the end of the aisle, which was giving him a bird's-eye view of the checkout counter. They both watched the kid reach into his coat.

And faster than a blink of an eye, Ms. Riley had her shotgun out and pointed at the kid's nose. "Go ahead, make my day, punk," she said, not missing Clint Eastwood's tone by all that much.

Here was the thing. Tae knew that the gun was all for show, that Ms. Riley, annoying as hell and mean as a snake, was not a murderer. She wasn't going to shoot the kid.

But obviously, the kid didn't know that. He tried to make a

run for it, making Riggs swear and head him off, with Tae right on his heels.

Suddenly a shotgun blast sounded. In the thunderingly loud echo of Tae's astonishment that the woman had actually taken a shot, ceiling tile dust rained down on all of them.

"And there's more where that came from!" Ms. Riley yelled, keeping the gun in motion so that it was always aimed at one of the three of them.

Tae couldn't hear past the ringing in her ears, but she slid in front of the kid, while at the very same second, Riggs pushed in front of them both.

"What kind of idiot jumps in front of a gun?" he growled at her.

"What kind of an idiot jumps in front of a woman who's jumped in front of a gun?" she growled right back.

Riggs looked incredulous. "I was trained by Uncle Sam."

"Yeah, and I got my education from the school of hard knocks. I've got this under control!" She looked at Ms. Riley. Not easy, since she had to peek around the big stone wall that was Riggs, which meant the diminutive Ms. Riley now had Dirty Harry pointed directly at his chest. "Okay, whoa," Tae said as calmly as she could with her blood thundering in her ears. "Let's all just calm down here and—"

"*No.*" Ms. Riley had the gun up to her cheek, one eye closed, the other clearly holding the three of them in her sights. "Hands up. All of you."

The kid was frozen in place, visibly shaking as he raised his hands.

Ms. Riley narrowed her eyes at Tae. "I *knew* you were trouble. You're with this little punk-ass thief, aren't you?"

Tae had faced a lot of questionable circumstances in her life, several that she probably shouldn't have lived through. She'd long ago decided she was like a cat and had nine lives. She sure as hell hoped she had at least one left. "Ms. Riley, please lower your gun."

"Dirty Harry stays until you all empty out your pockets on the counter right now. The big guy first."

Tae could feel the tension in Riggs's body, but he didn't move.

"I don't care who I shoot!" Ms. Riley said.

Tae started to take a step toward the counter, but Riggs gave her a hard look and she stilled. Then he slowly reached into his pockets and set the contents on the counter. Wallet. Keys. Phone.

"Turn around," Ms. Riley told him. "Slowly. Are you armed? You seem the sort to be armed."

"I'm not armed." Riggs raised his hands and turned in a slow circle.

Ms. Riley nodded her satisfaction and looked at Tae. "You next."

"Look at me. I had to shoehorn myself into this ridiculous dress. Do I look like I'm hiding anything?"

"Girl, I know you're carrying *something*."

Tae reached into her bra, pulling out the debit card she'd already revealed, along with two twenties and a small lip gloss.

The kid looked agog.

Riggs was showing nothing.

Ms. Riley gestured with the gun. "I know there's more."

"Fine." It wasn't often Tae felt thankful for her D's, but she was in that moment as she reached back in for her handy-dandy, fix-anything tool that would crack open a head nicely, and then under her dress for the pocketknife she had sheathed to a thigh.

"You still carry that thing?" Riggs asked.

"Of course."

The very corners of his mouth quirked slightly. "What else is in there?"

"Wouldn't you like to know." Tae looked at Ms. Riley. "We good?"

"*Everything*, Tae Holmes."

Tae sighed and pulled out a just-in-case tampon. "There. Happy?"

"Not until the kid empties his pockets."

The kid shook his head.

Tae eyed him. She'd been right. He looked to be *barely* four-teen, and he was definitely still a flight risk. "Listen, she's not kidding, okay? Whatever you've got in there is way less danger-ous than Ms. Riley with a gun, trust me."

He shifted on his feet and yep, it was in the whites of his wide eyes. He was going to bolt. "No!" she cried. "*Don't—*"

The little idiot darted for the door.

Ms. Riley swung her gun his way, and Riggs dove straight at the gun.

CHAPTER 4

In that moment, Tae's life became a slow-motion movie montage. Riggs literally flying through the air *toward* the locked-and-loaded gun. The kid running faster than the speed of light.

Ms. Riley taking aim . . .

On Tae's left was a bank of coolers holding last-minute-purchase items: eggs, milk, soda. On her right was a display of beer, the cans stacked like a castle turret against the end cap. She snatched a can and flung it, beaning the kid right between the shoulder blades. He went down just as Ms. Riley's gun went off with an ear-splitting *BOOM*.

More ceiling tile rained down on them, as well as glass from the overhead lights. Everyone but Ms. Riley hit the floor. Tae raised her head, her eyes locked on Riggs as he got to his feet. No holes in him anywhere, thankfully. She stumbled through the ceiling debris, insulation, and broken glass on the floor to the kid, who hadn't moved. *"Hey, are you okay?"*

Riggs tried to nudge her aside, his voice gruff. "Careful, we still don't know if he's armed."

Tae patted the kid's back, going for that bulge Riggs had seen, lifting up his jacket to find a sweatshirt rolled around his waist. She glared at Riggs. "Some weapon." Then she pulled two granola bars and a small carton of milk from the kid's various pockets and sent Ms. Riley a scathing look. "Shame on you."

"Stealing is stealing," the woman said, not looking sorry in the least.

"I swear I'll never do it again," the kid whispered.

Tae stood, feeling an ache around one eye and the sting of glass cutting into her skin from several different places. Since she'd had worse, she ignored all of it and pulled the kid upright. Glass and bits of ceiling tile rained off them both to join the mess on the floor. Miraculously, he didn't appear to be hurt. "You *really* picked the wrong place to steal from."

He looked panicked and tried to scramble free, but Riggs had him by the back of his jacket. "I was seventy cents short," the kid burst out with. "My little sister's been crying all day and there's nothing in the apartment."

Tae felt her heart squeeze, and she pushed one of her two twenties toward Ms. Riley. "Here. For what he's got. Keep the change." The other twenty she handed to the kid. "What's your name?"

"Jordy."

"How old are you, Jordy?"

"Fourteen."

She sent a scathing look at Ms. Riley, and for good measure also at Riggs. "Okay, Jordy," she said softly. "How about you go across the street to McGregor's market. Make sure you pay this time, yeah?"

The kid nodded like a bobblehead as he took a step backward, keeping a wary eye on Ms. Riley.

When the woman lowered her gun, the kid turned and hightailed it out of the store.

Tae felt blood trickle down her arm and looked at her now very dirty dress. And dammit, the slit had ripped up to near indecent heights. "I *knew* I should've bought the insurance!" She narrowed her eyes at Ms. Riley. "You're going to pay for this dress!"

"The hell I will! But *you're* going to pay for this whole mess." She pointed at her. "I should've called the cops on the lot of you!"

Riggs looked around. "You've got two ceiling tiles out, some insulation, and a few lightbulbs." He pulled money from his wallet. Two hundred-dollar bills, from what Tae could see. "This should cover it," he said to Ms. Riley. "We good?"

Ms. Riley snatched the two hundred bucks and shoved them into her pocket.

Riggs nodded and then turned his sharp and—*whoa*, seriously pissed-off eyes—on Tae. "You're bleeding," he said.

She took his left hand and turned it over, looking at his cut palm. "So are you."

"It's nothing," he said grimly. "You shouldn't have—"

"What? Not stood up for the kid who was stealing for his starving sister? Not given him money to get more food? Not let him go so he could feed her? Which?"

"All of it." He moved close, his eyes on her like he might be approaching a wild lioness. Then closer still, until they were toe to toe. Moving very slowly, he lifted a hand, tipped up her face, and turned it right and then left, studying her carefully.

She jerked her chin free. "I'm fine. And if I hadn't helped him, then who would have?" She turned to Ms. Riley. "You got a broom?"

Ten minutes later, she and Riggs had cleaned up the mess while Ms. Riley sat on her stool watching Netflix on her phone, ignoring them both.

Riggs looked at her face again.

"Still fine," she said.

"Is there someone I should call for you?" he asked. "Let them know you're okay?"

"Nope."

"*Someone's* got to be worried about you."

"Nope."

"No one?"

She slid him a look. "Are you fishing to see if I'm in a relationship?"

He almost smiled. "Are you?"

"No." She'd had boyfriends, but no one to write home about, and nothing lately. She wanted stability; she wanted a relationship—someday—but she didn't really even know what that looked like. Her last serious boyfriend had been a few years ago, and their relationship had been pretty great. She'd actually thought maybe he was the one, but it'd fallen apart when he asked her to set boundaries with her mom, saying that they were codependent, unhealthily so. She'd tried and failed, and he'd walked.

He'd shown up a month later, saying he loved her and he wanted to try again; she'd told him she hadn't missed him when he was gone.

Except . . . she had.

Okay, so not *him* exactly, but she'd missed having someone in her life, someone to have fun with, be physical with, someone to talk to.

Was that her problem? Was she lonely? Good God, that made her sound so pathetic, but she suspected it was true. But for so long, she'd been motivated by circumstances, money—or the lack thereof—and she'd told herself over and over again that nothing mattered but the security and safety money could bring her. Certainly not love.

At her continued silence, Riggs grabbed two pints of ice cream, taking the time to hold them up to her for approval. The double fudge chocolate *and* the Neapolitan.

She nodded, and then he slapped more money on the counter. Without looking at Ms. Riley, he grabbed a plastic-wrapped spoon and came back to Tae.

She raised a brow in disbelief, knowing he ate clean. Or at least he used to, which she remembered, because he'd always shared his snacks and lunch with her. Something she appreciated more than he could possibly know. "You're going to pollute your body with dairy and fat?"

"After what just happened? Yes." He gently pressed one of the containers against her aching eye. With his free hand, he offered her the other carton and spoon.

She nearly melted. *Nearly.* Instead, she narrowed her eyes. "This doesn't make us friends again."

"Agreed."

CHAPTER 5

After cleaning up the store and making sure Ms. Riley wasn't going to call the cops on them, Riggs followed Tae outside, where they stood in a sort of stunned silence under the overhang. The military had trained him how to process adrenaline quickly and efficiently, but he was worried about Tae. She stood in that dress, a little dirty, bleeding, rocking her glam look in much the same way she'd once rocked her moody all-black wardrobe, looking dangerous and gorgeous. Or gorgeously dangerous.

A warrior princess.

He pulled off his jacket and wrapped it around her shoulders as sheets of rain poured down from an angry, turbulent sky.

"Perfect," she muttered in a tone that gave away nothing of what the hell she'd been thinking when she'd stepped in front of a loaded shotgun. He could still feel his heart skipping beats over *that* stunt. So much for processing the adrenaline.

"Well, okay then," she said suddenly. "Gotta go."

He had to hustle to grab her hand and hold on to her. "Where are you going?"

"Home."

"You don't have a car here."

"I've got two feet, don't I?"

He looked down at the high heels that were going to fuel his fantasies for a long time to come. "You can't walk home in those."

"The last guy who told me what I can't do is still walking funny."

That gave him a smile. He was a sick, sick man, but damn, he loved her sass. "I'll drive you."

Looking unimpressed, she raised an eyebrow.

"Right," he said, reminding himself he wasn't a soldier anymore but supposedly a civilized civilian. "I'll rephrase. Can I *please* give you a ride home?"

This got him a long side-eye, as if she was assessing him for . . . God knew what. "Sure," she finally said. "Thanks."

Note to self: use "please" more often.

When they got to his car, she started to climb into the backseat, but he shook his head and opened the front passenger door for her. "Still not your Uber."

She slid into the front while he did his best not to notice that her dress had ripped all the way up now, revealing a long, toned leg and an intriguingly teeny-tiny strip of black lace across her hip.

He shut the door and shook his head at himself as he came around the front of the car to slide behind the wheel. *Not* going there. "Where to?"

She directed him through Sunrise Cove, across the train tracks and to the very last part of town before heading up a narrow street into an area that had been built in the early 1920s, back when the tiny cabins were for summers only, not the harsh winters. A few had been renovated, but most hadn't. She pointed to a duplex that looked not exactly up-to-date but was obviously well cared for.

He glanced over at her. "Is this your place, or are you messing with me again?"

She grimaced at the reminder of that long-ago night, when she'd not wanted him to see where she lived.

"I'd have done the same if I'd been you."

She looked so surprised, he smiled, which felt . . . unfamiliar. And how was it possible that all these years later she still had such an effect on him? He'd been prepared to be angry and frustrated at being back here in Sunrise Cove, but he wasn't either of those things. At least not right now. He was . . . actually, he had no idea what he was. "You didn't owe me anything back then. You'd just been trying to protect yourself."

She nodded. "But not from you. Life was . . . hard then."

"And it's been hard tonight too."

"That?" She let out a rough laugh. "That was just another Saturday night."

"You could've been killed."

"But I wasn't."

He shook his head. The words were right, her facial expression was right, but her eyes lacked her usual sass. "So you still do that."

"What?"

"Use bravado like a shield."

That won him a real smile, one that made it all the way to her pretty eyes. "I like to stick with what works. Thanks for the ride." She put her hand to the door handle, then paused when he turned off the engine. "What are you doing?"

"Walking you in," he said. "I want to look at you."

"I'm fine."

"Humor me. Those cuts need to be cleaned out. I don't want you to get an infection." He looked at her. "Or give me a bad review on Uber."

She snorted. "Trust me, I've got no intention of telling *any-one* about tonight. As for the first aid, I'm low-maintenance and take care of myself."

He looked at her shimmery dress and four-, maybe five-inch heels, and went brows up.

"Okay, so I'm *almost* always low-maintenance. Don't judge me by my clothes."

"I wouldn't dream of it."

She studied him in the ambient light. "I'm fine," she said again, softer now.

"Maybe I'm not." He got out of the car and met her on the curb. "Cute place."

She eyed the cabin-style duplex and let out a small smile, like she couldn't help herself. "My mom lives on the right. I'm on the left. If the guy behind me keeps his trees trimmed, and if I stand on top of my back fence, I can sometimes almost sort of see a tiny sliver of the lake."

He remembered how much she'd loved the lake, how she could often be found sitting on the rocks, watching the water.

He knew how she'd grown up—which wasn't all that different from the life of the kid she'd saved tonight. Her mom had been a baby having a baby, and they'd lived hand to mouth, sometimes couch surfing with friends, sometimes in a one-room rental. It made him happy to know she had a place to call home. "The lake's still one of your favorite places then."

She looked at him, her eyes narrowed. "How did you know that?"

"I used to see you out there sometimes. And you told me when we were partnered up on that Sunrise Cove Cleanup Day we did for extra credit."

Their gazes locked and held, and in her eyes he could see surprise that he remembered.

A front door opened across the street and a huge guy, at least six foot six, became a hulking shadow in his doorway. "Tae?" came his deep, booming voice. "You okay?"

She smiled and waved; a bedraggled, drenched, bloody, grunge princess. "Hagrid! Yes, it's me, and I'm okay, thank you!"

Hagrid—there was certainly more than a passing resemblance in the guy's thick, bushy beard and loose wild hair blowing around his face—took a step onto his porch and was suddenly fully visible thanks to the light adjacent to his head.

The handlebar mustache, leather vest, beat-up jeans, and heavy black boots said badass biker. The stature and stance said military. He had something tiny and furry in his arms, which looked like a stuffed animal until it gave a series of high-pitched yips. Hagrid made some kissy noises and spoke to the dog in a high-pitched baby voice that did not go with the rest of the big man. "Shh, Muffin, it's okay, baby, it's Tae, and you love Tae."

Muffin stopped yipping just in time to save Riggs's eardrums.

Tae waved and blew both the man and the dog a kiss.

"You're good?" Hagrid called out.

"All good," Tae promised.

With a long, hard look at Riggs, Hagrid vanished back inside.

"I think I've just sullied your reputation," Riggs said.

She snorted and unlocked her door, putting a hand to his chest when he made to follow her.

"You're still bleeding," he said. "I want to get a closer look."

She eyed him, the warning hand still on his chest.

"Okay," he said. "If you won't let me check you, then how about you check me. I might be bleeding out."

She cocked a single brow.

He smiled. "You're the most suspicious person I've ever met."

"Who's the one who almost tackled a kid for stealing a couple of granola bars and milk?"

"I nearly tackled a kid because you were going to get hurt."

She looked surprised at his answer, as if she wasn't used to being worried about. "I keep telling you, I can handle myself."

There was definitely something in her voice that betrayed her feelings whenever she said that, but if he coddled her, she'd retreat. "No shit. And good to know your trust issues are still firmly in place."

She glared at him. "I'm pretty sure I was the only one trusting in humanity back there. So what does that say about you?"

He had to laugh. She'd called him out on his own bullshit. No one ever did that. Not even Jake. "That I'm not fit for civilization."

Her gaze softened. "How long have you been home?"

"What day is it?"

"Saturday."

"It's still Saturday?" He scrubbed a hand down his face. "Hell, I'm not even sure what time zone I'm in."

"Understandable," she said quietly. She stepped inside and turned to look at him. "You can come in." Then she turned and vanished inside.

It'd been a long time since he'd been intrigued about much, but there was no doubt that was the emotion going through him now. Tae Holmes fascinated the hell out of him, and always had. But more than that, she impressed. Bad shit happened, he knew that more than most, and so did she, but she didn't let it faze her, at least not outwardly. She was no damsel in distress. She was resilient, tenacious, and brave as hell, and . . . damn. That was attractive.

Her place was small and the furniture sparse, but warm and cozy. Her couch was a soft gray corduroy, piled on with neutral-toned pillows. The scarred hardwood floors revealed the well-worn paths to the hallway and, he assumed, the kitchen.

That was where he found her, pulling vodka from the freezer.

"Medicinal." She took a sip right from the bottle, then handed it over to him. "I figured it was alcohol or a workout to burn off the excess adrenaline. I went with the obvious choice."

He took a shot that burned a path down his throat, then

handed it back with a nod. "Saw the workout mat in the living room in front of the TV. It has dust on it."

She snorted. "I signed up for a Zoom workout class that was too advanced for me."

The woman had kicked ass tonight. Hard to imagine anything she couldn't do. "Too advanced?"

"The instructor said to do a plank and bring my knee to the opposite elbow." She shrugged. "I did a modified version where I turned off the TV and took a nap instead."

He laughed. She was turning him into a regular Chuckles. "First aid kit?"

She headed down the hall, vodka in hand.

He followed her to a bathroom the size of a postage stamp. Her hair had fallen loose and wild around her face and shoulders as she stared at the pair of them in the mirror, she still wearing his suit jacket, he in a white button-down, the both of them wet, dirty, and a little bloody. "We look like we were in a bad horror flick." She set the vodka on the counter and bent to the cabinet below the sink, pulling out a first aid kit.

"You first." He patted the tiny countertop space between her medicine cabinet and the sink.

"We going to play doctor?" she asked with some amusement.

"I don't play."

With a roll of her eyes, she pulled herself up to sit.

Stepping close, he nudged his suit jacket from her shoulders, letting it fall behind her so that it still kept her warm from the waist down. Once again, he took in the dress. "I really do like the new look." He waited until she met his gaze. "But I liked your old look too."

"Right. You liked the all-black emo-girl thing."

"I liked *you*."

That had her going quiet, and he smiled. "Besides, it wasn't *all* black. You had blue streaks in your hair. Sometimes purple."

"Good times." But she gave a reluctant smile. "I don't think about those days very often. Not exactly happy memories, you know?"

Yeah, he did. He drew a deep breath and looked her over carefully.

She had shallow cuts along her right arm and hand where she'd landed taking down the kid. Also on her neck and above her right eyebrow. Cupping her face, he checked her pupils.

At his touch, she sucked in a breath, and the air between them seemed to shift. "I keep telling you, I'm fine."

Her pupils backed that statement, so he opened the first aid kit and pulled out the antiseptic and clean cotton. Then he went to work inspecting each cut for glass before deep cleaning and covering them. She sat there stoically, occasionally wincing as he worked, not saying a word or making a single complaint. The guys he'd served with would certainly be whining, but not Tae. She seemed reflective and . . . vulnerable? Maybe because, like him, no one took care of her but her. Yes, she had her mom, but his impression had always been that Tae did most of the caretaking. The deepest cut, the one over her eyebrow, kept oozing blood. "This one could use a few stitches."

"Just slap a Band-Aid on it, it's fine."

"Chicken," he teased.

"Do you have any idea how much an ER visit costs?"

That shamed the smile right off of him. He used Steri-Strips, and while he worked, she pulled her things from her bra, including her knife, setting it all aside. Somehow that seemed to bring back to him the danger they'd faced tonight.

As if she'd gone there too, she looked at him. "Seriously, no weapon?" she asked.

He held up his hands and wiggled his fingers. "These are multiuse tools of mass destruction."

"Don't I know it."

He smiled. "Is that supposed to mean something?"

She shook her head at him, but there was a slight amused light in her eyes. "You know damn well those hands also have other . . . talents."

He grinned. "I've been wondering if you remember."

"Burned into my brain." She hopped off the counter and pointed at him. "Stay." She vanished, reappearing three minutes later, the dress and heels gone, replaced by black leggings and an oversize, soft-looking sweater that was so big it fell off a shoulder. Her feet were bare. Reaching into a drawer, she pulled out a hair tie and twisted her hair into a knot on top of her head. Then she patted the counter. "Your turn."

He shook his head. "I'm okay."

She gave him a saucy stare. "You'd rob me of my turn to be the doctor?"

"I don't fit on your counter."

She nodded toward the closed commode, and to appease her, he sat. Oh hell, who was he kidding, he wanted her hands on him again, in any capacity he could get. She gestured for him to take off his shirt, pointing to some blood seeping through on his shoulder and elbow.

Unbuttoning the shirt, he shrugged out of it. She took a long moment just to look at him, and he thought maybe she was cataloguing him for injuries, but when she sucked in a breath and slowly let it out again, he realized she'd been taking in his body for a different reason entirely. "Everything in the right place?" he asked mildly.

She rolled her eyes. "Don't even pretend you don't know that your scrawny ass grew up to be hot as hell."

He grinned. "You like me."

Ignoring that, she shifted close, standing between his legs, her head bent as she poked and prodded at his wounds, carefully checking for glass. When she finally spoke, her voice was quiet. Reflective. "I was going to sneak out the back door of that store tonight. Without saying goodbye."

"I know."

Her eyes flew to his, and he let out a small smile. "Why do you think I kept my eyes on you through the store windows? Well, on you, but also on that dress."

She snorted and began irrigating his cuts, which, for the record, stung like a bitch.

"You've got some new scars," she said, sliding her finger over a round one along his rib cage, and then another, a straight one that started low on a hip and vanished beneath the waistband of his pants.

It took him a moment to speak instead of groan. "One's a souvenir from a bullet, the other a knife."

"From combat?"

He nodded.

She shook her head. "Damn." She still had her hands on him. His eyes locked with hers, and the air went heavy with a sense of intimacy, both present and past.

"This one might need stitches," she said of his shoulder, characteristically moving on from a difficult conversation.

He smiled. "Just slap a Band-Aid on it."

She snorted, proving she could laugh at herself—also attractive. She might be all mouthy sarcasm and cynicism, but she took very good care of him, her fingers both efficient and gentle.

"You're good at this."

She glanced at him, making him realize that their mouths were only a few inches apart. "Not my first time."

He nodded and held eye contact, knowing she'd been bullied in high school. Knowing also, she'd put out the appearance of not giving a shit. He remembered the time she'd been cornered on her walk home and beat up by four girls, who'd later gotten suspended. She'd been suspended as well because she'd pulled a knife to get them to back off. She hadn't used the knife, even as badly hurt as she'd been. He'd known then that she would understand his life more than he'd wanted her to. "In some ways," he said quietly, "my growing-up years weren't all that different from yours."

She chuckled. "Okay, Mr. Popular, who drove a cool truck and was loved by *everyone*."

Maybe, but no matter what he'd told Jake, his home life had been hell without his mom or his brother around to help buffer his dad's not-so-slow descent into the bottom of a liquor bottle. "People saw what I wanted them to see."

Her hands stilled, and she met his gaze.

"Yeah," he said, gently setting his hands on her hips and pushing her back so he could stand. Because suddenly having her so close was more torture than pleasure. "You're not the only one who plays their cards close to the vest."

"So if it wasn't your social life that sucked . . ." she murmured. "Your home life?"

He buttoned up, not answering. Not wanting to.

"I know your mom died when you were young. Was your dad . . . not a good guy?"

Reaching for his shirt, he shrugged back into it. "No."

She held his gaze for a long moment, apparently reading him in a way few others could. "I'm sorry," she said simply. "Some people don't deserve to be parents." She offered him the bottle of vodka in silent commiseration. "Were you scared you were going to get shot tonight?"

"No." He'd been scared *she* was going to get shot tonight . . .

She cocked her head. "Guess what happened must seem pretty tame to you after all you've been through."

Not wanting to go there either, he shrugged.

"Right." She nodded. "The big, bad warrior doesn't show weakness."

"Showing weakness is a good way to get dead." He took another pull of the vodka and then found himself hungrily watching her do the same, including when she licked her lips after.

"Oh boy," she whispered, staring at his mouth as well. "Don't go there."

"So you're a knife wielder, handy with a first aid kit, heartstoppingly beautiful, and also a mind reader?" He smiled. "I always knew you were an overachiever."

She rolled her eyes, clearly uncomfortable with the compliment. It made him want to give her more. "I thought about you, Tae. After that night."

"*Not* going there," she repeated.

"Right. You always were smarter than me."

She looked surprised at his quick acquiescence. But he meant it. They'd been too young. And yeah, okay, so maybe he'd hoped after their night together there'd be more, but whatever. It hadn't happened, which had probably been for the best. She'd have left him at some point anyway. That's what people he cared about did, and he had never gotten okay with it.

"The truth is," she said, "I did you a favor." And with that, she put away the first aid kit, gathered up the trash, and walked out of the room.

CHAPTER 6

The past always caught up with her, one way or the other. Needing a moment from the intensity of one Riggs Copeland, Tae headed to her dark living room window and stared out into the night, listening to the torrent of rain pummeling her roof. There were no streetlights or billboards in Sunrise Cove. They were against city code. As a result, the night sky above Lake Tahoe usually looked like a sheet of black velvet covered in brilliant, shimmering diamonds of all shapes and colors, and could stun and humble her into a peaceful silence.

But the storm blanketed the stars, revealing nothing, leaving her to relive tonight's adventure, including the look on Jordy's face when she'd handed him a twenty-dollar bill.

Like she'd just saved his life.

Once upon a time, her mom had been that kid, fifteen years old, kicked out of the house by her family, and left with an infant with little to no means to take care of them both. She looked across the driveway and saw her mom's car, parked safe and sound.

She wished she knew if Jordy and his sister were safe and sound too, and promised herself she'd find out.

Riggs came up behind her, keeping a respectful distance, which she appreciated more than she'd ever say. Everything about tonight had played into her old nightmares and angst, leaving her feeling far too . . . open. She could see his reflection in the window, watchful, quiet, a sense of easy confidence that belied how dangerous he could likely be. A man who'd put her life ahead of his in that convenience store. "I didn't thank you for tonight."

He gave a slow shake of his head. "I didn't do anything. You had it under control from the start."

There was something about the big, strong guy admitting such a thing that had her softening. But softening for Riggs was a dangerous thing indeed, far more dangerous than anything she'd faced tonight. So she put on her most polite smile. "I appreciate your help and the ride home. You give good Band-Aid, so thanks for that too." She moved to the front door to let him out. When he didn't follow, she looked back just as he sank to her couch. "What are you doing?"

He leaned his head back, his long legs stretched out in front of him. He looked . . . pale, and every line of his body tense and seemingly exhausted. He'd literally just come home from some likely hellhole. It was no wonder he'd reacted so aggressively to what had happened at the store. His head was probably still in a war zone. "Maybe you should go home and sleep for a few days. Get caught up."

He didn't say anything to this. Didn't so much as move a muscle.

With a sigh, she walked closer. "You're staying with Jake and Carolyn?"

This got her the slightest of nods.

"Maybe they're worried."

"If I leave, maybe you'll worry about my wounds opening again. Wouldn't want you to feel responsible if I black out on my way home."

She wanted to smile. Hell, she wanted to jump him. But the thing about being pummeled tonight by emotions she'd felt for him in the past was that it made her wary.

And afraid to reveal too much of herself. "I won't."

His eyes were still closed, but a smile curved his mouth. He always had been able to see right through her. And yeah, she remembered a lot about him as well.

Like how he treated her as if she were a real person, not the back-off-or-die person she'd pretended to be.

"I could also starve to death," he said. "Getting shot at made me hungry."

"You always used to be hungry."

"That hasn't changed."

Something deep inside her quivered and she wasn't even sure why. She felt like she was in the danger zone here, holding on by a thread. If he touched her, it was all going to come back, how he'd been a balm to her wounded soul that night, how his touch had made her feel, how she wanted to know if it would be the same amazing, scorching chemistry now . . . She glanced at his very still body. "Hey." Leaning over, she poked him in the chest. "No sleeping on my couch."

Before she could so much as blink, he'd caught her wrist and tugged so that she fell into him. "Okay," she said, pushing upright off his chest. "So your reflexes are still on point."

His eyes opened. Those usually sharp, assessing green eyes were soft with exhaustion now, and something else that made her breath catch. "Are you really not afraid of anything?" she whispered.

When he didn't answer, she nudged him. "Come on, *everyone's* got a fear."

He shrugged, which she was starting to realize was his go-to move when he didn't want to answer or reveal too much of himself.

"Not even death?" she pushed.

"I've faced death and I'm still here." He lifted a hand to brush his fingers gently over the Steri-Strips above her eyebrow. "It's bleeding through."

She touched the one on his shoulder. "So is yours."

Time seemed to freeze as they stared at each other. Two minutes ago she'd been wet and cold. Funny how her body temperature had rocketed up. Maybe she was coming down with something.

His hand came up to touch her jaw, but it was she who leaned in, meeting his mouth halfway in a soft, questing kiss that blew brain cells left and right.

Far before she was ready, he pulled back and studied her face, his own serious and assessing. At whatever he saw there, he groaned low in his throat and caught the back of her head gently, pulling her to him again, the kiss hot and serious this time. Desire washed over her in waves, reminding her of that long-ago night. They'd been each other's first. Neither of them had known much. It'd been awkward and fumbling and . . . *amazing.*

But he'd learned some new moves, at least in the kissing department, and in the very back of her mind she tried to remember if she was wearing sexy underwear.

And how does that matter if you get naked quickly?

Again, Riggs pulled back, taking a steadying breath. She supposed she should feel good that one of them was still capable of thought. Searing her with a heated look, he nudged her off him and stood.

And just like that, she remembered what it felt like to be sixteen years old all over again, starved for affection.

But she *wasn't* sixteen. She was twenty-eight and apparently *still* starved for attention. "You have something to say," she guessed.

"Yes." His expression was of regret and longing. "I want to be honest with you. Your friendship in high school was important to me. More than you could ever know. Then we slept together and I thought it might turn into more, but it didn't. You didn't talk to me again, and I got it. We were just stupid kids. But I worried about you."

Her heart kicked it up a notch. "And . . . ?"

"And . . . I'm leaving this time too. You deserve to know that."

Damn. Sometimes a good mood was *really* hard to maintain. "And?"

"And . . . we're no longer kids just messing around. I don't want to start something I can't finish. Not with you, Tae. You deserve so much more."

"Oh, and you've decided that for me, huh?" Feeling defensive, she crossed her arms. "What makes you think I was going to let you finish something tonight anyway?"

His laugh was wry as he tunneled his fingers through his hair. "Do you ever let your guard down?"

"No."

"Tae . . ." He appeared to struggle for words. "I want to be friends again. The real deal."

She blinked. They'd just nearly self-combusted from a holy-shit hot kiss, but if she was reading him right, he wasn't interested in that, and she had no idea how to feel about it. "Friends," she repeated slowly.

"Yes. Friends. Like we were in school."

"Are you going to finish my lab homework for me and every-thing?" she asked.

"You know what I mean." His eyes were serious, and she sighed, because for a moment she'd thought—hoped—things might be going in a decidedly different direction for the rest of the night.

Like to her bedroom.

But she was pretty sure she'd just been turned down, granted in the nicest possible way. Didn't take the sting away though.

Never good with rejection, she pointed to the door. "Goodbye, Riggs."

"Good night, Rebel." The distinction didn't escape her as she watched him head to the front door. He paused before turning to face her. His hands were shoved in his pockets, which she hoped meant he was having a hell of a time keeping them off her.

"It's just that more is a really bad idea," he said.

"*Obviously.*"

With a slight shake of his head, he was gone.

Good riddance, she told herself, feeling . . . a whole bunch of things she didn't want to feel. Worse, there was no acceptable reason why she'd felt so damn much from a few kisses.

She needed a man who wanted her, who'd open himself to her, heart and soul, and let her do the same—and still stick around after, regardless if her life felt like too much to handle. She wanted . . . stability.

Riggs was never going to be that guy.

She just needed to remember that.

Shaking her head, she locked up and went down the hall. She needed a hot shower, an orgasm, and sleep, and she didn't need a man for any of it.

CHAPTER 7

For all of her adult life and half of her teenage life, April Holmes had been one thing, and one thing only.

A mom to the best thing that had ever happened to her—*Tae.*

Standing on the shore of Sunrise Cove, she stared at the early dawn sky and felt her breath stutter in her chest. Streaks of pinks and magentas stretched above the deep, dark blue of Lake Tahoe's famously clean waters and stole her heart. Lifting her camera to her face, she began taking pics, losing herself in the moment.

She'd had to skip a lot of things in her life, college being one of them. But with Tae being a grown-up now, and better at taking care of herself than April had ever been, it had freed up a lot of time. It used to be that April would fill that time in self-destructive ways.

But she'd grown up too. Or so she liked to think. Her new goal was to be a better April Holmes, and that included being a better mom to Tae. She was working on that, but part of being a better mom was becoming a more well-rounded person herself instead of leaning on Tae to be her entire world.

So she'd enrolled in photography class at the local community college and had an assignment due. But that wasn't why she was up at the butt-crack of dawn. She was here because she wanted to be, assignment or not.

The public dock on which she stood was only ten minutes from home. She had no idea how she'd ever gotten so lucky to have this view whenever she wanted.

She must have done something right.

She'd liked to think it was that she'd been a good mom, but though she'd tried, she knew she'd had a lot of fail moments. She'd done a lot of things that she wasn't super proud of to make ends meet. Dated guys just so she and Tae would have a place to live, worked for cash under the table to avoid taxes, etc. She'd long ago stopped doing those things, and she comforted herself with the knowledge that she'd done what she'd had to in order to keep them off the streets.

But that knowledge didn't make it any easier to look back on.

She was just grateful that both she and Tae were in a good place now. Especially Tae. Her business was doing well, and April was so proud.

A hint of the brilliant sun teased the mountaintop far to the east, and her breath caught again at the sheer beauty. She snapped some more pics in quick succession, then lowered her camera to take in the moment.

There was a chill on the pine-scented air as she waited for

the sun to touch down and warm the high-altitude beauty all around her. At the moment, the lake was as still as glass, so clear and deep she could see schools of fish chasing each other. The only sounds were trees rustling and the occasional birdcall. Heaven on earth.

It'd taken a long time to get to this place in her life. Sure, she worked as a receptionist in a no-brainer job that she could do in her sleep. And yeah, okay, so she'd never followed any real dream of her own.

But she was pretty sure that was because of the guilt from the secret she kept.

It'd started out so innocent. It'd been the only surefire way to protect Tae and herself, but somewhere along that path, it'd ended up being something else entirely. And if she was being honest with herself, she carried a lot of shame around for how she'd handled it. Yes, she'd done a wrong for the right reason, but wrong was still wrong, and as she'd learned, some wrongs couldn't be fixed.

She'd accepted that. And because of it, all she'd ever aspired to in life was for her daughter to be happy. And if that made her and Tae what her daughter liked to teasingly call *codependent*, so be it. She was good with that. She loved how close they were, how they shared everything.

Correction: *almost* everything.

She lowered her camera again, the knot in her chest tightening, as it tended to do when she gave into introspection. But before she could dive too deep into it, the alarm on her phone buzzed, reminding her it was time to get to work, to a job she was lucky to have because she had a great boss and she loved Adrenaline HQ's mission statement.

And if the actual work—answering phones and keeping track of their client base—didn't exactly fulfill her, Jake allowing her to be their volunteer event photographer came a little bit closer to doing that.

It was enough, she told herself. She would make it be enough. So she put her camera away and headed to work.

RIGGS CAME INSTANTLY awake and then lay there, trying to figure out what had woken him from a dead sleep only a few hours after he'd gotten to bed. He was in his childhood bedroom, which might've given him nightmares, except it'd been renovated.

No evidence remained of his and Jake's wild and feral youth except the wood floors, which had been refinished and now gleamed and were dotted with throw rugs. But the rock band posters on the walls, hung to cover the holes from his dad punching through the drywall in fits of drunken rage, were gone, replaced with pictures of the gorgeous Tahoe landscape. His old, dark wood dresser was also missing, an oak bedroom set in its place, along with a little desk.

All of it looked like it belonged on a Pinterest board somewhere, which he only knew because his last girlfriend had been a Pinterest fanatic. She'd also been a soldier like him. But unlike him, she'd been sweet and gentle and open, and had expected him to be the same. Since he couldn't be what she needed, she'd used that sweet gentleness to dump his ass.

He hadn't been surprised. He didn't exactly have a track record of keeping the people he loved in his life.

The bed didn't creak like his old one, probably because it was also new. The sheets felt like he was lying on a silk cloud. There'd been a trillion little fluffy throw pillows, all of which now resided on the floor, but he was warm and comfortable, which was more than he could say about life before this bed.

He blinked blearily at the clock. Five A.M.

What had woken him?

A soft moan sounded in the still house, and he sat straight up. When the sound came again, he froze, then lay back down because it had been distinctly female, followed by a rough male groan. Shit. *Again?* Reaching over the edge of the bed, he gathered an armful of those ridiculously fluffy throw pillows and held them tight to his ears.

What he really wanted to do was bang on the wall and yell, "Knock it off," but his brother was having sex. No way in hell was he going to ruin that for him.

One of the moans penetrated his pillow earmuffs. *Hot dogs*, he thought a little desperately. Why did hot dogs come in packs of ten, but hot dog buns came in packs of eight? What kind of insanity was that? And he had a whole summer ahead of him here. Why had he thought coming back here was a good idea?

You hadn't been worried about that when you'd kissed Tae . . .

He'd kissed Tae. And it'd knocked him for a loop all over again. What was he doing? His mission had been simple—get in, help his brother, and get out. He could accept that missions sometimes changed, but he was cynical enough to know that he himself hadn't ever changed all that much and probably never would. He'd seen the military as an escape, and he'd been right.

This summer was just a quick side trip to the rest of his life, nothing more, no matter how sweet Tae had felt in his arms. Walking away from her had been hard, pun intended. But he'd meant it—she deserved better. *And . . . you don't want to get hurt when she leaves you, because at some point, everyone does . . .*

He could still hear himself telling Tae he had no fears, and he rolled his eyes at his own bullshit. He had *plenty* of fears. But as a Copeland, he wasn't good with showing them. His dad had squashed every ounce of emotion from him. When he'd been scared, he'd had to "suck it up." If he'd been hurt, he needed to "take it like a man."

Very tentatively, he let loose the pillows he was trying to smother himself with. No moans. With a sigh of relief, he lay back and willed himself back to sleep.

Two minutes in, the moaning started up again.

Rising, he pulled on sweats and went out into the early dawn to see if he could run off his demons.

When he got back—demons still firmly in place—Jake and Carolyn had already gone to work. Thankful, he showered and headed over to Adrenaline HQ's warehouse.

Riggs had gone over the building specs with Jake during the purchase of the warehouse two years ago, but he'd yet to see it in person. He wasn't sure what to expect, but when he stepped inside, he stopped short.

Because he hadn't expected a beautiful space, well organized, colorful, and . . . welcoming.

The warehouse had been divided into sections. The back portion appeared to be dedicated all to winter equipment, like skis and boards. The middle area had been set up for wheelchair polo. The front greeting area was wide open with love seats and comfortable chairs spread throughout, along with a few tables set at the right height for easy wheelchair access, all with charging stations.

It was a far cry from what he'd imagined for their small, fledgling start-up adventure company, that was for sure. He'd expected to see a desk for Jake and some winter equipment strewn about. Not this huge, wide-open, well-put-together playground. A warm wet nose smacked him in the crotch. A massive red Wookiee masquerading as a dog smiled up at him, panting happily in greeting.

"Hey, big guy." Riggs crouched to pet Grub, whom he'd met via FaceTime with his brother. "How you doing?"

"Well, he just ate my flip-flop so maybe ask him that again a half hour from now, after he yaks it up," the woman in a blue Adrenaline HQ T-shirt behind the front desk said sweetly, the pink metallic strips in her hair shimmering beneath the overhead lights. "Grub, sit." She smiled at Riggs. "Welcome."

There was something incredibly familiar about her, but he felt distracted as he took everything in.

"How can I help you?" the woman asked.

"I'm looking for Jake."

She clapped her hands together and then pointed at him with a smile. "I *knew* it! You're Riggs, Jake's brother." She waved at the wall nearest to her. "I recognized you."

Riggs glanced over and found it covered in pictures, some of them featuring his own mug. There were pics from when he and Jake had been little, on matching skis. Them in their hellion teen years—rafting, snowboarding, biking, climbing . . . One of them both in military dress uniforms—before Jake's accident. And for a moment, Riggs was brought back to a time when they'd both had the-world-is-still-our-oyster look in their eyes.

It felt like a hundred years ago. He was so far removed from that world, he'd forgotten what Jake, or for that matter, himself, had been like. It was like looking at two perfect strangers.

Grub had given up sitting and was trying to get more love from Riggs, who'd never been able to resist a dog. Crouching, he rubbed Grub's belly, who sighed in ecstasy.

The receptionist pulled her phone off her belt and made a call. "You've got a special guest here, boss." She listened for a few seconds, then laughed. "Yes, he looks like you, but not nearly as handsome, no." She winked at Riggs as she disconnected. "He'll be right out."

Riggs gestured to the handful of people moving equipment around, some in wheelchairs like his brother, some not, all wearing AHQ T-shirts. "What's going on?"

"What's going on is success," Jake said as he came out from the back, presumably from an office, looking like . . . a carefree kid.

So only one of them was hating life. Good to know. "Actually," Riggs said, "success was when you sold your boating company in San Francisco to come up here for the fresh mountain air, to relax and take things down a notch."

"Wow." Jake's smile didn't fade. "Most siblings would just say, hey, man, thanks for expanding our business." He turned to the receptionist. "April, this is my grumpy, curmudgeonly baby brother."

Riggs held his tongue while April smiled sweetly and said how nice it was to meet him.

"Come on," Jake said to him. "I'll show you the office. Don't slip on Grub's drool."

There was indeed a puddle of drool, which Jake swiped away with a mop that had been leaning against the wall, presumably just for that.

Riggs followed Jake through the warehouse, where everyone they passed sent Jake a smile and a friendly wave. More shocking, Jake smiled and waved back. The guy who'd been terse and stoic and bossy as shit for Riggs's entire life did seem relaxed and happy. Who knew? "What the hell's going on?"

"Not here." Jake swung directly toward a door along the back wall of the warehouse, Grub right at his side. Before contact was made, the door swung open.

Motion sensor.

They were in a hallway now, and at the end, Jake moved into what turned out to be a good-size office with a desk at the right height for Jake's chair, screens up on the walls, some of them running recorded videos without sound, clearly of AHQ events, showing wounded warriors and disabled athletes skiing, boarding, sledding . . . And for a beat, Riggs got lost in it, taking in all the wonder and joy on their faces.

"Now," Jake said, gesturing with one hand for Riggs to speak, the other on Grub's head. "Lay it on me. Oh, and nice to see you, by the way."

"You're expanding?"

"We need a summer program. And in the shoulder seasons, we've got this big warehouse, so I figured, why not use it? Now people can come play polo or basketball or . . ." He smiled. "Or whatever else we think up. It's a work in progress. I like the idea of having an event every few weekends through the summer, like we do for winter. We can operate here and also across the street at the park and beach. The rec center said they'd give us permitting for it."

This boggled Riggs. "I thought you were considering retiring at some point. That was the last conversation we had."

"No," Jake said. "That was the last order *you* gave. But I'm not one of your subordinates. I'm your older brother, who can still kick your ass."

Could you actually feel your own blood pressure rise? Because Riggs was pretty sure his was. "I'm fifty percent owner of this place." The minute the words were out of his mouth, he regretted them. Truly. But Jake had a way of making him feel like he was five years old and stupid all over again. He took a breath and ran a hand down his face. "I didn't mean that."

"Actually, that's exactly what you meant. And I get it, you put up half the money, blindly trusting me to do this. But I *did* do it, Riggs. *Successfully.*"

"I know. And you've put one hundred percent of the sweat equity in." Not to mention the heart and soul. "It's amazing. But, man, you're working too hard."

Jake shrugged.

"You got hurt twice this last year alone."

Jake's eyes went hard. The guy hated showing weakness, always had. "I'm fine."

"Jake—"

"I'm doing this with or without you, Riggs. And would you sit down? You're pacing like a wild animal and you've only been here a few minutes."

It was true, and Grub was following him faithfully step by step. He sat on a love seat against one wall and felt the fight go out of him. "Look, what you've done since coming home, starting up two successful businesses, it's nothing short of incredible. But you've worked so hard. *So* hard, Jake. It's not what I want for you after all you've been through."

Jake looked at him for a long beat, then nodded and softened. "I didn't think it was what I wanted either, but working with these kids and injured vets, giving them something back after all they've lost, it's the most fulfilling thing I've ever done. It's changed me. I'm happy."

The truth of that statement was all over Jake's face, so Riggs nodded.

"And maybe I'm the worried one," Jake said. "In the past four years, you've been dropped into just about every hellhole on the planet and had to shoot your way out of half of them."

Riggs shrugged. "So?"

"So maybe *that's* why I asked you to come for the summer. Maybe I want *you* to slow down. Maybe I wanted you to come because . . ." Jake's eyes were serious. "I need you here, Riggs."

Riggs's gut tightened hard. "What's wrong?"

"Nothing. *Nothing*," Jake said quieter, earnest. "Except we're not on the same page anymore and I hate it."

Riggs let out a breath, relieved to find common ground with the one person who knew him better than anyone else ever had. "I hate it too," he admitted.

Grub jumped up on the love seat and laid down his big, heavy head on Riggs's leg.

"So you'll stay for the summer? Spend time with me running AHQ?" Jake asked.

Riggs stared down at Grub's huge brown eyes. They'd never had a dog except the one he and Jake had rescued once and kept at a friend's house. He stroked a hand down the dog's body. Grub sighed in pleasure and closed his eyes.

"Riggs."

He blew out a breath. "What do you want from me? I'm here. I'm doing the best I can."

"And that's all I'm asking for."

They stared at each other for a beat. They'd never been talkers, and they'd certainly never been much for feelings—either of them, even when they'd dodged their dad's fists together. Actually, Jake had taken most of the fists, for both their mom and Riggs. He had no idea how to repay that favor. But all of it had happened so long ago. They'd not spent much time, if any, together since Jake had joined up with the military shortly after their mom had died.

Uncomfortable with the awkward silence, Riggs shifted and pulled a pillow out from behind his back. And then a second.

Both were sunshine yellow, so bright he almost needed his sunglasses to avoid retina damage. "I don't get the pillow fetish."

"It's not a fetish, weirdo."

"You've got them at the cabin too, *everywhere*, and coordinating curtains on all the windows. Hell, you even have flowers in the kitchen and bathrooms. I'd have just burned that place to the ground by now."

"I thought about it when I first moved back," Jake admitted. "But Carolyn taught me to focus on the here and now. And I gotta tell you, the here and now looks pretty damn awesome from where I'm sitting."

"Great, but what does that have to do with owning more throw pillows than actual furniture? I mean, these are migraine-inducing."

"It's a girl thing. I think . . ." Jake winced. "Just don't tell Carolyn, she picked them. And since when are you so emotionally bankrupt that you can't appreciate some color—" He paused as a tall, leggy blonde entered the office.

The woman lightly cuffed the back of Jake's head. "I thought the idea was to shower your brother with so much love he'd want to stay forever, not scare him off." Then she leaned over the wheelchair and kissed Jake on the lips.

Grub abandoned Riggs without a backward look to sit at Carolyn's feet, staring up at her adoringly.

Jake gave her the same look. "Hi, honey."

Riggs had met Carolyn via the occasional phone call with Jake. She'd done great things at AHQ, but more than that, she could go toe to toe with Jake. Riggs liked her for that alone.

He knew all about the rescue dog she'd pretended to adopt for herself—Grub had needed a home—but she had really done it for Jake, who'd needed but refused an emotional support dog. Which made Carolyn beautiful *and* brilliant.

When Grub jumped up into Jake's lap and licked his master's face, and Jake actually touched his forehead to the dog's, Riggs felt the oddest . . . pang, a longing for that sort of unconditional love Jake had so easily found here.

Carolyn smiled at him. "Nice to see you in person finally." She jabbed a thumb at Jake. "He causing problems?"

"Yeah." Riggs grinned. "Can you hit him again, a little harder this time?"

Carolyn eyed them both. "Just a heads-up, we've got pretty thin walls in here, and the gang is all *very* interested in the famed Copeland brothers. I'm going back to work, so you two behave."

Riggs waited until they were alone to look at Jake. "Speaking of thin walls . . . Maybe we should delegate some of the pillow acquisition fund toward insulation."

Jake threw a pillow and hit Riggs in the face hard enough to knock him back a step and into a wall. "And don't think you're getting away with changing the subject from you being emotionally bankrupt," Jake said.

"I'm not emotionally bankrupt." At least not all the way. "I'm just . . ." *What, genius?* "Choosy where I invest my emotions."

"Yeah?" Jake asked, suddenly very serious. "So when exactly did you stop investing in me emotionally?"

"Jesus, Jake." Riggs strode to the window, staring out at the azure blue sky that was so clean and pure it almost hurt to look at it. He hadn't seen skies like this since . . . well, since he'd left Tahoe. He hadn't allowed himself to miss it, or Jake. Hell, maybe he *was* emotionally bankrupt after all. "I haven't *ever* stopped investing or believing in you."

"Prove it."

Riggs lifted his hands. "How?"

"Like this." Jake met his gaze straight on. "I love you, Riggs."

Riggs blinked, startled. "Uh . . . right back at you?"

Jake jabbed a finger at him. "See? That right there. You just proved my point."

He was saved from responding when the door opened and another woman walked in, this one with her dark hair piled up on top of her head, her incredible whiskey-colored eyes and nose buried in her iPad.

Tae.

"Jake," she said. "I'm going over the notes for next weekend's inaugural summer program event and—" She broke off as she looked up and her eyes locked on Riggs.

And right then and there, he knew he was wrong about himself. He wasn't emotionally bankrupt at all. Because ever since last night he'd had the oddest feeling in his chest. A feeling he hadn't experienced in a long time.

His heart engaging.

"You're busy," Tae said after an awkward silence, and started to go.

"No, it's okay." Jake gestured to her. "Come in."

She didn't look at Riggs again, but he looked at her plenty. She was in white capris and a crisp white button-down, looking professional casual, until he got to the green beat-up sneakers, which made him want to smile.

Jake gestured to Riggs. "Tae, maybe you remember him from high school, since I think you were probably only a year or so apart, but this is my brother—"

"—*Riggs*," she said tightly.

Jake nodded, looking a little surprised at her reaction.

Not Riggs. He was realizing that asking her to be friends had meant rejection for her—not what he'd intended or wanted her to feel.

All he knew was that he was trying to preserve a relationship with her, and for that to happen, they needed to be friends. And hell, he was doing them both a favor of avoiding heartbreak.

"Riggs," Jake said. "This is—"

"Tae." Riggs smiled at her.

It was not returned.

Jake, his eyes narrowed now, studied them both for a terminally long beat before finally speaking into the tense silence. "You two know each other."

Tae nodded once. "As you already noted, we went to the same high school."

Still taking them in, clearly noticing their awkwardness, Jake slowly shook his head. "No, I mean you two *know* each other."

"Old history," Tae said firmly.

Jake didn't look happy. "Whatever it is, I'm going to need the two of you to deal with it because . . ." He looked right at Riggs now, like *he* was the problem. "We signed Tae's event-planning company on for the next two years."

Riggs wasn't surprised that Tae ran her own business and was successful. She was smart, intuitive, and resourceful as hell. She also liked to be in charge of her own fate. "I didn't realize we use an event planner now."

"We do," Jake said patiently. "We're adding the summer program to an already existing demanding winter program, and both will take up all my time. Planning the events, plus fundraising to support them, is exhausting, plus I'm shit at it. Tae's going to pay for herself, trust me. You'll see that firsthand, since you'll be here for the next three months. We want the summer program to be every bit as robust as our winter program. Gentle tubing, Jet Ski rides, kayaking, that sort of thing. And Tae had the great idea to add at-risk kids to our clientele."

Riggs looked at Tae, impressed whether he liked it or not.

She wasn't looking impressed. She was in fact looking horrified as she stared at Riggs. "*Three months?*" she asked. "You're here for *three months?*"

Riggs managed a laugh, suddenly vastly amused by this entire situation. "For better or worse."

"I've mentioned my partner before," Jake said to Tae. "Riggs is that partner. He's half of Adrenaline HQ."

The look on her face said she thought Riggs was the annoying half.

Tae was looking at Riggs, her eyes narrowed in Jake's wake. "So ruining last night wasn't enough for you, now you're going to ruin my summer?"

"*I* ruined last night?"

She looked away, a telltale flush creeping up her face.

He stepped closer, lifting a hand to the cut above her eye, but she batted his hand away. "Don't baby me."

That had him smiling. Another woman might still be traumatized by what had gone down, but not Tae.

"Are you really here for the whole summer?" she asked.

"Sounds like it. Excited?"

"More like disappointed."

He smiled. "Liar."

She gave him one of her eye rolls. "How's your ass?" she asked.

"What do you mean?"

"Well, you ran away so fast last night that the door surely hit said ass on the way out."

"You mean when you told me to go?"

"You know damn well you wanted to run," she said. "*Friend.*" And then she made a sound like a chicken, complete with a little arm-flapping action.

He smiled, but no way was he going to admit she was right. "I just realized something about you. You get snarky when you feel uncomfortable."

"I don't feel uncomfortable. Why should I feel uncomfortable?"

"You tell me."

"Argh!" She turned to leave, then looked at him again. "But really. The *whole* summer?"

He wasn't about to tell her that only five minutes ago he'd been trying to figure out how to get out of it. "The *whole* summer."

"But you *are* leaving after that, right?"

He laughed roughly. "Usually when two people go through a traumatic experience together, they bond."

She wasn't amused, nor was she playing. "So what . . . we're friends until the end of summer?"

His smile faded. Because though he didn't fully understand why, it was very important to him that she agree. "Yes."

She looked at him like he was nuts but hooked her pinkie with his. "To the end of summer then. Can't wait."

"To the end of summer." And to the months between now and then, which were suddenly looking far more interesting than he could have ever imagined.

"See you around, Riggs." And with that, she spun on the heel of one of her beat-up sneakers and headed to the door.

Riggs watched her go, let out a deep breath, and told himself he was doing the right thing. Turning to the window, he stared out at the mountains. He'd wanted to hate it here. There were certainly enough bad memories to ensure it. But he was having a hard time accessing them, now that their childhood cabin had been renovated into . . . well, a real home, and none of the ghosts of the past seemed to have stuck around. Plus, no matter how much he and Jake snapped at each other, it'd been damn good to see him. And then there were the mountains themselves. Tall, majestic, gorgeous . . . drawing him in every single time he looked at them. He'd had some of the best times of his life out there. Adventures he'd never forget.

He could hear Tae and Carolyn talking. Laughing. And he thought maybe there were also new adventures yet to make.

Shaking his head at himself for the odd reflection, he turned and nearly fell into Jake's lap. His brother sat there, his arms crossed over his chest in a familiar Big Brother Asshat stance.

"What?" Riggs asked.

"Details. *Now.*"

Riggs didn't bother to pretend to not understand. "High school," he said, speaking in the same staccato pattern as his annoying brother. "Past."

"What else do I need to know?"

"Nothing."

Jake stared at him for a long moment, then swore colorfully. "Look, she's important to me. I need to know—"

"No, you don't," Riggs said. "It's not up for discussion. But the first summer event is this coming weekend?"

"You're going to piss me off, aren't you?"

"Look, if I'm staying for the summer, then put me to work."

Jake went from being irritated to surprised, which was insulting.

"You've got a lot on your plate, Jake. Give me the summer program to build. I'll create the events just like I did our winter program. Everything you mentioned earlier is good, but you'll need more. You'll need a ropes course, zip-lining, dirt biking, off-roading, a climbing wall, stuff like that."

"Not sure I've got the time to get that all together," Jake said.

"Good thing then that I do. Look, I know you're swamped with the ongoing programs, not to mention the day-to-day operations and all the schmoozing and fundraising." Riggs looked his brother in the eyes, because Jake hated to accept help. "Let me do this for you."

Jake took a beat, and when he spoke, it was his overly calm voice, a sure sign he was angry. "You think I can't help plan those activities?"

"You hurt yourself twice this year. *Badly.*"

Jake's hands fisted where they rested on his wheels. "Yeah, pissing me off." He came right up to Riggs, nearly rolling over his toes.

"Hey!"

"You only see what I can't do, not what I can do."

Riggs opened his mouth to say that wasn't true, but Jake whipped his chair around—*not* missing Riggs's toes this time, which, for the record, hurt like a bitch—and then he was once again heading out the door.

"So that's a yes, right?"

"As long as you stop treating me like I'm your burden who needs help." Jake then slammed the door, leaving Riggs alone to feel like maybe *he* was the asshat brother after all.

CHAPTER 8

Tae left Adrenaline HQ feeling a whole bunch more than she'd planned on for this early in the morning. She lay the blame at the feet of one big, sexy, annoying Riggs Copeland, who'd clearly turned her brain inside out.

She drove to her office, which was the spare bedroom in her home. She'd had the early meeting with Jake but would now spend the rest of the day dealing with the fact that she had five events spread out over the next two weeks. And a bunch more after that. A good problem, a quality problem too, but one that was giving her heart palpitations, so she skipped breakfast and headed straight to her desk.

The second she sat down, Jenny, her longtime virtual assistant, FaceTimed her.

"I literally *just* got to my desk," Tae said. "How do you always know exactly when to catch me?"

"Catch you? Or drive you crazy?"

Tae smiled. "If the shoe fits."

"And it does." Jenny, a thirty-year-old grad student, lived in

New York and didn't take shit from anyone, not even her boss. "And as for how I know when you're home, I loaded you on the Find My Friends app, remember? So I don't catch you in the middle of a great adventure somewhere, which never happens, because you don't allow yourself a private life."

Tae sighed and pinched the bridge of her nose. "How do you *always* work that into the conversation?"

"It's a gift. Take some Advil for the headache. I had a new super-size bottle sent last week, along with electrolyte waters, which you should be drinking every day."

"You do know that I already have a mom."

Jenny smiled. "You need to eat something. An apple and peanut butter maybe, because you're hangry."

Tae had to laugh, because *true.* She grabbed some Advil from her drawer and drank from her ridiculously huge water bottle, the one her mom had gotten her that had lines on it every few ounces, like "you can do it!" and "keep going, you're saving yourself early wrinkles." Hell, she even started eating a granola bar, which she waved at Jenny. "There. Happy?"

"Ecstatic." Jenny swiped on her iPad. "First up—"

"Wait. Were you able to get anything on Jordy and his sister?" Tae couldn't stop thinking about them. She needed to make sure Jordy was okay and not traumatized by what had happened.

"Nothing," Jenny said. "The grainy pic you got from the surveillance tapes wasn't clear enough, and we don't know his last name. I'm sorry."

Tae had gone back to the store and talked Ms. Riley into letting her take a pic from the tapes, but she claimed not to know anything about him. "It was a long shot."

"I'll keep trying."

So would Tae.

"Anyway," Jenny said, "the Milligan's event in three weeks. Found you a caterer." She thumbed past a few screens. "As for Brown's charity ball next month, I've sent you over several possible locations. I took virtual tours and left you my thoughts in my notes, but you should probably go see them in person."

"I will, thanks." Tae smiled. "You've saved me a lot of time."

"The whole reason I exist. You still haven't said how your last date went."

"He wanted me to go skinny-dipping."

Jenny smiled. "*Ooooh*."

"More like ew. I declined. And then he declined to continue the date."

"A girl needs a heads-up before being expected to skinny-dip. And a wax appointment."

"A heads-up wouldn't have changed this outcome," Tae said.

"Been there, done that. Oh! I just found out, a friend of mine has a cousin in Tahoe. Supposedly, he's gainfully employed and hot. I could—"

"No thank you," Tae said quickly. "I'm no longer dating. If someone's interested in me, they'll need a five-hundred-word essay on how they won't waste my time."

Jenny laughed. "Considering my last date wanted to know if he could take a picture of my bare feet, I should do the same."

"Dear God."

"Right?" Jenny shook her head. "Tell me about this morning's meeting with AHQ. We still on for the inaugural Lake Days next weekend?"

Tae nodded at the mention of Adrenaline HQ's inaugural summer event. "Yes. Location is the state park. I'll send you all the notes."

"Great. I'll get an itinerary going, verify caterer and order decorations, and organize any other vendors needed."

"You're a godsend," Tae said.

"Just remember that at my next review."

Tae snorted and disconnected. Jenny wasn't just her employee. She was also her closest friend. Not sure what that said about Tae and her ability to connect, that her bffs were her mom and her assistant, who lived three thousand miles away, but it was what it was.

It was late in the afternoon when Tae finally pushed her laptop away. Stretching her aching back, she headed to her car and drove to the convenience store. Her heart skipped a beat just walking into the place, proving she wasn't quite as okay as she'd thought.

Ms. Riley sent her a baleful stare from her perch. "What now?"

"Have you seen Jordy?"

"Who?"

"You know, the fourteen-year-old kid you almost shot."

"Oh, you mean the thief. No. And good riddance."

Tae walked across the street to McGregor's market and showed the clerk Jordy's pic.

The clerk nodded. "He came in last night, and again today."

Tae's heart skipped another beat. "Do you know him? Can you tell me where to find him?"

The clerk's expression shuttered. "Why? He's a good kid who doesn't need trouble."

"I know. He's up for a scholarship for Adrenaline HQ's summer program. I just need to locate him."

"I know about Adrenaline HQ," the woman said. "My sister's girlfriend got hurt in Afghanistan two years ago. Her legs don't work very good now, but she skied on this cool seat thingy with Adrenaline HQ this past winter."

"Imagine how much Jordy would love a chance to do something like that," Tae said.

The woman bit her lip. "How about you leave me your info and I'll get it to him."

Knowing it was the best she could hope for, she left the woman a card.

Back at home twenty minutes later, she went straight through her place and out her back door. She stepped over the small hedge to her mom's yard.

Here the little patio had a picnic bench, potted flowers, and a string of fairy lights that transformed the very plain space into something warm and welcoming.

Like April herself.

Tae's patio was a stark contrast. She'd done nothing to it. She'd never had the time or inclination, so all she had was the eight-by-eight-foot concrete pad. Besides, why decorate when, if she was going to sit outside, she'd be doing it with her mom and probably eating and drinking wine while they were at it—all things that would come from April's kitchen, not Tae's.

Yes, maybe one of these days she wouldn't use her oven to store her pans, but that day was not today. She helped herself to her mom's key, hidden under a fake rock, and found a note.

The pint of cookies 'n' cream ice cream in the freezer is for you. Do not kill the spider in my bathroom. Her name is Queen and she's guarding the plant you gave me for Mother's Day.

Love, Mom

Hard not to madly love the woman. Tae let herself into the kitchen, carefully stepping over the small black cat sprawled across the throw rug right in front of the door.

At the ripe old age of fourteen, Storm had patchy black fur. She was also missing most of her teeth, and as a result, she was as cranky, moody, and destructive as a category 5 hurricane. Oh, and she hated men. All of them. She was also near deaf, so when she meowed, she sounded like she'd been smoking for five decades.

Tae crouched low and gave Storm some love. This was generally acceptable, but not always. It was a game of Russian roulette; Tae literally took her life in her hands when she pet Storm. Every time. But Storm started up her engines, her rumbly purr so loud it could've been a diesel engine. There was also a lot of drool, thanks to the missing teeth, but she closed her eyes in pleasure. After a few moments, still purring, the cat slowly sank her teeth into Tae's hand. Not breaking skin, just a loving warning.

Tae stood. "You know, you could just walk away."

Nose in the air, Storm went into the living room, where she climbed her way up onto the couch that she was forbidden to get on because she liked to sharpen her claws on the material. Not that Tae was about to stop her. "Mom?" she called out.

There was no answer, and she hadn't expected one. It was 4:00 P.M., and her mom rarely got home before 5:00. Dragging in a breath of relief and nerves, she looked around at the living room her mom had turned into a place as warm and comfortable as her back deck. Tae hadn't inherited that ability. Which had her thinking for the hundredth time . . . what had she *not* inherited from her dad?

She entered her mom's room and headed straight for the closet. In the very back, behind the hanging clothes, sat a wood chest where her mom kept all her old treasures: photo albums, mementos, clothes . . . When Tae was little, her mom would pull the chest out and they'd go through it together. Today, Tae opened the chest and went straight to the very bottom, to the small box the size of a shoebox.

Her mom had never opened the box in Tae's presence, saying only that it was paperwork she didn't need to worry about.

But for the first time in her life, Tae *was* worried about it.

She sat on the floor, drew a deep breath, and pulled out the box.

Storm nudged her elbow and then climbed into her lap.

"Excuse me, ma'am, I'm doing something here—"

Storm once again turned on her rusty motor and closed her eyes.

"Sure," Tae said. "You stay right where you are and I'll just reach over you." She eyed the box and told herself this wasn't about curiosity. She didn't have that luxury. It was about finding out the truth. She wanted to believe that Mr. Schwartz had been mistaken about AJ Strickland being her father.

But if he wasn't, that could mean only one of two things. Either AJ Strickland had lied about his name to her too-trusting mom, or . . . her mom had lied to Tae—which obviously wasn't an option.

So that meant, somewhere in this box had to be proof that Andy Jameson was her dad, because though trust was always Tae's very last instinct, she knew it was her mother's first. The woman had never lied to her.

She opened the box, and Storm gave her a judgy look.

"Yes, I'm snooping, all right?" She sighed. "Listen, the last thing I want to do is to tell Mom she's been lied to. It would break her heart. *That's* the only reason I'm doing this. To prove it's just a case of mistaken identity, which I don't have any doubts that it is. Not a single one."

Storm lifted a leg and began to clean her lady bits.

Tae rolled her eyes and opened the box. To her shock, it was filled with *her* stuff. A porcelain baby shoe with her birthday and weight written in pretty pink, matching the laces. A picture of her mom in a hospital bed holding a wrapped bundle with an already-annoyed-by-life face.

Good to know she hadn't changed much.

There was a little beaded bracelet, the kind babies used to wear in the hospital with their name and birth date on it. And . . . dear God.

An envelope labeled: TAE'S BIRTH CERTIFICATE.

She'd seen it before, but it'd been years. When she'd been ten, she and her mom had gotten passports for a Mexican getaway that had never happened. Tae had been young enough not to remember even looking over her birth certificate.

Now, she pulled the paper out of the envelope, then stared at it in shock.

Under FATHER it said: UNKNOWN.

This made zero sense. It should have said Andy Jameson, plain as day. He and her mom hadn't been married because circumstances hadn't allowed for it before he joined the military, but they'd loved each other madly.

So why didn't her mother put his name down? Was her dad alive and walking around, or was he a dead war hero? All she knew was that he couldn't be both.

Stunned, she sat back, thoughts racing, questioning everything she knew about herself. She was still sitting there, having a freak-out party for one, when she heard the front door open downstairs. She jumped and dislodged a sleeping Storm. She began shoving everything back into the box, guilt heavy in her chest when she didn't even know *why* she felt guilty. She was just looking at her own birth certificate, right? *Right.*

Still, she scrambled out of the closet.

"Honey?" her mom called out from what sounded like the kitchen. "Is that you?"

See? *Trusting*. Tae could've been a burglar or worse, and her mom would be down there making tea to share. How did someone who'd been forced to grow up as her mom had, then raised herself and a baby, all on her own, stay so sweet and trusting?

Just one of life's little mysteries, she supposed. "Yeah, Mom, it's me," she yelled back. "I'm coming."

"I picked up Chinese on the way home. Got your faves."

"Sounds good!" Tae stood up, still holding her birth certificate. She folded it in thirds, then in half again, sliding it into her back pocket. She and her mom were going to talk about it, in great detail, as a matter of fact. Drawing a deep, calming breath, she ran down the stairs, breathless and a little sweaty.

April stood at the kitchen counter, her back to Tae, peering into two brown bags that smelled delicious. Storm trotted in with a happy chirp, her belly swinging to and fro, and she weaved around her mom's ankles.

"Mom," Tae said. "We need to talk—"

"Oh my God, you have no idea!" Her mom whirled to face her. "After you left Adrenaline HQ today, I somehow managed to mess up their entire computer system. I was just attempting to do a restart, but instead I somehow shut it down and it wouldn't come back on."

"Yikes." Her mom was tech challenged, to say the least. "Do you need help?"

"No, Carolyn handled it, but it took her an hour that she didn't have." She went to the tea cabinet and began to search through her dozens of different brands, not making eye contact, which she tended to do when she was really rattled. "And then when I went to go home, I had a flat tire. Ran over a damn screw or something. Roadside service was backed up, so Jake came out and changed it to my spare in like fifteen minutes flat, but he missed a meeting."

"I'm sorry," Tae said. "But—"

"And then when I finally got on the road, some idiot blew through a stop sign and nearly T-boned me. I'm telling you, I need to skip the tea and go straight for a glass of wine. Maybe a whole bottle." She sighed, looking more than a little shaken as she met Tae's gaze for the first time. "I'm so sorry." She let out a long breath. "You wanted to say something and I'm just prattling on."

She'd definitely wanted to say something, but how to get to the topic at hand? "Uh . . ."

"Tell me something good, honey. I'm really not sure I can handle one more rough thing today without having a breakdown."

Tae let out a breath and managed a smile. "I'm just relieved you didn't get in a wreck."

April nodded. "Me too. I haven't even begun to make my medical deductible this year." She started to smile but stopped when she got a look at Tae's face. "Are you okay? What was it you wanted to say?"

Tae paused. "That I missed you this week." And she'd called Riggs a chicken . . .

April smiled. "Well, I'm all yours tonight. What did you need upstairs?"

"I was . . . looking at your shoes."

Storm gave her a slitty-eyed look that said *liar, liar, pants on fire.*

"Did you find any shoes you want to borrow? Did you see my new boots?"

"They're amazing." She hadn't seen the boots. She'd been busy panicking. But surely there was *a reasonable explanation* for her mom not telling her. And it wasn't like she'd never kept things from her mom. The truth was, she'd been lying to protect her mom her whole life. Stealing food. Chasing away the loser guys her mom sometimes attracted—once with her trusty baseball bat even, then telling her mom he'd left a note that said he was moving to Rio. The guy hadn't been abusive, or even mean. In fact, he'd been sweet. He'd also been a jobless loser who ate all their food.

But *this* lie, sneaking through April's things and not admitting it or what she'd found, didn't feel so innocent. In fact, it left her feeling a little sick.

Or maybe that was just her life.

CHAPTER 9

April might not know a lot of things, but she did know *one* thing. And that was her daughter. The girl had been born an old soul, though she'd lost her way in her teens for a while.

Who hadn't.

But today, right now, Tae didn't look like herself. She looked . . . worried and upset, both of which she was also trying to hide.

This told April that whatever it was, it was bad. But as much as she'd like to drag it out of her, no one had ever been able to rush Tae, who, when she wanted to be, was an unmovable stone wall.

Patience was the only way to get anything from her. April hadn't been born with patience, but after twenty-eight years with the most stubborn, wonderful girl on the planet, she'd learned to build up a decent reserve. She would wait Tae out. In the meantime, she showed her the pics she'd taken on the lake that morning.

"Beautiful," Tae said, appreciatively poring over each shot. "You need to print these and sell them, Mom. They're gold."

April felt herself flush with the praise. "Yeah?"

"Yeah. I bet Jake would let you hang them on the walls at Adrenaline HQ with little sale stickers."

The thought was a huge thrill, but she shook her head. "I couldn't ask him to do that."

"I could," Tae said.

That was her daughter. Bossy. Direct. Protective. Sweet. And April was so proud of her, but she knew her daughter too well to allow herself to be distracted. "Honey?"

"Hmm?"

"You going to tell me what's wrong?"

Tae froze for a beat, then said casually, "No, because nothing's wrong."

Uh-huh. And April was the Easter Bunny. Tae had always been able to hide her feelings better than April. But Tae wasn't the only protective one in the family, and a mama had to do what a mama had to do—and sometimes with Tae, that required stealth.

It was to that end that she'd . . . done a thing.

A thing Tae wasn't going to like.

But . . . but. Tae had been closed off for a long time. For goodness' sake, her closest friend was her virtual assistant. April had been pushing Tae out into the real world with their dating mission agreement. But April suspected that Tae picked poorly on purpose, probably because April hadn't exactly been a good role model and shown her what a relationship should look like.

April knew her daughter needed someone patient enough to wait for her walls to crumble. Hence the plan for tonight.

"Mom?" Tae lifted her attention from April's camera. "Do you ever think about Dad?"

April couldn't have been more surprised if the roof had just caved in. "What?"

"Because I do. I mean, I don't have actual memories of him, since he died when I was . . . ?" She met April's gaze. "One, right?"

April's heart was a staccato beat in her ears, anxiety changing her heart rhythm. "A little before your first birthday," she managed in a normal voice.

"Overseas, while in the marines," Tae said.

Her throat closed up tight, April nodded. It was . . . complicated. So complicated. And she'd compounded that tenfold. A mess of her own making, she knew, but she really hated, *hated*, that the one teeny tiny white lie she'd ever told had grown into something so big she could hardly contain it. But what else could she do after all this time but keep it up?

Tae was watching her carefully. "It hurts you to remember. To talk about him."

April nodded. It did hurt. It brought her back to a time when she'd felt powerless, deserted, terrified, and far too alone. Being young on top of that, and with no guidance, she'd made so many, many mistakes. It was no wonder that Tae was so messed up. April was working on that, on being a better mom, but she knew she couldn't erase the past. "Yes."

"Because you loved him very much."

God help her. Again she nodded, and thankfully, Storm began demanding her dinner with her do-as-I-say-or-I'll-leave-molten-hot-lava-poop-in-your-shoes *meow*.

April turned to the pantry—she'd never get over the thrill of that, having a pantry filled with food—and got out a can of cat food. "Here, baby," she murmured, filling the bowl, mushing it up good, since Storm didn't have much biting power.

Tae was head deep in the bags of Chinese April had brought home, her dad hopefully forgotten for the moment. "Mom, are you kidding me? Did you buy for a zombie apocalypse? We're only two people and you bought enough for—"

"Six."

Tae craned her head and stared at her.

April smiled. Her daughter was still in her work clothes, which were understatedly classy, and made her look . . . beautiful. But the fact was, she was always beautiful. Even back in the day when she'd dyed her hair jet-black to go with her black makeup and clothes. Even when she'd been mad at the world and withdrawn and sullen.

April loved Tae beyond reason, but sometimes a mama really did know best, and this was one of those times.

Tae was watching her and narrowed her eyes. "Oh my God, Mom. You *didn't* arrange a date without telling me."

"I did. I'm giving the baby bird a nudge. But also the mama bird." She really was trying to be a better example, and a more well-rounded human being. Tae not trusting or opening up to people was April's fault. So she was taking matters into her own hands. She'd invited a date for each of them, along with Jake and Carolyn. Because what could go wrong?

Tae backed away from the food like it was a coiled snake

poised to strike. "Mom, no. I promised I'd put myself out there, and I have."

"I know. But then Michael said that you were closed off and unwilling to let the universe fill your cup."

Tae snorted, and April let out a small laugh. "Okay, even I can't keep a straight face on that one, but I know what he meant, Tae. You're not even really trying. Why?"

"Mom . . ." Tae sighed. "My cup is so full it's spilling over. I'm running no less than five events over the next two weeks, working most of them by myself or with temp workers, since I can't afford to take on any full-time employees other than Jenny. I'm working around-the-clock since we bought this duplex—which comes with a big fat mortgage that's taking every spare penny we've got. So please tell me . . . when do I have time to let the universe fill my cup?"

April ignored the jab but accepted the rush of maternal pride at her amazing daughter. "You're working so hard because you insisted I quit two of my three jobs to concentrate on me."

"Yes," Tae said. "Which you deserve after spending your best years taking care of me."

April cupped Tae's face. "And they were just that, baby. The best years of my life. We spent them together. We raised each other. And I love that. I have no regrets." Okay, so she had one regret. A big, fat regret that still kept her up at night. But she'd made her choice a long time ago, and there was no taking it back now. Not without destroying everything. "But I'm still the mom. I'm supposed to take care of you."

"Just tell me what you did."

"I was looking into this new dating site because there was a two-for-one deal. And you know how much I love a deal."

Tae was looking resigned. "More than you wanted to have The Rock's love child?"

April smiled. "Exactly."

"Tell me you didn't invite two strange men to our home."

"Of course not. I mean, okay, so I haven't always made the best decisions regarding men, but I'm learning."

Tae gave her the universal go-on gesture with her hands.

April talked faster. "I was pinged on the site by someone I know, the head mechanic at the place where I took my car all last year when it kept breaking down on me? Anyway, Ethan was always so nice to me, but he'd been dating someone. He's single now, so it was an easy yes. Turns out his brother is also single, and so I thought why not make it a double date."

"And you know this guy well enough to have him here, at your house?"

"Ethan, and yes. He was the only one who could fix my car, and he refunded me all those other times when one of his guys couldn't seem to get it right. He's honest and he's funny, and . . ." She smiled. "Cute."

Tae sighed. "Okay, so that makes four for dinner. How did you get to six?"

"I invited Jake and Carolyn over as well. I figured the more the merrier."

"Mom, I'm exhausted. I spent the day on phone meetings,

pitching to two new clients and I already landed one, so I've still got a lot left to do tonight—"

"A new client! Oh, honey, that's amazing! Who is it?"

"The new pub on Lake Walk." Tae let out a proud smile. "So thank you for the oh-so-tempting offer of a blind date and socializing, but I'm going to head back to my place and shower before hitting the laptop."

"How about this: If after dinner you still hate everyone, you're free to go. Deal?"

Tae blew out a breath and looked at the bags of food longingly. "Did you get crab rangoons?"

"Of course."

The doorbell rang.

Tae nearly jumped right out of her skin.

"Honey, honest to God," April said. "You'd think you were wanted for murder the way you react to someone coming over."

Tae looked at the back door for a quick escape.

"No!" April pointed at her. "I'm going to go let them in. Do not run out the back. I repeat. *Do not run*. Promise?"

"If I get *all* the crab rangoons."

"*All of them*," April vowed solemnly, and rushed to the living room, quickly checking her reflection in the mirror over the tiny desk in the entryway. Her hair was down. She preferred it up, but this way better hid the gray coming in at her temples. Not that she was ashamed of the gray. She'd earned every single one. But her date was seven years younger than she was, and April had enough vanity left to want to look good.

She pulled the door open to the two handsome men standing on the porch.

Ethan sent her an easy smile, and April smiled back at the thirty-five-year-old mechanic. He stood maybe five foot ten, longish dark blond finger-tousled, wavy hair, neatly trimmed facial hair, and a smile that assured her that he found her as attractive as she found him.

"April." He brushed a kiss to her cheek. "This is Hunter, my brother."

The other man offered his hand. From his profile, April knew he was thirty-one and a local pediatric dentist. He was an inch taller than Ethan, devastatingly handsome in a very clean-cut way with his short dark hair styled into an artful disarray and his freshly shaved face creased with a sweet, genuine smile.

"Tae, darling," April called over her shoulder. "Our dates are here."

Tae appeared next to April, silent, but hey, at least she hadn't run out the back door. "This is Ethan."

"And I'm Hunter, his brother," Hunter said, holding out his hand. "Looking forward to dinner with you."

Tae blinked at him and appeared frozen in place until April elbowed her. Ouch. But she shook Hunter's hand.

Storm made her way onto the porch too. Ms. Nosey wrapped herself around Hunter's ankles until he bent to pet her.

Both April and Tae yelled "*no!*" at the same time.

Too late. Storm, clearly still a man-hater, opened her mouth and closed it on Hunter's hand.

"Uh," Hunter said, looking worried.

"Storm!" Tae scolded. "Let the nice man go."

Storm did just that, turned her back, and, tail up, reentered the house.

"Are you okay?" Tae asked Hunter.

"No blood," he said, examining his hand. "It's all good. She seems . . . sweet."

"As sweet as my daughter," April quipped, making even Tae snort out a laugh.

At the sound, April relaxed. Tae's laugh was rare but magical, and proving it, the sound of her amusement immediately dissipated the awkward tension.

They all moved inside, and April offered everyone a drink, which she knew would further break the ice. She adored her daughter more than life itself, but Tae wasn't much fun until she had a glass of wine in her. April headed into the kitchen to get a bottle, and Tae followed. "Mom," she whispered, "this isn't going to work."

"Of course it is." April opened a bottle of chardonnay. "Things are always awkward at first, but Ethan's really great, so Hunter must be as well. Give it a glass or two."

"My head just isn't in it."

April frowned. Something was still off with her baby, and it wasn't just about the unexpected blind date. But before she could press, there was a knock on the still-opened doorjamb of the front door. Both April and Tae turned to peek out into the living room just in time to see Carolyn walk inside, Jake behind her, a six-pack in his lap.

Followed by . . . Jake's brother.

"Mom." Tae ducked back into the kitchen. "Oh my God. You didn't."

April looked at her in surprise. "What?"

"That's Riggs!"

April shrugged. "Jake must've brought him along. He's been worried that his brother feels withdrawn and unreachable." She eyed her daughter carefully. "Is Riggs being here a problem?"

Tae thunked her head against a cabinet door.

"Honey?" April rubbed her back, worried. "Is there something you want to tell me?"

"Yes." Tae poured wine into one of the wineglasses and then gulped it down and refilled. "You're going to need another bottle."

CHAPTER 10

Tae waited until her mom left the kitchen with the bottle of wine to take another big gulp from her glass. Maybe it was more like a chug, but just as she did, Riggs stepped into the kitchen. "Interesting way to date," he said. "Being in two different rooms."

She promptly choked, then shoved him away when he tried to pat her on the back. "Why are you here?" she finally managed to gasp out.

"Well, when a mommy and daddy love each other . . ."

She narrowed her eyes, and he grinned.

Meow.

Storm had followed Riggs into the kitchen and was now rubbing her face against his denim-clad legs. He bent to her, and Tae panicked.

"No!" she said quickly. "It's a trick, she hates men and bites—"

But the traitor jumped into his arms with surprising stealth for a geriatric, and was now rubbing her face against his chest.

Riggs looked smug. "She bites?"

Tae rolled her eyes just as her mom came in to grab another bottle of wine. She did a double-take at Storm sitting in Riggs's arms like a princess. Recovering quickly, she said, "I need someone to take this out to the living room."

Riggs gently set Storm back down and took the wine.

"Thanks," her mom said. "We'll be right behind you."

He turned and walked out of the kitchen. Her mom looked at Tae. "You sure there's nothing you want to tell me?"

"Not right now," Tae said honestly.

Her mom sighed. "Honey, this will be fun, I promise."

Fun. She could hardly wait. But she followed her mom into the living room, and sure enough, in less than sixty seconds, her mom had spread her easy magical chemistry and had everyone chitchatting and laughing. It was her superpower.

Tae didn't have a superpower. She also wasn't in the mood for chitchatting. Or being on a date. Even though Hunter seemed nice and attentive, she was pretty sure he just wasn't her type. She accidentally met Riggs's gaze. Unfortunately, he *was* her type. Tall, dark, and dangerous. Maybe that was the problem. Maybe she needed to try a different type on for size.

Her mom led everyone to the table, still casting her cheerful, wonderful, amazing spell over the entire group, as only she could do. And not for the first time, Tae wished she could be more like that, able to shed the past that had molded her and be carefree and easygoing.

Hunter sat on Tae's right and handed her the container of garlic shrimp. "I don't mean to be presumptuous, but I don't want to eat anything with garlic unless you do too," he said with a very nice smile.

That actually made her laugh. Nice, attentive, and also confident. Okay, maybe she could work with that. She scooped up some shrimp, aware of Riggs watching her from across the table, his eyes unreadable. Friends. And yeah, that still stung. He hadn't said much, but then again, he never did. The man, pragmatic, impenetrable, and unflappable, could say more with silence than most men could with volumes of words.

What was it her mom had told her Jake had said about Riggs? He'd been withdrawn and unreachable . . . Her heart pinched, but she had other problems. Her birth certificate felt heavy in her back pocket. She needed to be alone with a computer to research what it meant not having a father listed on her birth certificate. But first, she took some garlic shrimp.

"You have beautiful teeth," Hunter said. "I hope that's not a weird thing to say."

From across the table, a corner of Riggs's mouth quirked sardonically, and that settled that. She beamed at Hunter. "Not at all. Thank you."

Hunter looked dazzled by her smile.

On the other side of Hunter, her mom was telling the story of the time she and Tae had gotten into a fight, back when Tae had been in high school. They'd been staying in a one-room hovel and were practically living on top of each other. Tae had gotten the bright idea to divide the tiny room into two sides with masking tape. "Only problem," she interjected into her mom's tale, "the light switches were on my mom's side and she wouldn't let me use them."

Everyone laughed, including Riggs. Even Tae felt a smile tug at her mouth as she looked at her mom. "I remember telling you I just wanted a little private personal space."

April lifted her wineglass in Tae's direction. "And *I* told *you* that you'd once come out of my private personal space."

Tae grimaced as everyone burst out laughing again. "Yeah, still not funny."

"It's a mom's job to embarrass her kid."

"Well then, mission accomplished," Tae said dryly. "Tenfold. Remember the job I had before I started my event company?" She looked at her mom, who was already smiling. "I got called into HR. I thought I was in trouble for something, but they wanted to let me know that my *mom* had been commenting on their Instagram every day, telling them I deserved a raise."

"Because you did," April said proudly.

Carolyn laughed. "That's so sweet. My mom still lives to embarrass me. Someday I hope to repay the favor to my own kid."

Jake smiled at Carolyn in a sweet and sexy manner that made Tae's heart hurt in the very best of ways.

"Are you two married?" Hunter asked.

"Not yet," Jake said, and it was Carolyn's turn to smile at him.

"You two are so great together," Tae's mom said. "And still so romantic after two years."

"Yep," Carolyn said. "Just last week I left him a heart made up of a bunch of Post-it notes on the bathroom mirror."

Jake laughed. "Yes, with chores written on each of them."

"Okay, hotshot," Carolyn said, grinning. "What's the last romantic thing *you* did?"

"The other night," he said, "we were watching TV and I heard a text, and realizing I'd left my phone in the kitchen, I went in there to check it. It was a text from you that said: please bring chips on your way back. Which I did."

Everyone burst out laughing at that, and Carolyn conceded with a toast of her wineglass. "You're right. That was the perfect romantic gesture on your part."

Still smiling, Tae accidentally met Riggs's gaze, and in spite of herself, she felt an almost unbearable electric pull. Effing annoying. She glanced at Hunter and waited for a spark. Then she waited some more. Nothing. Dammit. How annoying was that, because he was a smart, stable guy who worked with kids, and most importantly, he *didn't* seem like the kind of guy who'd turn her down for a no-strings-attached social orgasm.

"Honey, could you pass the chow mein?" her mom asked.

The chow mein sat directly between her and Riggs. They both reached for it at the same time, their fingers brushing. Tae sucked in a breath, and Riggs, holding her gaze, handed the container straight to April. Just because she could, Tae gave him a *you're-a-jackass* look.

It made him smile.

Hunter divided a look between them. Ignoring that, Tae snatched the whole container of crab rangoons.

"So, Riggs," April said into the awkward silence. "What do you think of all the wonderful things your brother's done with Adrenaline HQ?"

"He thinks I'm growing the business too fast," Jake said, passing the egg rolls to Carolyn. "And that I can't handle it without him."

"And that they don't need an event planner," Tae added, and popped her second, maybe third, crab rangoon into her mouth.

Riggs looked pained. "I didn't say any of that. I just thought it's a lot for him to take on by himself."

"He's not by himself." Carolyn held Jake's eyes with a soft smile. "He's one of the most savvy, hardworking men I've ever met."

Normally, blatant mushy romantic stuff made Tae want to gag. But seeing Carolyn's genuine love for Jake, and knowing it was real, moved her.

Riggs was looking . . . confused, and she got it. She and Carolyn had spent time together. She knew that before Carolyn had come along, Jake had definitely had a specific type. Tall, blond, busty—which, okay, described Carolyn to a T—but also gone-by-Monday. Not only was Carolyn still with him, but she'd also been at his side for two years now. They both were incredibly outdoorsy and active and were constantly pushing each other in the very best of ways, complementing their strengths and making up for their weaknesses. Carolyn was genuinely there for Jake no matter what. And in return, Jake boosted Carolyn's once-missing confidence and just celebrated her exactly as she was. They were meant to be. That simple. What Tae had found so elusive and hard for her came naturally to them. It left her wondering if, in spite of her cold, black heart, a happily-ever-after could ever be for her.

"What you two have," her mom said softly, also looking moved, "is nothing short of amazing." She smiled at Jake. "Hold on to her."

Jake had Carolyn's hand in his. "Count on it."

RIGGS HADN'T WANTED to come tonight, but both Jake and Carolyn had insisted, and so here he sat, not to mention being studied like a bug on a slide by the Good Dentist.

A fact he completely ignored.

He felt off his game. He also felt confined in tight quarters with people he didn't know, uncomfortably alert for a threat he knew wasn't coming but couldn't seem to turn off. The edginess that had saved his life more times than he could count wasn't serving him well tonight.

Nor when it came to reconnecting with Jake, his gruff, perpetually-in-control brother, who was currently smiling sweetly at Carolyn, none of his usual hard-ass self in sight.

But then Jake looked over and met his gaze head-on. There was a simmering tension between them, and Riggs felt guilty as hell for it. He felt guilty for a lot of things, like what had happened to his brother. Riggs had been on a mission at the time and unable to go home and help, leaving his brother to face all of his surgeries and PT on his own. By the time Riggs had gotten leave, Jake hadn't seemed to want him around. Riggs had felt pushed out. Still did. As for what Jake had felt . . . hell, Riggs had no idea. Nor did he know what to do or how to resolve any of it. He could only hope he'd figure it out before summer's end.

Somehow, he suffered through dessert, which were some

pretty damn fine double fudge cookies that Carolyn had made. He watched Tae work her way through two of them, sucking some chocolate off her thumb.

The Good Dentist had an eye lock on that action as well. Riggs glared at him, but apparently the man could only concentrate on one thing at a time.

Amateur.

"Did Tae tell you about Jordy?" April asked Jake, and Riggs looked up at the name of the kid from the convenience store.

"Yes," Jake said. "She invited him and his sister to Lake Days on full scholarship. It's great. Exactly the kind of kids we hoped to reach and help."

Riggs looked at Tae. "You found him?"

"She sure did," April said proudly. "She turned into a private investigator to do it too. Put out some feelers and got a call from his mom. Tae explained about the program and got the woman's permission for both Jordy and Sarah, his younger sister, to participate."

Tae lifted her gaze to Riggs, a little defiant and defensive. Did she think he wouldn't approve? Not that she needed his approval. "That's amazing," he said. "You're amazing . . ."

She shrugged and shoved another crab rangoon into her mouth. "Anyone would have done the same thing."

Not true. He hadn't even thought of it.

After dinner, he offered to clear the plates to escape his third-wheel status, but Tae followed him into the kitchen. "I'm going to ask you again," she said. "*What are you doing here?*"

"Existentially?" Riggs shrugged. "I try not to overthink those things."

"Oh my God." Tae smacked her forehead with the heel of her hand. "You *know* what I'm asking! Why are you here, in my mom's place, tonight, eating dinner with us?"

"Who doesn't like dinner?"

"Riggs, I swear to God . . ."

He had to laugh. She was so easy to rile up. And a lot of fun too. "Carolyn made me come."

She laughed. "Right. Like anyone could *make* you do something you don't want to do."

Actually, after seeing Carolyn and Jake, and her genuine love for the guy and what they gave each other, Riggs thought Carolyn could probably ask him for the moon.

Same with the woman in front of him. He just hoped she never figured it out. "She didn't want me to be home alone." The concern had been touching, so he'd caved like a cheap suitcase, not wanting to disappoint her. He lifted a shoulder, not wanting to admit any of that, or how it felt to have people care at all. "She thinks I'm having trouble adjusting to civilian life."

"Are you?"

"No." *Yes.* Not that he could admit it out loud.

"Riggs . . ." Her expression had softened. "I—"

"Didn't know you'd be on a date though," he said not wanting pity.

"Yeah, well, that makes two of us." She pushed him aside and began rinsing dishes. "My mom set this up."

He laughed low in his throat, oddly liking that she hadn't agreed to a date. "You could just send him home."

"He's nice." She paused. "*And* he probably doesn't have weird . . . 'just friends' rules."

At the mental image that invoked, he actually got a chest pain. "You know why."

"Do I?"

He opened his mouth, but she flicked on the garbage disposal and drowned out anything he might have said. Probably for the best.

When she turned it off, she nodded with satisfaction. "Love getting rid of all the excess crap."

That made him smile. Tactful, she was not. "You have something to say, Tae, just say it."

"Nope," she said, popping the *p*.

"Good."

"*Good.*"

He shook his head at the both of them. "Still as mistrusting and suspicious as ever, I see."

"Being suspicious isn't a weakness."

"Agreed," he said.

She looked surprised. "You do?"

"Being suspicious has saved my ass more than once."

"Huh," she said, and he nodded. Something they had in common. He hadn't seen that coming, and judging from the look on her face, neither had she. Then he realized the low hum of voices from the other room had died down to nothing. He craned his neck behind him.

From the kitchen table, all eyes were on them like they were Must See TV.

The Good Dentist stood up. "Well . . . thanks for dinner, but I think this is my exit." And he headed for the door.

Smart move. Riggs didn't know the guy, but anyone could see that he was far too much of a pushover for a woman like Tae. Plus, no matter what she wanted Riggs to think, there was zero chemistry between them. *Unlike* the electricity storm going on between Tae and himself. Hell, every time they so much as looked at each other, the air crackled. He hadn't yet decided if that was a good or bad thing, but he was leaning toward *bad*.

"Hold on," Tae called to Hunter, turning off the water and drying her hands. "I'll walk you out." And then, with a glare in Riggs's direction, she left the kitchen.

Riggs moved to the sink to take over the dishes, and only partially because the window over the sink was cracked and he could see Tae and Hunter heading out the front door.

"Honey, guests don't do dishes," April said, coming into the kitchen.

Damn. She was as silent as any soldier he'd ever known. "You bought dinner, I've got this," he said. "Go be with your date and my annoying brother."

She smiled. "If it's any consolation, I'm pretty sure he thinks you're annoying too."

"Family," he said with a shrug.

April's smile faded some. "Family's everything," she said with surprising vehemence.

He gave a slow nod. "I agree."

"Hmm," she said, and then she was gone.

Okay, so he hadn't made a fan out of her. Normally, he wouldn't give it a second thought, but oddly enough, it bothered him a lot more than it should that Tae's mom didn't like him. His gaze drifted back to the window.

"Sorry about that," Tae was saying to Hunter. "Thanks for coming tonight. I really did have a good time."

Hunter's back was to Riggs, but he heard the guy's disbelief in his voice. "You're kidding, right?"

Funny, Riggs was thinking the same thing. At dinner, if Tae hadn't been working hard to not fall asleep when the guy had droned on and on about all his volunteer work with kids, like he was trying out for the position of her boyfriend, Riggs would eat his own shorts.

"I did," Tae insisted.

"Are you sure?" Hunter asked. "Because it seemed like you and Riggs were kind of into each other."

Tae glanced over Hunter's shoulder and, *shit*, caught Riggs at the window. He had to resist the urge to drop to his knees and out of view.

"It's not like that," she said, whether to Hunter or Riggs was anyone's guess, but Riggs was pretty sure it was to him. "Adrenaline HQ is my biggest client, and Riggs is half owner."

"So it's business then." Sounding relieved at that, Hunter nodded.

"*Old* business," Tae said, and she gave Riggs a surreptitiously subtle *go-away* gesture with her hand.

He did not go away.

"So maybe you'd be open to seeing me again then," Hunter said.

Riggs mimed hanging himself with a rope.

Tae's expression changed, and damn, Rigs knew that look. Sheer obstinance. She was about to do something incredibly stubborn just to spite him, and it was his own fault.

"Maybe," she said with a smile. It was her polite smile, Riggs knew, but clearly Hunter did not because . . .

Hunter leaned in.

The asshole was actually going to kiss her and Riggs found himself holding his breath. But then, right before contact, Tae turned her head and . . . The Good Dentist's kiss bounced off her cheek.

She'd cheeked him.

Riggs grinned.

Tae pulled Hunter in for a quick hug. "'Night," she said, and behind the guy's back double-flipped-off Riggs.

Anytime, he mouthed. Anytime at all.

CHAPTER 11

Tae spent the rest of the week buried in work. With Jenny's help, she pulled off a midweek dinner and auction for Sunrise Cove's Chamber of Commerce; both a fiftieth anniversary and reunion party; *and* a gorgeous, intimate sunset wedding with two brides on the lake.

The one thing she hadn't done? Talk to her mom about her birth certificate. It was keeping her up at night, but the longer she waited, the harder it was to bring it up. She finally had decided it was a problem for *after* Lake Days.

She'd been working closely with Jake and Carolyn for days. They'd all said they'd feel lucky if they ended up with thirty-five guests this first time.

Seventy-five attendees had signed up.

The sheer logistics of handling that many, along with their families and friends, took up every single one of her brain cells, so it was just as well she didn't talk to her mom.

Or so she told herself. Because deep down, she knew it was

nothing but a stalling tactic. She was scared. No way around it. She didn't want to upset her mom, but the real truth was that she was terrified of what answers she might get.

On Saturday morning, day one of Lake Days, she was woken at dawn by a text.

JENNY: I've emailed you everything you asked for; the final itinerary, the group breakdowns, and all the other deets you'll need.

JENNY: Oh, and don't forget to smile.

TAE: Really?

JENNY: Yes, really. You know you forget to smile all the time. I drafted a thank-you letter to the event sponsors, including the cutie-pie dentist. You ever going to go out with him or what?

TAE: TBD

JENNY: How about the hot silent partner then?

TAE: We're just friends.

JENNY: Was that sarcasm?

TAE: A little bit. Long story.

JENNY: I googled him. There's a pic of him and his brother from a few years back. God, I love those tough military types. All intensity and testosterone.

TAE: Feel free to put the same enthusiasm you put into my non-existent dating life into the upcoming Boosters event. I need table assignments, a list of door prizes, inventory for decorations, and food options pronto.

JENNY: This is an auto-response. Your employee is hard at work and can't chat right now.

Tae rolled her eyes and showered. Then she armed herself with the biggest to-go cup of coffee she had and drew a deep breath.

You've got this.

She stepped outside and found her mom leaning against her car, wearing an Adrenaline HQ T-shirt and a cute denim skirt that made her look younger than Tae. She was sipping what Tae knew would be herbal tea, and she seemed her usual serene and happy self.

Normally, this would help Tae be serene, but not today, not with butterflies bouncing around in her belly. "I envy you the calm."

Her mom sipped her tea. "It's because I'm not holding on to anything."

Tae's heart skipped a beat, and she searched her mom's darker brown eyes, hoping it was true, that her mom really *wasn't* holding on to anything, like, say . . . a twenty-eight-year-old secret. That had guilt joining her butterflies because this was her mom, who told Tae everything. Always.

"Want to talk about it?" her mom asked.

"About what?"

"Whatever's going on between you and Riggs."

Tae let out a careful breath. "As I've told you every day since the night you held me hostage with a surprise blind date, *nothing's* going on between me and Riggs."

"Good. Because he's not the right guy for you. In fact, he's exactly the *wrong* guy for you."

Irritation spiked, even though she was right. Riggs *was* the exact wrong guy for her and he'd be the first one to say so. "Not telling me anything I don't already know, Mom."

Her mom brushed a kiss to her cheek. "You should've gotten up with me and done yoga on the deck as the sun rose."

"Yeah, yeah."

Her mom smiled. They'd also had this conversation a thousand times. That's when Tae took a closer look at her mom. Her smile was not all from just a few stretches at sunrise. "*Ethan?*"

"Yes, but it's not what you think."

Tae's first response was envy. She wouldn't mind having that kind of a smile this morning. Her second response was worry, because her mom tended to move way too fast and get hurt because of it. "Mom—"

"He needed a headshot for his website. I gave him a photo shoot."

Tae felt her brow raise in surprise. "And . . . that's the only 'head' you gave him, right?"

"Oh my God. *Yes!* I had a great time, *with* all my clothes on no less, *and* he paid me. He said he loved my work."

"Because you're one of the best," Tae said. "But—"

"But I go too fast. Yes, I know, and you know why I know? Because you always tell me so."

"Because you always go too fast."

"Hey, I'm a new and improved me," her mom said. "And this was really just a job, Tae. I'm not going to tie myself down again, don't worry."

Tae sighed. She'd heard it all before, of course.

"I mean it this time. I know what your goals are, your need for stability and security, and I also know that's because of me. I never gave you that."

Guilt flashed. "Mom—"

"No, honey, let me finish. I didn't know what I was doing, but that's no excuse. A kid needs to know their mom knows what she's doing so they can develop trust, and I . . ." She shook her head, her eyes shiny now from emotion. "I screwed that up."

"No, Mom—"

"Hush, baby." April sniffed and blinked away the unshed tears. "I had good intentions that I couldn't execute. But I'm turning this ship around. I realize you're a grown-up, more of a grown-up than me, in fact, but I'm still your mom, and I intend to be the best one on the planet from here on out."

Tae felt more feels than she wanted to, and a whole bunch of love. "You are the best mom on the planet."

"Good. Then you can stop frowning, you'll get lines. It's going to be a great day. People are going to *love* the activities, the food, being on the water, *everything*!"

The butterflies took up flight again. "Here's hoping."

"They will." Her mom got into the passenger seat, and when Tae was behind the wheel, she reached for Tae's hand. "Honey. Look at me."

Tae had been scrolling through her emails and messages. All of Adrenaline HQ's staff would be on hand today, every last one, along with a dozen volunteers, all executing the multitiered itinerary she'd put together for all the adventures Riggs had created.

No pressure or anything.

She didn't want to let anyone down, but the reality of what she had to pull off in the next eight hours, making sure everything ran smoothly, everyone stayed safe *and* had an incredible time, was giving her palpitations.

Nope, that's not all it was . . .

"Tae."

She glanced at her mom sitting there serenely, with seemingly no idea of the inner turmoil Tae had been grappling with. Which was no one's fault but her own. She'd gotten nowhere with Google searches. She'd even gone as far as ordering a 23andMe test kit, but it hadn't come in yet. She'd been racing home every day to get to the mail first because she didn't want her mom to see it. She'd rearranged her schedule to do so and was getting damn tired of cooking dinner because that was the rule, first one home cooked dinner. "I was thinking maybe we save up and take a trip next year," she said casually.

April smiled. "Yes! We've never traveled together. I've always wanted to go see Niagara Falls."

"I was thinking Europe." Tae took a casual glance at her mom, wanting to see her reaction. "I let my passport expire, so I'll need to renew. I'd like to get one anyway, just to have. Which means I'll need my birth certificate . . ."

"You could just use your REAL ID," her mom said, no weird pause or eye twitch or anything to make Tae suspect she knew something.

"No, I think I need my birth certificate."

Her mom's phone buzzed and she sent an apologetic look Tae's way as she answered to Jake, assuring him they were almost to the site and would have everything set up by the time he got there, no worries.

No worries.

It was her mom's mantra, but Tae couldn't get behind it for herself. Her own mantra was more like *always worry . . .*

"You've got this," her mom said softly, gesturing to the lake. "Trust me, the way Jake runs his winter events are chaos. Wonderful, but total chaos. *Anything* you bring to the table today will be an improvement. And since I know what you bring—organization, your innate talent of knowing what people need, and let's not forget your amazing ability to get people to do what you want them to do—a great time will be had by all, I promise."

Her mom's praise was lovely but overwhelming, so she concentrated on the road, pulling into the parking lot. Right behind them was the equipment van with the kayaks, rafts, and tubes to be towed by a boat that had been lent to them for the day. Tae turned off the motor and took a deep breath.

"Oh, and don't worry about getting me home after," April said, getting her camera backpack out of the back. "Carolyn's going to drop me off. She wants to borrow a dress for some fancy gig she and Jake are going to next week. Now, say it with me." Her mom lifted her tea, in a toast. "It's going to be amazing."

Tae gently knocked her coffee mug into her mom's. "It's going to be amazing."

"There. Was that so hard?"

Tae had to laugh. "After the life you've led, I'll never understand how you're so optimistic and hopeful."

April shrugged. "For the past twenty-eight years, my life's been *absolutely* what I wanted it to be."

Surprised, Tae glanced over. "But it was so hard on you. No support. Always working multiple jobs. Not able to have your own life because you were saddled with a kid when *you* were a kid . . ."

"I want you to listen to me very carefully," her mom said with warm steel in her voice. "*Nothing* about having you and keeping you in my life as my family has been hard on me. Sure, money was more than tight, and there were times we lived day to day, but we were together." She sat back. "And I'd do it all over again, no regrets."

So simple. And Tae 100 percent believed her.

Tell her.

Instead, she let out a long shuddery breath and smiled back through a tight throat. "Love you, Mom."

"Love you more."

She was *such* a coward.

CHAPTER 12

Tae and her mom got out of her car to find that the day was one of those stunning June days that had to be seen to be believed. The lake shimmered in a myriad of blues and green, surrounded by sharp, jagged mountaintops that stunned the breath right from her lungs.

An hour later, they'd set up everything and redirected the staff and volunteers to the guest-welcoming area. Each guest would wear a lanyard that had a pass, and the color of the pass would tell the adventure guides what level of adventure they could participate in. If they could hold on to something and keep their head up on their own, they'd be able to ride on tubes behind the boat currently anchored at the beach. If they couldn't, they could get on a wave runner with one of the adventure guides and be held secure for a fun, safe ride. Same with a kayak. If all that was too much, they could be helped into the water to sit in flotation devices and just enjoy the gentle swells and sunshine. There were also a variety of games on the grass and a sand castle station on the beach. They had something for everyone.

Jake and Carolyn had arrived and were huddled with their adventure guides, going over their stations and tasks. Grub sat faithfully at Jake's side, staring worriedly at one of the guides. It was Hagrid, a ski instructor in another life, who always volunteered in their winter seasons. Tae had talked him into joining the summer program as well. Today, he had Muffin in a small leather backpack against his chest.

Muffin, who wore a little pink ribbon that held the hair out of her eyes, was glaring down at Grub.

Grub was afraid of small dogs. Didn't understand their language. Or why they liked to run circles around him. Last time Grub had seen Muffin, he'd lifted a leg and peed on her.

Which was probably why Muffin was safe in a harness against Hagrid's broad-as-a-mountain chest.

Someone else who'd arrived?

Riggs.

She'd seen him twice this past week. The first time had been when she'd gone to Adrenaline HQ to meet with Jake and other staff about today. Riggs had been in the warehouse, standing on the rafters thirty feet above with two other guys, taking measurements and doing God knew what. "Building a climbing wall," he'd told her when he'd come down to join the meeting.

Two days later she'd been back to find him stripped down to shorts and athletic shoes, scaled halfway up the warehouse wall. She'd stood at the base of that wall, staring up. His brown hair was already growing out from his military cut. The rest of him came in varying shades of brown too. His skin had turned bronze from long days in the sun, and his eyes as they caught her staring were mesmerizingly green. He'd smirked and rappelled down. "Want to try?"

"No."

He studied her, then smiled. "You don't trust yourself around me."

Of course she didn't, not when her brain and her body wanted two very different things. "You keep telling yourself that. What are you doing?"

"Testing a climbing wall and apparatus system. I want to be sure we can keep everyone safe, whether they can grip or not. We want them to have fun, have an adventure, but not be in danger."

"And you know how to do that?" she asked.

"I know how to do a lot of things."

To her annoyance, certain parts of her quivered. "Trust me, the knowledge of the things you know how to do is burned into my brain." Along with just how "creative" he could be when sexually motivated.

His laugh was soft and husky, and she'd glowered at the things it did to her insides. Big, fat tease, that's what he was. But now that he'd taken control of creating the summer program's activities, they were going to see a lot of each other.

Like today. Only about ten feet away, Riggs ran a hand over the top of Grub's head. "It's okay, buddy. I've got you."

Grub pressed into Riggs's leg. Riggs crouched low and wrapped his arms around the eighty-pound baby. "The trick is to never let them see you sweat."

Grub licked Riggs's cheek, and Tae tried hard not to be jealous.

Riggs kissed the top of Grub's head and straightened. When he caught her surprise, he gave a half smile. "I love dogs. Wouldn't mind having one of my own."

"What's stopping you?"

"My life."

She would swear that he was sounding wistful, maybe even vulnerable. "Riggs—"

"Nice job with this event," he said.

"Maybe you should wait until the day's over to say so," she said.

He gave a slow shake of his head. "You put your heart and soul into whatever you do. I'd bet my last dollar on you any day of the week, Rebel."

And then, with that shocking statement, he turned and walked off.

Tae absolutely did not watch his ass as he walked away.

Five minutes later, she stood at the entrance to their cordoned-off area, checking people in. Her mom was doing the same, as were two other Adrenaline HQ volunteers.

Halfway through check-in, she froze at the sight of Mr. Schwartz standing in front of her with a tween-aged boy in a wheelchair. "Welcome," she managed.

He smiled. "Thank you. This is my grandson Denny."

Thoughts racing, Tae searched her iPad for their names to check them in. "Here you are," she said, pulling their badges and welcome packet from the stack in front of her. "Denny's group is meeting over at the big pine tree with the blue flag."

They both smiled, thanked her, and walked off.

She stared after them, then finished checking in everyone in her line. Soon as she was done, she casually made her way over to Mr. Schwartz, who was standing on the sidelines of the snorkeling group, where he could see his grandson. When he saw her, his expression went a little guarded.

Yeah, join my club . . . "Hi," she said a little breathlessly. "Um, sorry, but remember last week when you mentioned your son? Scott, I believe? And your son's friend, AJ Strickland?"

"Yes," he said after a hesitation. "But as I mentioned, I was clearly mistaken about him being your father."

"I have a picture I was hoping to show you." She pulled out her phone and scrolled to the shot she'd taken the day after she'd met Mr. Schwartz. The original sat on her mom's mantel and was a military headshot of Andy Jameson—the only pic Tae had of her dad. "Is this AJ Strickland?"

Mr. Schwartz stared at the picture for a long moment, taking in the clean-cut, short-haired, almost innocent-looking young man, and slowly shook his head. "To be honest, I can't really tell. I don't think so?"

She drew a deep breath. Not the resounding "no" she'd been hoping for. "Did AJ grow up here? Or was he mostly a weekender, like Scott?"

"I'm not sure what school he went to, but I do think he was local. Like I said, he and Scott were hellions together and got into some trouble. After that, I stopped allowing my son to come to Tahoe." His expression was regretful but firm. "And really, that's all I know."

She nodded. "Do you think you could check with Scott about

whether AJ was a local? I'm sorry to ask, but it's really important to me."

"He's on a trip overseas, which is why I have Denny this week."

Damn . . .

Mr. Schwartz eyed her for a long beat, then sighed. "But . . ."

She couldn't help the hope that filled her, a rare emotion for her. "Yes?"

"I suppose maybe the next time Scott calls to check in on Denny, I could ask him."

"That would be amazing. Thank you so much."

He looked at her for a long beat, and his eyes softened. "I know it's none of my business, but sometimes, the past is best left in the past."

She watched him go, having to give herself a mental shake. He was right. And anyway, she needed to be focused today, no distractions. Lake Days wasn't just important to Adrenaline HQ and their guests, but it was also crucial to the growth of *her* business as well. She couldn't afford to let her own past creep in.

And speaking of distractions, the *biggest* distraction of them all was only ten feet away from her, talking to a few guys—one in a wheelchair, one with a prosthetic arm, another with no visible injuries. Jake had told her earlier in the week that Riggs was personally bringing in some new guests today, friends of his, all wounded veterans. She couldn't hear what he was saying, but whatever it was had them all cracking up, including Riggs himself, and she stared at him, realizing she'd not seen him laugh like that since they'd been teenagers.

He caught her looking at him, said something to the group,

then broke away, heading toward her. He wore camo board shorts, an army-green Adrenaline HQ shirt, battered athletic shoes, and dark sunglasses.

Looking like sin-on-a-stick.

He came close enough that she had to tip her head up to look at him. She couldn't see his eyes and wished she had sunglasses to hide behind too. "What?"

That got her a small smile. "There's a hundred-plus people here."

"Was that a question?"

"More like a compliment. You did good."

She smiled in pleasure in spite of herself. "So did you. You've joined the dark side and brought in some friends."

"You and Jake were right about doing this. And they"—he gestured to his friends—"need this too. Now, because of you and my brother, they can have a day off from their troubles."

A kid came up to them. Jordy, holding on to the hand of a much younger girl.

"You said I should drop Sarah off at ten," he said, shifting his feet nervously.

"Jordy!" Tae smiled. "I'm so happy you came." She glanced at Riggs in time to catch his unguarded expression, which was soft and welcoming. His mouth turned up slightly, and he pushed his sunglasses to the top of his head before going down on his haunches, balanced on the balls of his feet in front of the little girl. "Hey, you. Sarah, right?"

Eyes huge, she nodded. "I don't want Jordy to leave."

"I hope he doesn't leave too," Riggs said. "There's going to be a sand castle–building contest, and then a lunch where you can pick out whatever you want to eat. Does that sound like something that might interest you?"

Sarah's eyes got even bigger, and her smile was sheer delight as she nodded.

Riggs looked at Jordy, standing there staring at his shoes like he knew he didn't belong. "There's plenty of stuff for kids your age too. You ever been out on a boat?"

"No."

"Want to?"

Jordy lifted his head, surprised. "Really?"

"Really." Riggs rose, looking around. He caught Carolyn's gaze, and she came over to take the kids to their respective groups.

And then it was just Tae and Riggs.

"So you're not such a hard-ass after all," she said.

He shrugged. "Maybe you're wearing off on me."

"You take that back right now," she said. "I'm one-hundred-percent hard-ass."

He let out a small smile. "You are, but you're also a secret softie." He watched Jordy and Sarah walk away with Carolyn, a surprisingly solemn look and something-else-she-couldn't-quite-place in his gaze.

She waited a moment to speak, more moved than she wanted to admit. "Most people don't see past the shitty situation to the good kid beneath."

He nodded. His body language said calm and relaxed, but she knew that wasn't true.

"I wish you'd had something like this to come to when you were young."

"Right back at you, Rebel."

"My mom didn't abuse me."

"There are all kinds of shitty growing-up situations," he said quietly. "And they mold us, make us different, no matter what we want to think."

She had no idea how it was that he could reach right inside her and touch her heart with so few words. She realized with a start that they'd shifted closer and were staring at each other's mouths.

"I thought we decided this was a bad idea," he said, his voice low. Husky.

She drew a deep breath. "No, *you* decided. But I agree. You're a bad idea. In fact, you're a terrible, horrible, no-good, bad idea. So thanks for turning me down."

He paused. "You know it's not because I don't want you, right?"

"Whatever."

"*Tae.*"

She reluctantly lifted her face.

His gaze held hers. "I want you, Tae. I want you bad too. But—"

"Oh good," she said with false cheer. "The but. My very favorite thing." She pulled free. "I don't want to hear it, Riggs. Let's just stick with you're a bad idea."

"Yeah—wait." He looked confused. "Why am I the bad idea?"

"Are you kidding me? You're a walking, talking bad idea." She tossed up her hands. "You make me forget myself and what I want in life."

This appeared to stun him. "I do?"

"Never mind." She turned to walk away, but he caught her hand.

Reeled her in slowly, looking at her with those intense green eyes. "What is it you want in life?"

"It doesn't matter."

"It does," he insisted.

"Fine." What the hell, she had nothing to lose except her pride, and when it came to their past, she didn't have much of that to begin with. "I want the three *S*'s: safety, security, stability— which I intend to get for myself, in case you were wondering. And a guy like you . . ." She shook her head. "Well, you'd threaten all of that."

She thought maybe he'd laugh and then she'd have to kill him, but he didn't laugh. He didn't smirk. He was very serious. "And the Good Dentist? Does he threaten it as well?"

"Does it matter?"

He stared at her for a beat. "It shouldn't." He slid his sunglasses back on. "So where does this leave us?"

This tugged a reluctant laugh from deep in her throat. "Just friends, remember?"

"Hard to forget."

"Is that regret I hear?"

"Buckets of it."

She sucked in a breath, somehow both mollified and shocked

at that. After a hesitation, he ran a finger along her temple, tucking a strand of hair behind her ear, and an electric shock went straight through her. Him too, if the look on his face told her anything. "You just tried to electrocute me," she said.

"I think that was animal magnetism."

Before she could respond to that, someone called her name.

She turned and came face-to-face with Hunter.

"Hey, you," he said with a welcoming smile, like she was the best thing he'd seen all day. "Thanks for inviting me."

She glanced over at Riggs in time to catch him giving Hunter a nod before walking away.

She drew a deep breath. *Buckets of it?* Shaking that off with difficulty, she smiled at Hunter. "All the sponsors were invited. So thank *you* for sponsoring some of the at-risk kids today."

"I was happy to do it." He wore a casual shirt, untucked over board shorts and flip-flops. His smile was genuine. He had volunteered his time and money to those in need. He was a good guy, a really good guy.

But there was no zing.

Buckets of it . . .

What was wrong with her?

The answer to that was undoubtedly more than she had time to think about. A lot more.

CHAPTER 13

Riggs strode away from Tae in her pretty sunshine-yellow sundress and sandals, her hair piled on top of her head, iPad in hand, looking like the girl-next-door, only bossier.

Sexier.

Calling himself all sorts of an idiot for the ball of emotion in his throat that felt a whole lot like jealousy, he moved faster. Like he could outpace those always-present demons.

Damn, he needed to get a grip. So he moved across the grass with purpose, the new summer program going on in joyful chaos around him, the program that had been developed and implemented in part by him, but didn't include him.

His own doing.

Apparently, he'd been gone so long, he no longer felt connected to . . . well, anything. Stopping in the middle of it all, he looked out at the water. At least he could admit to having some good memories of the lake, really good. He and Jake sneaking out on long summer nights, stealing his dad's piece-of-shit boat to take friends out on the water. In winter, working weekends with Jake at the ski resorts for free passes so they could snow-board to their heart's content.

Jake came up to his side, also looking out at the lake. Riggs wondered if he had the same good memories of this place as Riggs, or if his memories were tainted now because of what he could no longer do.

"If you keep looking at me like you feel bad for me, I'm going to punch you in the face," Jake said mildly.

"You can't reach my face."

Jake laughed. "Christ, I missed you. No one else will fuck with me, call me out on my own shit."

"Happy to help."

"Still going to punch you in the face later," Jake said fondly. "But for now, I need to put you to work." He gestured to the boat anchored right off the beach. "The guy who donated his boat for the day had to leave. I need someone to drive it."

"We've got a trillion volunteers and staff here."

"Yes," Jake said. "And I like the 'we,' but there's only one per-son here I trust to drive that boat around this lake while towing people with disabilities on tubes behind it. It takes a knowing touch to drive a boat with that kind of precision."

"*You* have that knowing touch," Riggs pointed out.

"But you do it better."

Riggs had to laugh. "You've been getting me to do shit all my life with that excuse. 'Riggs, you gotta do the dishes before Dad whups our ass because you do them better than me. Riggs, you gotta cook Dad dinner tonight because he's in a foul mood and you duck faster than I do. Riggs, you gotta get Dad up for work, he won't get as angry if you're the one to wake him up, you do it better than me.'"

Jake rubbed a hand over his jaw to hide his smile. "You always were too smart for me. But in this case, I'm being real with you. You'll handle the boat better than I could. I'll be onshore, helping to load and unload people from the tubes so you don't have to get in and out of the boat every time. I'll also put a volunteer on board with you to flag and help our athletes back onto the boat when they get tired, and also to handle the parents, siblings, or whoever is with our athlete."

Riggs looked out at the water sparkling under a warm sun, surrounded by 360 degrees of staggeringly beautiful mountains. He actually couldn't think of anything he'd rather be doing today. "Okay."

Jake gave him an actual honest-to-god smile. "Yeah?"

"Sure."

"Good. Oh, and one more thing."

Riggs looked at him warily. "What?"

"Keep your eyes and heart open."

"Seriously? You sound like a Hallmark ad."

"I want you to see how important Adrenaline HQ is to this community and how much it means to the people we're serving today."

"You think I can't see that?"

"I think you're trying to keep yourself closed off so you can say you came home and fulfilled your brotherly duty to make sure I'm okay, and to make sure it's easy for you to leave." Jake gave him a look. "How am I doing?"

That he was right on the money didn't help. "I don't think of you as a duty. You've got that backward. Growing up, I was *your* duty."

"So what? I was the big brother. I would've protected your ass no matter who you were. And if our positions had been reversed, you'd have done the same. It's how we're built, Riggs. Protect the weak. So, are you driving the boat or not?"

Off-balance now at the reminder of the long years he'd been the weak one, Riggs gave him a smart-ass salute, and on the boat he went.

He quickly familiarized himself with the controls and was checking all the gears as his volunteer came on board in a sunshine-yellow sundress, ponytail sticking out the back of an Adrenaline HQ ball cap, sunglasses on her face.

Tae stopped short and stared at him. "You're the driver?"

"Of all the boats in all the land . . ." he said.

She'd left her sandals onshore, so she was barefoot as she grabbed the red flag they would use to alert other boats when they had someone in the water. She then straightened and looked around, as if trying to decide where to sit. There was a spot right next to him, but she chose to kneel on the bench seat across the back, watching as fifty feet away, onshore, Carolyn and Jake helped two teenage boys onto the wide tube attached to the boat by a rope.

"That's Archie and Arlo," Tae told him, consulting her iPad. "Sixteen and seventeen. Brothers. Autistic. They requested their mom stay on the shore instead of coming on the boat. Also they want to go fast, but their mom says please don't. They're mostly nonverbal, so I'll read their cues and let you know how you're doing."

"And you?" Riggs asked. "Are you going to let me know how you're doing too?"

Apparently, she was only going to talk to him when necessary because she didn't respond. Instead she kept her gaze on her two charges as she held the flag in the air. She waited for a thumbs-up from the older of the two brothers and then called out, "Hit it," to Riggs.

He accelerated and the boys grinned from ear to ear, bouncing on the small swells, hanging on to the tube for dear life. The older one gave a thumbs-up sign, which Riggs could see because he was keeping one eye on the rearview mirror. A thumbs-up meant go faster, but Tae didn't tell him, which meant she was with the mom on speed then. Noted. But the boys were strong and clearly not novices, and they were *both* giving him the thumbs-up now.

So he went a little faster.

"Hey," Tae yelled at him over the sound of the engine, squinting because the spray was hitting her right in the face thanks to the way he steered. He liked to take his entertainment where he could get it.

"What are you doing?"

"Going faster," he called back to her. The boys were whooping and hollering and having the time of their lives, which had him grinning too.

Tae made her way to the seat beside him, still facing the back of the boat so she could see the boys. "Slow down!" she said, swiping water out of her face.

"Tae, you could jog faster than this." He carefully steered them away from an approaching boat and eyed the boys again. Still having the time of their lives. "They're good. They're better than good, look at them."

She gave a reluctant smile. "Yeah. But I'm drenched, thanks to you."

"It's the wind."

"Yeah, right," she said. Standing, she pushed her drenched summer dress off her body, leaving her in a one-piece sky-blue bathing suit. While he did his best to not swallow his tongue, she squeezed the water from her dress and tossed it to a seat to air dry, keeping an eye on the boys at all times.

"You're staring," she said without looking at him.

"I appreciate a good view when I've got one."

"Nothing you haven't seen before," she noted, and when he didn't respond, she spared a fraction of a second to give him a brows up.

He flashed a smile. "Let's just say you grew up right nice, Rebel."

She snorted.

"So where's the Good Dentist?" he asked.

"Jet skiing."

He waited for her to say something more, but she didn't. She went back to concentrating on her charges.

And he went back to watching *his* charges, all three of them, in the rearview mirror as he handled the boat. When the boys were done, Tae helped the brothers off and the next group on—a twelve-year-old girl named Lucy who'd lost her legs due to a rare infection at birth and her father. She and Tae wore the same color swimsuit, and Lucy was completely charmed by Tae.

Her dad had been prepared to sit on the tube and hold Lucy during the boat ride, but Lucy wanted only Tae.

So Dad held the flag and Tae got into the water and onto the tube, holding Lucy as Riggs took them on a ride that brought the biggest, sweetest smiles he'd ever seen.

From both girls.

And he had to admit, Tae was something to watch. She was so sweet and kind and loving out here, so giving of herself, and more open than he'd ever seen her. He hadn't even known she'd had this side of her; she certainly hadn't shown it to him.

After twenty minutes, which was the amount of time they'd allocated to each guest in order to give as many people a ride as they could, he stopped and made his way to the back of the boat to pull the girls in. Kneeling on the swim deck, he took Lucy from Tae's arms, handing her over to her dad, who wrapped her in a towel. Then Riggs offered Tae a hand, pulling her on board as well. She grabbed a towel—his—her gaze daring him to complain.

No idiot, he kept his mouth shut as he drove them back to shore.

And so the day went. They took out kids with a wide variety of medical conditions, at-risk teens who'd never been on a boat before, and wounded warriors, all of their stories heartbreaking. All wearing smiles today.

On the last run before the lunch break, they took one of the wounded veterans out. Ace had suffered a traumatic brain injury and wore a prosthetic arm thanks to an IED. Riggs nodded to him and did what he'd done for the others, took them on a rather sedate ride on the lake. But after one loop, Ace looked bored, so Riggs hit the gas and did some donuts, spinning the boat in a tight circle.

He heard Tae gasp and yell, "Slow down!" He ignored her, which—*shock*—she didn't like. She got right up in his face. "Stop this boat this instant! *Are you nuts?*"

He eyed Ace, who was grinning like he was on the ride of his life. But Riggs slowed, then stopped, brushing past Tae to pull Ace in himself. They hugged hard with some back slapping, then pulled back, laughed together, and then hugged again.

"Ahhh," Ace said on a blissful sigh, making his way off the sundeck to sink gratefully to the bench seat. "Man, it's good to see your ugly mug again."

Tae stared down at Ace in relieved shock. "You two know each other."

Ace smiled. "Yep."

Tae nodded. "You served together."

"Yep again. This asshole"—Ace gestured to Riggs, as if there could be any doubt who was the asshole on board—"saved my life. Once overseas, and once a few years back, when he nagged me into getting my private investigator's license to support myself instead of sitting around feeling sorry for myself."

"Yeah, well, he very nearly took your life again just now," she exclaimed.

"Nah. He knew what I wanted."

"And what was that?" Tae asked. "An early death?"

"Already stared death right in the face and won," Ace said easily. "And Riggs knows that sometimes after something like that, you gotta keep staring death in the face to remind yourself that you're still winning, even when it doesn't feel like it."

Tae let out some air. "Then I'm glad you're here," she finally said gracefully. "And that you can enjoy the day."

"Oh, I'm enjoying it all right." Ace grinned up at her. "So . . . are you his?"

Nope, Riggs thought. *Because I'm a spectacular dumbass.*

"Excuse me?" Tae said in a tone that any normal man would've backed up at. "I'm *nobody's*," she said. "I'm my own."

Ace didn't back up. He cackled. "Feisty. That's new." He glanced at Riggs. "I approve." Then he winked at Tae. "He usually goes for sweet. Gets bored. Needs to be kept on his toes."

Maybe not my toes, Riggs thought. But she could have him on his knees with a single look . . .

"I'm not *keeping* him at all," she said. "Not on his toes or otherwise."

Ace laughed again. "Yep, you're perfect."

"Oh, for God's sake." Tae turned and concentrated her sharp gaze on Riggs, who was still at the back of the boat on the swim platform, pulling in the tube and coiling up the rope. "And *you*," she said. "You could've told me you knew him!"

"What, and ruin your righteous anger?"

Rolling her eyes, she snatched up her sundress, stepped into it, and pulled it up her body. She consulted her iPad. "Time for lunch."

"One of my very favorite things," Ace said.

"I'd suggest not asking him what his *other* favorite things are," Riggs said.

"Spoilsport," Ace said.

Tae moved to the front and sat behind the wheel.

"What are you doing?" he asked, tossing the coiled rope and tube on board.

"Taking us to shore."

"Wait—do you even know how to—" He never finished the sentence because she hit the gas and . . . he went sailing off the swim platform and into the water.

When he surfaced, Tae was turning the boat around to get him, and Ace was doubled over with laughter. Good to know she could still make him feel like that stupid kid who was all thumbs.

Tae had her sunglasses on as she watched him retrieve his own ball cap and sunglasses, both floating on the water, and then swim the twenty feet to the back of the boat. He boarded and shook like a dog, water flying from his hair and getting her wet all over again.

While she gasped, he peeled off his now suctioned-to-him T-shirt. Tossing it aside, he realized Tae was staring at him. Specifically at his bared chest and abs. He raised a brow.

With a roll of her eyes, she very purposely stopped looking at him and turned forward to drive toward shore.

"You know how to drive a boat," he said, sitting next to her.

"I know how to do a lot of things."

How well he knew it.

She shrugged. "I dated a guy once who had a boat."

She went back to concentrating on driving, and Ace looked at Riggs. *Keeper*, he mouthed.

Yeah. But he wasn't. After all the people he'd loved and lost in his life, he couldn't help but think that relationships weren't meant to be permanent. He cared deeply for Tae as a friend, and knew trying for more would mean losing her at some point, if not when he left for D.C., then when she eventually walked away from him. That was just how it was. Taking this thing with Tae deeper would ruin everything. Expectations would change, and he could face a lot of things, but he didn't want to lose her. She deserved more than someone who couldn't give her the world. He knew her past and refused to play with her.

Which meant he had to be the strong one and protect them both.

On the beach, the crowd was happy and relaxed after a morning full of events, and the guests seemed thrilled to be here. Jake had asked Riggs to be open, but in truth, it was hard *not* to be moved by the day. And yeah, he got it. Jake really was doing something here, something important, something special. And being a part of it felt . . . good.

Really good.

He got in the lunch line with everyone else, realizing he was starving.

"Sorry about the accidental swim."

He turned and came face-to-face with Tae. "Is that the story you're going with? *Accidental*?"

"Yep." And then she cut him in line.

"Aw, there she is," he said. "That girl from school."

She snorted. "She's long gone."

"Not all gone," he said. "And I loved that tough-as-nails, 'tude-ridden girl."

She craned her neck and gave him a long look. "That was lust, not love."

"Maybe." But he knew that in his case, it'd been a bit of both.

AT THE END of the day, when all their guests were gone and everything was cleaned up, Riggs stood between the parking lot and the grass, doing a final check to make sure they were leaving the park as clean as they'd found it. He eyed the area that had been buzzing all day and shook his head. He'd had the time of his life, and he didn't even realize he was still smiling until Tae spoke from directly behind him.

"Did you actually have fun?"

He turned to face her. Still in the sundress, still barefoot. Her hair had fallen loose in wild waves around her face. Her cheeks were windburned from the boat, and there was a dusting of freckles across her nose. She was holding two big bags of trash, and somehow she'd never looked more beautiful. Fun? Hell, yeah, he'd had fun, which he hadn't seen coming. "Maybe." He took the bags of trash from her, setting them down for the moment.

She arched a brow. "'Maybe'? Still a word miser, I see."

"Maybe you just tongue-tie me."

She tilted her head back and laughed. He loved the sound, and the way her eyes lit up with genuine amusement, but . . . "You do," he said.

"Uh-huh."

He just looked at her, and her smile slowly faded. "I . . . tongue-tie you," she repeated, heavy on the doubt.

"Yes. And it turns me right back into that stupid, awkward teenager."

"You were never awkward. And I saw you today, you were so great with everyone, making them feel right at home."

He had to laugh. "What did you expect me to do? Be a brooding asshole?"

"Well, if the shoe fits . . ." she said demurely.

He snorted, then caught her staring at his mouth. Just the thought of her maybe thinking about kissing him put his mind on the same thing. And more. "You're right," he said quietly. "I had a good day. A great one, actually. But . . ."

"But what?" she whispered. "You can think of something that could improve it?"

Her gaze was still on his mouth, and suddenly, or not so suddenly at all, kissing her was all he could think of. "I can."

"Maybe you should tell me about it. In great detail."

He gently nudged her up against a tree, planted his hands on the trunk on either side of her face, and leaned in until their lips *almost* touched. "I want to taste you."

She left her eyes closed, but her mouth curved. "Too bad we're just friends. And why is that again?"

He was having a hell of a time remembering. "Because I don't want to ever be someone who hurts you."

She had her hands into his hair and tightened. "And if I told you you're hurting me by not kissing me?"

"I'm serious, Tae. I don't want to be a regret to you."

"You know what I think?" she asked. "That I want to be friends who kiss. How can a little kiss possibly hurt me?"

Well, when she put it like that . . .

She was smiling when he closed the distance between them, the kiss deep and drugging, quickly dragging him under. He moaned when she slid her hands down his chest and yanked him into her so that there wasn't any space between them. He lost himself until he heard an "ew!" and remembered where they were.

"They're kissing," a little girl stage-whispered.

Sarah.

Regretfully, he pulled back before he drowned in Tae, who he knew was driving Jordy and Sarah home.

"Is he your boyfriend?" Sarah asked Tae.

Tae appeared to choke on her own tongue.

"My teacher Mrs. Watson, she kisses her boyfriend too. But my bestest friend Kimmy says you get cooties if you kiss a boy. Do you have cooties, Ms. Tae?"

Tae's eyes were laughing as she hunkered down before the girl. "One day, you'll find the cooties are worth the risk. But not until you're older. Much older."

"How old?" Sarah asked.

"Twenty-eight," Tae said.

Riggs grinned.

Sarah looked vastly disappointed. "That's . . . ancient."

CHAPTER 14

April's heart was so full as she helped load the back of Jake's van, she could hardly contain herself. The day had been incredible, and she was so thrilled she could burst. She pushed the last box of extra supplies into the van, shut the door, and then she and Carolyn hugged.

"Today couldn't have gone better," Carolyn said. "Can't wait to see the pics you took."

April had easily taken hundreds. She couldn't wait to sort through them either. "I'll put together an album and email you the link."

Carolyn nodded. "And don't forget to bill Jake for your time. He wanted to make sure you got paid for that."

"He's already paying me to be here today."

"As an event worker, yes," Carolyn said. "The photos are a separate deal, and he was adamant about that."

Most likely because Tae had suggested it, and the thought filled April's heart even more. "Thank you."

"Creativity certainly runs in your family," Carolyn said. "Your daughter's amazing."

April smiled. "She *is*, isn't she?"

Jake approached. "I've tried putting her on my payroll, but she likes running her own ship. Can't blame her. She's good at it."

"Trust me," April said on a laugh. "She's better off being her own boss. She's not big on authority, likes to do her own thing, and doesn't always play well with others."

Carolyn laughed. "She'd fit right in with Jake then."

Jake rolled his eyes, tugged on Carolyn's hand until she bent over him, and kissed her.

Everything about Carolyn softened, and she cupped his face, then hugged him tight before pulling back.

April adored their relationship, but she also knew what they had was rare. She'd certainly never found it, despite desperately wishing otherwise so she could show Tae what a healthy relationship looked like.

Jake drove off in his van, leaving just Carolyn's car, but she turned to April. "Would you mind if I swam out to the buoys and back before we go? I didn't get a chance to run this morning."

"Go for it. I'd go with you, but . . ." She smiled. "I don't want to."

Carolyn laughed. "With your figure, you don't have to. But if I even look at food, I gain weight."

While she headed down to the beach, April moved back to the grassy area. Looking at the lake always calmed her, centered her, and now was no exception. The sun was getting lower in the sky, sending the late-afternoon light dancing over the whitecaps on the lake, making it shimmer like magic.

Gorgeous.

She inhaled deeply the clean mountain air, filled with pine and the slight scent of the hamburgers and hot dogs they'd barbecued for lunch. Then her attention got caught on something else and her heart jerked to a stop. Tae pressed against a tree, with Riggs's body flush to hers. It wasn't the fact that they were kissing that got her, it was more the emotion implied in their body language.

This was not just a kiss.

She looked away, thoughts racing. She couldn't deny that Riggs Copeland was dead sexy, but . . . but. He had an edge to him, an element of implied danger that she didn't want for Tae. And then there was the biggest reason she didn't like him for her daughter. When he'd shown up at the warehouse that first day, something about him, something deep in his eyes, told her he didn't think he deserved Tae.

Which meant he didn't.

And she'd heard Jake and Riggs arguing several times now, their voices hard and filled with resentment. Riggs had seemed cold and distant. Incapable of what she wanted most for Tae— someone to love her. Except . . . the care in which he held Tae now, his hands carefully cradling her head, made April doubt herself. Though he'd hidden it impossibly well, he was clearly more than capable of deep emotion.

She still didn't like it.

Because he wasn't going to stick around. And Tae had seen enough temporary in her life. She didn't need more.

She and Riggs were staring at each other now, the air thick with tension. On some level April supposed she'd known there was something between them, no matter what Tae claimed. But knowing and seeing were two very different things. There'd been an undeniable change in her daughter after the convenience store incident. She smiled more. And then there'd been the Chinese food date night. The difference between the way Tae had looked at Hunter and the way she'd looked at Riggs had been . . . well, very telling. But when April had asked her about it, she'd said nothing was happening except that Riggs drove her crazy.

April hadn't considered the fact that she might've meant crazy in a good way.

April sank heavily to one of the benches lined up between the parking lot and the grass. Someone started to walk by her, momentarily blocking the view she hadn't wanted anyway. She looked up to see one of the wounded warriors who'd been at the event. Most of his face was hidden beneath a ball cap and dark glasses. Tall and lanky lean, he was in cargo shorts and a T-shirt that revealed one of his arms was a prosthetic. He moved closer and looked at the empty space next to her.

"Go for it," she said.

He sank, as if exhausted to the bone. He'd spent his day doing the most active activities they'd had, while she'd been seeing to the families of their campers, helping out with the food tent, and taking tons of pictures, so their paths hadn't crossed since she'd signed him in that morning. "Ace," she said. "Right?"

He nodded. "And you're April."

"You remembered," she said, surprised.

He smiled, and his weathered face was transformed, making her realize he couldn't be older than forty. "I make it a habit to know a pretty lady's name."

There'd been a whole bunch of years where April wouldn't have recognized a nice guy if she'd tripped over him. Yes, she was online dating, but that was more for Tae, to get her out there. She herself had been concentrating on learning from her mistakes. So she gave him a small smile and let her gaze drift back to her current biggest concern—Tae and Riggs.

Ace's gaze followed hers. "Never thought I'd see that."

"What?"

"Riggs letting his guard down," Ace said. "He's got his back turned to the parking lot and no one at his six. She must be something."

"She is." She looked at him. "How well do you know Riggs?"

"To the bone. He bullied me back to life."

"So he's . . . a good man?" she asked.

"He's tough, fearless. And just about as badass as they come."

She met his gaze. "That's not the same as being a good man."

"He's a good man too," Ace said. "The best."

"So he's not . . . messed up?"

Ace laughed. "Oh, well, yeah. He's *totally* messed up."

Exactly what she was afraid of. She glanced back to Tae and Riggs, but they were gone. She stood up, noting Tae's car pulling out of the lot, but April couldn't tell if she had a passenger.

"You okay?" Ace asked.

"Always." It was her go-to answer. And given the look on Ace's face, he knew it, but he just nodded at her as she moved to Carolyn's car to wait for her ride home.

AN HOUR LATER, Carolyn had driven April home, picked out a dress to borrow, and left. April looked out her living room window at her daughter's car in their shared driveway. Seeing it there meant she hadn't gone home with Riggs.

It did not mean Riggs wasn't over there right now . . .

Mew, Storm said in her gravelly, old-lady voice.

She scooped the cat up and cuddled her close. "I know. I'm hungry too." She changed and headed—with Storm on her heels—into the kitchen to plate the Mexican takeout she'd picked up on the way home. Yes, it was takeout, but if she wasn't going to treat herself like she was special enough to use a real plate and silverware, then who would?

And besides, she needed the pick-me-up. She felt a little down, though she told herself she didn't have anything to feel down about. Nothing. Nada. Zip. First of all, Tae was a big girl, and plus interfering in her life only made them fight. And second . . . it was fine. It wasn't as if Tae would keep Riggs long enough to get hurt by him. She never kept a man for long, not even the good ones. Something she'd learned from April, to her own shame. She intended to fix that.

As for herself, she really was fine. For the first time in a long time, she and Tae were in a good place. They had roofs over their heads, roofs they actually owned. They had food. They even had a little cushion in their bank accounts, which meant they weren't living like animals. and there was that photography class she was taking at the local community college.

Things were good, dammit. Real good.

So what was wrong? Why did she feel like a hamster on the wheel, that her life was living her, and not the other way around?

Tae burst in the back door and into April's kitchen, and instantly her mood improved.

"I smell food," Tae said hopefully.

April couldn't help but laugh. "Grab a plate."

Her daughter loaded up, and they both sat to eat.

April looked at her daughter carefully, trying to read her thoughts or find even a hint at what was going through her mind, but the girl could be a stone when she wanted. "You were amazing today."

"Thanks. Right back at you." Tae kept shoveling in food. "Everything went off as planned, which is always nice. Perfect day, really."

"And . . . *after*?" April's mouth asked before her brain could stop it.

Tae stopped midchew. "After what?"

"What did you do after the event?"

"Showered, and then came over here to steal food."

"That's all?" April asked casually.

But not casually enough, because Tae stopped eating and met her gaze. "Why do I feel like you're fishing for something?"

Because she was stupid and apparently hadn't learned from her mistakes after all. "I'm not. Forget it."

An emotion crossed Tae's face that April couldn't quite catch, but it might have been pity, and there were few things in life that April hated more than pity.

"Mom—"

"Don't." April shook her head. "Don't say it."

"I have to, and I mean this in the best way possible because you know how much I love you. But you need a hobby."

"I have hobbies. They include rage-sighing and marathoning *Bridgertons* on repeat."

"And I like both of those hobbies." Tae put her hand over April's. "But you need *another* hobby as well, one that doesn't begin and end with me."

Dammit. "I know," she whispered, feeling herself getting choked up. She hated getting choked up almost as much as she hated being pitied. "You're right. I've been needing something just for me."

"And not a man," Tae said. "They're overrated."

"Are they?"

"You know they are." Tae looked up. "What's wrong?"

"Nothing." She paused. "I've been needing to find something to make me feel . . ." She searched for the right word. "Okay on my own." Damn, her voice wobbled. *"Fulfilled."*

A look of devastation crossed Tae's face, and she started to stand. "I've got a box of those cookies we love. The fake Girl Scout chocolate mint ones. They're in my desk drawer beneath my unpaid bills, hidden from myself until a cookie emergency came up, but I'll just go get them and—"

"I'm taking a photography class at the community college," April blurted out.

Tae froze halfway out of her chair.

"I started a few weeks ago but was too embarrassed to tell you about it."

Tae looked stunned. And hurt. "Mom, why would you be embarrassed? I think it's awesome."

April felt her chest swell. "You do?"

"Of course. You love to take pics. You take *amazing* pics. You could probably teach that class."

But she shook her head. "I'm just self-taught. I want to know the terminology and the right way to do things. But . . ."

"But what?"

April grimaced. "How in the world did I ever used to work multiple jobs and handle our lives? Now if I have one class and have to get groceries on the same day, I fall apart. Plus, I'm the old lady in my class."

Tae laughed. "Mom, you're forty-three."

"Forty-*four* in a month, which makes me a zillion years older than everyone in my class."

"So?" Tae laughed again when April just glared at her. "You're just used to being the hot young thing. And I get it, it's been your identity for a long time."

April sighed. "Now you're just making me sound egotistical."

"Well, you did use that coupon you found online to get that high colonic." Tae shuddered in horror. "If that wasn't for ego."

"Hey, I lost five pounds overnight." She sighed. "It was awful," she admitted.

Tae laughed, then met her gaze, smile fading. "Are you enjoying the photography class?"

April thought about the assignments, and how her heart raced with joy every time she used the excuse of an assignment to get out there with her camera. "Yes. I want to go out and get some sunset pics in a few."

Tae waved a hand, like *see?* "Then ignore everything else. And stop looking at goop for coupons." She took her dish to the sink, rinsed it, and stuck it in the dishwasher. "If you're going out to shoot, I'm going to get some work done."

"I thought maybe you'd go out with Hunter tonight," April said as casually as she could. "He was pretty great with the kids today."

Tae shook her head. "I'm too tired for a date tonight."

Let it go . . . But she couldn't. "Tired? Or confused?"

Tae frowned. "What does that mean?"

April really wanted to shut up, but she hadn't been born with the shut-up gene. "I saw you with Riggs today."

"Me too. We both worked on the boat."

When had her daughter gotten so good at evasion? "There's something going on between the two of you."

"There's really not."

"Then why are you really here instead of on a date with the very nice dentist, who, by the way, happens to *live* in Sunset Cove and isn't just visiting? A man who works with children and saves lives."

"Mom, he's a *dentist*," Tae said dryly. "Not that there's *any-thing* wrong with that. But technically, since Riggs fought to keep America safe, he's the one who saves lives."

April nodded, well aware she was stepping into the ring, but she felt strongly about this, that her daughter was about to make a gigantic mistake. "Yes, he did an amazing service for our country. But, Tae, it's in his eyes. He's jaded and closed off. And while my heart goes out to him for everything he must've seen and done, I want more for you."

"There are worse things than being jaded and closed off," Tae said.

"Honey, you're *not* jaded and closed off. It's just a front you use, a face you give the world because you're scared to let someone love you."

Tae let out a rough laugh. "I don't need a man's love to validate my life, Mom. And neither do you."

"Well, of course not. But being in love can be a lot of fun." And if he happened to be compassionate and patient enough to bring out her soft side . . . well, *that* was what she wanted for Tae. Someone to love her as she was, someone to be there for her because she was *always* there for everyone else. Was that so wrong? "I hate that I taught you love is something bad, something to be avoided."

"Look, I'm sure love is pretty great." Tae paused. "But it won't be with Riggs. We're . . . not like that."

April nodded, her chest tight because not only was her daughter not being honest with her, but she also wasn't being honest with herself.

"I'm going now," Tae said.

"Wait. You mentioned dessert. We could talk."

Tae's face went blank, the way it did when she was closing herself off. "Maybe another night."

"I've got ice cream right here in my freezer." April quickly pulled out a tub of rocky road ice cream.

Tae looked torn, but after a few beats she took out bowls and spoons, then moved to the fridge for the chocolate sauce, making April nod in approval.

They ate in silence for a moment, letting the sugar do its work. Sighing in pleasure as it hit their veins.

"Nothing makes me quite as happy as ice cream," Tae murmured, licking her spoon.

"I can tell," April said. "You're glowing. Although, somehow I don't think that's the ice cream."

"It's the glow of success for the event," Tae said.

"Or . . . ?"

"Or what?" Tae asked.

April hesitated. "Truth?"

Tae slid her a wary look. "Sure . . . ?"

"I saw you with Riggs after the event."

Tae stilled for a beat, then set her spoon down. "It doesn't matter. We both know he's the exact wrong man for me."

"Which is exactly what you're attracted to."

Tae laughed mirthlessly. "Hello, Pot, my name is Kettle." She paused. "Look, Mom, there's no need to worry about me, okay? Just worry about you, I've got me covered."

"It's hard not to worry when my daughter is about to follow in my footsteps and make my mistakes."

Tae shook her head. "I'm capable of making my own mistakes, Mom. Don't blame yourself."

"But I screwed up. A lot. I brought men home because I

thought I could make an instant family. But that's not how it works. Who knew?" She managed a smile, but Tae pushed her bowl away.

"Mom."

April's heart sank. "Yeah?"

"I love you. I love you so much. But it's frustrating when you try to tell me how to live my life, especially when . . ."

April's stomach fell when Tae trailed off. "When . . . you raised me, instead of the other way around?"

"That's not what I was going to say."

"But it's true."

Tae closed her eyes. "I'm too tired for this. You've got to trust me. There's no need to worry, I've got it under control."

April nodded. "Just . . . just promise me you won't do what I did, you won't give up your future for one moment in time."

"Is that what you did after Dad died?"

Everything inside April froze. "Why are you bringing up your father?"

"You said not to make the same mistake you did. I assume I'm that mistake."

April felt her stomach clench as she winced, because she *never* wanted her daughter to feel like a mistake. "Tae—"

"It messed you up, Mom. You've said that. Is it because *you* were stuck living in that one moment in time?"

There was something in Tae's voice now that scared her. When she'd been younger, she'd asked about her dad a lot. But she hadn't mentioned him in well over ten years. April knew, because she'd been counting. So why the sudden interest, worded so carefully? She got up and put water on for tea. Stalling, of course, as guilt and remorse flooded her. She'd tried to live her life up front and be honest about everything with her daughter. Because as she'd learned, lies only hurt.

And yet she'd told one. A big one.

And it'd led to another. Which had led to another. And now Tae's entire childhood, based on that original lie, was a house of cards in a windstorm. But that was the problem with a runaway train: once it caught enough speed, there was no stopping it. That's what this felt like, she was on a runaway train. No brakes.

Worse, there'd been plenty of times over the years to tell Tae the truth. But she hadn't. And doing so now would only serve to clear her own conscience. Because it would crush Tae and very possibly destroy their relationship.

The irony was that she'd started this whole thing to *protect* Tae. "Sometimes, I think that I was so caught up in what happened between your dad and me that, yes, it held me back." And that was God's honest truth.

Tae dipped her head and stared at her sandals for a long beat. She always did that when she was frustrated, and God knew, April had certainly frustrated her plenty over the years. Then Tae lifted her head, and for a moment it seemed like she was going to ask more about her dad, but she didn't. "People are entitled to their own mistakes," she said instead. "I've *always* supported your questionable choices. Remember Clyde?"

April grimaced at the reminder of the man she'd thought she'd fallen in love with on date one, only to find out that while he'd been a gentle giant and a very sweet man, he'd had not one iota of ambition in his entire body and had made a career out of living on women's couches, draining them dry. When she'd finally changed the locks on him one day, leaving his stuff in boxes on the front steps, he'd had the gall to try to sue her for mental distress. "God. Clyde."

Tae let out a mirthless laugh. "Exactly. So can you please find it in your heart to let me make my own mistakes? Without commentary?"

April moved closer to Tae and mimicked her stance, leaning back against the counter. Then she set her head on her daughter's shoulder. "I'll try."

Tae turned and wrapped her arms around April. "Thank you. And don't worry so much. I'm not alone, like you were. I don't know if you'd heard, but I've got the best mom on the planet. Okay?"

April sniffed and held on tight to the bestest thing in her entire life. "Okay," she whispered, and worked really hard at believing it, in spite of herself.

CHAPTER 15

After the talk with her mom, Tae stepped over the hedge and into her place. She showered and climbed into her bed, her mind racing too much to sleep. She'd missed an opportunity to tell her mom what Mr. Schwartz had said, to confront her about her birth certificate.

But her mom had seemed almost fragile tonight. Tae realized she couldn't do it, couldn't talk to her until she had more answers, answers *she'd* find on her own.

Her mind wandered to the day. They'd been so successful that Jake had already approved their next Lake Days, two weeks from now, a midsummer event that would include *two* days of lake fun, including a barbecue and auction on night one.

But that wasn't what she was thinking about. Nope, that honor went to the kiss. At just the thought, her heart started to race. She tried some calm breathing, but sleep still took forever to come for her, and when it did, it took her back in time.

* * *

Tae hated her mom's old Chevy truck for guzzling gas faster than she could fill up the tank. She hated high school for making her feel invisible. Hated too the one-room apartment she and her mom shared because she could hear her mom crying at night. Hmm . . . let's see. This was actually the most fun she'd had in a long time. What else did she hate?

Oh wait, she knew. She hated her life.

The Tahoe night sky, usually lit up by billions of stars twinkling like little diamonds scattered on black velvet, was dark tonight. Thick, turbulent clouds hung overhead, and in her little town of Sunrise Cove, where there were no city lights of any kind allowed at night, it felt a whole lot like the set of a horror flick.

Not a great night to go to her first party. She'd gotten the directions from a girl named Cassie in her English class. It'd been awkward because Cassie had never so much as looked at Tae before, but she was tired of being lonely.

The directions had been sparse:

Drive up Road 06 for two miles, turn right at the fallen tree the size of California. Half a mile in, stop before you go over the cliff.

Tae knew the 06. It was an unmaintained dirt fire road in Hidden Hills that led to the Tahoe Rim Trail, one that hikers and bikers used during the day to get out into nature. At night, it would be deserted.

And dangerous.

But her entire life had felt a little dangerous, so whatever. Knowing the trails well enough, she navigated the windy, rutted road in the truck, stopping well before the cliff and all the other cars revealed by her headlights. She even managed a seventy-five-point U-turn so she could park facing the way out, allowing for a quick escape if she needed. And since people were not her favorite things right now—or ever—needing an escape was highly likely.

She gave herself a quick peek in the rearview mirror. In all-black, including her dyed hair, not much of the real her was visible.

Not that she knew who the real her was anyway.

"Be normal," she told her reflection. She got out of the truck and walked up the dirt road to the large bonfire, already shivering. Damn, she needed a jacket, but she and her mom shared one, and Tae had insisted her mom take it tonight on her date with her latest loser.

She slowed when she realized there were close to a hundred kids standing near or around the fire in groups and clusters, laughing, talking, drinking, smoking pot. Tae wound her way through, trying to find someone, anyone, she knew.

A group of girls huddled in a circle nearby, and when one of them tossed her hood back, exposing platinum blond hair, Tae knew she'd found Cassie. Still unseen, Tae moved closer, then stopped short when she realized they were talking about her.

"Jonah told me Tae was all over him at last week's football game," Cassie was saying. "He said he had to fight her off and that she kissed like a dead fish."

"I didn't see Tae at the game," another girl said—Ness, from Tae's PE class. Why the hell Ness would've noticed Tae at the game when she'd never acknowledged her before, Tae had no idea. She opened her mouth to say something, she wasn't sure what, when Cassie spoke again.

"They were behind the bleachers, and since you stayed in Eric's car the entire game, you wouldn't know."

Ness shrugged. "Why did you invite Tae here if she's screwing your boy toy?"

"Because I've leaked it to everyone what she did. She'll get the message tonight."

"What message?"

"That when you try to steal my boyfriend, you get erased."

With that, Tae turned and practically ran back toward her truck before she did something stupid. Like try to defend herself by telling Cassie that what she said happened wasn't even close to how it'd gone down at the game. Jonah had come on to her out of nowhere, and she'd said no. The end.

Okay, not quite the end. Jonah hadn't wanted to hear her "no," forcing her to not-so-accidentally put her knee to his kibble and bits. The rest was a blur as she continued to move fast. She was on the other side of the campfire now, just far enough away from the party that the sounds of voices had died down, blocking out everything but her own breathing.

And the sound of someone coming up behind her.

"Tae."

Oh, perfect. Just who she didn't want to see. Jonah himself. And he wasn't alone this time, but with his pack of friends. A collective bag of dicks, all of them. They stopped her progress by making a semicircle around her. She tried to step clear, but Jonah got in her way. He was bigger than she was, much bigger, but she told herself she didn't feel threatened because there were a ton of people only a hundred feet away. Even with his four goons, he wasn't stupid enough to try anything. But if he did, she had her trusty knife in her boot.

The knife had never seen bloodshed, but it would make an impression, and sometimes that was all that was needed.

"You owe me," Jonah said.

"I owe you nothing." She made sure there was an implied "you idiot" at the end of her sentence.

He stared at her, looking surly and mean, but then suddenly he laughed and looked at his friends. "Think her black lipstick will leave a circle around my d—"

She pulled her knife. Brandished it where they could all see it, and though she wanted to take a step back, she stood firm, even as her knees quaked.

"What's going on?" another male voice asked, disembodied in the dark. Tae recognized the voice and used the distraction to shove her knife back into her boot and take off running in the direction of her mom's truck.

God, she was so stupid, thinking she could be normal. She never should have come—

She plowed right into someone, and that someone's hands came up to her arms, holding them both upright. Tae gave him a hard shove.

"Whoa," he said, dropping his hands from her. "I come in peace."

It was true. He was Riggs Copeland, and one of the very few people who'd been nice to her at school. They'd had PE together, and he always had good snacks, which he shared with her. Still, she took another step back, needing space, needing air, needing to be far, far away from here. She shouldn't have come, and now thanks to Cassie, everyone would believe she'd slept with Jonah. The joke was on them. She hadn't slept with anyone. Ever.

"Hey." Riggs, tall as hell, ducked his head a little and looked into her face. "You okay?"

She pushed past him, shoulder checking him with the huge chip she carried, and headed toward her truck.

"Tae—wait up."

Nope. Not doing that. Because no matter that he'd always treated her well, her mistrust ran deep. Otherwise, why would one of the town's best athletes, a decent student and liked by all, teachers and students included, be so nice to her?

She could hear him jogging to keep up with her, so she ran faster. And great, now her eyes were tearing up. Not because she was sad or hurt, she never cried over emotions, she'd gotten over that a long time ago. She'd built an ice block around her heart, protecting her.

But she did cry when she was mad.

And how she hated that.

Somehow Riggs got out in front of her and turned to face her, jogging backward, since she never stopped moving. His eyes were unusually serious. "Did they hurt you, Tae?"

"No."

Clearly not believing her, he ran his gaze from her black roots to her black boots. "Are you okay?"

She slowed, not because she wanted to talk, but because she hated to run and was already out of breath. "If I say yes, will you go away?"

"If I believe you."

Rolling her eyes, she moved around him and kept going. At a walk this time.

"Cassie's been drinking," he said, keeping pace but giving her plenty of room. "She's always mean when she drinks. Don't listen to her."

"What makes you think I was listening to her?"

He flashed a smile in the dark. "Smart girl. I'd say come back to the fire where it's warm, but somehow I think that would be a waste of breath."

"Smart boy," she said, heavy on the sarcasm. Finally, she got to her mom's truck. She hopped in, turned the key, and . . . nothing but a click and then an odd whining and then grinding sound. The engine didn't catch. "No," she whispered, and tried again. But because her life sucked, the truck still didn't start. "You've got to be kidding me."

"Sounds like a bad alternator or starter," Riggs said.

Tae could change a tire and the oil. Beyond that, she was out of her league. Deflating, she set her head on the steering wheel.

"I can help."

"I'll just walk home and get the truck fixed tomorrow." Or never . . .

"Or . . ." he said. "I could give you a lift."

"No thank you." And with that bravado, she hopped out, locked up, and strode off into the pitch-dark night. Without a jacket and at least a five-mile walk ahead of her.

"It's too far to walk in the dark," Riggs said behind her, "Plus, there're bears and mountain cats and—"

"Raccoons oh my?" she asked, turning to face him.

"I'm not trying to scare you. I know you can handle yourself. But why should you have to do it alone when I'm willing and able to help?"

Because she hated needing help. Hated it more than she hated school and everything in it.

In the distance came the howl of a coyote and the answering howl from its mate. Tae jerked, and Riggs went brows up. Wrapping her arms around herself, she glared at Riggs. "Fine. You can give me a ride. But if you try anything funny—"

He held up his hands. "I know, I know, you've got a knife in your boot and you're not afraid to use it." He led her to a truck, also beat-up. He waited for her to buckle up before hitting the gas. "Where to?"

She directed him back to Sunrise Cove, to a ritzy neighborhood, where she picked out a house at random—a huge, gorgeous cabin, clearly well taken care of and loved. She figured once he drove off, she'd walk home. It was still a couple of miles, but she doubted a coyote would dare eat her in this fancy area. "That one," she said.

Riggs glanced at the place in surprise, then pulled over.

"Thanks," she said, reaching for the door.

Riggs turned off the engine and also reached for his door, and she started to panic. "What are you doing?"

He looked surprised at the question. "Walking you to your door."

"No!" She took a deep breath. "Not necessary," she said more quietly. How the hell did she get herself into these situations?

He looked at her for a long moment, then nodded. "Okay. I'll just wait here until you're inside safe."

"What are you, a Boy Scout?"

He smiled. "Maybe I want to ask you out sometime. What kind of a future boyfriend would I be if I didn't make sure you were safe after dropping you off?"

He had longish, shaggy brown hair and was lanky lean, almost to the point of too skinny, and had the greenest eyes she'd ever seen. "Look," she said. "I wasn't supposed to be at that party, okay?" The lie rolled right off her tongue. "You'll only get me in trouble. And anyway, I'm going to sneak inside through the backyard."

"Or," Riggs said, "you're going to sneak into the backyard, hop the fence, and start walking to where you really live."

She put on her best haughty face. "Are you calling me a liar?"

He smiled. "Mr. Ward lives here. I do his yard for him, and I know for a fact he's got two kids, both grown, both male."

Oh, for God's . . . She drew a deep breath. "I didn't say I lived there, I said I lived . . . there." She pointed to the next house over from Mr. Ward.

Riggs nodded agreeably, just as from behind the front window of that house, the curtains were pulled back by a man in his forties, who peered out at them in the truck with a scowl.

"Looks like your dad caught you," Riggs said. "Come on, I'll try to help you smooth things over."

Jesus, this guy. "No, you can't. My dad's . . . deaf. And grumpy. He doesn't like people."

"And your mom?"

She looked at him and found him almost, but not quite, smiling. He wasn't buying a word of what she was selling. "You do realize it's none of your business," she said.

He studied her for a moment, and that's when, in the quiet interior of the truck, her stomach rumbled loud enough to rattle the windows. Horrified, she clapped her hands to it.

"Hungry?" he asked.

"Nope." She'd passed hungry hours ago and was well into Hangry-Land. "Not even a little."

"Well, I'm starving." He put his truck back in gear. "What's open this late?"

"The diner," her mouth said without permission.

And with a nod, Riggs pulled back into the street.

"My dad—" she started.

"That wasn't your dad."

She sighed and didn't speak again until he pulled into the diner's parking lot. Mostly because she really was hungry, but also a little curious about this unflappable guy.

The diner had been built from an old railroad car, which was the front part of the diner. She stared into the front windows, registering that the place was surprisingly busy for midnight. She recognized a few kids from the high school, who'd either forgone the party or come here to get some food, same as she and Riggs. "I'm not going inside," she said. "I don't want to be around anymore dicks right now."

"What if I promise to keep my dick to myself?"

She almost laughed but still shook her head.

Unruffled, he nodded. "Okay, I'll get it to go. What would you like?"

She shrugged, like her stomach wasn't eating itself. "You're the hungry one."

"Right," he said. "Okay then, what do I want? Burgers? Tacos? Wings?" He stopped and smiled, and she knew she'd somehow given herself away. "Everything," he said, and opened his door. After a quick pause, he grabbed his keys and pocketed them. "I figure I've got half a shot at you actually being here when I get back. But I'd really like it if you were. I hate to eat alone."

And maybe it was because of that, she actually waited for him. And ten minutes later, Riggs was back with a big bag of food. He set it on the seat between them and drove them up a road she didn't recognize. And up. And up. Finally, he pulled off and parked. There were no other cars. She had no idea where they were, and she bit her lower lip. "I'm going to remind you that I have a knife."

"Thank you for the reminder, but you aren't going to need it." He pointed, and she stared at the unbelievable, heart-stopping view of the lake far below, lit by a half-moon and more stars than she'd ever seen.

"So what is this, your make-out spot?"

He laughed low in his throat. "No, and if you knew me, you'd know why that was funny." His smile faded. "We're at Hidden Falls. It's where I go when I need to get away."

She stared at him.

He stared right back, steadfast, open. And she believed him. "I have a spot too," she admitted. "Sand Harbor."

"That's a pretty good spot."

She agreed. It'd been her secret spot for years. They ate burgers and fries, and because it was past midnight, which meant it was practically morning, they also shared a stack of blueberry pancakes. It was the best meal she'd ever had, and then . . . God, the then.

It started with sweet kisses that unexpectedly set her on fire.

"Tae . . ."

She didn't want him to stop kissing her, but he pulled back and met her gaze. "You should know that I've never . . ."

She took a shaky breath of relief. "Me either."

"I didn't bring you up here for this, Tae, I promise. I can take you home right now."

"Please don't . . ."

They ended up sharing a whole lot more than a meal in that truck. More than she'd ever shared with anyone. She'd meant to only share her body and hold everything else back.

But she lost herself in his kisses, the ones that had started out sweet and had so quickly set her on fire. She lost herself in the way he'd so sweetly fumbled right along with her, so steadfast and careful to bring her pleasure before himself. Lost in the reverent way he looked at her, held her, touched her . . .

Two hours later, she allowed him to drop her off in front of the apartment building she and her mom lived at, probably having no idea how much trust that had actually involved on her part.

Her smile remained on her face for a week, during which she'd had lunch with Riggs a few times. She was almost disturbingly happy—until she missed her period. Panicked, she used her week's lunch money to buy a pregnancy test, which she took right there in the convenience store bathroom.

It was negative, which didn't have her smile returning. She'd been stupid, putting everything on the line for pleasure. Her mom had done that and look what it'd cost her—everything.

From that moment on, she refused to talk to Riggs. She knew he was confused, but he'd seemed to get over it pretty quickly. And then he'd graduated and left Sunrise Cove.

And Tae promised herself she'd never let a man dictate her life. Never.

She'd kept that promise.

CHAPTER 16

That night, Riggs walked into an ambush. It wasn't the usual kind, on some foreign soil, with his unit at his back. *That* he could have handled. But, of course, it wasn't anything as simple as that, and he stopped in surprise in the entryway to the kitchen.

Jake sat at the table, nursing a scotch, brooding, Grub sleeping at his feet.

Riggs recognized Jake's expression all too well, as he often saw the same look in the mirror.

"What the hell do you think you're doing?" Jake asked.

His tone said *fight*, and even Grub raised his head, his eyes sleepy, but frankly Riggs was too tired. "Uh . . . about to raid the fridge?"

"And?" Jake asked in a calm-before-the-storm voice.

Jake gave him the Older-Brother-Pissed-Off look and Riggs shook his head. "Look, let's skip to where you just ask me what you want to know."

"All right." Jake leaned back. "You're sleeping with Tae."

Riggs felt something stir in his chest. An ache at the thought of sleeping with Tae, but also that his brother was acting like the father of a teenage girl. "That didn't sound like a question."

Jake looked pissed off. "You're a real asshole, you know that?"

"Sure. You've certainly told me enough times."

Jake pushed back from the table and moved across the kitchen, before turning back to Riggs. "She's our employee."

"Actually, she's not. What she is, Jake, is her own boss. She's a strong, independent woman in charge of her own life. A concept you should get, seeing as you're with a woman who's equally strong and independent."

"Yes, I'm *with* Carolyn, in every sense of the word. I'm going to marry her, if she'll let me. You're not *with* Tae. You're just messing around until you get to leave. And that's bullshit, Riggs. She deserves more than that."

Normally it took a long time to light the fuse on Riggs's temper, and even then, it was usually a slow burn. He'd always thought of anger as an unproductive emotion, much like love. "So you know everything I'm up to then, huh, Jake? You've got me all figured out?"

"Always have."

"What the hell does that mean?"

"It means that even when we were kids, your motive was to never engage, at least not all the way. But you possess Mom's effortless charm and ability to bullshit with that easy smile on your face. People fall over themselves to please you, never realizing you don't really give a shit. But Tae . . ." A muscle twitched in his older brother's jaw. "She deserves a hell of a lot better. She's one of the good ones, Riggs. The kind of woman you're *lucky* if you get to keep. Which you'll never do."

Riggs let out a short laugh, because the hell of it was, his brother was right. On all counts. "Your intel on Tae is faulty."

"There were eyewitnesses. Stay away from her, Riggs. You won't be good for her."

That it was true didn't make him any less angry. "And you know that how?"

"Because I know *you*. And I know you've never stuck in a relationship for long. Not once."

Riggs stared at him in disbelief. "A lot you know. I was dumped by my last girlfriend, not the other way around."

Jake blew out a breath. "It's your commitment and trust issues. Mom left you. I left you. And then Dad."

"Mom died. You had to go, before either you or Dad killed each other. None of you left me on purpose."

"Yeah, now, see, I know that," Jake said. "The question is, do you?"

The hell with this. He turned to go.

"Riggs."

He stopped at the door.

"Tae's the real deal," Jake said quietly. "And she's been through a lot. She doesn't need your I'm-leaving-in-two-months bullshit."

"You think I don't know that?" Riggs had the oddest sensation in his chest, like a hot poker had been stuck right through him, and he wasn't sure if it was because he was angry at Jake or if it was the thought of leaving Tae behind. He should just go now. But he'd never possessed the good sense to know when to walk away. Or, for that matter, when to shut up. So he gave Jake a suggestion on what he could do with his advice and where he could shove it.

For a beat, he actually thought Jake might throw a punch. They'd certainly fought before, many times, and though Riggs could handle himself and had in the past, Jake had always been able to take him.

It'd never stopped Riggs from trying though.

But Jake didn't come for him. Instead, he said, "For once stop thinking about yourself. Think about who you're going to hurt."

And then, while Riggs was reeling from that blow, which, for the record, hurt more than any fist in his face would have, Jake was the one to leave.

ON MONDAY MORNING, Riggs came awake feeling like an elephant was sitting on his chest. Maybe he was having a heart attack. Maybe this was how he was going to go.

Should've slept with Tae so you could've died happy . . .

That was when something warm and wet landed on his chin and stroked upward, catching his mouth, up his nose, his eyes, all the way to his forehead. Since he couldn't move under what felt like a Mack truck, he cracked one eye open and sighed. "Grub."

Grub grinned and blew his doggy breath into Riggs's face, his tail wagging so hard the entire bed moved with it. "Someone needs to cut back on the doggy biscuits."

Grub's tail moved even faster, those huge brown eyes full of so much love and even more mischief. Riggs couldn't help but laugh and hugged the huge lug close. Dog hair flew about in the air, creating a cloud around them. "Oh, man. Your mama's going to kill me. You know you're not supposed to be on the bed."

Grub cocked his head to the side, one ear flopping over his eye. Command not computing.

"You gotta get down, bud."

This won him another lick, which was more like a really wet French kiss. "Wow, you need to brush your teeth. Okay, how about this. You get down and I'll feed you."

Grub was gone so fast, the only thing left in his wake was more dog hair and the putrid scent of morning doggy fart.

Riggs sat up, fanning the air. Which was when he heard the rhythmic banging. Shit. *Again?* But then he realized it seemed more like a hammer than a headboard hitting a wall, which was a relief. Yes, he was actually jealous of his brother, which made him an asshole twice over because whose fault was it that he wasn't having his own headboard-banging good time? *His.* Whatever Jake believed, Riggs had walked away from Tae without taking what they'd both wanted. He'd done that for her. He'd told her they were a bad idea, and he'd meant it.

Didn't mean it didn't hurt like hell.

He was a temp in his own world. Everything was temporary: being in Sunrise Cove, staying with his brother, helping at AHQ, Tae . . . all of it. In two months, he would leave for D.C. and start a new life, putting all of this in his rearview mirror, and it would be time. He was away from the world he'd known for so long, feeling a whole bunch like he didn't fit in, not here, and not in his own skin either. The only time he'd relaxed had been every second he'd spent with Tae.

Yep, he was screwed, and not in the good way. He would go irritate Jake some more, but Riggs was pretty sure after the other night that they weren't speaking. He tried to catch some more sleep but gave up after half an hour. Tired of his own bullshit, he staggered out to the kitchen, where he tripped over Grub waiting for him.

When Riggs was growing up, the kitchen had been a shithole. But he would say this for Jake and Carolyn, they'd turned the place completely around, so much so that it felt like a home now. A real one. The kitchen was warm and welcoming, and someone—he suspected Carolyn—kept it fully stocked.

The woman herself was hanging a few framed photos on the wall behind the kitchen table. "Don't let Grub fool you," she said. "He's already been fed."

Grub gave her a reproachful look and hit the floor, making the house shake like an earthquake had hit.

"You mad at me too?" Riggs asked Carolyn.

"Oh, I don't do mad." She set down her hammer and went to the coffeemaker. She poured a mug, added nothing, and handed it over. "Black, as your soul," she said on a smile.

Riggs arched a brow at his dad's old saying tumbling from her lips.

"The Copeland motto, right?" She smiled when he laughed roughly. "There's also bagels and fruit and eggs," she said. "Whatever you want."

"Thanks." He drank some more coffee, letting the caffeine do its magic. "Does my brother know you're the best thing that ever happened to him?"

She smiled. "Yes. I think the real question is do *you* know that your brother's the best thing that's ever happened to you?"

Riggs snorted coffee out his nose.

Carolyn just looked at him, steady. Curious.

He mopped himself up with a napkin. "You're perfect for him, you know."

"I *do* know. And nice deflection, which is something you have in common with Jake. So . . . do you? Know he's the best thing that ever happened to you?"

Riggs hated to think about his growing-up years. Hated. But on the few occasions he allowed himself to do just that, what he remembered most was how many times Jake had stepped between Riggs and his dad. So yeah, he did know Jake was the best thing that had ever happened to him. More than he could ever say. "Yes."

"Hmmm." She opened her mouth to say more, but then shut it again.

He arched a brow. "You've got something to say."

She smiled. "I *always* have something to say."

He gave her the go-ahead gesture.

"Okay," she said. "Why did you come?"

He ignored the little stab of what might have been hurt. "Because Jake asked me to."

"Do you know why he did that?"

"No idea," he said honestly.

"Did you ever think that maybe he missed you?"

He gave another rough bark of laughter. "No. That's definitely not it."

Carolyn stared at him. "Why would you think that?"

Riggs shrugged, finding it harder to say than he thought it would. "When he got hurt, it took me a bit to get leave time. Soon as I got it, I went to see him. He lived in San Francisco then, and was in a rehab facility, learning to handle his new life. He told me to go away and not come back. I tried again a few years ago, when he moved back here to start up Adrenaline HQ. He said we could be partners, but that I should stay where I was. I offered to come again last year. Radio silence."

Carolyn stared at him. "I didn't know any of that. But it changes nothing. You still could've come and just . . . I don't know . . . *made* him accept your help."

"Right." Riggs shook his head. "You've met him. He's . . ."

"Stubborn? Pigheaded? Obstinate?"

He smiled. "Those are all the same things, but yeah."

She laughed low in her throat and muttered something about them being two peas in a damn pod. Then her smile faded and she held his gaze, and he knew she was going to say something he didn't like.

"He's had some trouble, Riggs. Health trouble, beyond the broken leg and concussion."

Shit. He actually put a hand to his chest. "What kind of health trouble?"

"Neuropathic pain. It's a condition where his neurotransmitters transmit nerve impulses from one cell to the other, with no rhyme or reason or regularity. It often accompanies paralysis, which of course is the cruelest of ironies for people who lack sensation to then experience agony in those limbs."

Riggs absorbed that for a beat, trying to imagine his brother suffering pain on top of pain. "What can be done?"

"Nothing. Because he's a Copeland, which means he doesn't always admit when he has it . . ."

"Meds?"

Carolyn shook her head. "He's tried everything. Hates them anyway, hates the way they make him feel. So he pushes through. Until he can't."

Riggs took a deep breath. "What happens then?"

"He lies in bed until it passes." She shook her head. "Sometimes it's hours. Sometimes it's days. He can go weeks without having a problem, and then suddenly it's constant. We never know when it'll come or how long it'll last."

Riggs drew a slow breath. "He's never said a word."

"He won't. And before you ask, he never will."

Riggs's chest felt too tight again. Maybe he was having a heart attack after all. "He should've let me know."

"Oh please," Carolyn said on a laugh. "You're just as bad as he is, waiting to be asked home, like you need a written invitation. Maybe he wanted you to just show up, so he'd have family around."

Riggs's secret shame, and he turned to leave.

"Riggs."

He stopped but didn't face her.

"Jake uses his broody briskness to push people away. You use yours to be an impenetrable asshole for the same reason."

At that, he turned and even managed a small smile. "Not my first time hearing that."

It was her turn to snort coffee out her nose. He magnanimously handed her a napkin to clean herself up. "You and he really are alike," she said.

"Not *that* much."

"*So* much," she said. "Go talk to him, Riggs."

Riggs knew Carolyn was right, he and Jake did need to talk. That was if he could find the right words and not mess it up. He grabbed the keys to Jake's old truck, which he'd been driving since that first night in town when he'd turned in his rental car. He drove through town, turning on Lake Walk, which ran along the north shore side of the lake. It was lined by a walkable downtown community with a quaint and quirky mix of unique shops, places to eat, and bars that supported a lively nightlife for tourists and locals alike. A mile later, just outside of Sunrise Cove, he pulled into AHQ.

April was behind the front desk and nodded politely. "How can I help you?"

The muted greeting told him he was still on her shit list. He was really on a roll. "Is Jake here?"

"He's working out."

Riggs nodded and started to head back to the gym.

"He asked not to be disturbed," April called after him.

Riggs looked toward the other end of the warehouse, to the

hallway that led to Jake's office and, beyond that, a gym. Two guys exited in workout clothes, both employees he recognized from the lake event. He slid April a look.

"By you," she said. "He doesn't want to be disturbed by *you*."

Perfect. "I've got a direct order from Carolyn to go talk to him."

April studied him for a long beat, the both of them knowing that if he wanted to go talk to Jake, he didn't need her permission. But she seemed to appreciate that he was seeking it, because she gave a single nod.

He nodded back and then started to walk off, but curiosity stopped him again. "Do we have a problem?"

"Only if you hurt my daughter."

What the hell was it lately? Did he have a sign on his head that said he was both untrustworthy and an asshole? "I'd *never* hurt your daughter."

"Time will tell."

He met her gaze straight on so she could hopefully see his honesty. "*Never*," he repeated.

She stared at him, then slowly gave a single nod. Then she turned back to her laptop.

He headed through the warehouse and into the gym. Alone, Jake was working a lowered punching bag. There was little to no chance he hadn't heard Riggs come in, the guy never missed a damn thing, but he didn't stop or look over, just kept beating the shit out of his demons.

And there were demons. No matter what Jake wanted him to think. Inhaling a deep breath, knowing if he did as Carolyn had asked, if he pushed for a conversation here to get some things out in the open, there was zero percent chance of it going well.

But he'd given his word.

And damn. Carolyn was great. Great for Jake, great for the business, which meant she was more than worthy of being taken seriously by Riggs. But it was more than that. He'd long ago stopped giving a shit what people thought of him, and yet he wanted to be on Carolyn's good side for reasons he didn't want to admit, even to himself. Reasons that involved wanting to be a part of the family she and Jake were creating.

Dumb.

Beyond dumb. All of this was. Even knowing it, he moved closer to a shirtless, impressively built, sweaty Jake in his chair, still going at the punching bag like maybe he was imagining Riggs's face on it. The weights were across the room. The only thing close to Jake was a jump rope lying on a mat. With a sigh—he *really* didn't want to do this—he scooped up the jump rope.

Jake snorted.

Riggs slid him a look. "What?"

"Nothing, just remembering the time you nearly killed yourself with a jump rope. *Tinkerbell.*"

Riggs grinded his teeth together at that old childhood nickname Jake had given him when he'd turned thirteen and had grown eight inches in one year, leaving him off-balance and completely out of whack. For months, he'd walk into walls, tripped over his own damn feet . . . he couldn't do anything physical without injuring himself. The doctor had suggested jump rope for hand-eye coordination, and the one and only time he'd given it a try, he'd tipped over. He'd fallen face-first into the doorjamb, knocking himself out cold.

"Maybe you should put that dangerous tool down," Jake suggested with a smirk, still punching the bag, never breaking rhythm.

"I was thirteen." And great, he sounded like he was still thirteen.

"And now you're an old man," Jake said. "Seriously, be careful. You've probably got brittle bones and shit."

Riggs rolled his eyes and eyed the jump rope in his hand. No way was he going to walk away now. "I just turned thirty. Which makes you thirty-eight. *You're* the old man who should watch out for brittle bones." The minute the words were out of his mouth, he regretted them.

"Nice," Jake said mildly, finally letting his hands drop.

"I didn't mean—"

"Shut up, Riggs. I'm not some sensitive, special snowflake." He rubbed a towel over his face. "God, you piss me off like no one else can." Dropping the towel, he went back to punching the bag. "You think I don't know that you feel sorry for me? That you think I should sell because I'm weak?"

"I don't—"

Jake stopped punching the bag again but only long enough to pull out his cell phone and crank the music, which now boomed into the room with enough bass to nearly knock Riggs's fillings out.

Fine. He'd tried. Shaking his head, he started to jump rope.

It took a lot of concentration, so it was a moment before he realized the music had come back down and Jake was sitting there watching him with amusement.

Feeling stupid, Riggs rolled his eyes. "If you're waiting for me to fall over, I've got a lot better hand-eye coordination these days."

"You going to tell me about you and Tae or not?"

Riggs tripped over his jump rope and fell flat on his ass. Well, shit. He sat up and found Jake staring at him speculatively. "What, no smart-ass comment?"

"I'm starting to think I've got this all wrong," Jake said slowly. "Maybe you're not playing Tae. Maybe your feelings are playing *you*."

Riggs's heart sped up. "Meaning?"

"Meaning you like her. As in *like* her like her."

"What, are we in high school?"

Jake was looking at him like he was more than a little surprised. "Wow. I didn't see this coming. She really means something to you."

More than he could possibly explain even to himself.

Jake let out a long exhale and shook his head. "Riggs, if this is real for you, that changes everything."

"It changes nothing."

Jake looked at him like he was crazy. "You could make it real. Like what I have with Carolyn."

"Too late for that."

"Why?"

Because he was a dumbass. Because he'd thought he was being

chivalrous when he suggested they not sleep together. Because
she deserved more than a one-and-done guy who was leaving at
the end of the summer, no matter how much he felt for her. Because when she looked at him, when she rolled her eyes at him,
when she called him out on his shit, when he kissed her . . . he
lost himself, and that scared the shit out of him. And . . . Jesus.
He resented like hell he'd ever suggested that stupid Just Friends
Pact. He was such an idiot. He'd done it to protect her.

Nope. That was a lie.

He'd done it so that he could keep himself from falling too
hard, from having to trust her with his damaged heart.

Jake was brows up, waiting on an answer.

Riggs sighed. "We're just friends." He paused, then admitted,
"It was my suggestion."

Jake just shook his head. "You could go talk to her. Explain
that you're a dumb son of a bitch."

"She already knows."

His brother looked at him evenly. "You could try telling her
the truth, that you have feelings for her. That you want to be
hers."

"You really think I could possibly be the right guy for her?"
Riggs asked in disbelief.

"I think you could be whatever you want."

This stunned Riggs for a moment. "I was trained to point out
a clusterfuck in the making before it happens. And you *know*
this would be a classic clusterfuck in the making, Jake."

Jake was quiet a long moment. "The past is the past," he finally
said. "So answer this—what are you really afraid of?"

Riggs went back to jumping rope. "Nothing."

"Do you even hear yourself? You sound just like Dad. Controlling everyone and everything because you know best, and you don't feel the need to share with the room."

Riggs risked falling on his ass again to jab a finger in Jake's direction. "You need to shut up."

"Or," Jake said, "you could tell me what the real problem is here."

"The real problem? It's *you*! I came to Sunrise Cove thinking you'd be enjoying life and taking it easy. Instead you're working harder than ever, like you're trying to finish the job that IED started." This was actually a lie. Riggs's *real* problem was that Jake was in a wheelchair and it should've been *him*. All his life, Jake had protected Riggs. Stood between him and his dad.

And the one time when Jake needed him, he'd been stuck overseas unable to come home.

Not that it mattered because suddenly Riggs found himself flat on his back, staring at the ceiling. Jake had knocked his legs out from beneath him. "Damn. You're faster than ever."

Jake looked down at him. "Nearly getting blown to Timbuktu or not, if anyone's got a death wish in this relationship, it's *you*. Stop patronizing me."

"Is it patronizing to tell you the truth? That you're jeopardizing your health?" At the shocked look on Jake's face, Riggs nodded. "Yeah. I know."

Jake grinded his teeth. "You fucker. You sanctimonious, know-it-all, fucking prick."

Riggs got to his feet. "Because I'm right?"

That got him a fist to the face, and it knocked him back a step. He put a hand to his throbbing eye. "You kiss Carolyn with that mouth?"

Jake came at him with another punch that Riggs barely shifted and swung a punch of his own, satisfyingly connecting with his brother's face.

They both lay panting, Jake with his head back, still in his chair, Riggs flat on the floor. "That escalated quickly," he muttered.

"Our family motto." Jake put a hand to his bleeding mouth and pointed at Riggs with his other. "Whatever emotion that was in your eyes a minute ago, the one that looked a helluva lot like pity? Don't you dare send it my way ever again. Direct it at yourself. Because even without the use of my legs, I can still kick your ass."

True enough.

Jake just looked at him, slowly shaking his head. "We've both spent too much time being pissed off at the world."

Also true. "Are you saying you're not pissed off anymore?"

Jake hesitated. "Something happened to me when I was rehabbing my body. The anger just . . . left. I didn't even feel it happening, but I'm definitely a different guy now." He met Riggs's gaze. "But you're still the same. Which makes you the old me."

That statement hit Riggs harder than the punch, and the bleeding cut over Jake's eyes gave only minimal satisfaction. "All I was trying to say is that you're working yourself too hard."

Jake's gaze was serious, assessing. "Okay, maybe. But you

don't get it. The truth is, I . . ." He let out a long exhale, his emotions more visible than Riggs could remember ever seeing. "I need to do this, Riggs. I can't just lie down. You might as well shoot me if that's what you expect."

Riggs drew a rough breath and swallowed hard. How had he not seen that? Feeling like a first-class asshole, he nodded. "Okay."

"Okay what?" Jake asked warily.

"Okay I'm in. No more fighting. You keep working on the funding and the business end, and I'll finish building out the summer program before I go. Yeah?"

Jake held his gaze, ignoring the buzzing of his phone in his pocket. "Yeah." Finally, he pulled out his phone. "I've gotta go. We 'bout done punching each other?"

"I think so."

Jake laughed shortly and left.

Riggs let out a breath. His brother was right, about all of it. Riggs had been pushing Jake about the business because he thought he couldn't handle it. Thought Jake needed to be coddled. He'd also been keeping Tae at arm's length because she made him feel things he didn't want to feel.

Maybe it was time to be done with walking away from things that mattered to him. Moving to the weights, he began a workout, and when he was done, he remained seated on the bench, eye aching, heart pounding. And Jesus, what was happening to him that he could feel his heart at all?

Disgusted with himself, he left the gym and headed down the hallway, stopping when he heard his name.

Tae was leaving Jake's office, and she stopped to stare at him. "Is that a black eye?"

"Nope."

She arched a brow.

"Okay, maybe."

"What happened?" she asked.

"Ran into a door."

From inside the office, Riggs heard Jake snort.

Tae turned back to the office, hands on hips. "And *you*," she said, presumably to the unseen Jake. "You told me the same thing. What do you think the odds are of that happening to both of you at the same time?"

Jake didn't answer.

She looked at Riggs again.

Riggs didn't answer either.

Shaking her head in disgust, muttering something about how stupid men were, she gave Jake a hard look. "I'm sending Carolyn in here to look at you." Then she turned to Riggs and gave him a nudge to the chest that was more like a hard shove. "And you. You're with me."

She dragged him into the hallway bathroom and pointed to the closed commode. Amused, and also wondering why he'd been trying to avoid her, because somehow she always lightened his day and made him smile, he sat. And then watched as she dropped to her knees and pulled a first aid kit out from under the sink.

"We going to play doctor again?" he asked hopefully.

Ignoring this, she searched through the kit. Then she rose

up on her knees to get a good look at his eye. She was up close and . . . beautiful, and he thought maybe . . . *maybe* his brother was on to something after all when it came to holding on to a good woman. "What's the verdict, Doc?"

"The verdict's that you're a dumbass."

He grinned. "But you like my dumb ass."

"I don't."

"You do."

"Because we're . . . *friends*?" she asked in a dry tone.

Kissing friends. "Remember when you cheeked Hunter?"

"He *missed*," she said.

"Because you cheeked him."

"I don't kiss every man who crosses my path, you know."

"You didn't cheek me." Cupping her face, he brought it up to his and smiled at the combo of annoyance and reluctant heat in her eyes. "You didn't."

She shook her head. "Why do you always have to take it there?"

"You're on your knees in front of me. It's hard to think of anything else. Emphasis on hard."

She rolled her eyes, slapped an ice pack against her palm to activate it, and set it against his eye with surprising gentleness. "Hold it there."

"For how long?"

"Until you get brain freeze."

He laughed softly. "You're cute when you're bossy and cranky."

"You have a very odd idea of what's cute. And our . . . *predicament* is all your own fault."

As he well knew. "Just how serious is your . . . predicament?"

"No way. You first."

He held her gaze. "My predicament is as serious as it gets."

She looked at him for a long moment, as if trying to ascertain his level of honesty. He kept his eyes on hers, letting her see everything.

She sucked in a breath.

"Now you," he said.

She narrowed her eyes. "You suddenly talk a whole lot for a guy who likes to hold his own counsel. If you're feeling so chatty, let's talk about *you*. Who did *you* last kiss, cheek or otherwise? Actually, when was the last time you even had a relationship?"

"My last kiss was you."

She rolled her eyes.

"And the one before that was . . ." He shrugged. "Maybe three months ago? I was with someone, at least until she dumped me because I didn't want to get serious enough to move in together."

"Hmm," she said, not sounding surprised. "Did you get hurt?"

"You mean, did she break my heart?"

Eyes on his, she nodded, attitude gone, looking like she actually wanted to know, looking a little worried too. Worried for him, he realized, which hit his heart. The organ was going to be bruised as hell. "Maybe a little," he admitted. "But I wasn't in love, if that's what you're asking."

She shook her head at him. "Because . . . ?"

He'd started this conversation, so he shouldn't be surprised that they'd ended up here. He just wasn't sure what to say.

As the seconds ticked on, she moved to get up, but he caught her. "Because I have a trust problem," he admitted. "I'm . . . working on it."

She raised a brow. "That was pretty honest."

"I've never lied to you, Tae."

"So what are we doing?" she asked softly, her hand on his thigh.

"Whatever you want." He covered her hand with his. "You're in the driver's seat here, Rebel. Always."

"Like you let anyone drive . . ." But she leaned in and kissed him, coaxing a surprised groan from deep in his throat. Unable to help himself, he set down the ice pack and pulled her in closer, holding her tight until they were both breathless.

"You didn't cheek me," he said, his voice husky even to his own ears.

With a laugh, she pushed him back. "Let it go." Then she put the ice pack to his eye again. When he pulled it free, she was gone.

CHAPTER 17

On weekdays, Tae tended to get up early. Today she got up extra early because she and Jenny had a bunch of work to do. There was the upcoming Lake Days for Adrenaline HQ, plus four other events for different clients as well. Typically, they used video to chat, but today Jenny signed on with audio only.

"You know I don't care what you're wearing," Tae said. "This isn't a classroom."

"It's embarrassing."

"Well, now I've got to see."

Jenny paused. "I'll go on video if you open yesterday's snail mail."

"How do you know I haven't?"

Jenny laughed. "Because you would've called me about the package I sent you."

Tae ran outside, gathered the mail that she'd indeed forgotten to get. She had a stack of bills and a box. She made her way back to her office. "I'm back."

Suddenly Jenny appeared in the Zoom chat. Wearing a uni-corn onesie, hood up, a rainbow horn attached.

Tae burst out laughing.

"Hey, don't mock it until you try it."

"Not happening."

"You don't know what you're missing." Jenny turned in a cir-cle to give Tae the full effect. The onesie material was black and dotted with a zillion little colorful rainbows and had a fluffy tail.

"I'm not even sorry," Jenny said. "It's baggy enough to hide my trouble areas and the material is light and airy."

"I'll take your word for it."

Jenny smiled. "That's the beauty of this. You don't have to. Open the box."

Tae opened the box and looked at a matching unicorn onesie.

"I'll wait," Jenny said.

Tae shook her head but stood up and stripped off her sundress and stepped into the onesie. When she zipped it up, she looked at a laughing Jenny. "Can we get to work now?"

"Soon as you say you love it."

Tae sat back down, the material kind of floating softly around her, not restricting or bunching. "Okay, maybe I love it."

"You're welcome."

Tae laughed. "Thank you."

They then spent the next two hours working, just two regular unicorns, getting through their to-do list. They'd just discon-nected when Tae's phone buzzed an incoming call from an un-known number. Normally, she wouldn't answer, but something compelled her to anyway, and she was glad she did because it turned out to be Mr. Schwartz.

"I promised to let you know if I talked to my son," he said. "Scott just called. He said he and AJ haven't spoken in years, except that one time two years ago when they ran into each other at a coffee shop in south shore. AJ had apparently just retired from the military, and they spoke only for a few moments. Scott asked about his daughter because it'd been well known back in school that he'd gotten his girlfriend pregnant. AJ said his daughter, named Tae, was a grown-up now, and how time flew by. That was it. Scott said he had no idea how to get a hold of him now, or even if he stayed in the Tahoe area."

"But . . ." Tae's mind was whirling. "AJ grew up around Tahoe?"

"Sounds that way. I'm sorry I don't have more to share," he said, then paused. "I wish you the best, Tae."

She felt more confused now than ever. "I really appreciate the call, thank you." She disconnected and leaned back in her chair to stare at her ceiling.

It'd been weeks since she'd . . . *commandeered* her birth certificate from her mom's closet. Two weeks to be exact, during which time she could have, *should* have, talked to her mom.

So why hadn't she?

Because the longer she waited, the harder it became. That was her excuse, and it was a poor one at that and she knew it. The truth was, she was afraid to rock her and her mom's little boat for two. Afraid of change. Afraid to know that maybe her mom had kept secrets of her own.

Tae had received her 23andMe kit and had already sent it

back, but she hadn't heard anything more. Social media had been a fat waste of time, she could find nothing of AJ Strickland *or* Andy Jameson. She needed another angle.

And she thought maybe she'd figured one out.

Yearbooks. She needed to see the yearbooks from the years her mom had gone to high school. Needed to see if there was any Andy Jameson registered around the same time, and if it was the same man as in the few pics she'd seen of her dad. After that, she could only hope there'd be some other clues as well.

To that end, she grabbed her keys and ten minutes later found herself in front of the town's high school—her old stomping grounds. Just standing there had her skin feeling itchy, and her stomach in her toes. She didn't belong here, she'd *never* belonged here. She'd actually hated this place. Hated that she'd not fit in as she was, and then when she experimented with who she was, she hadn't fit in then either. Nothing had ever worked, and she shuddered at the memories.

Is the truth worth it?

She didn't know. What she *did* know was that she'd promised herself after graduation to never look at this school again, and she'd kept that promise. She had only a very few happy memories here, and her gut told her that wasn't going to change.

But she had lots of questions and zero answers. The idea of her dad being a known troublemaker was something her mom had never mentioned. Was it true? She intended to find out. She intended to find out *everything*. And with that resolve, she lifted her chin, channeled her inner badass, and strolled up the stairs to the high school's front doors.

School was out for summer, but the doors were unlocked, and a woman sat behind the front reception counter.

Mrs. Yorkshire.

She wasn't small like her name might imply, but she was territorial. Back in the day, she could pack more mean into her formidable frame than anyone Tae knew.

The woman's sharp eyes narrowed in displeasure at the sight of Tae. "Ms. Holmes."

Nope. Nothing had changed. Even the woman's hair hadn't dared to gray. "Mrs. Yorkshire. Nice to see you again."

The woman gave a short cackle. "I see your lying skills are still intact."

Do not squirm. Do not engage. Do not show weakness.

"Never thought I'd see the day where you crossed our threshold again," Mrs. Yorkshire said.

And don't take the bait either! "I'm here about a student."

"Is your child enrolled in our fall schedule?"

Holy crap. Was she actually old enough to have a high school–age kid? Since her mom had her when she was fifteen and had been thirty when Tae started her years here, she supposed the answer was yes, she was old enough. *Yiiikes.* "I'm here about a past student. I was hoping to look through some of the old yearbooks."

"The library's locked."

"But you've got a key, right?"

"I do."

Tae waited a beat, but the old woman wasn't budging. She did her best to swallow her pride but couldn't get it all down. "*Please?*"

Mrs. Yorkshire's eyebrows raised at that. "The last time I left you alone in the library was during detention, where you hacked into the computers and changed my picture to a Yorkshire dog. A very old dog."

Yep. Guilty as charged. She grimaced. "That was a long time ago. And I'm . . ." She worked at swallowing the last remnants of that pride she was currently choking on. "Sorry."

Mrs. Yorkshire gave a tight smile. "In order for an unauthorized adult to be on campus, we'd need a copy of your driver's license, a security deposit for the key to the library, and you'd need to be chaperoned while in the library—which can only occur during official school hours."

"But that's not until September," Tae said.

"Correct."

She stared at the woman. "Seriously?"

"Those are the rules, Ms. Holmes."

"All I need is five minutes."

Mrs. Yorkshire smiled without showing teeth and lifted her bony-ass shoulders, like *what are you going to do?*

Oh, for God's sake. Tae turned and strode back to the front double doors, shoving them open, practically running by the time she reached the top step—where she collided with a brick wall.

The wall turned out to be Riggs, who wrapped his arms around her, absorbing her forward motion, keeping them both upright.

"*You,*" she said.

"In the flesh." He pulled back, leaving his hands on her shoulders, and gave her a slow once-over. "Cute."

She looked down at herself and nearly screamed. She was still in the unicorn onesie. And Mrs. Yorkshire hadn't so much as blinked an eye. She closed her eyes, but she could still *feel* Riggs's amusement.

Mrs. Yorkshire, who'd come to the door, probably to see what the commotion was, gasped like an eighteenth-century schoolmarm at the sight of them locked together. Recovering quickly, she smiled brightly at Riggs. "Well, look at you. How lovely to see you again, dear."

"You've *got* to be kidding me," Tae muttered.

Riggs, still holding on to her, pressed—actually more like smothered—Tae's face into his chest so she couldn't talk. But her nose worked just fine and he smelled . . . damn. Amazing.

"Lovely to see you too," he said. "And how is it you haven't aged a single minute?"

"Oh, aren't you the one," Mrs. Yorkshire said, all verklempt. "Is there something I can help you with?"

Tae tried to lift her head, but Riggs was holding her in place, so all she managed to do was eat some of his shirt.

"Yes," he said. "You most certainly can help me, but first I need a quick moment with Ms. Holmes, if you don't mind."

She must have complied because Tae heard the doors shut again. Shoving free of Riggs, she blew her hair out of her face. "Are you following me?"

"Of course not. Someone decided it was a great idea to expand

Adrenaline HQ's client base to include at-risk youth, so I'm here dropping off forms."

"It *was* a great idea," she said.

"I just said so, didn't I?"

She stared at him for signs of sarcasm, but there were none, so she took a deep breath and looked at his black eye, which was fading to a nice yellow and green. "Sticking with your running-into-a-door story?"

"Actually, it was a ro-sham-bo gone wrong."

"Uh-huh."

He touched the very small scar above her eye, left over from the convenience store incident on his first night in town. Then he looked into her eyes, smile gone. "You okay?"

"It hasn't hurt since that first night."

"I don't mean the injury. Are *you* okay?"

How did he always do that? How did he know to ask? No one *ever* knew, and there was a good reason for that. She'd gotten really good at putting on a brave face, her *armor* as her mom called it, so good that even *she* believed it most of the time. "I'm fine. Or I'll be fine as soon as you're out of my way. I've got some research to do in the library."

Riggs lifted his hands from her and stepped back, and she turned to the front doors again, gathering her courage.

"I could help you get what you need," Riggs said.

"You know I used to go here too, right?"

He gave her a small smile. "From what I could tell, you cut class more than you were in it."

True story.

"Let me help, Tae."

"I don't need, nor will I *ever* need, your help." Determined to get her answers even if she had to beg, she reached for the double handles and tugged.

The doors had been locked. She set her head to the steel.

"Problem?" Riggs asked.

"You mean other than my life sucks and I'm wearing a unicorn onesie?"

He chuckled, and she knocked her head to the door a few times until a warm mouth brushed her ear. "Move aside a second, Rebel. Or is it Ms. Unicorn now?" Without waiting for a response, Riggs gave her a nudge and then knocked. "Mrs. Yorkshire?"

The doors immediately opened. Riggs sent Tae a smile that luckily for his own life didn't have an ounce of smugness to it. Then he looked at Mrs. Yorkshire. "Can we come in?"

"Of course, dear." She called to someone over her shoulder. "Look who's here, you remember Riggs Copeland . . ."

The other woman had been an aide when Tae had been in high school but had apparently worked her way up to the office. Tae had long ago forgotten her name, but the woman's face creased in a smile. "Of course I remember Riggs. Don't you look handsome. We've missed your face around here. You were always one of our favorites."

Tae was standing there, a grown-ass woman wearing a unicorn onesie, and she was *still* invisible. But she supposed she wasn't surprised in the least the ladies were falling all over themselves to let Riggs in. "Suck-up," she whispered out of the side of her mouth.

He squeezed her hand. "You should try it," he whispered back.

And the ridiculous thing was he was right. She could either walk out of here with her pride and nothing else, or she could let Riggs help her to get into the old yearbooks. Dammit. She gave him a nod.

He turned to the ladies. "So Tae and I have been working together with Adrenaline HQ to help some of the at-risk kids in the community, and—"

"I heard!" Mrs. Yorkshire said. "You have no idea how many kids you and your brother are helping."

"Actually," he said, "it was all Tae's idea."

The ladies both stared at her.

Not Tae. She was staring at Riggs.

"We'd love to get into the library and do some research," he said.

Unbelievably, Mrs. Yorkshire handed him a library key. No questions asked. "Just leave it on the counter here when you're done."

"Wait, what about the background check and key deposit?" Tae asked.

Mrs. Yorkshire ignored her and leaned forward toward Riggs. "We're just about to leave for the day. Could you make sure the doors lock behind you? The janitor already left, and there's no one else. I shouldn't be letting you in so close to end of shift, but—"

"No worries. I'll make sure it's locked up tighter than a drum," Riggs promised.

Mrs. Yorkshire patted his hand. "You were always such a good boy. You overcame so much, I'm so proud of you."

Tae went brows up, but Riggs just smiled, waved at the ladies, then turned and headed toward the library.

Tae found herself jogging to keep up with him. "Hey."

He didn't slow down, not until he got to the library door.

"Okay, let's have it," she said breathlessly. "What's the catch? Why are you helping me?"

"It's called basic human decency."

"Or . . . ?"

He tsked low in his throat. "Such a suspicious thing."

She thought about that for a second and decided he was right. She *was* a suspicious thing. "Look, we both know I haven't been all that nice to you. I've actually been kinda snotty."

"It's how you show affection."

"Funny."

"I wasn't going for funny," he said. "It's just what people who care about each other do. They help."

She stared at him. "We . . . care about each other." And what she really meant was . . . *You care about me?*

"Don't we?" He said this in a question, as if he was just as surprised as she was, and if she hadn't still been off-balance, she might've laughed at the slightly confused look on his face.

"No." But she immediately sighed. Dammit. "Yeah."

He smiled. "Admit it. I'm growing on you."

She was very afraid that was true, but the simple fact was that she hated being beholden to people.

Riggs dangled the library key in front of her. "You going to tell me what we're up to?"

"*We're* not up to anything. *I'm* going to go through the old yearbooks."

"Gonna need more than that."

She reached for the key, but he held it above her head.

She narrowed her eyes. "Hand it over."

"Sure," he said. "Soon as you trust me with what you're up to. And/or why you're in that adorably sexy . . ." He cocked his head sideways to take her all in. "Unicorn onesie?"

She ignored the way her face heated. She was never going to live this down. And as for trust . . . the only person she trusted was her mom, and there was now no way she was telling her mom anything about any of this until she had answers. She wanted to make sure her dad was good and dead, or if not, that he wasn't going to come back and try to break her mom's heart.

"Talk to me, Tae."

"Fine. I think my dad might be alive. Which means he's an asshole, and I want to find out the truth before my mom gets hurt. Again."

"Wait." He shook his head. "Didn't your dad die in Desert Storm?"

"Maybe. But maybe he visits a bar in south shore."

"What?"

"At the last AHQ fundraiser, I met an older gentleman whose son used to hang out with my dad. Apparently he saw my dad in a bar a few years ago. Maybe. Or maybe he's mistaken. It's complicated."

Riggs's amusement from earlier was gone, his eyes serious as he studied her. "What does your mom think?"

She sighed. "I haven't told her. She thinks he's dead. So on the off chance he's not, I need to find him and tell him to stay the hell away from us. That's why I need to look at the old yearbooks. I need to see if there was an AJ Strickland in school when my mom was."

"I thought your dad's name was Andy Jameson."

"Me too, but Mr. Schwartz seemed so sure that his name is AJ Strickland, and it rattled me."

"Okay," he said simply, and unlocked the library.

"You remember my dad's name?" she asked.

"I remember everything about you."

Tae laughed, heavy on the disbelief. In her experience, she wasn't all that memorable to people. "Like I left any sort of lasting impression on you."

He put his arm out to stop her from entering the library and waited until she met his gaze. "You did, Tae."

The words, and the look in his eyes, made her insides feel squishy. And warm. And . . . nice. Pushing away from him, she crossed the threshold.

"I never spent time in here," he said behind her. "I'm not sure where to even look."

"They used to keep every yearbook displayed on a shelf in the back room."

"How do you know?"

"Because I came here a lot." She kicked herself for giving him that little reveal as she headed into the back room. "Still in the same place." She breathed with relief at the sight of the bookshelf filled with the school's past yearbooks. She ran her fingers along the labels, looking for the year her mom had been a freshman. "Here."

Her fingers trembled as she pulled it from the shelf. She located her mom first. The sight of April Holmes as a teenager wasn't completely new; Tae had seen pictures before. But the sweetly smiling fifteen-year-old staring out at the camera still choked her up a little bit. "She was pregnant in this picture." And she'd given everything up—college, her family . . . *everything*. All to keep Tae.

Riggs didn't say anything, and whether it was out of respect for her obviously overwhelming emotions or something else, she appreciated it. Because as she stared at the picture, she suddenly felt like her entire life was as out of her control, as it had been the last time she'd been in this room. Knowing from her mom's stories about her dad that he'd been a junior when she'd been a freshman, Tae flipped a few pages to the juniors section, heart pounding.

No Andy Jameson.

She nearly staggered back a step. Her legs felt that weak. And how was it that she felt like she was losing a dad she'd never had? Why did it even matter?

She flipped to the *S*'s page, looking for AJ Strickland.

And found him.

AJ Strickland. He was skinny, even scrawny, long hair sticking out from a backward baseball cap, dressed in an oversize hoodie, eyes sullen and angry.

Tae pulled out her phone and accessed her photos. She stared at the shot of Andy, a young man in military dress, hair in a buzz cut, head high, eyes shining with pride, looking strong and capable.

Were they the same guy?

Mr. Schwartz had been right. It was hard to tell.

Riggs's breath was warm on her neck. So was the hand that covered hers. "All this proves is that there was a guy named AJ Strickland who went to the same high school as your mom."

"But why isn't Andy Jameson in the book too?"

Riggs shook his head, watching her carefully. "Tae."

"I know," she said softly. "His eyes." They were *her* eyes.

"There's something else," Riggs said. "AJ Strickland. AJ . . . short for what?"

She gasped. "Oh my God. Maybe . . . Andy Jameson?"

He nodded.

"Holy shit," she whispered.

He nodded again.

"I've got too many questions and zero answers." She shook her head, not sure why she was telling him all this. "If AJ Strickland is my dad, why isn't he on my birth certificate?" And why had it been so easy for him to tell a long-ago friend that his daughter was grown now, and yet he couldn't be bothered to contact her? Maybe he hadn't been ready to be a dad when he was a kid himself? Because he's an adult now. Why not get in touch? Unless he just doesn't care . . . Which hurt more than she wanted to admit.

"Maybe your mom could fill in some blanks—"

"No." She was firm on this. "It would only hurt her."

He hesitated. "Are you sure she doesn't know?"

"*Yes.*"

Riggs's silence said he wasn't, but Tae knew her mom wouldn't, *couldn't*, be hiding all of this.

"What do you want to do?" Riggs asked.

She wanted to lose the knot in her chest. She wanted to go back in time and not have talked to Mr. Schwartz that night at the charity event. She wanted . . . hell, she wasn't even sure. How many times had she fantasized about having her dad around? Too many to count. But she'd never mentioned it to her mom. She hadn't wanted her to feel like she wasn't enough, not when she'd been so much more than enough. In fact, maybe it'd been *Tae* who hadn't been enough.

The bottom line was that her mom would be either devastated by all this or . . . Well. She couldn't think about the or. Not yet. If this was really somehow true and her dad was alive and living under a different name, it would tear them all apart. Completely. She pulled out her phone, snapped a pic of AJ Strickland on the page. Then she put the yearbook back and turned to go.

"Whoa." Riggs put a hand on her arm. "Where are you running off to?"

"To find him. I want answers."

"Of course," he said, not letting go. "But you don't even know what kind of guy he is. We need more information before you go confront him, guns blazing."

"Hey, I've got more tact than that."

"Do you?"

"You know what?" She shrugged free. "Maybe me coming in hot is exactly what this situation needs."

"We need more info," he repeated softly.

"We?"

He just looked at her.

Oh boy. Her heart went a little squishy. "We're not a we, Riggs."

Gently, he nudged her unicorn hood off and she blew out a self-conscious breath. "I'm going to kill Jenny."

"We're a *something*," he said, not letting her change the subject. "Even if you are the most stubborn, suspicious woman on the planet."

She let out a rough laugh, dropped her head to his chest, and closed her eyes. Because he was right. They *were* most definitely a something.

He stroked a hand down her hair. "Still don't trust me."

"Don't take it personally," she said into his shirt. "I don't trust anyone."

"You can trust *me*, Tae."

She lifted her head and met his gaze. "With my body? Or my heart?"

He cupped her face. "What do they each tell you?"

Her body told her "yes please!" Her brain told her to run for the hills. Neither was helpful. "They say they wish you wouldn't push for answers you don't really want."

CHAPTER 18

Riggs just barely managed to catch Tae's hand before she escaped the small back room. Around them, the rest of the library was dark and silent, much like the woman in front of him. Some women cried when they were upset. Some railed. Not Tae. The more she hurt, the quieter she got.

She slayed him with her strength. He knew she was confused and hurting. Riggs had lost his dad too, to complications due to liver failure, the year after he'd left Sunrise Cove—though he'd never mourned the man, not for a single day. His dad hadn't deserved it.

But if what Tae thought was true, she'd spent her life mourning a man who might still be alive, and that sucked. Slowly reeling her in, he leaned back against the wall, widening his stance so that her feet fit between his, their hips snugged up against each other. "Tae."

She closed her eyes. "Don't."

He gently stroked a strand of hair from her face. "Don't what?"

"Say my name like that. It makes it harder for me to stay in the friend zone. I'm trying to deny you really do care. It'd help if you let me."

"You know I care," he said. "More than I want to." A truer statement had never been told. Didn't change anything about their situation though, so he tried to keep it to himself.

Staring at him, she slowly shook her head. "I forget myself with you, Riggs. I lose myself." She fisted her hand in his shirt. "I've got a mission. I need to go."

What this mission needed was someone standing between Tae and a potential heartbreak. Or worse. For all they knew Andy Jameson wasn't a good guy. "The mission needs a plan," he said. "And caution. We aren't even sure it's him."

"It's him," she said with certainty.

Yeah. His gut told him the same thing. Not only did Tae and this guy have the same eyes, they also had the same way of holding themselves, like they knew they were alone against the world. Looking into her eyes now, he also saw something he'd never seen before—betrayal. It made his gut clench, and the need to try to solve all her problems for her was strong. But he was evolved enough to know how well *that* would go over. "We don't know for sure what happened."

"We know what *probably* happened."

"You still don't have to do this, Tae."

"Yes, I do. You know I do."

He did know. She wasn't ever going to be the woman who walked away from a fight or from protecting someone she cared about. Hell, she'd protect a perfect stranger if that stranger needed it, even to the detriment of herself. "We could leave this library right now and never talk about it again," he said quietly.

She looked away. "And a part of me wants to do just that." Her gaze met his again, hers shimmering. "Dammit." She blinked rapidly before any tears could fall. "But it's the chickenshit way out." She drew a deep breath. "There's no walking away from this, Riggs, not for me. In order for me and my mom to move forward, I have to know the truth."

"You *know* the truth. It's that you and your mom not only survived, but you've also succeeded in life, in spite of circumstances. What this guy did or didn't do doesn't change anything."

"Are you kidding?" She was practically vibrating. "It changes *everything*. It changes all those years my mom mourned him. It changes everything about who I thought my dad was and who *I* am as a result. I thought he died a war hero, but for all I know, he's really just a deadbeat dad who got his teenage girlfriend knocked up, a guy who pretends I don't exist rather than be a dad."

The sheer emotion in her eyes was killing him. "He's an idiot, Tae, and it's *his* loss, because you're amazing."

"And stubborn. And suspicious . . ." she said, ticking off the adjectives he'd used to describe her before.

He smiled. "Also smart, and resilient, and beautiful."

Hard to believe, but her cheeks actually flushed. "I've got a lot to do," she said. "I'm not even sure how to go about finding this guy."

"I know a guy who can help. And, in fact, so do you. Ace. He's using his military tracking abilities as a private investigator now. When he was on the job, he was a bulldog with a bone. He never gave up until he found his man."

Tae let out a shaky breath. "I appreciate that, but no. I've got this. It's something I need to do myself. And speaking of that, I also really do need to go. I have to think about what to tell my mom."

"Sometimes the truth only leads to more hurt."

She met his gaze again. "Which you know from experience."

It was his turn to look away. And as he had, she touched his face and brought it back to hers. "I know you've been hurt."

The genuine warmth in her eyes was like a sucker punch to his gut. "This isn't about me," he said.

"Right, because your biggest fear is opening up."

He grimaced. "What is it with you and fears?"

"What is it with you and emotions?"

Touché.

She was still looking at him, *into* him, and it was disconcerting as hell. As were her next words. "Do you hold back, keep women in the friend zone, because of how you grew up?"

Very little could surprise Riggs anymore. But Tae had a way of always doing just that. She could read him, and crazy as it seemed, she *knew* him. Which meant she could cut right through his defenses. Always had. After high school, he'd purposefully gone for the sweet, girl-next-door type, because it would never last. Not when deep, *deep* down he craved the edgy, tough, would-take-on-the-world-if-she-had-to type.

Tae, of course. It'd always been Tae. Which, talk about fears, scared the ever-loving shit out of him. If she only knew. "Seems like we both lost out on the lottery when it came to our dads."

Tae didn't say anything for a moment, just gave him a small, solemn smile and squeezed his hand. "His loss," she said softly. "Because you are smart, resilient . . ." Going up on tiptoes, she pressed a kiss to his black eye. "Beautiful."

"*Shit*," he muttered.

She laughed. "Don't worry . . ." She kissed his jaw. "I won't tell anyone." Then she kissed his mouth.

The kiss was gentle and reached to the depths of his soul, reminding him of their long-ago night. He wasn't sure what was happening here, but it felt like they were in a bubble out of time and place.

No matter what they pretended, they understood each other. They connected with each other, on a level he'd not been able to do with anyone else.

Hell, maybe *that* was his biggest fear.

Tae pulled back and stared at his mouth, pulling her lower lip in between her teeth, like maybe she wanted more. His body was on board with that, but his brain . . . it wouldn't shut up. "Tae, you're going to give me ideas."

"No worries, I've got plenty of my own."

He pulled in a deep breath. "We've tried this before."

Her eyes met his, filled with desire and hunger. "That was a long time ago."

He couldn't resist her. He'd tried. And even though he was up a river without a paddle, he didn't care, because when it came to how he felt about her, reason and logic were in low supply. "So I've got just one question for you," she said softly.

"Hit me."

"Do friends sleep together?"

"If the female half of our duo wants to."

"Why the female half?"

He laughed. "Because the male half always wants to."

She gave a slow smile that pretty much made it impossible to breathe. "But now I have a question," he said.

"Hit me."

"You going to be gentle?"

Her eyes met his, hungry, heated, as she pressed him against the wall of hardwood half shelves anchored to the wall. "Not even a little bit."

"Good." He was goners. "My safe word's *cookie.*"

Tae laughed and kissed his jaw again, then worked her way to his ear, nearly melting at the rough groan that rumbled up from deep in his chest.

"*Tae—*"

Not wanting to talk, she nibbled at his earlobe. Hard.

Sucking in a breath, he entangled a hand in her hair and forced her to look at him. He met her gaze, his own dark with hunger and a sexy edginess that nearly gave her a miniorgasm.

"I wasn't expecting this," he said gruffly.

"It's okay if your legs aren't shaved, or if you're wearing laundry day panties. I mean, I'm in a unicorn onesie, so . . ."

His laugh was rough. "I mean I don't have a condom."

"I do." She backed away, slapped the lock on the door to the library, then dug around in her purse, coming up with a foil packet.

"Damn," he said. "That's sexy."

"Don't get too excited." She walked back to him. "I only have the one, and it's purple, but at least it's . . ." She eyed his jeans at crotch level. "XL."

He snorted, and she smiled. "Awhile back, my mom went to a friend's bachelorette party and she got a bag of these as a door prize. About a month ago, she dropped one in my bag, telling me I should use it before my parts shrivel up and die from being neglected."

He grinned. "I like the way she thinks."

"Would you still say that if you knew she wasn't a fan of yours?"

He shrugged. "She's a smart woman."

"Agreed." She gave him a nudge until his back hit the half wall of shelves.

He settled in, his butt resting on the edge, his arms snaking around her waist, hauling her in and kissing her like he meant it, until they were both breathing like they'd just run a marathon. He pressed his forehead to hers. "I was here to help you."

If he hadn't been hard as a rock against her core, she might have believed him. "And now . . . ?" she murmured, sliding her hands beneath his shirt to roam over warm skin and all smooth, hard muscle.

"I definitely feel my priorities shifting." He turned, then lifted her up to sit on the shelf before stepping between her legs, where he kissed her with more intent and more emotion than she'd ever felt in her life.

Yep, his priorities were *definitely* shifting. She tried to wriggle closer to those "priorities" and moaned in protest when he pulled back an inch. "You're sure?" he asked.

"Riggs?"

"Yeah?"

"Shut up and kiss me."

The kiss detonated. He lost his shirt. She kicked off her shoes. He swiped the books behind her aside, making more room, the movement giving her a ridiculous flutter. As did the intent look on his face as he reached for her and unzipped her onesie all the way down to her feet, revealing a slice of her in nothing but a bra and undies.

He groaned at the sight. "And you wonder why I like the onesie."

She shrugged it off her shoulders, and he stepped in to help, promptly encouraging it past her hips to the floor. He made short work of her bra and undies before dropping to his knees and letting out a rough male sound. "Damn, Tae. You're gorgeous." Leaning in, he kissed an inner thigh, then turned his head and kissed her other inner thigh.

And then in between.

He took her completely apart in a shockingly short amount of time, and when she came back to herself, she was gasping for air. She opened her eyes to find his head resting on her thigh, his eyes closed. He didn't open them as she cupped his cheek with her hand, just turned his head into her touch, and she took a steadying breath at the wave of affection joining her hunger for him. Tugging gently on his hair until he rose, she pulled him in and kissed him, trailing kisses toward his ear.

His hand came up to tangle in her hair, moving her mouth back to his, lips curled up into the hint of a smile. "Maybe one of these days we'll make it to a bed."

"I don't need a bed." She tore open the condom and eyed his hard length doubtfully, making him laugh and take it from her. He protected them both, then slowly, exquisitely, slid into her. A low sound of pleasure escaped in his throat, but it was the undisguised emotion in his face that told her he was as lost in her as she was in him.

"You okay?" He breathed, breaking the kiss to stare intently into her eyes, his gaze searching.

"Very."

As if finally believing her, his hands gripped her hips, guiding her movements into a rhythm that really, *really* worked for her, his head bent so he could watch himself slide in and out of her. The intensity in his gaze was the hottest part, and then he covered her mouth with his and she could think no more as he took them to heaven and back.

WHAT COULD'VE BEEN a minute or a week later, Tae stirred and, finally having caught her breath, opened her eyes.

Riggs had fastened his jeans but not put his shirt back on, and the view was . . . magnificent. The full-body Riggs experience was very distracting indeed. Smooth, tanned muscle stretched over lean, hard muscles. He was currently bending down and picking up her discarded clothes, and even though she'd just had two handfuls of his ass, she couldn't help but take another appreciative look.

Riggs gave a soft laugh. "Didn't get enough?"

She felt her face heat. "It's involuntary."

He rose to his full height and handed over her things. When she just sat there, still a little stupefied, his hands went to her waist, his eyes on hers. "I like the way you look at me," he said.

"Like I'm planning your murder?"

"Like you want me inside you." He kissed her just beneath her ear. Her hot spot, which he damn well knew. "It's flattering."

Ignoring this, she hopped off the shelf and got dressed in the onesie again. Riggs smiled. Hmm. Maybe instead of killing Jenny, she should give her a raise. And how was it that he looked even better with his hair standing up in spikes from her fingers and his shirt wrinkled from where she'd fisted her hands in it? "I gotta go."

He nodded. "I know." He tipped her face up to his. "I like you, Tae. A lot. You're important to me. Please don't use what just happened between us to make you retreat."

Like she had last time . . . "Once upon a time, walking away was the only thing I knew how to do."

"I get that, and ditto," he said. "But we're not dumb kids anymore."

She nodded, then shook her head. "Back then, I'd never had a boyfriend, but from what I'd seen of my mom's life, they did nothing but complicate things." She paused. "I'm not sure my stance has changed all that much. And also? I think you're not all that different from me on the matter. I mean, you are still leaving, right?" An emotion crossed his face quickly and was gone. Regret? "I am," he finally said.

Something inside her stilled. It wasn't pride. Pride was what had her nodding in agreement. "Good thing then that this was just friend sex and not I-love-you sex." She searched for her shoes, incredibly aware of Riggs quietly watching her.

He pulled her shoes from under the shelves and handed them to her.

She snatched them, painfully aware that she'd made a mistake here today, a big one, and had no one to blame but herself. She turned to the door.

Very gently, he turned her to face him. "Are you running off because I've made you angry by being honest, or because you're scared?"

She choked out a laugh. "I'm not scared."

He ran his fingers along her jaw. "Don't start lying now, Tae."

She closed her eyes. Damn. Damn him. Because she *was* scared. Terrified, really, of her feelings for him. They felt out of her control, which she hated. "Look, I'm on a fact-finding mission about my dad, and that's all I have bandwidth for right now."

"I told you I'd help."

"I need to do this alone."

"No one needs to do anything like this alone."

"I do," she said firmly. "Look, there's something you need to know about me. I talk a good game, but it's all bravado. I'm not good with showing my feelings."

Riggs looked surprised. "And you think I am?"

"Better than me."

He laughed roughly. "That's a first," he murmured. "A woman even thinking I have feelings."

She had to laugh. "I'm trying to warn you that I'm every bit as screwed up now as I was when we were younger. I'm not a good bet, Riggs."

He ran a finger along her temple. "I think you're wrong. But as always, this is your choice."

"So . . . no pressure?"

"Not ever," he said quietly. "Not with me."

"Not even if we're having quickies in the library?"

"It wasn't *that* quick."

She refused to laugh. "Riggs, I'm a little scared of this."

"What's there to be scared of? Just friends, right?"

"Okay, admittedly friends . . . with benefits."

He gave a small smile. "*Great* benefits."

She knew it wasn't, couldn't be, that simple, but she really wanted to believe it. "Right. As long as we're honest with our real emotions."

"I believe I just showed you a whole bunch of my emotions a few minutes ago. I'd be happy to show you again, anytime."

She gave him what she thought was a rather impressive eye roll and headed out the door. He caught her, slid a warm hand to the nape of her neck, and tipped her head back. "You want to know what I really feel, Tae? I feel like I wouldn't mind upgrading our friendship pact, to me being what you wanted for the rest of the summer."

And then on that shocking note, he took her by the hand and pulled her out of the library.

Her brain whirled as she let him lead her along. She'd asked for honesty, and she'd gotten it. Which meant she should be honest in return. Did she want the summer? Did she want more? How could she be honest with him when she wasn't ready to admit to herself what she wanted . . . ?

They strode down the quiet, dark halls in silence. When they got to the front doors, Tae started to pull free, but Riggs had a grip on her hand and wasn't letting go. She could've tugged free if she wanted, but in spite of what she'd learned from the yearbook and the knowledge that her world was on tenuous hold until she knew more, she felt . . . mellow. Maybe it was the orgasm. Okay, *two* orgasms—which, for the record, she'd deny if asked. She understood some women faked their orgasms to make their man feel better, but Tae belonged to the opposite philosophy. *Fake nothing, demand more.*

They walked outside and stood on the front steps, blinking in the bright sunlight.

"Gotta say . . ." Riggs looked at her. "Best school day ever."

When she laughed, he smiled and leaned in, but she put a hand on his chest. "What are you doing?"

"Kissing you. Thanking you. That was amazing." His mouth was still curved in amusement, but his eyes were serious. "I was serious about amending the pact, Tae. To being each other's until the end of summer."

"Each other's what?"

He just smiled. "I think I'll let you wrestle with the details."

CHAPTER 19

April sat in class, feeling . . . ancient—at least compared to everyone else here. The other students were either teenagers or in their very early twenties.

What was she even doing here? She was way too old to chase a career. But as she was packing up to walk out, Professor Stone strode into the classroom.

Like her, he was in his midforties. Unlike her, he'd made a name for himself locally for capturing the personality of his subjects. When anyone in the Tahoe region needed a photographer, he was their number one choice.

"Every picture you take says something about you," he said, setting down his briefcase. "So to that end, everyone take out your phone. Bring up the last picture you took. We're going to try and figure out what it says about you, the photographer." He opened his laptop, hit a few keys, and looked up. "When you're called upon, you'll AirDrop your pic and I'll cast it to the big screen for everyone to analyze. Remember, it must be the last pic you took, no cheating. Now. Who's going first?"

No one volunteered.

He looked around, his brows raised. April knew she was his favorite student. Mostly because she always showed up on time and gave him the respect of listening to every word he said instead of not-so-secretly playing a game on her phone. Normally, she'd bask in that knowledge, but not right now. Right now she was too busy panicking because she knew the very last picture she'd taken was of her shopping cart in the grocery store, because she'd sent it in a text to Tae to see if she'd missed anything on their list. She ducked her head to avoid his gaze.

"No volunteers?" Professor Stone asked.

No one raised their hand.

"Okay, how about this—*everyone* AirDrop your photo. I'll load them, sort them randomly, and we'll talk about what each one has to say about the photographer based on the quality and content of the shot. *Last* photo taken, people."

Everyone bent over their phones and AirDropped their picture. April hesitated, then figured what the hell. It was anonymous, right?

Professor Stone loaded a photo onto the big screen, and April took a big breath of relief because it wasn't hers.

It was a selfie of a woman in a barely there string bikini—emphasis on string—no face showing, just body. Also no cellulite, no stretch marks, no rough tummy from birthing an eight-pound, big-headed baby (thanks, Tae, the gift that kept on giving).

The room immediately erupted with a few catcalls and a *whoop-whoop* from some guy in the back.

Professor Stone ignored all of it. "We've got our mission," he said calmly. "And someone in this room trusted us to stay on that mission. So. What does this shot say about our photographer?"

"That she's hot as hell," someone said.

"Thank you," a girl said from behind Tae.

Professor Stone closed his eyes and looked pained. "I said *anonymous*, Karissa."

Karissa was nineteen years old, perky, pretty, and always smiling. "Oops. My bad. I was just trying to take a picture of the lake, but the camera was front facing." She gave a little embarrassed giggle. "I didn't plan for anyone to see it. Well, except my one thousand five hundred Instagram followers, of course. But I didn't touch it up or anything. Hashtag no filter," she said on another laugh.

Professor Stone was looking like maybe he was wishing he'd done this differently. "What does this picture say about you the photographer, Karissa?"

"Well . . ." She bit her lower lip. "That I could belong behind or in front of the camera, I guess. Hey, you're in the biz, right? Do you know any talent scouts?"

Professor Stone drew a deep breath. "Moving on." He loaded another pic and . . .

Oh dear God, it was April's, revealing her shopping cart. In it sat a jumbo package of toilet paper, control-top leggings, a historical romance novel with a nearly naked man on the cover, three bags of assorted potato chips—the family size—a few frozen Lean Cuisines, a box of organic tea specifically formulated to fight hot flashes, and a bottle of MiraLAX—which she'd taken and texted to Tae to see if she'd forgotten anything.

The room was silent except for a few snickers.

Professor Stone's lips twitched, but he didn't say a word.

And where is a huge sinkhole when I need it?

"Okay, so what does this photo tell us about the photographer?" Professor Stone asked.

A scrawny, pimply kid raised his hand. "It says this person is middle-aged, single, lonely, and possibly constipated."

Everyone in the class turned to look at April.

She *thunked* her head to her desk.

The guy next to her leaned in. "Dude, I knew you were old, but I thought you were, like, thirty tops."

When class was over, April sat still through the rush to get out the door, slowly putting her things into her backpack.

Professor Stone came over. "Can we talk?"

"The MiraLAX wasn't for me." *Good God, April, shut it.* She gave an embarrassed smile that was really more a grimace. "And I know. I should've cheated and sent a different pic."

He smiled kindly. "No, I'm sorry. I'll definitely do that differently next time. But that's not what I want to talk to you about. A local gallery in town holds an art show made entirely of local students to showcase their best work, and while normally this honor goes to a few grad students at UNR, your work is really outstanding." He smiled. "And varied."

She moaned and covered her face.

"No, I'm serious. You're amazing at landscape, but working at

Adrenaline HQ like you do, you've done some incredible people shots. I'd really love to include you."

Her mouth fell open. "Wait. Me?"

He smiled. "You're the most talented in this class, by far. So yes, you. I'd need ten of your best asap. The gallery donates the matting and framing. Think you can handle that?"

Her heart pounded in her ears, her blood thrumming through her veins in excitement. "Yes! Thank you. Thank you *so* much."

"Don't thank me, your work speaks for itself."

April practically floated out of the classroom, feeling euphoric for the first time in . . . well, a damn long time.

You need a life for yourself, Mom . . .

Tae had been right. And this was it—a kick start to her new life.

To celebrate, she stopped off and bought an extra-large pizza to share with Tae. She even got a salad for a side to make the meal downright healthful and texted her daughter to meet her at home for dinner.

Ten minutes after she'd walked in her door, Tae showed up wearing a unicorn onesie and an honest-to-God smile.

It didn't take a genius to figure out that the smile—and the glow that came from either a week in the Bahamas or sex—meant her daughter had been with a man. "New fashion statement?" she asked lightly.

"Jenny sent it. I didn't mean to go out in it. It was just so comfortable, I forgot I was wearing it."

"You look adorable. And the smile?"

"I'm not smiling." Tae moved directly to the pizza box. "Oh my God, pepperoni. I love you so much."

"You can't distract the master," April said. "Were you on a date?"

Tae paused, and April's mom-meter went through the roof.

"I was working," her daughter finally said.

April felt a deep unease. "Since when do we lie to each other?"

Tae had taken a slice of pizza and was eating it standing up, no plate. "Since you don't want to hear the truth."

Damn. "It was Riggs," she guessed flatly. "A man who's leaving and will never love you the way you deserve to be loved."

"We're not having this conversation again," Tae said, but then turned to look at her. "And what exactly is so wrong with Riggs?"

April wanted to say *everything*, but that wasn't true. She'd seen him in action now at Adrenaline HQ. And like Jake, he was at heart a good guy. A *very* good guy. He was also an island of one: impenetrable, implacable, stoical, and utterly unavailable emotionally.

The very *last* thing she wanted for her daughter.

Tae took one look at her mom's face and sighed. "Forget it. It doesn't matter. We're not a thing."

"The postcoital glow to your complexion suggests otherwise."

"And you know better than anyone that a 'glow' does not require a relationship," Tae said.

Touché.

"So you're . . . *not* in a relationship with him?"

Tae looked over the salad but didn't touch it. "I'm not even sure *Riggs* is in a relationship with Riggs."

Her heart actually hurt as she whispered, "Oh, baby."

"Stop." Tae shook her head. "There's nothing to worry about. I've got it under control."

This was Tae's go-to statement. *I've got it under control.* Whenever they'd had to move, when there'd been barely enough food, whatever the problem, Tae always said, *I've got it under control.*

Taking on April's problems as her own.

It put a big, fat, unswallowable lump in April's throat. Because her precious girl had always had to be the grown-up for both of them. But it was her turn, as she was desperately trying to make up for lost time and be the mom she'd always wished she'd had. "Tae—"

"I'll get the drinks," Tae said quickly. Code for *I don't want to talk about it.* She turned to the fridge.

"But—"

Tae held up a hand. "I love you, Mom. I do. To the moon and back. But we're dropping this."

If there was one thing April knew, it was when to cut her losses. She nodded and brought the pizza and the salad to the table. "Then there's something you should know."

Tae had been in the act of reaching for a wine bottle, but at April's words, she smoothly shifted and took the bottle of vodka from the freezer. Because yes, they had one in each side of the duplex. "It's good news," April assured her.

"Okay." Her daughter came to the table, still looking wary.

"It is. Really." April patted Tae's chair.

Tae sat.

"Eat some more, and I'll talk," April said.

"Talk, and then I'll eat," Tae countered.

April nodded, the age-old guilt and regret reaching up and choking her, because Tae had every reason to be cautious. April had put her through a lot of shit in their past. "I was selected to put up my photos in a gallery display this month," she said, unable to hold back a smile through the words. "The honor almost always goes to a grad student from the university, but my professor said my pictures were good enough to be included."

Tae's entire demeanor shifted from skeptical suspicion to sheer joy in only the way her mercurial daughter could. "Mom! That's amazing!"

April grinned. "I know! Something good finally happened to me!"

Tae's smile faded, and she reached across the table and gripped April's hands in her own. "This didn't happen to you, Mom. *You* did it. *You.*" Her eyes were fierce with love. "Don't you get it yet? Life isn't about letting things happen to you. It's about going out and getting what you want. And you've done that. I'm so, so, so proud of you."

April burst into tears.

Tae grimaced, and if April hadn't been busy crying, she'd have laughed. Her precious daughter hated tears. "I'm okay," she promised. "You're just so sweet. And the truth is, I'm the proud one. Of you, Tae. You're my everything. I love you so much."

Tae hugged her tight. "I love you too, Mom."

April hugged her back, her tears streaming for another reason now. Because always, always, Tae repeated back, *You're my everything too.* But this time she hadn't. She'd always known the time would come when Tae wouldn't need her as the center of her universe anymore. She'd told herself to be ready.

But she wasn't ready, wasn't sure if she ever would be.

AFTER THEY ATE, Tae cleared the table, handled the dishes, and hustled out, claiming she had a ton of work left to do.

But what she really meant was that her brain was so full, it was giving her a headache. She needed to think about things. Such as what she and Riggs had done in the library . . .

And what she'd discovered there, and how it'd changed everything. It'd been on the tip of her tongue the whole time she'd been eating with her mom. She felt like the biggest asshole on the planet for keeping it from her, but . . .

She couldn't shake the feeling that her dad had pulled a fast one on her mom. But telling her before she knew more now felt . . . selfish. Besides, this was what she'd done all her life. Protected her mom. And she'd keep doing it too, until she had answers.

Though she had no idea how. She knew she didn't have to do this on her own. Riggs wanted to help her, a fact that both grated and also gave her the oddest sensation, one she wasn't exactly used to.

Comfort.

Which was a whole bunch more important than the orgasms—not that *those* had been anything to sneeze at. Nor what he'd said after.

I was serious about amending the pact, Tae.

Such a stupid idea. And yet . . . a part of her wanted that. Bad.

The memory of him, his eyes intense and focused on her as he moved them in rhythm, his mouth on hers, his hands everywhere, that sexy, deeply male sound he made in his throat, his breath whispering in her ear . . .

Damn. *Don't get caught up. Let it go . . .*

As if it were that easy.

But having Riggs assist in the search for her dad would feel even more personal and intimate than what they'd done to each other in that library. The bottom line—she wouldn't, *couldn't,* accept his help. This was something she had to do on her own. Just like always.

CHAPTER 20

Tae gave up on sleep. Every time she closed her eyes, she had dreams. Vivid dreams. Either some version of her recurring childhood nightmare about not being able to find her mom, or the kind of dream that had her hot and sweaty and trembling in the very best of ways, thanks to one far-too-sexy Riggs Copeland.

It was midnight, several days post–Library Gate, as she'd decided to call it, and she tossed off her covers and stalked into her kitchen. No cookies. Why the hell didn't she have cookies?

She looked down at herself. Her pj's consisted of an old T-shirt and flannel bottoms. She pulled on an even older, baggier sweatshirt, shoved her feet into her fake UGGs, and grabbed her keys.

She decided to avoid the convenience store because . . . well, memories. She hit up the grocery store instead, and as a bonus, it was nearly empty at this time of night. She dropped a family-size bag of Double Stuf Oreos into her cart, and then a bag of carrots, because nothing said PMS like buying just a family-size bag of cookies. She was studying the wine selection and eating a cookie—yes, she'd lost all impulse control—when she felt like she was being watched. Removing her tongue from the icing in the middle of her Oreo, she turned.

Riggs stood in the aisle wearing dark jeans, a dark T-shirt, and dark eyes. The urban commando riding the night. If he was trying to look badass so no one would approach him, he was doing a great job as he stood very still, watching her, unsmiling.

They hadn't seen each other since Library Gate, and she studied him, searching for a hint at where his mind was. She knew he'd been putting in long days at AHQ, building the zip line and bike track. He looked tired. She could see it in the tiny lines that appeared around his eyes. But he wasn't unhappy to see her. Hope, his posture told her, that was . . . *wary*?

Interesting.

She moved toward him and nudged her cart to his. "Hey."

He smiled instantly, looking relieved.

Even more interesting . . .

She eyed his cart. Eggs. Veggies. Tortillas. Damn. A grown-up cart.

He looked into hers and smiled. "Nice deflection with the carrots."

"It's to offset the impending diabetic coma."

He laughed softly, the sound scraping at all her good spots.

"Having trouble sleeping?" he asked.

She liked the fit of his T-shirt, how it was stretched taut across his shoulders and chest, loose over what she knew to be kissable abs. With a shrug, she lifted her gaze to his mouth, remembering just how talented it was.

"Tae." His voice was low, almost rough.

"No, I'm not sleeping, and it's your fault."

This got her a very small smile. "I could help with that."

Her gaze flew to his, where she saw the same heat and hunger and spiraling need she knew was reflected right back at him. "*Yes.*"

He added her cookies and carrots to his cart. "Go home. I'll meet you there."

She barely remembered the drive home. She ran inside and kicked off her boots and tore off her sweats, replacing them with soft booty shorts and a barely there cami. Then she quickly scooped up the clothes all over her room and shoved them into her closet.

She'd left the front door unlocked, and when she heard it open, then the quiet, unhurried footsteps in her hall, she lay back on her bed, pretending her heart wasn't threatening to burst out of her chest.

He took in the thin cami and teeny booty shorts. "Is that for me?"

"Nope."

He came to her bed. Setting a knee to the mattress, he leaned over her for a long, hot, deep, drugging kiss. When they tore apart to breathe, she was wrapped up in him. He held her gaze as one hand slid inside her cami, the other in the back of her shorts. When he found no bra and no undies, he smiled. "This was so for me."

She smiled back. "Maybe."

That was the last time they spoke.

When she woke up, it was morning, and she was alone.

But she'd slept dreamless . . .

FOR A SECOND straight week, Riggs's life was taken up with work. Specifically on the five acres AHQ owned behind the warehouse. The flat part of the land made a perfect dirt bike course. The steep hill at the back—covered with a thick grouping of tall, towering, proud trees—was the zip line course. The design had been the easy part. His days were now spent out in the high-altitude summer sun, the air warm and fragrant with pine, working his ass off clearing out the sagebrush beneath the line, and building the apparatus and landings needed.

The manual labor wasn't anything new. But this time he wasn't in some hellhole on the other side of the planet. He wasn't in constant danger. He wasn't wondering if he'd live through his deployment. He was at one of the most beautiful places on the planet, working outside with his hands, and . . . loving it.

"I think you took out more bush than you had to," Jake said from twenty feet below him.

Riggs looked down. "You push yourself up that hill just to correct me when you could've called?"

"Would you have answered?"

Good question.

"I want to be able to call you and have you answer."

Riggs looked down again. "Then maybe you should talk *to* me instead of *at* me."

Jake was in dark-mirrored sunglasses, but he didn't need to take them off for Riggs to feel the eye roll. "You sound like a chick."

"*Excuse me?*" Carolyn asked, coming up beside Jake with Grub at her side.

Riggs grinned. He'd seen them coming.

"*He sounds like a chick?*" Carolyn repeated to Jake, heavy on the disbelief. "What does that mean exactly?"

Jake looked at Riggs, as if seeking help.

Riggs shook his head. "Definitely not on your side on this."

Jake sighed. *Sighed.* And then looked at his girlfriend. "I didn't mean anything by it."

Carolyn seemed unimpressed.

"Okay, I just meant that we're *guys,*" Jake said. "We don't have to tiptoe around a boatload of emotions when we talk to each other."

Carolyn's eyes narrowed. "But you have to tiptoe around a *boatload* of emotions when you talk to me?"

"Shit." Jake scrubbed a hand down his face. "No. I mean . . . sometimes. You've got a lot of emotions is all." He caught her hand when she started to walk off. "Babe, come on. You know I love you, *all* of you, including your emotions."

Carolyn looked into his face and gave in. "I do."

"I didn't mean to insult you."

"But you *did* mean to insult your brother."

"Well, yeah." He smiled at her. "That's what brothers do."

"As well as punch each other," she said.

"Sometimes."

Carolyn bent over Jake and kissed him. "Do you remember what I said the last time we fought?"

"That the way I speak to you sometimes hurts your feelings?"

"Yes, that," she said. "And . . . ?"

"And . . ." Jake appeared to search his memory. "That I need to use the words 'I'm sorry' more often."

She smiled at him. "Riggs," she said while still looking into Jake's eyes. "Does the way Jake speak to you sometimes hurt your feelings?"

Jake looked pained.

Riggs grinned. "Yep."

Carolyn looked at Jake.

"Fine! I'm sorry if the way I speak to you sometimes hurts your feelings," Jake said. Maybe growled.

"Apology accepted," Riggs said brightly.

"Whelp, my work here is done." Carolyn turned to head back to the building. Grub followed, and so did Jake, but not before flipping Riggs off.

Riggs went back to work, smiling.

The only thing that could make the day better would be seeing Tae. Other than the grocery store, and then the ensuing night at her place, where the only words they'd exchanged had been things like "yes, oh my God, yes, *there*" and "don't stop, *please* don't ever stop," he'd not seen her at all.

And not for lack of trying.

There'd been two meetings about their upcoming July events, both run by Tae. The first, he'd gotten stuck at city hall trying to get extra parking permits for their next Lake Days event. He'd also missed the second meeting because he'd been at the lake, walking through the logistics with the rec center park commissioner for the event's evening barbecue and auction. Both errands had been handed to him by Tae—via email.

Yep. She was definitely avoiding him. After the library, and the shocking connection they'd had, he'd felt more open, more vulnerable, than he could remember ever feeling. If she felt even a fraction of that, he got the need to take a minute. But he'd been fooling himself. He didn't need time. Not from her.

But if she did, he could give that to her.

Only, as the days went on, he began to think he'd made a mistake. He wanted to talk. He wanted to know she was okay. That they were okay. He'd checked-slash-stalked Jake's schedule and found a meeting scheduled with Tae today at 11:00.

He went inside at 11:05 and planted himself right outside Jake's office. When Grub saw him, he came running. He had some speed going on the hallway's concrete floor, too much. He tried to slow down by dropping his butt, but his forward momentum was too much, and his back end slid out from under him, flipping him onto his back, where he skidded to a stop at Riggs's feet. He flopped like a fish for a few seconds as he tried to right himself, then with a *wuff* gave up and stayed on his back, his tail wagging like crazy and his tongue hanging out of the side of his mouth, smiling up at Riggs with sheer joy.

"That was some landing." Riggs crouched low to rub the dog's belly before helping him roll over.

April appeared. "Can I help you?"

Still not a Riggs fan. But then again, if he were Tae's mom, he wouldn't be either. He smiled. "No, but thank you."

April eyed Jake's office. "I could let you know when he's done."

"I don't mind waiting."

April nodded and walked off. Riggs leaned against the wall, pretending to go through his email, one ear cocked to the door. Was he crazy? Clearly. But suddenly he needed to see Tae more than anything. He wanted to look into her eyes and see no regrets.

Ten minutes later, Tae strode out in a denim skirt and a sleeveless white button-down, but it was the wedge sandals, the ones that emphasized her long, lean legs, that got him.

She stopped short at the sight of him and watched as he closed the distance between them.

"Hey," he said.

"Hey."

And because they were chronic idiots, they just stared at each other, then started to speak at the same time. She gave a rough laugh and gestured for him to go first.

He shook his head. "You."

"It's nothing. Forget it. You go."

"You've been avoiding me," he said.

"No." Then when he gave her a long look, she grimaced. "Okay, maybe. A little."

So it *was* regrets then. Damn.

"But it's not what you think," she said.

He wanted to see her eyes soften for him, the way they did when he had his hands on her. But they were at work, so he kept his mitts to himself. With difficulty. "What do I think?"

"That I regret when we . . . um . . ." Her cheeks flushed. "Well, our incident." She paused. "Incidents," she clarified.

He arched his brows. "We're an . . . incident now?"

"My point," she said, lifting her chin, "is that whatever they were, I don't regret them."

He smiled because he was glad to hear it. "I thought maybe I scared you off when I suggested we let this thing between us play out for the summer."

"You mean when you said you'd let me wrestle with the details?" she asked.

"Well, you are good at details."

"So are you," she said, making him laugh. "And . . . I don't scare easily," she added.

"Good to know." Very good.

"I guess I was thinking that maybe the . . . *details* don't need to be spelled out," she said.

Ambiguity. He could work with that, and if he was a smidge disappointed, well, he could keep that to himself.

Tae's phone had been buzzing steadily throughout this conversation from a pocket on her somewhere, and she sighed. "The auction is killing me."

The auction was going to be at the end of day one of their upcoming event, right after the barbecue, and hopefully be a huge fundraiser for them—and he knew it was a lot of work to put it together. "Need help?"

She bit her lower lip and stared at his mouth. "Depends on what you're offering."

He ran a hand up her arm and slid his palm to the nape of her neck, urging her to tilt her head up to his. "Whatever you need."

Her mouth curved. "Well . . . I'm still short a few auction

items, so if you're available for, say, an evening out on the town, then yes, I'd love your help."

He blinked. "You want me to auction myself off."

She smiled. "Scared?" She gave him a daring look. "No, that can't be it, because you're not afraid of anything. Right?"

Well, he'd walked right into that one. And damn he loved when she challenged him. "Right. And you?"

"Oh, I have plenty of fears," she said.

"Name one."

"Falling for you."

This stunned him into silence.

She smiled. "That was worth it just for the look on your face."

His heart skipped a beat. "You're messing with me."

She held his gaze for a long minute. "The auction. You in or out?"

"*In.*" *In for everything that you'll give me* . . . "On one condition." He shifted closer. "Meet me for lunch. You choose the place."

She looked at the time. "It's lunchtime now."

"And . . . ?"

Her gaze dropped to his mouth. "My place. First one there chooses . . . the menu."

TAE OPENED HER eyes and looked at the clock. Holy shit—2:00 P.M.? "Oh my God," she gasped, and jumped out of her bed and hunted for her clothes, which were scattered far and wide.

Riggs sat up, hair wild from her fingers, eyes heavy-lidded and . . . damn. Sexy as hell.

"Two hours! We've been here for two hours!" She threw his jeans his way and hit him in the face.

He let them hit the floor. "Where's the fire?"

"We fell asleep!"

He just smiled, looking lazy and satisfied in a way that made her want to jump him. Again. "That's what happens when you're a sex fiend," he said. "I tried to leave an hour ago, but you weren't finished with me."

True, but she pointed at him. "This is all *your* fault! You make me stupid with lust."

With a grin, he rose and came at her naked as the day he'd been born, and not concerned in the least, damn him. "Oh no you don't!" She backed away. "You keep your magic wand away from me. I have work to do, and so do you! People are going to figure out what we're up to."

"News flash," he said. "I think they already know."

She blinked at him. "Well, can they share with me? Because I'd like to know too."

His smile faded as he pulled on his jeans but didn't fasten them. "Has something changed?"

She looked up into his face, caught the unguarded concern in his gaze as he pulled her against him. *Had* something changed? Maybe not yet, but she knew herself, knew that what they seemed to share when they were together like this didn't come around often. Or ever. So she also knew that the more intimate they were, the more her heart would engage.

But she didn't want to give him up yet. "No. Nothing's changed."

He looked like he wasn't sure if he believed her or not, so she said, "I'd just rather that no one know about us. It'll make it easier when you leave next month."

He stared at her, and she wondered if those two words had sent his heart reeling the way they had hers. Next month was going to come soon. Way too soon.

"Have you gotten anywhere in your hunt for AJ Strickland?" he finally asked.

"No. I've been too swamped with work. But as soon as Lake Days are over, I'm on it."

On her nightstand, her phone vibrated across the wood surface with an incoming text.

MOM: Spilled my soda, coming home to change. I'm going to grab your cute peach sundress, just fyi . . .

"*Crap.*" She tossed her phone aside and whirled around, looking for Riggs's shirt. She found it draped over her lamp. Good God. She tossed it at him.

He pulled it over his head, then studied her as he—slowly—shoved his arms into it. "You look panicked."

"My mom's going to be here in four minutes! So yes, I'm panicked! Join me, won't you?"

He pulled on his beat-up athletic shoes, watching her the whole time. "Embarrassed? Or regretful?"

"What?"

"About me. This. Us . . ."

She blew out a breath and sat next to him, bumping her shoulder to his until he gave her a little smile. "Neither," she said, and then repeated it when he looked at her skeptically. "I'm not. I just . . ." She shook her head. "It's like I said. I like that it's just us, that no one's trying to impose their thoughts or wishes or whatever."

"I'm not sure we've been all that stealthy."

Maybe not, but she wanted to live in denial land. Because that teeny tiny little seed of doubt deep inside her, the one that said her mom was right, that she was going to get hurt in all this, wasn't going away.

"You're serious about not letting anyone know about us," he said after a moment.

"We decided there is no us."

"There's an us. We even have a pact about it."

"A pact with an expiration date on it," she pointed out.

"No," he said. "There's no expiration dates on friends like us. That's why I wanted a pact. So I wouldn't lose you."

Her heart skipped a beat, but her brain couldn't even go there. "We've gotta go."

He nodded but caught her close and tugged her ponytail until she met his gaze. "So . . . we're okay?"

She went on tiptoes and brushed a kiss across his lips. "We're okay."

As she said it, she realized she wanted that to be true more than anything.

CHAPTER 21

The morning before the Lake Days event, Riggs was on the phone, pacing the length of his childhood home. He was glad the lovebirds were out for brunch and he had no one to overhear him talking to Ace.

Because Riggs knew damn well that Tae wouldn't be thanking him for putting Ace on the hunt for AJ Strickland. She'd straight up told him that she didn't want help on this. But he was bothered by something he couldn't quite put his finger on, and he hadn't been able to stop himself.

"Sorry it took me so long," Ace said. "Andy Jameson had some precautions in place, enough to tell me he didn't want to be easily located. But luckily for you, it wasn't enough to foil me."

Riggs stopped pacing. "So on a scale of one to deadbeat dad, what are we dealing with?"

"Andy Jameson, aka AJ Strickland, was born Andrew Jameson Strickland. Growing up, he went by AJ. But he went into the military as Andy Jameson."

"He dropped his last name," Riggs said. "Why?"

"No idea. He actually has a stellar military record. And from what I can tell, he retired two years ago and moved to south shore, where he lives a quiet life, only about an hour from Sunrise Cove."

Tae had said she needed to find out about her dad to protect April. But Riggs's goal was to protect Tae. And he was definitely missing some pieces of this puzzle. "What made April think he was dead?"

"That I don't know," Ace said.

Yeah, and that didn't sit well. Just because Andy led a quiet life now didn't mean he was a good guy. "How deep did you go?"

"He's got a juvenile record," Ace said. "But it's sealed. From then on, his nose has been clean. What are you going to do?"

"I want to know why the hell this guy decided to come back after all these years. He stayed away for what, nearly three decades? So why now?"

"Maybe he wanted to be back in Tahoe," Ace said.

Maybe, but there had to be more. Riggs could feel it. Tae's dad was using a different name. That didn't seem like a guy who wanted or needed the creature comforts of a childhood hometown. It was all too coincidental, and he didn't believe in coincidences. Tae had started her business last year and it was becoming successful, and now this guy resurfaces? No. There had to be a reason, and he was going to find it.

"You going to tell her?" Ace asked.

"After I make a little visit to Andy. I've got some questions."

"Oh boy," Ace said. "An interrogation."

"Problem?"

"I've seen you *interrogate* someone before, remember? And are you sure that's how you want to take this? Because I'm telling you, man, any woman I've been with would have my ass on a platter for taking this matter out of her hands and keeping her out of the loop."

"Sometimes it's better to ask for forgiveness than permission."

Ace snorted. "You poor, dumb bastard. You've got a lot to learn about relationships."

Riggs disconnected. The only thing he wanted to *learn* was what this asshole was up to. Grabbing his keys, he headed out. And yeah, okay, he knew Tae would be furious, and that he needed to bring her into the loop. Especially as the loop was hers. But she'd been through so much disappointment and loss. Too much. So first he needed to know that this guy even deserved to be in her life.

Then he'd share.

An hour later he was in south shore, parked across and down the street from a row of small A-frame cabins. A truck sat in Andy's driveway. No sign of activity going on, but when he walked closer and felt the hood of the truck, it was warm.

Someone had just recently gotten home.

He headed to the front door and knocked. A man opened the door, looking a lot like the aged version of the kid he'd seen in the yearbook. "AJ Strickland?" he asked.

The man said nothing.

"You have a daughter," Riggs said. "Tae."

The man's expression went cold. Hard.

Riggs gave it to him right back. He could out-mean anyone any day of the week.

"You have the wrong man."

"And you were clearly never trained in interview and interrogation, because you're shit at lying," Riggs said.

The guy paused. Considered Riggs. "Marine?" he finally asked.

"Yeah. Same as you. *Andy.*"

He looked at Riggs for a long moment, giving nothing away. "What do you want?"

"To talk."

With a single nod, Andy backed up and gave Riggs room to enter.

The interior of the cabin felt small and closed in. Andy went to the kitchenette and brought two beers from a small fridge. They each leaned back against opposite counters and stared at each other.

"Tell me how a guy walks away from his daughter," Riggs said.

"I never said I had a daughter."

"Still shit at lying."

"How did you find me?" Andy asked. "Who are you to Tae? And why should I tell you a damn thing?"

"I found you through a friend who's a PI, and if it makes you feel any better, you weren't all that easy to locate. As for who I am to Tae, I'm someone who cares deeply about her, enough to do what I can to protect her from you if I need to. And you're right, you don't have to tell me a damn thing, but I'm hoping you care about her too, enough to want to keep her safe."

Andy Jameson took a pull on his beer, then finally met Riggs's gaze. "What if I'd rather you think I'm a terrible liar than break a promise?"

This comment sent up a big red flag, because shit, it implied that they definitely didn't have the whole story. He set his beer aside, unopened. "Just so you know, your daughter's as stubborn as you are. And she's going to find you, whether you want her to or not. Before she does, I need to know why you walked out on her and her mom, letting them think you've been dead for twenty-eight years."

Andy staggered to the couch and sank heavily to it. "I've made a lot of mistakes in my life. One of those mistakes was not pushing April to let me stay in Tae's life when she wanted me gone."

Riggs stilled in rare surprise. "What?"

Andy nodded. "You heard me."

"April knows you're not dead?"

"Of course she does."

Holy shit. Riggs's stomach bottomed out. It was the same feeling he'd always gotten when he'd been given bad intel and knew things were about to go FUBAR. He sat in the beat-up armchair across from Andy. "You need to give me the whole story, because I wasn't kidding, your daughter's one step behind me, and this is going to crush her either way."

Andy started to shake his head. "I promised—"

"If you promised for the greater good of your kid, you can trust me. If you promised because you're a deadbeat asshole of a dad, then by all means, stay silent and destroy her when she finds you."

Andy leaned his head back and closed his eyes for a long moment. Just when Riggs thought that was going to be it, the guy lifted his head and met his gaze. "Who are you really to her?" he asked.

"Right now, I'm the unmovable brick wall standing between you two, protecting her."

Andy blew out a long exhale. "I'm going to need more than that. You her boyfriend?"

Boyfriend had always been one of Riggs's least favorite titles, and before Tae, it was one he'd never wanted. Now that he wouldn't mind it, he actually had no right to it. "This isn't about me."

Looking frustrated that Riggs wasn't answering questions, he said, "I'm not telling you a damn thing until you give me a good reason to."

"Assuming my fist in your face isn't a good enough reason," Riggs said lightly.

Andy, who, given his build, could probably handle himself, surprised him by saying, "I understand the impulse. When I think of what I did, walking away from my own daughter, I'd like to punch myself in the face too." He shook his head and got up to pace the room. "I wasn't expecting this." He drew a deep breath and turned to face Riggs. "What do you want from me?"

"The truth."

Andy laughed roughly. "The truth." He tossed up his hands. "I was a complete screwup as a kid. Had parents who didn't give a damn, so I got in with the wrong crowd, did stupid shit on dares."

Something Riggs could understand, more than he wanted to. "And?"

"And . . . it was all fun and games until I was seventeen." Andy shook his head. "I went to a party, got bombed off my ass on hard liquor that I had no business drinking, and sweet-talked a cute girl I'd never met before out of her clothes."

That Riggs had sweet-talked Tae out of her clothes at the same age suddenly didn't sit well.

Andy ran a hand over his jaw, his gaze internal, as if he was reliving that time. "A few nights later, me, along with two punk-ass kids up here on vacay with their rich parents for the weekend, somehow decided that boosting a car was a great idea. The stupidity was then amplified when the gangbanger drug dealer who owned the car ran alongside of us and jumped on the hood just before I crashed it into a telephone pole."

"Jesus," Riggs murmured. "What happened?"

"The gangbanger was thrown off the car. I was stupid enough to try to flee the scene and got caught. I'm lucky that he didn't die, but regardless, the two weekenders pinned it on me, the local kid, and a known punk looking for trouble. By the time I got out of juvie, April was six months pregnant and wanted nothing to do with me. She told me that the only thing I was going to bring to her was heartache and trouble, and at the time, she was right."

"Would she still be right?" Riggs asked.

"No, but trust me, no one had any way of knowing I'd get scared straight."

"So you let April make that call for you?"

"There's more." Andy's expression was grim. "The gang whose car we stole? The one I flung fifty feet into the air? His entire gang were after me. They wanted my head and didn't care who they had to hurt to get to me. They caught me one night, beat the shit out of me. Said I was going to do whatever they wanted, or die slowly and painfully."

"And what did they want?" Riggs asked, knowing he wasn't going to like this story.

"Me to run drugs, steal cars. All sorts of bad shit."

"And you agreed?"

"No." Andy shook his head. "I didn't. I told them to go to hell. That's when they went after April."

Riggs had been right. He didn't like this story.

"She found them waiting for her one night after work," Andy said. "Thank God, they didn't do anything to her, just scared her half to death. After that, she wanted me to vanish from her life, and I couldn't blame her. I had no money, no job, and no way to support her and our unborn baby, much less myself. She said the only thing I could possibly bring her was more trouble, not to mention another mouth to feed. So we decided that I'd enlist, that she'd be out of danger without me around. To add another layer of protection and a way to separate April and the baby from anything to do with AJ Strickland, I went into the military as Andy Jameson."

"And you walked away," Riggs said. "Just like that."

"No." Andy's jaw was tight. "Not just like that. But April and I were never a couple, and as I said, she had no reason to believe that I could get my act together. She didn't trust me, and I couldn't blame her. So when she wanted me to vanish from her life, I felt like I owed her."

"Why did April tell Tae that her father was Andy Jameson, who died overseas?" Riggs asked.

"Look, she really believed my past would never leave her alone. And think about it. All the shit I put her through? She wanted me gone, and she wanted me to stay that way. So I guess it made more sense to her to tell her daughter about Andy Jameson, the soldier, rather than AJ Strickland, the fuckup."

"I get the why," Riggs said. "And the lengths you went to in order to protect them and get your life straight is admirable. You were man enough to go into the military to keep trouble away from your family. So I hope that now, when Tae finds you, you're going to be man enough to take responsibility for your part in all this, including the lie."

Looking grim, Andy nodded. "I know. When I retired two years ago and came back, I went to April. I wanted to see if . . ." He sighed. "I don't know what I wanted exactly. To meet Tae, hopefully. But April flipped out. Reminded me that we have a deal."

Shit, Riggs thought. When all this came out, Tae was going to be destroyed. "What was her objection to you meeting your daughter now, all these years later?"

"I'd promised to go away and stay away. If she has to tell Tae that she's been lying all these years . . . ?"

"Yeah." Riggs scrubbed a hand over his face. "She'll be risking her relationship with Tae."

"Much as I regret agreeing to vanish from my daughter's life,

I can't do that to April, not after all she's been through. All *I* put her through. So I made the promise and I kept it. She deserved that much for my ruining her life."

Riggs hadn't expected to feel for the guy. "Why didn't you send child support? Or marry April when she turned eighteen so she and Tae could share your military benefits? They had some seriously rough times, and there were plenty of things you could have done to help them."

"I tried, believe me. But April refused all efforts of mine to marry her for the benefits or to give her money. Even threatened a restraining order."

Riggs felt so angry for Tae, who'd been unaware of all this the whole time. "Tae deserved better. From both of her parents."

"Agreed." Andy set his beer down. "Look, if this is really happening, if she's about to find me, I'm not going to hide. I want it to happen." He met Riggs's gaze again, his suspiciously shiny now. "Let it happen," he said quietly. A question. A hope. A plea.

What right did Riggs have to make this decision for Tae? *Zero.* "She's had enough drive-by relationships in her life, she doesn't need one more." God, listen to him. Such a hypocrite. Because *he* was one of those drive-by relationships, and he knew it. Which, for the record, he hated.

"What are you going to do?" Andy asked.

Riggs shook his head. "This isn't up to me."

"Then why are you here?" Andy stared at him, then slowly sat back and let out a rough breath. "You want me to stay dead until you're convinced I deserve her."

That had been the plan, but Riggs knew he had no right to

decide that either. "It's not up to me. You need to talk to April and together figure out a way to tell Tae the truth. Because if you don't, chances are you'll both lose her."

Andy took that in and nodded.

"And whatever happens," Riggs said, "be worthy of her." Advice he needed to take for himself. He too needed to be worthy of her and own what he really wanted and what that might look like—which was a whole lot more than he'd ever allowed himself to hope for.

Andy nodded again.

"There's one more thing," Riggs said. "Right now, Tae's looking for answers. She thinks she's protecting her mom from you. So you need to promise me that when she finds you, *she* gets to decide what kind of a relationship you have. If she wants you in her life, *she* makes it happen. Not you."

"I promise," Andy said solemnly. "And I think I've at least proven I can keep a promise."

Yeah. But could Riggs? That was the question. He'd made his own promise—to stay out of this so Tae could handle it on her own. *Not* to go find her dad and then wait for the cards to fall.

He was as screwed as Andy.

CHAPTER 22

April kept her shit together on the days leading up to the local art gallery showing, but on the night of, her nerves bounced around in her belly, worse than the time she and Tae had gambled one day on expired ranch dip and got food poisoning.

Tae parked the car on the Lake Walk, but April didn't move to get out. The dusk sky had all the colors in the rainbow, and the street was lit with twinkling fairy lights. They lined every storefront window and wrapped around the potted pine trees lining the sidewalks.

The place looked like a postcard.

Her fingers itched for her camera, but for the first time in a long time, she didn't have it on her, not tonight.

The art gallery had its front doors wide open and a sign announcing the display of local talent.

She was *talent* . . . It boggled and thrilled, and she had to swallow hard.

"We ever going to go in?" Tae asked, sounding amused.

April watched people enter the gallery. They would see her work, and suddenly it was like she'd gone to school without pants. "TBD," she managed.

Tae laughed and squeezed her hand. "Mom, this is a good thing. No, this is a *great* thing."

April nodded, then shook her head. "I'm not used to great things happening to me," she admitted.

"Aw, Mom." Tae reached over the console and hugged her tight, rocking her a little, the way April always did to Tae when she was trying to console. It made her eyes sting. Her baby, her precious girl, was comforting her, as always stepping up to be the adult. So she took a deep breath, squeezed Tae back, and kissed her cheek. "Thank you. I'm okay now."

Tae raised a brow.

"Okay, so my bones are trembling and I feel like I swallowed a bunch of butterflies, but it's the good kind of butterflies."

Tae nodded in approval, making April even more determined to buck up.

"It's the excitement," Tae said. "The reality of a dream coming true."

The words sank in and heated her up from the inside out. Not like a hot flash, thankfully, but more like a warm glow. "You're right," she murmured, marveling at the truth of that. "And hey . . ." She looked at Tae. "What would be your dream come true?"

Tae looked surprised at the question, which made April's gut hurt. She hadn't asked this question enough, which meant she still had a long way to go on the Being a Better Mom train.

"Honestly, I don't know," Tae said slowly. "Maybe to have enough money socked away that I don't have to worry about the future."

April felt her eyes sting again, but not in joy this time. She hated that Tae had always taken on that burden for the both of them. "It isn't about money."

"Since when?" Tae asked. "It's always about money. I want to have enough so that Future Tae and April are all set up."

Worried, deeply worried that she'd created this fear in Tae of not having enough, she shook her head. "Honey, it's not sup-posed to be like that."

"Well, not for tonight anyway," Tae agreed. "But, Mom, you more than anyone know that life's not all rainbows and kittens."

April thought about all those warm, wonderful Hallmark movies she loved to inhale. "Maybe it's about love."

Tae laughed at that, and even April had to smile. "Okay, okay," she said. "So neither of us have had much luck in the love department, but love could still happen for us, for both of us."

"Or it could be walking out the door for D.C. soon," Tae said, and April felt her heart ache. She opened her mouth, but Tae immediately shook her head, holding up a hand. "Disregard that, please. Tonight's about you and your incredible success. You deserve it, so let's get out there and enjoy it."

And then she got out of the car, leaving April to do the same or get left behind.

They stepped inside the gallery together. People were mill-ing around, holding wineglasses and taking in the pictures. The dark wood floors and light-colored walls showed off the art

JILL SHALVIS

beautifully. Everywhere April looked was a photo that stole her breath.

"Mom." Tae grabbed her hand and pulled her into the next room and then pointed.

April's ten pictures of local landscapes, matted and framed and hanging on the wall.

"They're beautiful," Tae whispered. "Oh my God, Mom, look at them. That's *you*, that's *your* work hanging on the walls. And look, this one you took up at Eagle Bluffs has a sold sticker on it!"

April covered her mouth with her hand so she didn't scream in excitement.

"Hey, babe," a guy off to her right was saying to the girl with him. "Check this out, these pics are from that chick in my photography class I told you about, the old lady who showed everyone a shot of her grocery cart filled with her MiraLAX."

"Oh my God, it wasn't *filled* with MiraLAX," she whispered to Tae, who was trying not to bust a gut laughing.

"Wow," the guy's date said. "Well, the old chick can certainly take a photo."

"Probably because she had like a million years of experience."

April felt her ears flame. Tae was now laughing so hard that no sound was coming out, and she had to bend over and put her hands on her knees.

April glared at her. "Hey, you use that MiraLAX sometimes too."

"*One* time, and I was on pain meds from breaking my wrist *eight* years ago." Tae straightened and swiped away her tears of mirth, but she was still smiling. "Mom, you're famous."

Infamous, maybe . . . She needed wine.

But just then a gallery employee came over and put a SOLD sticker on the picture in front of them, and it was better than any wine she'd ever had.

OVER THE NEXT week, Tae and Jenny worked almost around the clock. She didn't have time to continue the search for her dad, or so she told herself. But the truth was, she was scared. Scared she'd dig up something she didn't want to know.

Maybe she just needed to give herself permission to let go of all the what-ifs and the disappointments of the past and focus on appreciating what she had in the here and now. Because the here and now was pretty great. Besides, even if she found her dad, he'd probably not be so thrilled, and she didn't think she could take that either.

The good news was that ever since the gallery showing, her mom seemed to be on top of the world. She'd sold six of the ten photographs so far, and Tae had never seen her so happy before—especially for something that didn't involve a man.

Tae was uncharacteristically happy too. But she suspected a whole bunch of that came from her nightly visits from Riggs. With her crazy work schedule, and the hours he'd been putting in at Adrenaline HQ, those visits came late.

The long hours they spent in her bed lit by moonlight, doing things to each other by the soundtrack of the Tahoe forest as he held her like maybe she was the very best thing that had ever happened to him, his green eyes telling her what his mouth never would, she felt like nothing could go wrong. She and her mom both doing well at the same time felt like a turning point in their lives.

A positive one.

So she'd told herself, no more worrying. Not about Riggs, and not about her dad either. If she learned more, then great, but she was fine if she didn't.

But in the deep recesses of her mind where denial lived, she knew she was just kidding herself. About . . . well, everything. Her house of cards would come down in a storm. And there *would* be a storm. There always was.

On the morning of day one of their midsummer Lake Days event, Tae picked up Jordy and Sarah, who were so excited to help set up. When everything was ready, she helped register all the incoming guests, then moved from one station to the next, checking, assisting where it was needed.

At the shoreline, the first thing she saw was Riggs standing on the swim deck of the boat anchored at the beach, coiling rope, wearing only board shorts, and Jordy's little sister Sarah hanging off his broad back, her arms wrapped tight around his neck.

One would think Tae'd be used to the effect he had on her by now, but note to self: she was not.

As if he felt her presence across the sand he looked up, those sharp green eyes unerringly landing on her. And then he smiled the smile of a man who'd been in her bed only an hour ago.

"Tae."

She turned at the unexpected male voice just behind her and came face-to-face with Hunter. He was wearing a volunteer name tag, as was the pretty, petite brunette at his side. Her tag said EMILY, and Hunter smiled sweetly at her. "Em, this is Tae Holmes. Tae, Emily."

After the introductions, Hunter turned to Emily, squeezing her hand. "I'll catch up with you at the games station?"

"Of course," she murmured before kissing him on the cheek and walking off.

"New girlfriend?" Tae asked as he watched Emily go.

"An old friend." He smiled. "Turned something more now. I think."

"I'm happy for you."

His smile widened. "Thanks. You look great. You're . . . glowing with happiness. I don't think it's any secret why." He glanced over her shoulder, presumably to Riggs.

"Oh, we're not . . . what you might think."

Hunter nodded, but his smile faded, like maybe he felt sorry for her. "Tae—"

"No, it's all good," she said quickly. "And so nice to see you." And then she moved off toward the lunch tent, definitely needing a cookie. Possibly a box of cookies.

Delicious Deli, a mom-and-pop deli on the Lake Walk, was sponsoring lunch today. The owners, Suzie and Eddie, had a daughter with cerebral palsy and were frequent guests at Adrenaline HQ.

Suzie was putting out snacks, including cookies.

"Bless you." Tae grabbed one, then on second thought took a second. "It's a two-cookies sort of day," she said, catching Suzie's smile.

"Hey, no judgment here. I ate my weight in cookie dough just making those."

Tae laughed and moved to the games station, where she played cornhole with Jordy and lost. Twice.

"Where's your dude?" Jordy asked.

"Who?"

"Riggs."

"Oh . . . he's not . . . we're not . . ." She broke off, realizing she kept saying that to people and she was tired of being on defense. Especially since her gaze landed right on Riggs where he stood on the boat, looking far hotter than a man had any right to look. But that wasn't what made her feel soft and mushy. It was the care with which he was helping load one of the wounded warriors onto the boat, carrying the guy in his arms, saying something that had them both laughing. Letting out a breath, she turned back to Jordy.

Who was already playing his next game.

She had to laugh at herself. She was such a sap. When had that happened? She supposed her mom could be right, and that she'd made a stupid decision letting Riggs in. It certainly wasn't the safe decision, but if life had taught her anything, it was that she'd rather go with her gut than have regrets.

And besides, she'd never been interested in safe choices. Back in that convenience store all those weeks ago now, rather than doing the safe thing and leaving the store at the first sign of danger, she'd stayed to make sure Jordy didn't get shot over a granola bar. And she'd do it again. Just like this thing with Riggs. If she hadn't spent time with him, she'd always wonder what if.

No more regrets.

The day flew by, and by late afternoon, things were winding down. She took another peek across the beach. Riggs's eyes were locked on her as he anchored the boat. He never gave much away. He liked the world to think he wasn't ruled by anything so volatile and unpredictable as emotions, that maybe he didn't even have emotions to begin with because that would make him vulnerable. And being vulnerable was not on his to-do list.

But by now she'd seen him bare all, physically *and* metaphorically, and she knew better. You just had to know what you were looking for. The slightest quirk of his mouth or movement in his gaze were his tell if you could read him.

And she could. She was pretty sure what she was reading right now was genuine affection, but also something more. He wasn't smiling or anything, just projecting a general air of easygoing charisma, and damn . . . it looked really, really good on him. And that's when she realized. He seemed different because he was . . . happy too.

So she crossed the grass toward the beach, aware of Jake and Carolyn at the kayaks watching her, and her mom over at the registration table, also watching. Tae wasn't a public person, at all, but as Riggs jumped from the boat to the sand, straightening, eyes on hers, she headed right for him. "You know how you said the details about us were up to me?" she asked when they were face-to-face.

He gave a single nod.

"And how I said that maybe we didn't need to define the details?"

Another nod.

"Well, I figured something out. There's only one detail. And that is that I was wrong before. I *don't* want to hide this, whatever this is. You okay with that?"

Something changed in his eyes. She thought maybe it was affection with more than a dab of relief mixed in. "Yeah, I'm okay with that."

So simple that she wondered why she'd ever fought it. She took the last step and walked right into his arms. As they closed around her, she went up on tiptoes, slid her hands into his hair, and tugged his face to hers so she could kiss him.

He was warm, and still wet, and her clothes got soaked, making her laugh when she pulled away.

Riggs was much slower to pull his hands back.

"Thanks," she murmured. "I get tired of hiding myself."

He never took his gaze off her. "Even when you do your best to hide, I always see you, Tae. Always will."

Warmed by the look in his eyes, which had nothing to do with physical intent, she smiled. "So what do you see now?"

"A woman who makes me want things I've never wanted before."

CHAPTER 23

April stood at the lake's edge, enjoying dipping her feet into the cool water under a warm sun. It still boggled her that she was lucky enough to be here in front of the extraordinary, pristine beauty of the highest alpine lake on the North American continent. She took a deep breath and just took it in.

The day had been long but amazing. Right now they were between the day and evening events. The barbecue and auction would start soon. Her heart felt full in the very best of ways, and her cheeks hurt from smiling so much.

So when she caught sight of Tae walking across the grass with purpose, and then right into Riggs's arms, it took her by surprise. So did the longing and desire practically crackling in the air around the two of them, so personal and intimate she had to turn away, running blindly into someone.

"Hey," Ace said, then cocked his head. "You okay?"

She managed a smile. "Always."

He craned his neck to see what she'd been looking at and then met her gaze. "You might want to work on your lying skills."

She gave a little laugh. "Definitely not my forte."

He shrugged. "Not being able to lie is much preferred to the opposite."

"You think?"

"I know," he said. "Not being able to lie is . . . attractive."

She paused. "Are you flirting with me to take my mind off Tae and Riggs?"

"No. I mean, yes, I'm flirting with you. But not because of Tae or Riggs."

She took a deeper look at him. His light brown hair was long. Wavy. Messily finger-combed at best. He wore an unbuttoned short-sleeved shirt over a T-shirt advertising some dive bar in the Turks and Caicos, and the loudest, most obnoxiously bright-colored cargo shorts she'd ever seen. He was leanly muscled, emphasis on lean. He had a long scar down the right side of his hairline almost to his jaw, and his right arm was a prosthetic. All of that created an aura that said he was badass to the core and not to be messed with. But confusingly, layered over that was a charisma that drew her in like a moth to a flame.

He smiled, and she felt a reaction low in her belly. It made no sense. Rough and tumble and tough to the bone wasn't her type. Not to mention she wasn't on the man train right now. And yet there was something about Ace she couldn't ignore. Maybe it was his nonchalant air of *whatever happens, happens*. He was in no rush, for anything, and it was damn appealing.

"You really don't have to worry about Tae," he said. "At least not with Riggs. He won't hurt her. Ever."

She drew a deep breath and let it out. "I'm pretty good at obsessing about Tae's life rather than worry about my own life. She hates it, of course, but I was a terrible example for her."

"Everyone makes mistakes."

"But I made so many. So, so many. I pick out lemons. That's my big talent. For all I know you're a lemon—I can never tell until you pick your jeans up off my bedroom floor and walk out of my life. So I really want to tell Tae what to do and what not to do, but . . ."

"But you're trying not to obsess."

She gave him a wry smile, no longer surprised that he just seemed to get her. "Yes."

"And it sucks."

Yes." She looked him over. "You seem to know a whole bunch about having a kid."

"I do." He looked out at the lake. "I was married once for about fifteen minutes, a zillion years ago. I've got a nine-year-old son I don't get to see often enough because his mom moved to England for her new husband. And when I do see him, I spend way too much time overcompensating for that. My ex tells me to just be there for him, to not try and have teachable moments, that he'll make his own mistakes." He shook his head. "The hardest part is knowing she's right."

April's laugh was wry. "I bet you're a good dad."

His eyes met hers. "I try."

Her throat got a little tight, because she'd often wondered what kind of a dad might Tae's have ended up being if he'd turned his life around in the military . . . She'd been too scared to find out, and now all she could think was . . . what if she'd been wrong about him? "That's all anyone can ask," she said softly as her phone buzzed. "Excuse me a second." She pulled it out just to make sure Jake or Tae didn't need her and was startled to see a text from Professor Stone.

April, great news. The Tahoe Tourism Alliance—the company that creates the local tourism magazines—is seeking someone to produce photos of local favorite spots for their fall edition. They've picked you. They pay per photo. If they like what you give them, there's also a shot at an in-house position. Attached is how to connect with your liaison. Best of luck and congratulations, the competition was fierce. Be proud. Professor Stone.

April gasped out loud.

"What?" Ace moved closer, his eyes narrowing as he looked around them, as if searching out any possible danger.

"Oh my God." She put her hands on Ace's arms and beamed up at him. "They like me! They really like me!"

He studied her face, and his own softened. "Well, who wouldn't?"

"You'd be surprised," she murmured, aware that she'd shifted closer to him and that she was still holding on to his arms, one warm skin and hard sinew, the other cool, hard prosthetic. When she backed up a step, a look crossed his face. Pain? Embarrassment? Realizing he thought she was backing away from him because she'd touched his prosthetic, she once again closed the distance between them and put her hands back on his arms.

"I just startled myself because I haven't touched a man in a while," she said softly. "Can I keep my hands on your arms for a second? I'm wobbly with adrenaline."

He stepped closer in silent acquiescence. "What happened?"

"I might've just gotten a dream job."

"Your photography?"

"Yes!" She blinked. "Wait— How do you know?"

He smiled. "I saw your showing downtown. You're amazing. My favorite was the shot you did of Eagle Bluffs. I wanted to buy it, but it was already sold."

"I'll make you another."

It was fascinating how those silver eyes of his could warm. "Darlin', you're not supposed to give away the goods. You need to be celebrating."

She laughed. "I wouldn't even know how."

"I do. It's a full moon tonight. After the barbecue and auction, let me take you up to Eagle Bluffs. We can take a mental picture, with us in the shot this time."

"It took me an hour and a half to hike up there."

"Then we'll need to backpack in food for a midnight picnic to keep up our strength."

She laughed. How long had it been since she'd done something like that? Or maybe the real question was, how long had it been since she'd felt this kind of a spark, one that came from conversation and common ground, not from just a need to scratch an itch? Too long. "But . . ."

"What?"

"Maybe you're a lemon."

He nodded. "Maybe. But maybe you're smarter than you give yourself credit for. Maybe you could go slow and see what happens."

"Slow," she repeated. "That would be new . . ."

He smiled but didn't try to influence her decision one way or the other.

It was maybe the nicest thing a man had ever done for her. Her phone buzzed again, this time with a text from Tae, requesting assistance. She looked up and discovered Tae was no longer standing on the beach in Riggs's arms.

"You gotta go," Ace guessed.

"I do. Tae needs my help."

He nodded.

"Ace."

He met her gaze, his own carefully blank.

"I'll meet you after the event," she said softly.

He looked down at her hand, now holding on to his, then back up at her face.

She smiled. "Don't stand me up."

He laughed softly as she walked away. She headed across the grass toward Tae.

"Hey," her daughter said the minute April got within hearing range. "So I don't want to hear about—"

"Riggs is your own business." And April was going to try very hard to actually believe that.

"Oh." Tae blinked. "Um, thank you?"

April stared at her, and then let out a breath. "Okay, so you didn't call me over here to talk about kissing Riggs in front of God and everyone."

"Uh . . . no. I was really hoping to skip that convo. I was going to say I screwed up and I need a few more badges for some guests who are coming just for the auction and was hoping you had extra."

"Oh. Well, of course. I've got everything I need in my car. Come with?"

Tae held back and looked at her.

"Don't worry. Still not going to bug you about Riggs."

Tae got into gear and followed April to the lot. "Did you just . . . skip?"

"Yes." April laughed. She couldn't slow down. She felt so excited.

"Mom, what's up? You're practically running, which you won't even do to catch the ice cream truck."

April stopped at her car and turned to Tae, unable to keep the smile in. "I've maybe got another job lined up."

"Mom." Tae's face fell. "You no longer have to work multiple jobs. We're both keeping our heads above water these days. If you're short on money, I've got a small savings going, and—"

"No, this isn't a full-time job, it's a photography job!"

Tae gasped, knowing exactly what this would mean. "Tell me everything."

"My professor got me a gig with the Tahoe Tourism Alliance to take pics of some local hot spots. It could turn into a permanent, in-house position. They pay per picture, but we both know I'd do it for free because . . . *they like me! They really like me!*"

"But . . . you're *not* going to do it for free, right?"

April laughed out loud. "*Nope!*"

They grabbed each other and screamed and jumped up and down. Then got a hold of themselves when a family hustled away from them.

"This is just the beginning for you, Mom," Tae said, her eyes shiny with emotion. "I'm so proud of you."

April cupped her girl's face. "Thanks for believing in me."

"*Always.*"

With that single word spreading warmth and joy in her heart, April got the extra passes and walked back into the park with Tae. She was doing what she loved, she and Tae were in the best place of their lives, and she had just made a new friend who felt like an old friend . . . which was the very best kind.

She was on cloud nine and planned to stay there forever.

MANNING THE BARBECUE, Riggs took a moment to look around and soak up the day. It'd gone amazingly well, and he felt something stir in his chest for what they'd accomplished. Adrenaline HQ was doing something amazing here, giving back to people who could only dream about having days like this. He felt exhilarated, and something else too. Like he was a part of something that fulfilled him in a way he couldn't remember ever feeling.

His gaze settled on Tae, who'd worked her ass off all day, doing whatever had been needed, and was still working. One of her helpers said something that made her laugh, and she hugged them. Then someone tapped her on the shoulder.

Jordy.

Tae turned and hugged him, making him laugh a little, like maybe his sense of humor was rusty.

His little sister came out from behind him, smiling up at Tae shyly, and she hugged her too, whispering something in Sarah's ear that made her giggle.

Then Tae grabbed two hot dogs from the platter Riggs had just brought to the picnic tables, offering them to the kids. Both were snatched with a quick smile and inhaled in a blink.

Riggs heard Tae laugh again, and it warmed him in a way nothing else ever had. At some point between high school and now, she'd learned what he hadn't—to open up, to share herself, her *true* self. It was humbling as hell. He looked around, really looked, taking in the lake shimmering so stunningly blue it almost hurt, dotted with whitecaps and lit up from the sun slowly making its way down for the evening. He took a deep breath of air filled with pine and the unique scent of Lake Tahoe and realized something else surprising.

Being back here for a summer, for the first time since going into the military, he'd been prepared to hate it.

But he didn't.

In fact, without the weight of his shitty growing-up years, and his dad fucking things up, it kinda felt like home. His bright spot. Which was a sensation he hadn't had . . . ever. But it was true. All the best parts of home were here, the worst parts having moved on.

He wondered what would happen if he didn't leave. Because maybe he had something of value to add here. To Jake's life. To Tae's.

To his own.

Maybe his value didn't have to come from work as he'd always believed.

Jake came up beside him and handed him a beer.

Riggs took it, then held it out. Jake knocked his bottle to it in a silent toast. They drank, and Riggs's gaze drifted back to Tae.

"You haven't slept in your own bed for the past week," Jake said quietly, no rancor.

Technically Riggs hadn't been sleeping much in Tae's bed either. They'd done a lot of things, but sleep hadn't been one of them.

"Seems like it's the real deal with her."

Riggs looked over in surprise. "Does that mean we're done fighting?"

"I'd like to be." Jake studied the water. "Carolyn wanted me to tell you that she hopes you know you could stay if you wanted."

"I'm *already* staying with you."

"I meant if you decided not to ditch us for D.C."

Riggs looked at him. "I'm not ditching you. It's for a job, a good one."

Jake turned his head and met his gaze. "Are you going to tell me you haven't considered it?"

"Considered what, giving up my dream career?" he asked, as if he hadn't just been thinking that very thing.

"Yes," Jake said. "Stick around instead and take on the *real* dream career, side by side with me as a family. A real one."

The look of yearning in his brother's gaze made his chest tight. "And what would that really look like? Because you don't need my help running this thing, you're doing just fine on your own."

"Just because I don't *need* help doesn't mean I don't want it," Jake said. "Besides, *you're* the one who needs help."

Riggs rolled his eyes, partly to cover the unexpected emotion clogging his throat from hearing Jake say he wanted him to stay.

Never in a million years had he ever thought Jake would ask.

Or that Riggs would want to do just that—stay. "I made a verbal commitment to the D.C. job. I was pulled for it out of more than five thousand worthy candidates. I can't just walk away from it."

"Can't? Or won't?"

Riggs let out a long breath. "Both, I suppose. But it doesn't mean I don't think about it."

Jake nodded. "I suppose that's all I can ask. But only an idiot would turn this life down for the intense, life-consuming job you'll be taking instead."

Riggs opened his mouth, but Carolyn beat him to the punch. Coming up behind them, she wrapped her arms around Jake's neck, pressing a kiss to his jaw. "I'm sure you were about to say something super supportive about your brother's choices. Yeah?"

No fool, Jake nodded. "Absolutely."

Riggs snickered, and she leveled him with the same look. "And you were going to say something sweet and kind back to your brother, right?"

"Yes, ma'am."

Carolyn smiled and kissed Riggs too. "Look at us. Getting along."

"Babe, you get along with everyone," Jake said.

"Duh. I was talking about the two of you. Let me sweeten the pot. Continue to be good and get along and I'll make more of that sourdough bread you inhale the minute it comes out of the oven."

"A bribe?" Jake asked, sounding amused. "Of bread?"

"Well, for you, the prize would be more rewarding."

Jake laughed the laugh of a man in love. It looked good on him.

Tae was waving at them. "Need help getting the auction started," she called out.

It was all hands on deck as they switched gears from barbecue to auction. Riggs had been to several car auctions in his day. All extremely serious.

But this was no ordinary auction. Organized and run by Tae, it went fast, ran smoothly, and was full of laughter and good times.

She'd hired her neighbor Hagrid as the auctioneer, and the badass biker had come dressed in his leathers and holding a gavel, which he slammed down every time someone won an item. He talked superfast, like a professional auctioneer would, in that singsong chant that had people jumping up and down as they bid, the mood loud and jovial.

Items like buckets of wine, golf passes, ski passes, and Tahoe hotel stays went like hotcakes. When Hagrid paused, looking over his list for the next auction item, and then chuckled in his low bass, Riggs knew.

He was up.

"Folks, you don't want to miss this one. Adrenaline HQ's own Riggs Copeland is auctioning himself off for an evening of fun, including but not limited to dinner . . ." Hagrid waggled his eyebrows suggestively. Everyone laughed.

Riggs wondered how the hell he'd gotten talked into this.

"Opening bid is fifty bucks," Hagrid said, and at least twenty people jumped to their feet and started waving their bidding paddle.

Hagrid grinned and said, "Wouldn't mind bidding myself if it wasn't against the rules," and then began his singsong chant of managing the bids. It was fast and furious, and Riggs looked at the lake instead of watching the process.

Jake, sitting next to him, was laughing his fool ass off as he bid.

"Two hundred!" his stupid brother yelled.

"What the hell are you doing?" Riggs hissed.

"Bidding on you for Carolyn. She wants to go out to that new froufrou restaurant in south shore, and you know I hate froufrou. I figure if I win you, you can take her."

Riggs had slunk down in his seat, but he choked when he heard a female voice yell, "Five hundred dollars."

He knew that voice. Stunned, he sat up and whipped his head around to find, yep, Tae standing in the back, waving her auction paddle.

"*Sold*," Hagrid yelled. "For five hundred dollars! Honey, make sure you get your money's worth out of him!"

"Don't worry, I will!" And then she winked at Riggs. *Winked.*

The auction continued on, as if his heart hadn't stopped. But the rest was a blur for him. Afterward, everyone headed out for the night. They'd all come back in the morning for day two, but for now, they all scattered. Many of their guests were in nearby hotels or rented homes, others camped—whatever their pleasure.

Riggs's pleasure was tied up in the woman who was walking toward him, looking like a woman on a mission. A woman who knew what she wanted and wasn't afraid to go after it.

The epiphany hit him in the face. Forever now, his future, and where that future would take place, felt . . . murky. But his future wasn't a place at all.

It was a person.

Tae.

She smiled up at him, looking . . . well, exhausted. But happy and beautiful, and a whole lot like everything he'd ever wanted. "You've got to be done in," he murmured, pulling her into his side. "Want me to take you home?"

"Take me? Yes. But not home."

He looked into her smiling eyes. "You have a plan."

"Oh, I've got quite the plan, don't you worry. Come with?"

He'd follow her anywhere. Right off a cliff to his certain death. Which might be easier to do than admit that his heart 100 percent belonged to her. She was letting him in, and it was the most amazing gift he'd ever received, even as he knew he didn't deserve it.

"Follow me," she said.

"Uh-oh." He smiled. "Am I in trouble?"

Her return smile said yes, he was most definitely in trouble, the very best kind of trouble there was. So he followed her to . . .

His truck?

In the back was a sleeping bag, a blanket, a tarp, an ice chest, a few grocery bags, and a duffel bag. "What's this?" he asked.

"I'm kidnapping you. But I sort of need your truck to do it."

Amused, he pulled his keys from his pocket. "You want me to drive to my own kidnapping?"

"I mean *I* could drive, but you remember that old Chevy I used to drive in high school? I took out our mailbox."

"That's not so bad."

"Three times."

He laughed. "Okay, so I'm definitely driving." He got behind the wheel and looked at her. "Where to?"

"North."

He slid her a glance. "Hidden Falls?"

"Do you need to call and check in with Jake?" she asked instead of answering. "Cuz you're not going to be home by curfew."

"Naughty," he said. "I like it. And no, I don't need to call Jake. What about your mom?"

"She went off with that marine friend of yours."

"Ace?" he asked in surprise.

"Yeah." She looked at him. "Is that a problem? He's an okay guy, right?"

"He's a great guy. But he's not on the people train right now."

"Well, apparently he bought a one-way ticket to April-ville for the night. And I definitely don't want to talk about my mom right now."

He stole another look at her, curious. "What do you want to talk about?"

She unzipped her sweatshirt to reveal an athletic-type tank top with thin crisscrossed straps over her chest and back, leaving a lot of smooth, bare skin.

Only two of his wheels hit the dirt meridian. He was proud of that. "Jesus, Tae."

"Turn right."

He turned right. The road wound along for about five miles until it turned into a dirt fire road.

"Right at the second fire road," she murmured.

He slid her a glance, catching her staring at him by the ambient light from the dashboard. There were no other lights anywhere. He didn't need any because he knew exactly where they were going.

Back to the spot where they'd gone their first night together, all those years ago now.

CHAPTER 24

Tae's heart pounded as Riggs parked off the trail between two huge house-size rocks to keep them out of view on the very off chance anyone else made it up to this spot tonight. In front of them was the dark, cloudy night, obscuring the stars and moon, though she could still see the faint outline of the lake far below.

"Not quite the same view," Riggs said quietly at her side. "It was clear that night, and I'd never seen so many stars in one place."

"It's definitely way darker tonight. I almost can't see my own hand in front of my face."

She heard him shift to face her, sliding an arm along the back of the bench seat. His warm fingers brushed the nape of her neck, making her shiver in the best of ways.

"Your move, Rebel," he said softly, his voice husky. Affectionate. "Are we here to talk?"

No. She didn't want to talk. She didn't want anything to burst her bubble. "I wanted to make a new memory up here, as adults."

He smiled. "I'm incredibly grateful you walked back into my life."

As far as admissions went, it felt like a doozy, one that left her a little overwhelmed. "I didn't walk back into your life."

"No you didn't," he said on a laugh. "You slid into my car and demanded I hit the gas. And I've loved every single minute since."

She felt . . . stunned.

"Tae."

She looked at him.

He smiled. "You've got a way of leaving me out here hanging, with no idea where I stand."

"You know where you stand," she said softly. "With one foot here in Sunrise Cove, and the other in D.C."

His fingers ran along her jaw. "That was something we both knew going in. But we're friends now. The keeper sort of friends. We don't have to lose that."

She nodded but looked away so he couldn't see how pathetically deep she'd fallen, right past friends and into love. But she'd known going in what would happen. He'd never lied to her. Never.

"Talk to me, Tae."

She drew a deep breath, then leaned into him, settling her hands on his chest. "I'm not sure I can keep my heart out of this." Her smile was wry. "Whatever *this* is. I thought I could, but now . . ." She shook her head.

"Do you want to stop? Let each other go before it gets any deeper?"

No. She wanted to hear him say it'd gotten deep for him too, but he was always *very* careful not to lead her on. And the hard truth was, she didn't think it could get any deeper for her. Losing him now versus later wasn't going to solve anything.

His finger gently lifted her chin. "Tae?"

Tears welled, but she smiled through them. "No, I don't want to quit you. Not yet, anyway. I like being with you like this."

That got her a full two-hundred-watt smile. "Yeah?"

"I think you know just how much."

She shivered, the good kind, and he tightened his arms, pressing a kiss to her temple. "I was going to say remind me, but . . . not here. As much as I'd like to stay, it's too cold for an overnight."

He was right. The temps had dropped to below freezing, which wasn't all that unusual at this altitude, even in the summer. But still disappointing.

He was running a hand up and down her back, soothing her aching muscles, making her body all tingly, and she nearly purred, curling into him. "I mean . . . how dangerous is hypothermia anyway?"

He laughed. "Jake promised Carolyn they could camp out at Sugar Pine Point tonight. Which means you could come home with me for a change."

She lifted her head and stared into his eyes. Maybe his voice had been easygoing, but what she saw in his gaze said that he felt anything but. It hadn't been just a polite offer. He really wanted her to spend the night with him. "I'd like that. Are you going to do me on your childhood bed? Do you have any embarrassing posters up? Porn stashed under the mattress?"

"Yes. No. And no . . ." With a smile, he kissed her, and they very nearly never made it home at all, but neither of them had a condom.

Half an hour later, they were in Riggs's driveway. The cabin was dark when he unlocked the front door. Grub was camping with Jake and Carolyn. He led Tae to his bedroom. They quickly stripped each other by the moonlight slanting in the window and ducked under the covers, when Tae wrapped her arms around him tight.

"You're still cold," he said with a frown, and slid his hands down her body as he snuggled her closer to him.

She practically purred as she wriggled all her good spots against all his good spots, smiling up at him with erotic promise. "I'm maybe getting a little warmer."

He rolled them and pinned her to the mattress. "And now?"

"Hmm. Maybe. Keep working at it."

With a laugh, he lowered his head and did just that.

At some point, much later, Riggs opened his eyes just in time to catch an edible ass leaving his bed. "Tae?"

"Oh!" she murmured, like he'd startled her. "Um . . ."

He glanced out the window. Still pitch-black outside. "Thought you were spending the night, which implies staying until morning time."

"Four a.m. *is* morning."

"Cheater."

She stopped in the act of pulling on her clothes and studied him, her expression softening. "Sleeping with you is one thing.

Doing boyfriend/girlfriend stuff—like waking up together—is another thing entirely. I'm just trying to put up boundaries so I don't forget that you're leaving."

"Okay . . ." He sat up. "But what would happen if I wasn't?"

The quiet words he couldn't believe he let escape seemed to echo between them in the predawn air.

"Are you . . . thinking about staying?" she whispered, as if afraid of his answer.

"Truth?"

She nodded, and he reached out a hand for hers, pulling her back into his arms, pressing his face into her hair, closing his eyes. "When we're like this, I can't imagine going anywhere."

WHEN MORNING ARRIVED, the real morning, complete with daylight, Riggs very reluctantly disentangled himself from a still-sleeping Tae and padded into the kitchen for caffeine. He made a pot of coffee and was just pouring some into a mug when he heard her come padding into the room behind him.

"Wow," she murmured. "Pouring hot coffee while buck-ass naked. Brave man."

He turned to find her already dressed. Disappointing. He handed her the mug.

"Not to rush you," she said. "Because believe me, the view from over here is top shelf, but I gotta get to the lake for setup."

He got them out the door in thirty. It would've been ten, but they decided to shower together to save time, and then once in it decided also on a quickie, which turned into *not* a quickie . . .

When he pulled in the parking lot at the lake, Tae went to hop out of his truck, but he grabbed her hand. "Hey."

She smiled. "Hey. I really gotta go—"

"Last night was real for me."

Her eyes went wide. "What?"

"Very real."

"Oh." She breathed softly, looking touched and . . . happy. She opened her mouth and he hoped to hear "me too."

"Thank you," she said.

He took a beat. *Thank you?* Really? "And . . . ?"

"And . . ." She gave a dreamy sigh. "It was real for me too." She pointed at him. "So don't screw it up."

The ball of nerves dissipated, and he laughed with relief and a whole bunch of other emotions he didn't want to name right now. "I won't."

An hour later people began to arrive. Riggs was at the shoreline, prepping the boat, when Carolyn came over, looking for him. "A guy just showed up, asking to talk to you."

Riggs turned and caught sight of a man standing under a tree on the grass off to the side. He had a ball cap on and dark sunglasses, but to his utter disbelief, he realized it was Andy Jameson.

What the hell?

Riggs quickly scanned the area for Tae, who was setting up the giant chess game, her back to him. With a grimness in his gut, he headed over to Andy. "What are you doing here?"

Andy held up his hands. "Listen, some of my friends work with your brother, and I asked to come along. I didn't know for sure Tae would be here. When I saw you, I figured I should let you know . . ." He took a breath. "I can leave. I mean, unless you think it'd be okay . . . ?"

Shit. He looked again to make sure Tae was still busy. She was, but that could change in a second. "You should've turned around and left the second you saw she was here," he said flatly. "You're fairly unrecognizable, but she's got an eagle eye."

"I know. I know." Andy removed his ball cap, ran his fingers through his hair, then replaced the hat. "I was selfish to come."

"Incredibly."

"I just . . ." Andy shook his head. "I just wanted to catch a glimpse of her."

"Well you've done that, so—"

A warm, female arm slipped around Riggs. *Tae.* He'd know the feel of her, the scent of her, anywhere. She set her head on his shoulder and smiled up at him. "Hey."

His heart stopped.

And Tae laughed. "This is where you say, 'Hey, Tae, this is my friend so-and-so.'"

Andy stuck out his hand. He looked as gobsmacked as a man could look, but he smiled and gently said, "Hi, Tae."

"Hello." Tae's smile was warm and generous, and Riggs still couldn't move, couldn't draw a breath. Because he'd done this. He'd opened the can of worms and was about to pay the piper for his stupidity. When she figured out who she was talking to, she'd probably never want to see him again, and he'd deserve it.

So it was one hell of a time to realize that not only had he fallen for her hard and irrevocably, but he was *deeply* in love with her.

"Are you here with one of your kids, or the wounded warrior program?" Tae asked Andy.

"Actually, I'm here to check on my daughter," he said.

That statement released Riggs from his mental paralysis, and he sent the guy an I'm-going-to-rip-your-throat-out glare.

Andy didn't so much as look at him.

Which meant he had only one move left. Plan B: *come clean.* "Tae, I need to talk to you. Privately."

Before Tae could respond, April joined their group, smiling at her daughter. "Honey, Jake needs you—" She broke off with a small exhalation of breath, like it'd been knocked out of her lungs against her will. She paused, staring at Andy like she'd been poleaxed, the blood draining from her face.

And right then and there, Riggs knew Andy's story was true. April had indeed asked him to go away, and if Riggs thought Tae was going to be crushed before, he knew now, with Andy standing right here, it would all be so much worse.

"Tae," he said urgently. "We really need to talk. Now."

She nodded but was looking worriedly at April. "Mom? You okay?"

"Uh . . ." April blinked. Forced a smile. "Of course I am," she said in a high, unnatural voice. "But Jake needs your help right now, so maybe Riggs could wait a minute."

Tae glanced at Riggs. He did his best to smile and nod reassuringly, when what he wanted to do was throw up.

"Okay, Mom," Tae finally said. "I'll be right back."

When Tae was far enough away, April, still staring at Andy, grabbed onto Riggs's arm like she couldn't stay upright on her own.

"This is messed up," he said quietly but still supporting her. "You two need to get your shit together in the space of the single minute it's going to take Tae to get back, or worse, recognize Andy. Because no matter what happens next, *she's* going to be the one who gets crushed."

April just kept staring at Andy.

Andy wasn't speaking. Maybe wasn't even breathing.

"Hey." Riggs nudged him. "Did you hear me? Get it together, man." He looked at April. "You too."

She drew a shaky breath, but she nodded. "We . . . need a moment."

Riggs nodded and went to turn away, but she still had a grip on his arm, pulling him back around.

"*I'm* the one to tell her," she said fiercely. "Do you hear me?"

Riggs gave a head shake in the negative. "I never should've kept this from her in the first place. I won't continue to do so."

"No! You don't understand!" April's eyes filled. "If it doesn't come from me, she'll hate me."

"Not my problem."

Andy stirred. "Hey, man, watch your tone."

Riggs wanted to tell the guy to watch his fist plow into his face, but . . . he was right. He drew a deep breath and looked at April.

"Please," she entreated. "This is all my mess and I know it. I need to come clean, I know that too. I just don't want— I can't lose her, Riggs."

He nodded tightly, uncomfortable to realize that they all had the same goal. "Whatever you do, do it quickly or all bets are off. And when I say quickly, I mean right now, *here*. Because your daughter deserves so much more than this."

From all of them.

CHAPTER 25

April's existence had slowed to a complete stop. She could feel her heart beating in her ears and the blood pumping through her veins, but she couldn't move. Unfortunately, she was all too familiar with the sensation of her life teetering on a precipice, of what *real* fear was. Like when she'd given birth to Tae and the hospital staff had first laid her in her arms. Knowing it was just her and this wrinkly, grumpy infant staring up at her with huge, unwavering eyes, the two of them alone against the world. Or when she'd lost their one-room apartment. Okay, so that had happened more than once. Or those times when her meager paychecks hadn't spread far enough to keep them fed until the next.

So yeah . . . there'd been years where she'd been best friends with terror, panic, and anxiety. And right now, standing at the lake, staring at Tae's biological father, she was suddenly back to holding hands with those emotions all over again.

Don't lose Tae.

That was the only clear thought running through her head as

she looked at Andy. The catalyst. Without him, this wouldn't be happening.

And without him, you wouldn't have Tae at all . . .

"April," he said quietly.

"No." She shook her head. "We're not doing this."

"We have to do this," Riggs said.

And she knew he was right. She nodded, but pointed at Andy. "Back up. I need a minute, and you need to back the hell up."

Andy nodded and walked a short distance off. Maybe ten feet. Far enough for privacy, but she'd have preferred he leave entirely. But she knew he wouldn't. He was here because he wanted something, and it didn't take a genius to know what.

She felt Riggs's hand come up and cover her fingers, which were still digging into his forearms. His touch was warm and surprisingly kind, considering how much he must hate her right now.

"April."

She managed to look up at him.

His eyes gave nothing away, but the tension in his body suggested he was every bit as pissed off at her as she was at herself. "You know the last thing I want is for you to shatter Tae's world, or your relationship with her. But you're already threatening both by doing nothing."

"No. Andy threatened both by coming here. If he'd held up his end of the bargain, it'd have been fine."

"Really?" Riggs asked. "Because you've raised a woman who's independent to a fault, terrified to let anyone into her life, and even worse, doesn't trust anyone except you. *You*, April. You're it for her, and you've lied to her every single day of her entire life.

How's she supposed to feel about that, the one person she's allowed herself to trust has been lying to her all these years?"

April caught a quick glimpse of Andy closing his eyes at Riggs's words and covered her face. Dear God, how was this happening? "It wasn't supposed to come out." She shook her head and dropped her hands. "I thought this could stay buried." She was trying so hard to hold it together, but she was feeling sick to her stomach at the thought of Tae hating her.

"The past never stays buried," Riggs said flatly. "And she already knows something's up. If you can't, or won't, tell her, I will."

"I'll do it!" Panic made breathing all but a distant memory. She realized she was gripping one of his hands in hers, squeezing hard. His expression was every bit as hard as her grip, and she swallowed and made herself let go of him. "I just need the time to do this in the right way."

He shook his head. "Don't you get it yet? The only right way would've been to tell her years ago."

God, her heart hurt. "How do you know so much about all this?"

Something crossed his face. Guilt? Remorse? "It's Tae's story to tell," he finally said.

"What the hell does that mean?"

A muscle ticced in his jaw. "Once Tae had the name AJ Strickland, I went digging for her."

She blinked, the shock going through her. "Digging."

He nodded curtly, but she was boggled. "How in the world did she get the name AJ Strickland?"

"Her story to tell," he repeated.

She stared at him, waiting for him to say more, a *lot* more, but he said nothing. "Oh my God—do you conserve words on purpose?"

He grimaced, like maybe he'd been asked the question before. "Look," he said. "I'm not proud of my part in this, but once I found out where Andy was living, I went to talk to him, to make sure he was a good guy."

April stared at him and realized with a shock that not all of his anger was directed at her. It was for himself too. "And?"

"He's a good guy."

She nodded, then realized what she'd missed. "You kept the visit from Tae," she guessed.

Riggs shoved his fingers through his hair. "I shouldn't have." He let out a rough exhale. "Do you get how much this is going to hurt her? And trust me, I already feel like the biggest asshole on the planet for not telling her the minute I found Andy. The fact that I did it to keep her safe won't matter to her. The bottom line is that I kept your secret, which doesn't make me any better than you."

Tormented by that unhappy truth, she nodded. "I'm sorry. I'll tell her."

"I could do it," Andy offered from where he still stood, ten feet away from them. "I'm ready to face her with the truth."

April had no idea if Riggs was right, if Andy had really turned out to be a good man, but she couldn't let it go down like that. "*It has to be me*," she said, trying not to sound firm and forceful, not panicked.

"*Today*," Riggs said.

"I can't just spring it on her, not here. Give me twenty-four hours. *Please*," she said, and felt grateful when after a long pause, he gave a reluctant nod.

Oh, how she hated having her hand forced, but . . . *but*. Riggs being a hard-ass was exactly what she'd want the man in Tae's life to be, for him to stand up for her and look out for her best interest.

Which meant she'd judged him far too harshly and unfairly.

He didn't seem bothered or concerned by what she thought of him in the least. He stood there, just over six feet, muscles everywhere a woman wanted a man to have muscles. His hair was mostly brown, but highlighted by long days in the sun. It was messy, like he hadn't bothered with a comb. His eyes sparkled when he laughed. She'd seen it, though he was nowhere close to laughing now. But what really mattered was how surprisingly sweet and gentle she'd seen him be with Tae. Patient and kind. It was those things that made her admit to herself that she knew why her daughter was having a hard time steering clear of him, even if she didn't want to admit it.

Catching her staring at him, he went brows up. Alpha-speak for *what*?

"You don't have any way of knowing this," she said. "But I didn't think you were good enough for her."

His laugh was humorless. "Oh, I know." He looked around, clearly searching for Tae's location. She was with Jake and a few others, seemingly deep in conversation. Riggs shoved his hands into his pockets and gave April a chin up. "It's okay. Let me have it."

"Have what?"

"The inquisition. You know you want to."

God help her, she did. She really did. "I don't think I have a leg to stand on with that."

"*Ask*."

Fine, if he was giving her carte blanche, she'd take it. "This is not a question. Just a fact. Despite what it looks like and what you must think of me, I love Tae more than anything in the world. So if you hurt her, I will kill you."

He didn't laugh. He didn't smile. He nodded his head very solemnly. "Hurting her is the very last thing I want to do."

"Are you faithful?"

"Yes."

"Are you loyal?"

"Yes."

"How long have you been in love with Tae?"

That finally tripped him up, and he tipped his head back, staring up at the sky. "Good one."

She let out a breath. "You don't have to answer."

"You just caught me off guard."

She nodded. "I can be pushy sometimes."

He gave her a very small smile. "*Sometimes?*"

"Okay, all the time. I'm not going to apologize for being a mama bear. Tae's had a rough life and she takes care of herself the only way she knows how. She's flip and sarcastic about it, but she has emotions like anyone else, and yearnings. In spite of herself, she wants to believe in the fairy tale."

He acknowledged that with a bow of his head. "Then you

should know, on some level, I fell in love with her when I was seventeen years old."

Surprise filled her. "Oh." She breathed softly, feeling her eyes well up. "I . . . didn't know."

"Neither did I. Fix this, April." Then he nodded in Andy's direction and walked away from them both.

APRIL AND ANDY left the lake at the same time, with Andy following her to the Sunrise Cove Diner. They sat across from each other, April drowning in guilt and remorse and fear.

They stared at each other until the waitress came over with her order pad. She looked at April first. "Hey, darlin', what are you having?"

A heart attack for one . . . "Just some hot tea, please."

"Absolutely." She turned expectantly to Andy.

"A coffee, thank you," he said.

When they were alone again, they stared at each other some more. It'd been a hot minute, and April tried to find a glimpse of the young thug in the quiet, hardened man in front of her, but couldn't. When she finally started to speak, he did so at the same time. They both gave a nervous laugh, easing some of the tension.

"You look like you're walking to your execution," he said and, reaching across the table, put his hands on hers. "It's okay, April. We're just talking. It's going to be okay."

She nodded, then shook her head because nothing was going to be okay, not ever again. She had to pay the piper. Accept her fate. She knew this. "I know I saw you briefly last year, but . . . I've always wondered what you'd look like all grown up."

He spread his hands out, like *here I am*. He was being so nice, and she thought maybe Riggs was right, Andy had grown up to be a good man.

Which made this all far worse.

"We'll figure it out," he said. "I know you. You won't accept any less."

She felt her eyes fill. "You don't know me. Not anymore. And in any case, what I did, asking you to go away and not come back . . ." She drew a shaky breath. "A good person wouldn't have asked that of you."

He held her gaze for a long moment. "You did what you had to do."

Oh, how she wanted to believe that. "Are you really back in Tahoe to stay? I thought you'd never come back after all that happened."

"You mean when I took advantage of a sweet fifteen-year-old girl one night, seducing her and knocking her up? Then being stupid enough to not only get myself in trouble with the law, but also get a gang after me as well?"

"You didn't take advantage of me," she managed through a tight throat. "I wanted a walk on the wild side and I got it. We were both responsible for what happened that night, and neither of us had any intention of seeing each other again, much less wanting a relationship. We were on the same page."

"Doesn't make it any easier to swallow what came next." He looked at her for a long moment. "I nearly ruined your life. You had to move just to stay safe. I never blamed you, April, not for any of it."

And she'd repaid the favor by extracting the promise from him that he'd never come back.

"As for why I'm here now," he said, and shrugged. "For better or worse, Tahoe was the only home I knew. I stayed away as long as I could, but after I retired, I wanted to come back."

April stared at him, realizing that not only had she stolen his chance to be a father, but she'd also taken his home. Or at least held it hostage. She knew how much this place meant to her, and she couldn't imagine being forced out. And yet that was what she'd done to him. "You must hate me."

"I could never hate the mother of my daughter. You did what you had to do." He paused when the waitress brought their drinks, waiting until she'd gone again. "You've raised an amazing woman. You gave her what I'd always wanted growing up."

"What's that?" she asked.

"A loving mom."

He said this without any rancor or apparent ill will, and April took a deep breath. "Did you get married and have kids?"

"Tae *is* my kid."

"Yes," she said softly. "I'm sorry, that was thoughtless of me. She has your eyes. And your fierce loyalty to those she cares about."

He nodded, then shook his head. "And the answer's no, I never married or had more kids."

"Why?"

"Because I wasn't brave enough back then to fight to stay in Tae's life. I wasn't about to have another kid, because if Tae ever found out, I didn't want her to think I walked away from her just to start another family."

"I'm so sorry," she whispered, trying to hold it together. He didn't need her falling apart on him.

He'd given her the best, most amazing thing in her life—*Tae*.

And what had she done? Kept one of the most important people in Tae's life away. Selfish. So selfish, and she hated herself for that. "Andy—"

"You once told me that you knew what it was like to be abandoned. That you weren't going to allow that to happen to Tae. You knew there was every chance that I'd end up in and out of jail, so you asked me to walk away and never come back. What you did, you did out of love," he said. "I got it. I understood. Still do." He paused. "How about you? Did you ever get married or have more kids?"

She snorted. "Not for lack of trying. I wasn't always good at picking for myself. But I hope that's changing."

He cocked his head. "You're with someone."

A soft laugh escaped her, and she looked away, thinking of Ace. She wasn't with him. But it felt like they had a very small kernel of something, even with them both as damaged as they were. "No." She lifted a shoulder. "Maybe."

He nodded, accepting this with the same easy grace he'd accepted everything else.

"What do you want out of this?" she asked, and held her breath for the answer she knew was coming but didn't want to hear.

He didn't hesitate. "I want to get to know my daughter."

Yep. That was the one. Her biggest fear. Her biggest nightmare come true.

"April, I let you make a decision all those years ago because I knew I didn't deserve you," he said. "Either of you. To my shame, walking away was easier than making the decision to stay and fight." He held her gaze. "But I'm not a kid anymore. I have something to offer her now. A relationship, if she's interested."

April had a hand to her heart, pressing hard. "If I tell her, she's going to hate me."

"She might be angry," he agreed. "But she won't hate you. Your relationship is too strong for that."

"How do you know?"

He went through his phone, then turned it around to show her pics. Tae's kindergarten graduation, her high school graduation, her college graduation. All taken from afar. "She's smart, our kid," he said quietly.

She sucked in a breath and then looked up at him. "Tae's college scholarship. That was you."

He just looked at her.

Dear God, it *had* been him. When Tae had been accepted into Cal Poly San Luis Obispo's business school, they hadn't had the money for her to go. Tae had applied to every scholarship she'd been able to find, but the competition had been so fierce, she hadn't gotten anything. Then just days before the admittance deadline, a scholarship suddenly came through. Full ride.

April hadn't questioned it at the time, she'd been too busy being thankful and overwhelmed with gratitude for the found pot of gold.

"You wouldn't take my money," Andy said. "As a dad, I needed to be there for my daughter in the only way I could at the time."

If she'd accepted help instead of stubbornly refusing anything to do with her teenage baby daddy, she wouldn't have struggled to make ends meet for Tae for so many years. Things would've been a lot easier on their daughter. And that was her own personal shame to bear. How was Tae ever going to forgive her? Simple. She wasn't. "I'm so sorry. I—"

"Stop." He pushed the napkin dispenser toward her, making her realize she was crying. "We both made some questionable decisions," he said. "Decisions that might've been different if we'd been older and smarter. Or had anyone in our lives give enough of a shit to guide us."

Nodding, she blew her nose and dried her eyes as Andy looked at her with a good amount of remorse. "I know I was a punk-ass kid who didn't even try to get to know you, but I did eventually grow up, April. As you know, regrets suck, and I have buckets of them too."

She felt relief at that at least, knowing they were on the same page. At least as much as they could be. "I've grown up too," she said. "Now my decisions are made with only one person in mind—Tae."

"Of course," he said.

"I have to make this right. I *will* make this right." God knew how, but she would find a way.

He nodded again, and this time there was a small smile with it. "Maybe we can make it right from the same page this time."

She let out a breath and found a small smile. "I'd like that."

CHAPTER 26

April stood in her kitchen, staring bleakly out the window at the most glorious purple- and blue- and red-streaked sunset she'd ever seen. Not that she could enjoy it, not when she stood there waiting for Tae to come home, listening to the clock on the wall *tick, tick, tick*ing. Like an impending bomb.

Andy sat at the table behind her, drinking coffee. They'd agreed to tell Tae the truth together, instead of April doing it herself. At the time it'd seemed like the smart thing to do, but at some point while waiting for Tae to come home—during which she'd opened her refrigerated store-bought cookie dough and baked the entire tub—she'd changed her mind.

So now she was drowning in guilt and stress and . . . 120 cookies. But she had clarity. She knew Tae better than anyone, and doing it this way with Andy here was not the right way to do this. Tae was going to feel ganged up on, and if there was one thing her daughter hated more than lies, it was walking into a situation she wasn't prepared for.

"No," she said, and shook her head, turning from the window.

"This is wrong. I'm sorry, but you being here is going to blind-side her, which is way worse than me telling her by myself."

Andy nodded. "I hear you, and you know her best, but, April, we're *both* at fault. I don't want you to be the bad guy. Ruining your relationship with her is the *last* thing I want."

"I really don't understand why you're worried about my rela-tionship with her."

He drew a deep breath and pushed his coffee away. "Please don't take this the wrong way, but this isn't about just you. It's also about the relationship I want with my daughter. I—"

Tae came in the back door. "Oh my God, do I smell cookies? Like actual baked cookies? What's the special occasion?"

Andy stood.

Under any other circumstances, April would have laughed. A baker she was not, and they both knew it. "Tae," she said softly instead, heart in her throat.

Tae looked up from her phone and froze at the sight of the man in April's kitchen. Unlike at the lake, he wasn't wearing sunglasses or a ball cap. He was clean-shaven, hair still military short, standing there at parade rest, looking very much like the young soldier in the photo on April's mantel.

"Who are you?" Tae asked slowly, like she already knew.

"You met him at the lake," April said, her heart in her throat.

Tae never took her eyes off him. "Yes," she said. "But you're also . . . *him*."

Andy nodded. "Yes."

Everything about Tae's demeanor changed in an instant. She

went from smiling and carefree to tense as a sheet of glass in a hailstorm. Smile long gone, her eyes unreadable, she whirled on April.

And in that moment, April knew. She'd indeed waited too long and was about to lose the only thing that had ever mattered in her life.

"I'm going to give you and your mom some private time to talk—"

"Wait." Tae's eyes were narrowed as she took him in. "How dare you show up now, after all this time. We thought you were dead. You lied to my mom, left her to raise me without any help—"

April shook her head. "Tae—"

"No. Get out," Tae said to Andy, pointing to the door. "Just get the hell out and don't come back."

"*Tae*." April moved to block the door so Andy couldn't leave.

Tae whirled on her, her expression going from anger to shock to a heart-stopping betrayal that took the air from April's lungs.

Tae stared at her. "You . . . invited him here?"

"Yes. Because we needed to tell you something. Something *I* did."

Tae moved close and took April's hands in her own. "Mom? What do you mean?"

That even now, staring the truth in the face, Tae would side with her, comfort her, made it almost impossible to speak. But she was done hiding the truth. She gently squeezed Tae's hands in her own. "I've made such a mess of things, baby. A long time ago, I made a very rash decision, one that led to a lie, which led to another, and then another. And now . . ." She sucked in a breath. "Now . . ."

Tae blinked, dropped her mom's hands, and stepped back. "Does this have anything to do with why my birth certificate doesn't have a name listed under 'father'?"

April closed her eyes for a beat, then opened them again. She'd known this day would come. "Yes. And it's . . . complicated. I—"

"No." Tae held up a hand. "Did you know all this time I was actually afraid to ask you about it because I didn't want to bring up a painful time for you? That it never once crossed my mind that *you'd* lied to me? I thought by staying quiet until I had the answers that I was protecting you, but wow. The joke was on me."

Heartbroken, April drew a breath. "Tae—"

"Just tell me one thing. Whose decision was it to lie to me about him being dead?"

"Both of ours," said the "him" in the room.

April knew it would be so easy to let him shoulder some of the blame, but she couldn't do it. This was her chance to own up to everything, regardless of what Tae did with the information, even if it meant Tae leaving her. She had to allow her daughter to make her own choice. "No, this was *my* mistake, Tae, and my mistake only. He wasn't the liar. I was."

Tae closed her eyes, and when she opened them, they were ice. "A *mistake*? *That's* what you call the lie that has affected every single day of my entire life? Are you serious right now?"

Aril reached for her, but Tae backed away. "Let me see if I've got this right. You not only knew the truth, but you also kept it from me."

Throat aching, April nodded. "Yes. But—"

But nothing. Tae spun and walked out the door, slamming it in her wake.

April started to go after her, but Andy stopped her. "Give her a minute to think. She'll come back."

She could barely speak with the sheer amount of emotion choking her. "How do you know?"

"Because she'll want answers. And you're the only one with those answers. Plus," he said, giving her a very small sympathetic smile, "I've seen the way you two love and care for each other."

April shook her head. She knew better than anyone love wasn't always enough. Once upon a time, her parents had loved her. Until they hadn't. Same with every man she'd ever fallen for. But she had always believed she and Tae would be forever. She had to fix this. There was no choice. "I'm going to do whatever it takes to earn her trust back."

Andy nodded, his eyes filled with the same resolve she felt. "That makes two of us."

"You're pacing the wood floors bare," Jake said.

Riggs ignored him as he continued to prowl around the living room. It was late, nearly ten o'clock, and he'd heard nothing from Tae. He'd called, texted, gone by her place . . .

She'd vanished, and he had a very bad feeling deep in his gut.

When he'd been knocking on Tae's door, April had stuck her head out of her side of the duplex, her eyes red, skin blotchy. "She's gone," she said.

"You told her."

She'd nodded and shut the door.

Riggs had driven home, berating himself. He should've told her everything two days ago, when Ace had given him Andy's address. Then he'd compounded his error by agreeing to wait for April to tell her. He'd made himself complicit. An accomplice.

She'll always resent you now. You've screwed this up the same way you've screwed up everything else in your life. When will you learn to be content being alone?

But God, he was sick of being alone.

"Not trying to repeat myself here, but you really should have told her," Jake said.

Riggs gave him a death look.

"If you're wondering if you can take the first swing at a man in a wheelchair, you can try . . ."

Riggs heard himself snarl and took a step toward his brother, but Carolyn slipped in between them, her back to Riggs as she glared at her boyfriend. "Really? You're going to kick him when he's down?"

"Be honest," Jake said. "If I'd pulled something as stupid as what Riggs did, holding back something important, something that involved you directly, you'd—"

"Kick your ass," Carolyn said smoothly. "But let's face it, you've made *plenty* of your own mistakes with me and I'm still here."

"What kind of mistakes?" Riggs asked, needing to know if there was any hope for him at all.

Jake didn't respond.

Carolyn snorted. "He told me his life didn't lend itself to relationships. That he didn't believe he could even fall in love because he wasn't made that way. He left me on our first anniversary because he got freaked out that he'd somehow ended up in a relationship in spite of himself."

Riggs went brows up at Jake.

Jake ignored this as well.

"Should I keep going?" Carolyn asked.

"Yes," Riggs said.

"*No*," Jake said.

"Shit." Riggs shook his head. "We're both so stupid."

"Well, give the man an A plus," Carolyn said. "A Copeland male with some self-awareness."

Jake gave a tug on her hand, and she landed in his lap. He wrapped her up in his arms and nuzzled his face into her neck. "Thanks for not giving up on me."

"Never."

"I just wanted to get her some answers," Riggs said to the room. He'd thought that if he made sure Tae's dad was a good guy, she'd see how much he cared about her. How much he loved her. Maybe she'd also understand the mistakes he'd made and forgive him.

But that was a whole lot of maybes to hitch his heart on.

"You *did* get her answers," Jake said. "You just kept them from her."

True. And in the process, he'd thoroughly screwed himself. Tae was a whole lot of really great things, but trusting? Not one of them. Nothing hurt her like betrayal, and that's exactly what he'd done.

Someone knocked at the door. *Please be Tae.* That was his only thought as he yanked it open.

And it was Tae, trembling and looking utterly devastated. She'd reached her breaking point. She needed answers, and she didn't care what it would cost her. He knew what it would cost him.

Everything.

He felt a pain so deep in his heart that he didn't think he could survive it. This was his fault. He had done this.

"It was all a lie," she said thickly. "My dad's not really dead."

Heart aching, he reached for her. "I know, baby. I'm so sorry."

Behind him, he heard Jake and Carolyn discreetly move into the kitchen and out the back door, and a minute later, Jake's truck roared off. Riggs moved Tae inside and held her close. She was gripping him like he was her lifeline, and then suddenly she stilled, slowly lifting her tear-streaked face to his. "Wait. You . . . *knew?*"

In his head, he could hear pounding. The hammering of nails in his coffin as he sealed his own fate. But he would tell her everything he knew and give her everything he had.

TAE STARED UP at Riggs, still shaking, still locked in misery, and now holding her breath for his response.

He met her gaze, regret swimming in his, and she knew the answer before his husky voice said, "Yes."

And here she'd thought she couldn't hurt any more than she already was. "Oh my God." She whirled back to the door, no idea where she was heading, just that she had to leave. Now. She was just barely holding herself together, but she could feel the cracks inside widening. She was going to break.

But she'd save that for when she was alone.

"Tae—"

"*No.*" She whipped back around. "Did everyone know? Was I the last to find out?"

He didn't have to answer, it was all over his face. "And you didn't tell me." She put a hand to her heart, thinking maybe pressure would keep it from shattering. "Why? It's *my* life, Riggs, and it's not like I'm some fragile peach."

He held a hand out to her, but she stepped away, putting a hand up to hold him off, because no way was he going to touch her right now.

Or ever again.

"How long have you known?" she demanded.

"Tae—"

"*How long?*"

He looked as devastated as she felt but she did. Not. Give. A. Crap. "Did you know that day in the school library?" she asked.

"No."

She stared into his eyes and decided that was the truth. "How about last night?"

He winced. "I—"

"*When*, Riggs? When did you find out?"

"Two days ago, when Ace located your dad's address. I wanted to go meet the guy to see if he was on the up and up."

Her mouth literally dropped open. And, as it turned out, red-hot fury gave her heartburn. Good to know. She put her hand to her chest and pressed. Answers first. Heart attack later. "*Ace?*"

"He's a great investigator. He can find anyone and anything."

"So he found my dad—clearly at your request, even though I told you I wanted to do this on my own—and then you went to go see him. Without me. Do I have that right?"

She had to give him credit, he held her gaze. "Yes."

She drew a shaky breath. "I *introduced* myself to my own dad at the lake."

Again regret crossed his face. "I didn't know he'd show up. I told him it was up to *you* to make contact, not him."

"You told him . . ." She stopped and shook her head, confused on top of furious, and hurt on top of all of it. "Why didn't you tell *me?*"

He drew a deep breath, like *he* was stressed. "Your mom made me promise to let her fix this. I agreed to give her a day. I told her if she didn't tell you everything, then I would."

And the hits just kept coming. "Is any of that supposed to make it better? You withheld info that you *knew* I was seeking. You knew that my father was alive and my mom was a liar."

"Tae, I didn't do it to hurt you. Neither did they. I really believed the truth would be less painful coming from your mom."

"Well, you thought wrong." She turned to the door again,

then closed her eyes, letting the pain seep into her, and the realization that not only had her relationship with her mom just gone up in flames, but her relationship with Riggs had as well. "Not only did you lie to me, you found my dad alive and met him before I did. You stole that moment from me, Riggs." She set her forehead to the door and willed the tears off for another minute. That was all she needed. A minute.

"I'm so sorry," he said softly, with more emotion than she'd ever heard before. "I was trying to protect you."

She shook her head and turned to face him. "No." She jabbed a finger at him. "*You had no right.*" She tore her gaze from his face, the person she'd come to trust more than anyone else, and hugged herself. "Dammit," she whispered. "It was good with you, so good. Better than good. I really thought we had something—"

He stepped closer, into her. "We do."

She shook her head and gave him a little shove, while also keeping her hands fisted in his shirt, her mind and body at war again. With a sigh, she let him pull her into him. He kissed her forehead, and she closed her eyes. "I'm so mad at you," she whispered through a thick throat.

"I know. I just wanted to protect you, but I can't. Not from something like this." He sounded genuinely remorseful for not being able to spare her this pain and causing her more. He was big and warm and solid, and, dammit, comforting.

She wanted nothing more than to lose herself in him. He could do it too, make her forget. But she couldn't allow herself to forget. Not this. After a far longer moment than she should've allowed herself, she pulled away.

"Tae, don't go."

Surprised at the vehemence and emotion in the words, she tipped her face up and looked into his eyes as her entire heart turned over in her chest, exposing its underbelly. But her spine snapped ramrod straight. "I don't want to," she said truthfully, then had to swallow hard. "But you didn't trust me. And now, I can't trust you."

His expression was grim. And pained. He knew it was over. He lowered his head and kissed her, sweet and loving, with the same spark as always, and she clung to him for one more minute before stepping back. For good this time. "Goodbye, Riggs." And then she did what for the first time in her life she *didn't* want to do. She walked away.

CHAPTER 27

Tae drove with no destination in mind through the dark night. But in the end, there was only one person she was sure hadn't lied to her. Pulling over, she texted Riggs:

I want my dad's address.

Her phone immediately rang but she ignored his call. Two seconds later came the text with the address.

Her dad lived in south shore. She drove along the lake on a narrow, curvy, stunning highway. Under normal circumstances, she'd have let herself be awed by the heart-stopping view of the mountains cradling the gorgeous lake by moonlight. But tonight she drove with a single-minded purpose.

To find out what the hell was going on.

It was nearly midnight by the time she turned onto a narrow road and found her dad's place. He lived in a tiny cabin, the third in a row of ten about five blocks back from the lake. It was an old A-frame style, dark thanks to a thick grove of pine trees all around them, but the yards were neat if sparse.

Tae walked up the path to number 3 and knocked.

AJ Strickland, aka Andy Jameson, answered in a pair of jeans, a dad sweater, mismatched socks, and reading glasses perched on his nose. His surprise at seeing her was clear. "Tae."

"Can I come in?"

"Always." He stepped back. The living room was small, well lived-in but surprisingly welcoming. She stood in the middle of the room and turned a slow circle, trying to see what his life was like here, a life that hadn't included her.

"Do you want to talk about it?" he asked quietly from behind her.

"I thought I did, but . . ." She turned to face him just as her damn eyes welled up. "Not yet," she whispered. She tossed up her hands. "I don't even know what to call you. Andy? AJ?"

"I go by Andy these days. My real name is Andrew Jameson, so either works."

She nodded and then shook her head as a little sob escaped.

"Tae," he said in a pained, regretful voice. He tossed aside the book he was still holding, along with his glasses, and opened his arms. And before she knew what she wanted to do, she'd sort of crumpled into him. His hug was warm but careful, as if she were made of glass, and it made her cry a little harder.

This might not have been how she'd wanted the first meet with her dad to go, but this hug was everything she'd imagined it might be over the years. And even though he was a complete stranger, he felt . . . familiar. "Sorry," she murmured soggily, pulling back.

"Don't ever be sorry, not with me."

She nodded and swiped her cheeks. "I wanted answers, but I'm . . ." She thought of Riggs and felt devastated. "Tired."

"I've got a spare bedroom."

She looked at him in surprise.

"It's yours," he said.

She wasn't sure she understood. "You . . . have a room for me?"

"Yes." He paused. "Is that weird?"

"Yes." She shook her head, a little speechless. "And no. But . . . why?"

"I'm eternally optimistic?"

She almost laughed. "I definitely didn't get that gene."

He smiled a bit sadly. "You're welcome to go hole up if that's what you need. It's okay."

She was stunned by how badly she wanted just that, or that she'd even consider it, given what she'd thought of him only yesterday. "I might not want to talk tomorrow either," she warned.

"So we won't talk tomorrow."

She just stared at him. If she walked away now, she wouldn't want to go home. She'd have to get a hotel, which was fine, except . . . except she didn't want to. The bottom line was that she was too curious to leave.

"We're on your time, Tae."

Her mom would never have been able to just sit and let her be. But Tae needed just that. Time to think about her mom's lies, about walking away from Riggs. Finding a dad . . . It all felt so overwhelming. "I think I'd like to stay, thank you," she said, and knew by his nod and smile that he was happy to have her. It shouldn't have mattered, but it did. A whole bunch.

TAE WOKE UP to the scent of coffee and bacon and realized it was morning. Given that she hadn't fallen asleep until well after 3:00 A.M., it wasn't a shock. Staggering out into the kitchen, she found her dad at the stove.

"I hope you like eggs," he said.

"Yes." She paused. "Do you ever make pancakes?"

He turned and looked at her, almost into her, as if trying to assess if she was okay. Apparently deciding she was, he gave a little smile and shook his head. "I suck at pancakes."

For a beat, she felt sad because she herself rocked a good pancake. So why the flash of disappointment? *Because you wanted to know what you'd gotten from his side of the gene pool . . .*

He served her bacon and eggs and straight black coffee so strong it curled her tongue, and she nearly coughed up a lung.

"Sorry," he said ruefully, after getting her some water. "That's how we did it in the military. I rarely drink it anymore, but thought you might want some."

She shuddered and laughed, which eased the tension in the room. "The eggs are amazing," she said around a mouthful. "What's the trick?"

"Real butter and lots of cheese."

She nodded. "So you're a vegan then."

"Not hardly—" His smile faded. "Damn. Are you?" He started to rise. "I can make something else—"

"I'm not a vegan." She smiled. "But thanks for offering to cook again, if I was."

"Did you sleep okay?"

She nodded. Then shook her head.

They stared at each other, then both looked quickly away. He laughed again, roughly this time. "I've got to tell you, I haven't felt so awkward and desperate to impress since . . . well, since I was a punk-ass teenager. I'm nervous as hell."

Her smile faded. "I don't want you to try to impress me. Or feel awkward."

"What *do* you want?"

She shook her head. That seemed to be the question of the day. She had a phone full of messages from her mom. From Jenny. From Riggs . . . She'd texted each, assuring them she was okay, that she'd be back online soon, she needed a minute and hoped they could respect that. Because the truth was, she had no idea what she wanted.

"I know it doesn't feel like it," he said. "But we're family. You can talk to me."

"Family isn't whose blood you carry. It's who you love, and who loves you back."

"Then you should know I've loved you since before you were born." He nodded to her phone, which had just lit up with another text from her mom. "I guarantee your mom feels the same. She did the best she could with what she had, Tae. She was fifteen."

The reality of that statement hit her, maybe for the first time. Tae herself was nearly *twice* that age now, and she *still* didn't feel old enough for the situation her mom had found herself in. "I understand that," she said quietly. "What I don't understand is the lie."

"It's complicated." He was quiet for a moment. "I want you to know you're always welcome here, and I mean *always*, for as long as you want."

She looked up and found his eyes shiny but incredibly solemn. "I meant what I said about the room being yours," he said. "And I'll give you a key to come and go. But I want you to promise me you won't come here if it's only because you're running away from your mom."

He was protecting April. Just as Tae herself had always done. "I used to dream about running away to find you," she said quietly. "Even though I really believed you were dead."

"You can't imagine how many times I dreamed about you too." He paused. "I wanted you to know about me. I wanted you to know me."

"What stopped you?"

He studied her. "Are you ready to talk then? Because I'd like to, but I won't rush you."

Was she ready? Hell, she didn't know. Her chest felt tight, and there was a ball of emotion stuck in her throat, but she knew that would be status quo until she got answers. "I'm ready."

He dumped the coffee and made tea. Peach, and she stared down at the mug in surprise. "How did you know?"

"Know what?"

"Peach tea is my favorite."

For the first time, his smile, when aimed at her, wasn't sad or regretful. "I didn't know. But it's my favorite too."

She stared at him, into those light brown eyes that were her own, and let out a short laugh. "I always wondered what parts of me were from you."

"Probably more than is good for you." He spread out his hands. "I'm . . . impatient."

She nodded. "Same."

"I also used to be impulsive and quick-tempered as well. And those three things don't go well together. I was a rotten kid, Tae, and an even more rotten teenager. In and out of the system."

"What happened to your parents?"

He shrugged. "My dad peaced out before I was born. My mom did the best she could for a few years, then OD'd on pain-killers."

The teeny tiny part of her that had been hoping for the classic, loving, fleece-wearing grandparents who visited on holidays dissipated. "I'm sorry."

He shrugged. "I didn't know any different. And to say I wasn't an easy foster kid is an understatement. I was curious enough to get into trouble, but not smart enough to get out of it." He paused. Looked away. "You want to know who your dad is? By seventeen, I was a gang-wannabe. I was trying to impress, so I did stupid shit. Lots of it. Then I went to a party one night, met your mom by sheer accident, and we—" He broke off and scrubbed his hands down his face. "She was sweet and pretty, and . . . *shit*," he muttered.

"You slept with her."

He nodded. "After, there weren't regrets, but there was no real spark either. Neither of us intended to ever see each other again. I continued to work my way into big trouble. A month later, April showed up in tears with a positive pregnancy test." He met her gaze. "You need to know that staying together was never on the table, for either of us. I was a night on the other side of the tracks for her, and for me she was . . ." He smiled. "A moment in time; a single, sweet, unforgettable moment in time that wasn't meant to be. Still, I would've married her in a heartbeat to give her my military benefits, but she was too young. The court wouldn't allow it. And frankly, she—and you—were better off not being associated with me. But I still wanted to support you." He paused. "That didn't work out."

She didn't understand, and she could tell he knew she was confused, but he didn't say anything else. And that was when she got it. "You tried, and Mom refused to take anything from you." She sat there, letting that soak in. All the money problems they'd had, all the times they hadn't known if they would make rent or have enough food money . . . More emotionally touched than she'd thought possible, and also more angry at her mom than she'd thought possible, she set down her tea. "You said you two weren't meant to be. Why was that?"

"Tae . . ." He shook his head. "Don't romanticize it. You need to believe me that there wasn't a hope or yearning, for either of us. There just wasn't. After the party, where I met your mom? Me and two guys stole a car. I drove the car into a pole and nearly killed a gangbanger, got caught and went to juvy, and by the time I got out, your mom was six months pregnant. I got a job, intending to give every penny I made to April to take care of you, to visit whenever I was welcome. I intended to do that forever and be a part of your life, but trouble came knocking. The gangbanger I'd nearly killed wanted retribution. He wanted me under his thumb, and he wasn't about to let that go. He expected me back. He . . ." He paused, looked her right into the eyes. "He threatened to hurt you and your mom if I didn't comply."

Her heart stopped. "Oh my God. What happened?"

"I talked to April. I talked to my juvenile parole officer and my state-appointed lawyer. It was decided the best thing for me to do was to leave town. So I enrolled in the marines, because even though I was an idiot, I knew my current path would either kill me or land me back in jail. And the cost would be for you and April to be in constant danger. So when April asked me to go and not come back, I understood and did just that."

"So you *chose* to go away."

"No. I chose you."

She took in his very solemn, intense expression and drew a breath before slowly letting it out again. Not only had her mom known he was alive, but she'd also asked him to go. "She had no right."

"Tae, she had *every* right. Try to imagine what it was like for her. Her family had turned their back on her. She did what she thought she had to in order to protect you, and she did it out of love."

Tae swiped at a tear. "She should have told me everything."

He was quiet for a moment. "Look, you're right that family

isn't whose blood you carry, it's who you love. It's also not just the good times. It's got its ups and downs. And sometimes we try so hard to protect those we care about, we end up hurting them. But that doesn't make that love any less real."

She stared at him, struck by the realness and truth of what he'd just said. Her mom had lied to her, but Tae still loved her. And even though Riggs had withheld information, and she'd always said there couldn't be love without trust, she *did* love him.

Her dad was watching her carefully, and he gave a small smile. "Life's good at curveballs, isn't it?" He handed her a photo album.

It was one of those four-by-six-inch books that held single photos in clear plastic sleeves. The first picture was a wrinkly, screaming infant in a hospital nursery bed. She recognized the pic, as her mom had one identical to it. It was herself at one day old. "I don't look like I was finished being baked."

"You were beautiful."

She snorted and turned the page. Her heart caught at the sight of herself in a red dress, white tights, and black boots, her hair up in pigtails, her smile revealing no front teeth. "My kindergarten graduation." She looked up. "You were there?"

"No." He paused and smiled wryly. "I begged it off your mom via a million letters from overseas."

The next pic had been taken at her high school graduation. "Now that I was there for," he said. "Your mom didn't know. I was in the very back, behind the bleachers. I was so proud of you."

She ran a finger over the pic, remembering how excited she'd been to go off to college. She hadn't expected to be able to go. They didn't have money for it. But then . . . She gasped. "The scholarship—" She looked up and found the truth in his eyes. "I've always wondered why after getting turned down for so many that I finally got the one I did. It was awarded only to me, even though I wasn't the top student in my class. A full-ride scholarship. Basically a miracle." She took a deep breath. "You were my miracle."

"I never intended for you to find out."

She stared at him, her chest tight. "Thank you."

There were no other pictures slipped into any of the remaining sleeves.

"I was still gone," he said quietly.

She nodded, feeling a little too choked up to speak, because even though she'd thought she'd missed out on having a dad, he'd actually tried to be there all along. "Is it weird that I've loved you all my life even though I didn't know you?"

He took her hand. "Not even a little bit."

CHAPTER 28

Riggs didn't sleep much that night. Tae hadn't called him back or returned a text. Not that he blamed her.

Nope, this was all on him. At dawn, he gave up on sleep and nudged Grub off the bed. Grub waited for Riggs to stand up before jumping back on the bed and plopping his big head on Riggs's pillow.

"Get up," Riggs said. "We're going running."

Grub closed his eyes. Grub hated running. Or any form of exercise at all.

"All right, it's up to you, but you're getting a little pudgy, man, a run would be good for you."

Grub didn't budge.

"Fine. I'll be back."

Grub wagged his tail. With a laugh, Riggs pulled on sweats and did his best to outrun his demons, only, as always, they kept pace with him.

But he was a logics guy, not an emotions guy. So he worked the problem. One, he'd messed up. Two, Tae had left him and would probably never want to speak to him again. He tried to go with the logical conclusion, that it was for the best, because he could go to D.C., to the life he'd laid out for himself. He could forget the feeling of running his fingers through Tae's silky hair or how his lips tingled for what seemed like hours after he kissed her. He could forget how his heart did a somersault in his chest whenever she smiled at him.

But he knew he'd forget nothing.

He kept running, going farther along the Lake Walk than usual, pushing himself punishingly hard. His legs were already wobbling before he turned back. By the time he let himself into the house, his entire body felt rubbery and he couldn't feel his face. Not wanting to get sweat on the couch, he collapsed onto the rug in front of it and stared up at the ceiling. Interesting. He couldn't feel his heart either.

Definitely for the best.

He felt a big, furry body wriggle in close. Grub, going off the hot doggy breath in his face. Resistance was futile, so he wrapped his arms around the dog and accepted the hug.

"What's wrong with you?"

He didn't answer Jake as he came into the room. Riggs had been hoping he was alone, but hey, he'd had a lot of hopes dashed in the past twenty-four hours, so what was one more?

Jake bumped his wheelchair into Riggs's feet. "Is this about Tae? You two worked it out after Carolyn and I left last night, right?"

He didn't answer. He couldn't go there.

"Talk," Jake said.

"I'm going to be leaving," Riggs told the ceiling. "You sure about not selling Adrenaline HQ, so it's not all on you to run after I'm gone?"

Jake stared down at him. "It's like you *want* me to give you another black eye. You're such a jackass."

Riggs shook his head. "I'm not trying to be a jackass. But we added an ambitious summer project, which essentially doubles your workload. It's just a thought."

"Don't even try to pretend that this is about me." Jake was sounding good and pissed off now. "What does Tae think about you leaving?" He paused, but when Riggs didn't say anything— couldn't, because he felt dangerously close to losing it—Jake went on, twisting the knife. "You know damn well the second you get on a plane, you're going to regret leaving her. *And* me."

"Feeling awful sure of yourself," Riggs managed.

"Just admit it. You're running."

Riggs sucked in a breath. Held it. Let it out slowly. How like Jake to go for the kill shot. "You don't need me here."

"Bullshit," Jake said. "I know Dad used to call us worthless sacks of shit who'd never amount to anything. I know too that he showed us, over and over again, that we weren't worthy. And apparently you bought into the program. But fuck that, Riggs. Why would you let him win? Do you even know why I wanted you here? Because I want my family back. Life without you just doesn't work for me anymore. It's been good to be together, and you know what? I think you feel the same. So stay. Or don't. But stop looking at me like I'm a burden you have to fix."

Riggs was stunned, and he cranked his neck to look upside

down at his brother. "What the hell are you talking about? I don't think you're a burden. I've never thought that."

"Okay, then tell me what I am to you."

"Tell you? I worked my ass off half of this summer at your side. I *showed* you what you are to me, with actions, day in and day out."

"Words, man. I need the words."

"You want *words* on my feelings for you?" Riggs sat up. Elbows to his knees, he shoved his fingers through his hair. "I want to go back in time and be there for you."

Jake looked confused. "What the hell are you talking about? You've *always* been there for me."

"No, I haven't." Riggs shook his head. "If I had, you wouldn't have almost died."

"So you're God now? Because I was blown up on an *op*, Riggs. You weren't even in the same country as I was. How could you have stopped that?"

Riggs opened his mouth and then shut it.

Jake nodded. "See? You couldn't have done anything, and the truth is, what happened to me turned out to be a favor."

"Now *I* call bullshit," Riggs said.

"No." Jake shook his head. "Before that op, I was angry and holding on to resentments about how we'd grown up. It tainted everything, including my relationships. And okay, yeah, even afterward, for a long time I stayed angry. But slowly I realized that for whatever reason, I suddenly couldn't hold on to all that old shit. And the minute I let it go, things changed. Look at me," he said, gesturing around them. "I've got a woman who loves me enough to try and drown me in throw pillows. I run a business where I play all day long while helping people. I've got a damn sweet life. Sweeter than yours, in fact."

Riggs look at Jake, really looked at him, and saw the truth. His brother believed every word of what he'd said. And something else—he was right. Jake did have a sweet life, much sweeter than Riggs's at the moment.

"Yeah," Jake said, shaking his head with a small smile. "My legs might be paralyzed, but your heart is. You're such an idiot."

"And you're a dick, but do I complain? No."

But Jake wasn't playing. "Look, I know I wasn't the best brother to you. That I wasn't always there for you."

Riggs shook his head in disbelief. "Jake, you were the *only* one who was there for me. Always."

Jake thought about that for a minute. "Remember when we used to steal Dad's boat and go out at night?"

"You mean when you were a teenager and you and your friends would steal it and bring me along so there were no witnesses left behind?"

"Yeah. That." Jake's smile faded slightly, because they both knew the truth was that they'd sneak off on the nights their dad had been shit-faced in the hope it would save Jake from taking a beating for the both of them. Because more often than not, Riggs would do something to infuriate his dad—hell, it could have been just Riggs breathing—and Jake would step in and take whatever their dad had been intending to dish out to Riggs.

"You always saved my ass," Riggs said quietly.

"No." Jake shook his head. "You saved mine. If it hadn't been for you, I'd have grown up just like him."

"You have never been like him."

"I was heading that way, Riggs. It was going to happen. I had to stay human for you."

"Those nights on the water," Riggs said quietly. "They're the best memories of growing up here that I have."

"And then I just walked away from you," Jake said, just as quietly. "I went into the military and left you here with Dad."

Riggs stood, shocked at the torment and guilt in his brother's voice. "You had to go, or he'd have killed you for sure." He looked Jake right in the eyes and lied his ass off. "I was fine. He left me alone after you were gone."

"You were ten."

"I learned to hold my own, and mostly I just stayed out of his way. I promise you, it was okay."

Jake took that in, and then finally gave a nod and let it go. "So what's going on with Tae? I'm assuming you somehow screwed it up."

Riggs leaned back against the couch. "You assume correctly."

"You know what your problem is?"

Riggs closed his eyes. "I will *pay* you to not tell me," he said.

"You're not giving her what she wants."

"What the hell are you talking about? I'd give her anything she wanted."

"Except, I'm guessing, actual words," Jake said.

"Huh?"

Jake gave him a you're-so-slow look. "Come on, you know

this. You're the master of monosyllabic answers. You hoard words like they're bars of gold. A woman like Tae needs more."

"Which you know *how*?"

"Because this is one of those areas in which I'm far superior to you." Jake smirked. "Watch this." He met Riggs's gaze straight on. "You're my brother and I love you. I'll always love you, even when you're being a complete idiot, like right now."

Riggs blinked.

Jake raised a brow.

"What?" Riggs said, feeling irritated as shit.

Jake pointed at him. "You didn't say it back."

"I already told you. I show you how I feel for you all the damn time."

"Yep," Jake said. "By shoving my face in the things I can't do, making me feel inadequate."

Riggs stared at him. "That's not what I'm doing. I'm trying to help. I . . . couldn't help you get better."

"No, you couldn't. But, Riggs, *no one* could. And it sucks, but do you know what I'd be doing if I hadn't been blown halfway to Timbuktu?"

Dumbly, Riggs shook his head.

"I'd probably still be over there, chasing the adrenaline rush, living an empty life."

Riggs shook his head, boggled. "I've . . . never looked at it that way."

"That's okay. You're the aforementioned idiot. You can't help yourself."

Riggs paced to the window. He couldn't see the lake from

here, just woods. But he didn't have to see it. It was in his blood. "That's why you never wanted to sell Adrenaline HQ. I wanted you to have a life, but this *is* your life. Helping others."

Jake smiled. "Look at that. You're only *half* an idiot. You do know this could be your life too, right?"

Riggs turned to face his brother. "I've been thinking . . ."

"Dangerous."

Riggs rolled his eyes but refused to be redirected. Instead, he tested the waters. "Maybe we could find a way to make AHQ more far-reaching, where we could help even more people."

"I'm all ears, but it would have to involve you staying."

Riggs nodded his head.

Jake gave a slow smile. "Then I'm all in. And because you just finally evolved, I'm going to help you win your girl back."

"I don't deserve her."

"You mean you're terrified she'll leave you at some point."

Riggs looked away, because that too. Shit. Who knew he could feel the cold tendrils of fear just standing there thinking about it?

"So that's it," Jake said. "You're just going to let it fall apart."

"I'm not good for her," he said.

"Riggs, you're the best man I know."

The best man Jake knew was speechless.

"You've got this," Jake said softly.

"*How?*"

"What did you say to me when you came home that one time, when I was learning to get out of bed and into my chair?"

Riggs had to think about that. "'Try again.'"

"Actually," Jake said, "your exact words were 'Try again, you jackass.'"

Riggs grimaced. "Yeah, okay. Maybe." What could he say? They'd been raised on tough love. Minus the love.

"So now it's my turn," Jake said. "What are you going to say to Tae?"

"I'm guessing not 'Try again, jackass.'"

Jake gave a rough laugh. "You know what I want you to say. Say it. Say 'I love you.'"

"You love me."

"I swear to God." Jake looked down at his shoes, whether to fight another laugh or to resist the urge to beat the shit out of Riggs, he had no idea. Finally, he lifted his head, his eyes serious. "You can do this. I know you feel it. And she needs to hear it."

"She doesn't want to hear it," Riggs said, humor gone. "And I'll lose her all over again."

"I hate to point out the obvious, but you've already lost her. So really, what do you have to lose?"

Riggs stilled at the utter truth, and he realized . . . he had *everything* to lose. He pulled his keys from his pocket.

"You going to go get her?"

He was already halfway to the door. "Yeah."

"Wait."

Riggs turned back.

"The words. Practice the damn words."

Riggs drew a deep breath, let it out. "I love you."

Jake grinned. "Look at that, it didn't even kill you. Now go get your girl."

CHAPTER 29

After breakfast with her dad—which was a sentence Tae had never said to herself before—she realized she had already forgiven and understood what he'd done.

And since she'd done such a good job with facing that ghost from her past, it was now time to face her mom. As she drove home, her eyes caught on the dark, turbulent clouds coming in from the summit, slowly churning the sky above and the lake below, whipping up some serious swells.

It matched the storm within her. She told herself it'd worked out with her dad, so she wanted to think she could get to the same place with her mom, but she honestly didn't know how. And in far too short a time, she stood at her mom's front door, a panicked hot mess.

Normally, she'd just walk in. Her mom's casa was her casa, and vice versa. But for the first time ever, she felt uncomfortable just letting herself in. That was the thing about anger: it made it impossible to make a rational decision. She raised her hand to knock, then . . . didn't. She started to turn away, but didn't do that either. So she raised her hand again just as the door opened, eliciting a startled gasp from her.

"I'm sorry," her mom said. "I didn't mean to scare you, but you were standing there muttering to yourself for so long, I was afraid you'd leave."

Her mom was in baggy pj's, hair piled up on top of her head, no makeup, eyes puffy like she'd been crying, and Tae felt her heart squeeze in spite of herself. "I was definitely a flight risk," she admitted.

Her mom's face crumpled, but she never took her eyes off Tae. "It's really cold this morning. There's a storm on its way."

"I think it's here already." Or at least it was inside her.

"Please come in?" her mom asked. "If you want, you can keep talking to yourself. I promise not to listen. But I'd love to listen. If you're ready."

Was she? Tae had no idea. But she knew she looked every bit as thrown off axis as her mom. So she managed a small smile and nodded, and inside they went.

Her mom had a fire going in the woodstove, and Tae gravitated to it, holding out her hands to catch the heat.

"Get any closer and your boots will melt," her mom said quietly.

That had actually happened to her once when she'd been sixteen and had just bought herself a new pair of boots that she'd been in love with for months. She'd melted them on night one and, at the memory, gave a half laugh. Her mom too, but then they stood there in an odd awkward silence, which killed Tae, because there'd never been any awkwardness between them, ever.

"Tae—" her mom said at the exact same moment Tae said, "Mom, I—" She stopped, but her mom shook her head.

"You get to go first," she said. "I don't think I have that right."

Tae drew a shaky breath. "Actually, I think you should go first. I need to hear you say . . . stuff."

Her mom nodded, her hands clasped tight together, knuckles white. "I should've told you. I know this. But I was afraid you'd hate me—"

Tae held up a hand, trying not to get automatically irritated at the excuse. "You know what? I do need to go first." She drew a deep breath. "I want to preface this by saying I'm still angry at you. Very angry. I don't know how long I'll be this way, but I need you to know that."

Her mom, regret in every line of her body, nodded.

Tae nodded too. "I'm starting to understand why you did what you did. It doesn't make it okay, but if I'm being honest, if it'd been me who'd been fifteen and pregnant and all alone, I . . . can't even imagine." She met her mom's gaze. "You could've gotten an abortion. You could have given me up for adoption. But you didn't. Instead, you gave up your own adolescence to keep me. I can only guess how terrifying it must've been for you, and I'm sorry you went through that." Tae shook her head. "I hate that you went through all you did."

"Baby," April whispered. "I've got zero regrets."

They stared at each other some more. April's eyes were shiny, her voice ragged, and Tae ached for them both. "Why don't you just tell me the truth from the get-go?"

April nudged her aside and added more wood to the stove. "I wanted you to grow up with a good father figure," she said. "Even if it was only in your head. I wanted to protect you from the ugly truth."

Tae's heart painfully thawed a degree. Or ten. Because the truth was, she'd also done things she wasn't exactly proud of to protect her mom over the years. Including not telling her mom about the birth certificate and searching for her dad. "I understand more than I thought I would. But how about when I got older? Why not tell me the truth then?"

April's eyes filled. "Because of this." She gestured between them. "I didn't want you to hate me."

"I don't hate you." Tae wasn't sure she even could. "But it hurts that you lied."

"I wanted you to believe in love," her mom said. "I wanted you to have at least one happily-ever-after in your past."

"Oh, Mom." She sighed. "I would have liked seeing an HEA, for sure. But that wasn't in the cards for us."

"Because of my bad choices." Her mom swiped at her tears. "Because you often had to protect me from those bad choices, making you the adult in our relationship. I made a lot of mistakes, and I've got a lot to make up for." She clasped her hands together. "I'm sorry, Tae. I'm so damned sorry. For all of it. I just . . . I was so bad at being a mom, constantly triaging our lives . . . I used to think, *Just look forward, take one step at a time, don't look back.* I didn't want to lose you. Still don't."

Tae's chest hurt, because who was she to judge her mom's choices? She'd done the best she could with what she'd had. "You'll never lose me."

Her mom exhaled, as if she'd been holding her breath this whole time.

"But there can't be any more secrets."

"Agreed," her mom said. "They're too heavy to carry. Honey, will you stay? I can call for takeout—" She turned to the drawer where they kept all the local menus. "Maybe a Mexican brunch—"

"Mom, food can't fix this." But even as she said it, her stomach growled at the thought of a Mexican brunch.

April gave her a small smile. "I know food can't fix this. I know it's not going to be that easy." She hesitated. "But how *is* it going to be? Where do we go from here?"

Tae knew it came down to what she needed, which was the full story. "We go to the beginning. Tell me the story about you and Dad. The whole story."

THREE HOURS LATER, Tae was still on the couch with her mom in front of the fire. Her mom had told her everything, and it all matched her dad's account, so Tae knew she finally had the truth. And when she put herself in their positions, she also knew she couldn't judge either of them, not when they'd each given up everything for their baby.

Her mom was watching her carefully. "Please talk to me. Where are we at, you and me?"

Tae reached for her hand and squeezed it gently. "Where we're always at. Together."

Her mom smiled, lost the battle with her tears, and hugged Tae tight. "I love you, Tae. So much."

"I know, Mom. I love you too."

Her mom pulled back a little. "And you and Riggs?"

Tae felt the ball of grief return to her throat and shook her head. She'd very, very carefully not thought about Riggs this morning, because it hurt too much.

"Oh, honey." April pushed some of Tae's hair back from her face.

"He knew everything, Mom. I feel so stupid."

"Stupid . . . or hurt?"

Tae took stock of her feelings. "Hurt."

Her mom nodded and looked her in the eyes. "I overstepped and asked—no, actually, I *begged* Riggs to let me talk to you first. The whole reason being because he didn't want you hurt. I did that, Tae. Not him."

She stubbornly shook her head. "He should've told me right away."

"And believe me, he knows that, but he really thought he was protecting you."

Tae gave a low, disbelieving laugh. "Are you *campaigning* for him now? I thought you disapproved."

"I was wrong."

Tae just shook her head. "What happened? Did hell freeze over?"

Her mom gave her a small smile. "He loves you, Tae."

"Sometimes love isn't enough." But even Tae didn't believe

that. She hated that she'd walked away from him, *again*. But she'd just been so hurt and surprised at what he'd done . . .

No. That wasn't it. She'd been hurt and surprised by what her mom and dad had done, and she'd conveniently laid all of it on Riggs, blaming him for everything. She stilled. Well, damn. He had done the same thing she'd done to her mom, kept something from her to protect her from getting hurt.

With the best of intentions. "I'm a hypocrite."

"You acted from your heart," her mom said. "And that's never a bad thing. You could act from your heart some more and go talk to him."

Tae looked at her, wanting to believe that to be true. "Do you really think so?"

"After this morning with you, I know so." Her mom smiled and cupped Tae's face, using her thumbs to swipe away the lingering tears she hadn't even realized she'd shed. "You've got this, baby."

Did she? In the past when she'd screwed something up, she'd just moved on. Simple. No muss, no fuss. But she'd been a fool to think she could just move on from Riggs. He owned her heart. Riggs. She pulled out her keys.

"You're going to talk to him?"

"If he's willing." She headed to the door, but before she opened it, someone knocked.

"Tae," Riggs said through the door, making her jump in shock. She whipped around to her mom.

"How did he know?" she whispered.

"Because I can feel the skepticism, cynicism, and suspicion coming at me in waves," Riggs said through the door.

She laughed. Actually laughed.

"Tae." Softer now. "Can we talk? *Please?*"

She was astonished. The word miser himself knew the word *please*? Helpless against the onslaught of emotions his soft entreaty caused, she opened the door.

He stood in the doorway, palms up, braced on the doorjamb. He'd been looking down, but he lifted his head to meet her eyes, his own shadowed.

It was snowing good now. A freak surprise snowstorm in July wasn't unheard of. The only predictability of Lake Tahoe's weather was the unpredictability about Lake Tahoe's weather. But seeing big, fat flakes drift slowly down, sticking to the grass and street, still felt strange and disorientating. Riggs's hair was dusted white, as were his dark eyelashes and broad shoulders. She stepped back so he could come in, but he didn't move.

He looked into her eyes searchingly. "You okay?"

The simple question, asked in a low, intense voice, like maybe her answer was everything, touched her unbearably. Unable to speak, she nodded.

He looked past her and gave a nod of his chin to her mom before his gaze came back to Tae. "You sure?"

When she nodded again, he let out a breath like he'd been holding it on her answer. Then he stepped into her and cupped her face. "I'm so sorry, Tae. I never meant to hurt you. You mean so much to me. In fact, you mean everything to me." He drew a breath. "I know I handled this badly. Jake says it's because I'm an idiot."

This made her laugh through her tears. "You're not the only one. I handled this badly too, at every turn." She swallowed hard and met his gaze. "I was coming to find you."

He looked stunned. "You were?"

She nodded and took his hand. "Can we go talk?"

"Yes." He pulled her in. "Where to?"

"Anywhere," she said, and meant it.

They took his truck. She had no idea where they were going until he turned into the entrance for Sand Harbor and parked. It'd stopped snowing, and the sun was reasserting itself, with sunrays slashing through the clouds and into the water. The snow dusting the shoreline had steam rising off the rocks and into the air. She'd been coming here, to this very spot, for as long as she could remember. It was her happy place. "You remembered," she said as they walked to the water and sat side by side on a large boulder.

"You're hard to forget."

When he said stuff like that, her heart felt so full and happy, she almost didn't know what to do. He was looking at her like . . . well, like he loved her more than anything else in the world. "How did I *not* know you were my person back then?" she asked.

"We weren't ready for this." He slid an arm around her so that she was snuggled to his big, warm body. "I was a coward when it came to emotions. I was afraid to reveal myself to you."

"Wow. Admitting to a fear." She looked at him. "Thought you weren't afraid of anything."

"You really have no idea, do you?" He let out a rough laugh. "Tae, my biggest fear is exactly what happened—losing you."

Her heart skipped a beat as she stared at him. "I'm sor—"

Gently, he laid a finger against her lips. "No, don't apologize to me. You had every right to feel that way, and to need space." He turned to face her fully, bringing her hand to his chest. "I was so afraid to lose you, I had to make that friendship pact. I knew I wanted more, much more, but fear isn't reasonable. I think a part of me keeping what I knew a secret is me actually manifesting that fear to reality. I'm the sorry one, Tae. I never should've kept what I knew from you—"

"I understand why you did it."

"You do?"

"You were trying to protect me." She grimaced. "Exactly what I did to my mom."

"Because you'd been protecting her all your life. I don't have that excuse." He didn't look away, just held her gaze, letting her see his honest regret. "I was wrong, Tae. Very wrong. You don't need protecting. You actually don't *need* anything. That's what makes you so attractive to me. You want someone to stand at your side, not at your back."

"Yes." She breathed. Maybe he didn't talk much, but boy when he did, he made the words count. He got it. And he got her.

"I'm that man, Tae. I can promise you that."

Little tendrils of cautious hope unfurled within her. "How do you know?"

"Easy. I can't remember what my life was without you in it. I wasn't . . . whole. I was a bunch of broken edges and mismatched pieces, and . . ." He smiled. "You're the glue. I can't imagine being without you. You're a part of me now, a part of my heart and soul—the very best part."

She absorbed that for a wondrous moment, marveled and overwhelmed in the very best of ways. "That's some big talk for a man who doesn't like to acknowledge that he even has a heart and soul."

"I've got both," he assured her. "I just never knew what to do with them. Jake taught me something this morning."

She gave him a slow look over. "I don't see any new bruises."

"We used words this time instead of fists."

She smiled. "I bet Carolyn was relieved."

Still holding her hand in his, he kissed her palm, watching her over their tangled fingers with more in his eyes than she'd ever dreamed possible. "I'm the one who's relieved," he said. "I thought you and me were over, and I didn't know how to face that."

She gripped him tight. "Me either. So . . . about when you're in D.C. . . ."

Lowering his head, he kissed her softly, then not so softly. When they came up for air, he said, "I'm not going back to D.C."

The words sank in and spread warmth through her entire being. "You're not?"

"No."

"But . . . the State Department job. It's what you wanted—"

"What I want is you. What I need is you." He shook his head, looking a little overcome. "It's always been you, but I let my past mess with me. I'm done with that. Jake learned to let it go, and so can I."

"Must have been some talk with him," she murmured. "Tell me the truth. Your injuries are internal, right? Maybe a concussion from flying objects?"

He laughed. "The only things that flew were words." He dropped a kiss to her lips. "Lots of words. Like . . . it's never too late to get off your ass and reach for your dreams. So, here it goes." He met her gaze, his own filled with so much emotion it took her breath away. "I love you, Tae."

Her heart skipped a beat. Actually, it skipped a whole bunch of beats, and when it started back up again, it went straight to full-out pounding, complete with the *whoosh* of blood racing through her veins, so it took her a moment to react.

"Shit," Riggs said, pulling back at her pause, or lack thereof. "I've been practicing all the way over here. Did I do it wrong?"

"No." She slid her arms around his neck and pressed her chest to his, gratified to find his heartbeat at stroke level as well. "You did it exactly right."

"You sure?" He was studying her expression carefully. "Because I can keep trying."

"Good idea," she said. "How long do you have?"

He pressed his forehead to hers. "How does forever sound?"

She smiled through her tears. "Like even that might not be long enough . . . Oh, and one more thing. I love you too, Riggs."

EPILOGUE

One year later . . .

Riggs tossed another log on the campfire and accepted the beer Ace handed him.

"You look disgustingly content," Ace noted, lowering himself to the log next to Riggs.

Content—a word that Riggs had never associated with himself before this last year. He'd followed his heart and given up the D.C. job without looking back. He and Jake worked AHQ together, and he'd never been happier. He tipped his bottle in a toast, and Ace knocked his lightly to it.

"Who'd have thought we'd end up here?" Riggs said.

"Not me." His old friend's gaze searched out the woman sitting on the other side of the fire.

April turned, caught Ace's gaze, and winked.

Ace grinned back like he'd won the lotto.

April was still putting in time at AHQ too but also working

successfully as a popular local photographer. Ace's PI firm had grown, and he was adding a satellite office in London to be closer to his son. Much to everyone's surprise, he and April had actually built a meaningful, if deceptively casual, relationship, accepting each other as is, no expectations other than that they love each other for as long as it worked.

It looked good on both of them.

Riggs let his own eyes travel to Tae, who sat with Carolyn and Jake. Andy wasn't here tonight, but he and Tae had gotten close over the past year and had a weekly dad-daughter date. At the moment, she was laughing at something Carolyn was saying, her smile lighting up her whole face. Her hair was loose and flowing over her shoulders, her skin glowing by the fire's light, and she made him ache by just being.

As if she could feel his gaze, she caught his eye and smiled at him, melting his heart. She liked to tease him about being a man of few words, but he could've stood up then and there on one of the logs and shouted to everyone here at her birthday party how much he loved her and why.

"Man, you've got it bad," Ace said on a laugh.

Okay, so apparently he didn't even need to tell anyone how he felt, it was clearly obvious. He and Tae were made for each other, even Jake had known it before Riggs himself had come to believe it. And in the biggest miracle of his entire life, Tae loved him back. He handed his beer to Ace and rose.

"Where you going?"

Riggs just headed with purpose around the fire.

"Ah, man, you're going to make me look bad, aren't you?"

Ignoring that, he kept going until he was in front of Tae. When he dropped to his knees in front of her, April gasped.

"Oh my God. He's going to ask you to marry him!"

"Mom." Tae laughed. "You know he already did that just last month."

Indeed he had, after asking both Andy and April for their blessing. He reached for Tae's hand, looking at the ring he'd put on her finger. The main diamond was circled with smaller ones, symbolizing the love he had for her, no beginning and no end. Leaning in, he brushed his lips across hers. "Need anything?" he asked.

"Just you."

If he hadn't had a dopey grin on his face before, that did it for him.

"When do you think it would be appropriate to leave my own birthday party?" she asked.

"Hey," Jake said. "We're all sitting right here."

Riggs hadn't taken his eyes off Tae. "Whenever your heart desires."

With a grin, she rose and pulled him up too, going on tiptoes to kiss him to the tune of the catcalls and woo-hoos of everyone around them.

He held Tae, smiling as she stared up at him, marveling at how she made him feel. "What are you thinking when you look at me like that?" he asked.

"That you're the best choice I've ever made."

"Right back at you." Leaning down, he kissed the woman he was going to spend the rest of his life with. "Happy birthday, Tae. And to many more."

"All of them with you."

"Always."

Insights,
Interviews
& More . . .

About the author

2 Meet Jill Shalvis

About the book

3 Letter to the Reader

4 Reading Group Guide

Read on

6 An Excerpt from *The Backup Plan*

Meet Jill Shalvis

Susan Zweigle, ZR Studios.com

New York Times bestselling author JILL SHALVIS lives in a small town in the Sierras full of quirky characters. Any resemblance to the quirky characters in her books is . . . mostly coincidental. Look for Jill's bestselling, award-winning books wherever books are sold, and visit her website for a complete book list and daily blog detailing her city-girl-living-in-the-mountains adventures.

Letter to the Reader

Dear Reader,

You may remember Jake from my Heartbreaker Bay series, where he appeared in a walk-on role in *Sweet Little Lies* and *Wrapped Up in You*. He only appeared a few times, with only a few lines, but apparently he left his mark, as I've received a lot of letters begging for more of him. And so . . . he appears in this book! I hope you don't mind, but I did have to take some creative license with his backstory for the sake of *this* story (for instance, he no longer has a sister, but instead has a brother). But I promise you that he's still the tough, pragmatic, take-charge guy you loved. And if you've never read any of my earlier books, no worries! You can start right here! All of my Wildstone and Sunrise Cove books are stand-alone stories. ☺ ∽

Reading Group Guide

1. Tae and April have a close relationship, but Tae has felt that she sometimes takes on the maternal role in their relationship. Is this fair, or do you empathize with April's situation?

2. Was April right in lying about the identity of Tae's father? Should Tae have forgiven her?

3. If you discovered your mother hid the truth about your childhood, would you be able to forgive her?

4. How would you go about rebuilding trust between yourself and a family member or close friend?

5. Is there anything your parent or parents could do that you would consider unforgivable?

6. Was Riggs right in pressuring his brother, Jake, to retire early? Were his concerns warranted? Why are sibling dynamics often complicated?

7. Most people remember their first crush or first love. Tae and Riggs are lucky enough to get a second chance at first love. Would you go back and give your first crush or first love a second chance?

8. In a similar situation, would you have made the same choices as teenage April?

9. Have you lied to someone you love in an attempt to protect them? Was it the right decision?

10. If Tae hadn't run away after their first night together, do you think they would have had a successful relationship then? ∾

An Excerpt from
The Backup Plan

**Keep reading for an
exclusive excerpt from the
next novel by Jill Shalvis,
The Backup Plan,
coming in January 2023**

Chapter 1

Alice's To Do List:

1. Buy potato chips. The family-sized
   bag. If anyone eats them, act
   appropriately grief stricken at their
   funeral.

After two days of driving, Alice Moore
needed to make a pit stop to stretch her
legs but ended up in a drive-through
instead. Hey, it wasn't her fault that
exercise and *extra fries* sounded alike.
She'd just finished licking the salt off
her fingers when she realized she was
nearly at her destination.

She was either experiencing heart
palpitations or her tummy had regrets
about super-sizing her order.

Probably it was both.

What was it people said about the past? "Don't look back"? Well, she'd tried not to. Valiantly. But as she drove along the north shore of Lake Tahoe, surrounded by three hundred and sixty degrees of sharp, majestic, still snow-covered peaks, she felt her past settling over her as heavily as the storm swirling overhead.

It'd been four years since she'd been in Sunrise Cove, the small mountain town where she'd been born and bred. She'd spent most of her adolescence at her dad's work, the Last Chance Inn, nestled in the hills above the lake. But that'd been a long time ago. She'd been braver back then, full of hope. These days she was more of a slap-an-out-of-order-sticker-on-her-forehead sort of person.

She'd been driving for two days, blasting old '80s rock so she wouldn't think too much. But the closer to Lake Tahoe she got, the more her heart began to pound in her ears. Or maybe it was just the squealing of the clutch in Stella, her 1972 Chevy Blazer, proving that she needed a throw-out bearing replacement even more than she needed gas.

Turning off Lake Drive, she headed up Last Chance Road. At the end of the street, the ostentatious gate in front of her was wide open. She drove along the ▶

muddy and still snow-patched land surrounded by thick groves of towering pines that made the place smell like perpetual Christmas.

The old Wild West Last Chance Inn had been standing tall and proud since 1885, complete with a wraparound porch and wooden signs above the windows labeled Saloon, Jail, Graveyard, etc., all making her feel like she'd just stepped back in time. She knew every nook and cranny of the place like the back of her hand. She'd learned to drive here and was proud to say she'd only hit the mailbox three times. She'd ridden her bike here and had helped her dad fix up anything with an engine. Convinced she could fly, she'd climbed the trees and jumped from the high branches. It'd taken a broken ankle at age ten to figure out that maybe she wasn't meant to be airborne.

She parked in front of the inn, but her gaze went to the barn, a hundred yards to the south. Beyond that was a creek where inn guests had once panned for gold, but it was the barn that had always called to Alice. Along with her car-racing older brother and dad, she'd lost hours and weeks and months working on the inn's incredible collection of antique and old muscle cars.

If there was a heaven, it looked just like the inside of that barn. At least in

Alice's mind. With a sigh, she stared out her windshield at what had once been the very best part of her childhood. Not the buildings, but the searingly intense woman who'd lived in them. Eleanor Graham had been a lot of things to Alice: pseudo grandmother, teacher . . . enforcer. Her recent death had blown Alice's heart into little bits, leaving her feeling a whole bunch like the inn in front of her.

Badly in need of fixing.

And now she, a woman who owned little but the big, fat chip on her shoulder, also owned one-third of the Last Chance Inn and all its surrounding property. Boggling and . . . *terrifying*.

The stipulation of the will stated that all three inheritors needed to come to the inn for the necessary renovations or forfeit their individual one-third of the holdings. Today was the deadline in which to show up. Decisions needed to be made.

Not exactly Alice's forte, at least not *good* decisions anyway.

She slid out of Stella just as a light snow began to drift down from the turbulent sky. Par for the course for April in Tahoe. Or maybe it was because her armor of choice—three coats of mascara—wasn't waterproof.

There was a metaphor about her life in there somewhere, and her stomach ▶

An Excerpt from *The Backup Plan*
(continued)

tightened the way it did whenever she had to go to the dentist, murder a spider, or face her past, because it seemed no matter how hard she tried, the past *always* caught up with her. And right on cue, hers pulled up in an electric Nissan LEAF, a big decorative sunflower on the dash.

Lauren Scott.

Her one-time BFF got out in a clear rain jacket, hood up over her shiny blonde hair, a pretty white sundress with pink tights, an open matching pink cardigan and dainty ballerina flats. The heart-shaped sunglasses perched on her nose were a nice touch. Lauren was as cute and adorable as ever. In contrast, Alice wore faded, ripped jeans and a beloved old Bon Jovi concert tee, her wild, dark brown hair pulled back in a ponytail. Alice felt decidedly not cute nor anything close to adorable.

Just getting eyes on Lauren after all this time made her ache for the days when things had been easy. And good. Back to when they'd been each other's person through thick and thin, when Lauren had been in love with Will, Alice's brother, and they'd all felt like a family. A real family.

But Will was gone.

She missed him. And she missed Lauren, so much so that she felt both a little nauseated and unbearably happy at the sight of her.

"Wow." Lauren leaned back against her car. "You actually showed up. I'm shocked."

And obviously, *not* the good kind of shocked.

Lauren drew a deep breath, like just looking at Alice pained her. "The last time I saw you," she said, "you made it quite clear that you were never ever coming back."

Yep, Alice had definitely said that, and a whole lot more. She'd said and done some horrible and unforgivable things, and the pain in her chest told her she wasn't going to escape her own demons any time soon. "I can't do this, not right now."

"Or ever, right?" Lauren asked.

Truth was truth. "Look, we've got a lot to figure out here, and we can't do that if we're fighting. Let's just do what we're here to do. For Eleanor."

"You know how I feel about Eleanor."

Yes, and Alice knew why too. "And yet you came."

"I had to." A little bit of Lauren's carefully neutral facade crumbled as she searched Alice's gaze. "I have questions."

Questions Alice hoped to avoid.

Lauren pulled off her sunglasses. ▶

"So you still like to avoid talking about any *real* problem, especially between us."

Alice laughed roughly. "The real problem between us is that Will is dead." Something she still blamed herself for. "But you're right, it's not something I want to talk about, *especially* with you, and—"

And shit. Lauren's eyes went suspiciously shiny, causing guilt and grief to slam into Alice. "See, this is why we can't do this." Rocked by the emotions battering at her, she spun on a heel toward the front door, noticing for the first time the nice, brand-sparkling-new dark gray Chevy truck parked off to the side. Perfect, because she could guess who it belonged to—the third inheritor. Even as she thought it, the front door of the inn opened, and there Knox Rawlings stood in the doorway, casual as you please.

Alice, head still spinning from seeing Lauren, stopped dead in her tracks, her brain skidding to a complete halt. Apparently her feet too, because Lauren plowed into the back of her.

Giving her a dirty look, Lauren moved around her and kept going.

Not Alice. Her feet had turned into cement blocks. She'd expected Knox to be here. She'd warned herself, promised her awkward inner tomboy teenager that certainly he'd have lost his easy, effortless, charismatic charm by now, that maybe he'd also grown out of those good, rugged looks as well, hopefully having gained a beer belly and lost some hair, and maybe also a few teeth.

But nope, none of the above.

Knox was six-feet-plus of lean muscles and testosterone, and damn, of course he'd gotten better with time. Alice, on the other hand, felt like a train wreck. She could only hope he didn't remember her as the creeper teen, four years his junior, who'd once spent every free second she had spying on him as he worked for Eleanor too.

Lauren hit the front steps first, swiping at her tears. Alice followed, fighting her own. Stupid sympathy crying gene.

"I'm so sorry," Lauren murmured to Knox. "It's awful to meet you under these circumstances. I'm Lauren Scott."

"Knox Rawlings," he said and turned to Alice with absolutely zero recognition in his eyes.

Just what she'd wanted. So why did that irritate her? Ordering her feet to move, she promised herself ice cream, cookies, pies, whatever, as long as she moved with grace and confidence. *Lots* of confidence.

Instead she tripped over a loose rock and had to catch herself. Stupid feet. "Alice Moore," she managed as if she ▶

was completely calm. But the truth was, she'd not been calm a single day in her life. "Maybe we could get out of the crazy storm and get this over with?" With that, she brushed past them both and into the inn.

She got a few feet into the wide open living room, but before she could process the emotions, she was greeted by a huge scruffy brown mutt, who ran straight at her with exuberance.

"Pickle," Knox said calmly behind her, and the dog scrambled to stop, sitting politely in front of Alice, tail swishing back and forth on the floor, a wide smile on his face.

She melted. It was her heart; it beat for animals. Her heart was as stupid as her feet.

"Meet Pickle," Knox said. "When I rescued him, he went by Tiny, but for obvious reasons the name didn't stick."

Alice looked the dog over, a good hundred pounds past "tiny," and let out a choked laugh.

Pickle tilted his head back and *woo wooed* at the ceiling.

"He's sensitive about his size." Knox ruffled the top of his head fondly. "When I first got him, he was skinny and sick and, well, tiny. Good thing he loves food. Oh, and if you're ever eating a pickle, be prepared to share. He lives for them."

Alice absolutely refused to be moved that he'd rescued a dog.

"Oh my God." Lauren stopped in the doorway behind Alice and gasped dramatically. "Tell me that's not a dog. Tell me it's a bear or something."

"Okay, he's a bear," Knox said. "Or something."

Lauren sneezed and backed up, right into the wall while pointing at Pickle. "That's a *dog*!"

They all looked at the oversized scruffy fur ball.

"I mean, it's kinda hard to tell the difference isn't it?" Alice asked.

Pickle gently headbutted Knox's hand, asking for love. Knox obligingly bent down to hug him, and Pickle licked his face in thanks.

Lauren, looking like she was afraid she'd be next, tried to back up some more, but she was already against the wall.

"He's harmless," Knox assured her. "I rescued him from Puerto Rico last year on a job site. He'd have ended up on death row."

"Okay, that's very sweet," Lauren said. "But maybe he could wait in the car since I'm deathly allergic."

"It's a phobia," Alice said. "A well founded one, but it's definitely not an allergy." ▶

An Excerpt from *The Backup Plan*
(continued)

Lauren gave her a keep-talking-and-die look. "I'm *allergic*." And then, as if to prove it, she sneezed three times in a row.

"I hear if you do that seven times, it's as good as an orgasm," Alice said.

Lauren narrowed her eyes, but before she could respond, Knox spoke. "I had him tested for breed. He's a Samoyed, and Samoyeds are hypoallergenic."

"Wuff!" Pickle said, clearly proud of himself.

Lauren tried to back up some more, but a wall was . . . well, a wall. "If he's hypoallergenic, why am I still sneezing?"

"Because you got bit by your dad's evil girlfriend's dog when you were ten," Alice said. "I'd be afraid too."

"I'm not afraid!"

Knox stepped between Lauren and Pickle. "I promise, you're safe with Pickle. He's never bitten anyone. He can be shy, but that's because he's a rescue. He's actually drawn to shy people."

"I'm not shy. Nor am I scared of dogs."

Alice raised a brow and nudged her chin in the direction of Lauren's hands. Which were now gripping Alice's arm tight.

"Whatever," Lauren said, jerking her hands off Alice. "I'm a grown woman. *And I'm not scared of dogs!*"

Uh-huh. And the Tooth Fairy was

real. Alice dropped to her knees and opened her arms. Pickle walked right into them, nuzzled his face at her neck, and she promptly died and went to heaven. "Oh, look at you," she murmured. "So handsome. So sweet."

"Okay, all of that, but he's not going to stay, right?" Lauren asked, her voice registering at least three octaves higher than normal.

Alice wouldn't mind if Pickle stayed, but hoped Knox would go, for no reason other than just looking at him reminded her of a time she didn't want to think about.

Knox patted his leg, and Pickle immediately deserted Alice for his numero uno. Both man and dog turned to the door. "You going to leave?" Alice asked hopefully. "What a shame. A terrible, horrible, no good shame."

Knox gave her a long, unreadable look. "I'm putting Pickle in my truck and coming right back. But nice to know where you stand." ⌒